Bad English
the III

Bad English
the III
The ^Mostly True Tales of a Son of a Brit

JM DAVIS

To:

J.E.W.

"So I...

        ...Never Caught...

                ...the Faker...

'Changes' - David (Jones) Bowie

Prologue

The Interviewer, dressed smartly in a powder-blue power suit, took one last look around the posh So-and-So hotel room in Soho before pulling her N-95 mask over her nose and mouth. Answering the light knock at the door, she found the Subject, unusually bundled up for an early August evening. Adorned with mirrored sunglasses, a rainbow-coloured scarf and a wool cap, the lower half of her face was covered with a black cloth mask, prominently displaying a yellow sunflower. Seemingly paranoid, she looked up and down the hallway before practically pushing her way into the room.

Given it was the year 2021, the world in the throes of a global pandemic, the Interviewer backed behind the door in lockstep with the Subject to maintain the new world order's practice of social distancing. They both stopped dead in their tracks, pulling on their respective masks to catch their breaths. The Subject checked the back page of a folded-up Evening Standard newspaper, comparing the best she could, the paper's artistic rendition of the half-concealed reporter's eyes and hair with the woman standing before her.

"Britt Starling...and you are?"

"I said no cameras or photos of any kind," the Subject firmly said, pointing to a camera on a tripod.

"Of course. But if you change your mind," the Interviewer said, allowing the door to slam shut. They both jumped. Starling spun the camera off the tripod and set it on the glass coffee table between them. The Subject checked the room out high and low before her shoulders finally dropped, but the tension, however, was still palpable.

The Interviewer squinched her eyes in a welcoming smirk, outstretching her arm, indicating the settee. The Subject hesitated for a moment, still a bit stand-offish. "And no recording devices of any kind," she reminded the reporter as she slowly had a seat. The only other thing on the glass coffee table between them was Time Out magazine's Summer Edition, featuring an image of Queen Elizabeth wearing a surgical mask.

The Interviewer nodded, holding up her pen and notepad; the Subject nodded her appreciation.

"What I'm about to tell you, I have on good authority is the *true story* of the, you know, what we discussed on the blower.

———

Looking every bit like the two legitimate business-men their plan called for, I chewed on my fingernail as I watched my grandfather and cousin, their modified umbrellas and weirdly fitting suits bouncing up and down upon their every step. They approached the building with Y & T Goldbroker's - Established 1968, embossed in gold on the window. I took notice of the banner: Bank Holiday Precious Gems Auction - Today at Noon.

My heart pounded as fiercely as the wind blowing outside. I sat watching through the windshield of yet another stolen automobile as the two disguised men disappeared behind an alcove, the only storefront on the entire block whose door did not face the street."

"Wait, I'm sorry. Is the whole story going to be like this? This...style?" The Interviewer asked the Subject.

"It's exactly how it was written, virtually verbatim," The Subject of the interview informed.

"I see. So, I didn't know you were going to jump right in. Do you mind starting at the beginning? Maybe, tell me a little bit about yourself. How you came into--"

"Nofink about me," the Subject insisted, her accent rough as her demeanor. "Ian, Ian Jones, who you'll 'ear about soon enough, was me boyfriend at the time."

There was a purposeful pause by both the Interviewer and Subject.

———

"Oh, the way I dress," she said, taking herself in with a long leer—T-shirt and jeans under a flowing skirt combined with her large gold hoop earrings. "Yes, I've come to prefer the ladies," the Subject proudly informed.

"So, what can I call you?" The Interviewer inquired.

"Quite a lovely room. Smells lovely. Even under the mask," the woman said in an unusually manly voice. Another long pause. "Robbin."

"Just Robin?"

"Jus' Robbin. Two B's."

"Two B's? Two B's or not two B's?' the Interviewer asked, followed by an awkward chuckle, her half-baked attempt at injecting some levity to get Robbin to feel comfortable.

"Is that the question?" the Interviewer looked up only to have Robbin wink at her, letting her know she got the Shakespeare reference.

"No, oh," the Interviewer said, looking down at her notepad. "R-O-Double-B-I-N. So, okay, um, start where you think we should start."

"As I mentioned, this all combined took place in the summer of eighty-nine. June, one can reasonably presume. One year later, me and me boyfriend read the book our flatmate was writing at the time..."

'The Queen, looking rather poorly as her health was in drastic decline, sat up in bed, clapping as she watched her little Prince do sleight-of-hand tricks, including a burst of fire from the palm of his hands. The King burst through the chamber doors, catching the Queen most off guard and fearing the King's wild outbursts, The Prince dove under his mother's bed.

The Queen smiled sheepishly as The King approached with open arms. Instead of embracing her, though, he wrapped his large, coarse hands around her throat and squeezed, tightly lifting her in the air. Her eyes bugged so far out of her pained face that they seemed sure to pop right out of the sockets. Alas, with her last breath escaped, he dropped her like a rag doll back onto the bed.

The King dropped into his throne, thrust it back like a modern-day recliner, and proceeded to drive it around the castle as if it was somehow electric. The Prince stayed put.'

"Is this...?" the Interviewer inquired.

"Page 1, Paragraph 1, I kid you not."

The Interviewer nodded twice in understanding and once further for her to continue.

The Subject pulled again on the tip of her mask, taking a long and loud breath, perturbed by the interruption.

Chapter

1

Rolling into his teenage son's dark bedroom like a bat out of Hell, Mr. David Jones burst through the door driving his new motorized wheelchair.

"Wakey wakey!" he said, speaking with a heavy Midlands accent.

DJ, as his son preferred to be called, had surrounded his bed with stacks of 12"x12" cardboard boxes, making what he deemed to be an impenetrable fortress.

Pulling the drawstring to open the curtains, Mr. Jones was instead met by a black beach blanket with Pink Floyd's iconic Dark Side of the Moon logo, which strategically blocked the morning sun.

"Lunatic," he grunted, possibly alluding to the lyric from one of the album's songs, "Brain Damage." One never quite knew with Mr. Jones. He always kept his cards close to his chest.

———

He yanked the blanket down as if he were a magician revealing an illusion only to find another blanket, the Led Zeppelin Swan Song logo, that of the falling fallen angel. He scoffed before whipping it from the curtain rung with another flick of his wrist.

Mr. Jones spun his chair into the wall, careful to only pull down the boxes marked "MAGS," which consisted of "CIRCUS," "CREEM," and "HIT PARADER," magazines chock full of the era's rock gods. Not the boxes labeled "LPs."

Dust and atoms swirled in the swath of morning sunlight, illuminating his seventeen-year-old son lying seemingly lifeless on his back. His left leg dangled over the side. His tongue slightly protruded, regurgitated bile down the front of his shirt, appearing to have choked on his own vomit. As opposed to someone else's (a veiled Spinal Tap reference when the idea first occurred to him.)

Mr. Jones gasped.

"Oi," Mr. Jones grumbled with his distinguished Midlands accent, "f---in' vey."

He sidled up alongside DJ with a few forward and reverse shifts of his electric joystick and brought a punishing, open-handed slap down on his son's young, baby-faced cheek.

Quickly drawn back from dreaming to consciousness (a column fell on him after the Queen spontaneously burst into flames). DJ held his breath under such excruciating pain; a single tear ran unseen down the far side of his cheek. He quickly recalled his elaborate plan to play possum.

Mr. Jones draped the Zeppelin blanket over his son's body from head to toe.

"Sure, you don't want a lift?" No reply. "Suit yourself, mate," he said before doing a one-eighty, popping a wheelie, and banging into a few more boxes at the end of DJ's bed. He stopped with a squeak at the bedroom door. Jones buttoned his work shirt up to the third button from the top, beside the Exotic Autos patch with his name underneath in fancy font – David Jones, Proprietor.

"C--t," DJ said with a yawn.

"I heard that!" Mr. Jones shouted from the hallway. "And I'm not a c--t!"

"None of that! Not today," DJ heard his mother say.

From his crotch, the Led Zeppelin blanket began to rise as if the angel was ascending back to his place in Heaven. Either that or DJ was experiencing morning glory.

Like Adam said to Eve, DJ thought, '*Stand back, I don't know how big this thing's going to get!*'

The blanket fell to the side, revealing DJ, with a Sid Vicious-like sneer, flipping the bird, first with just his middle finger but then, lifting his index finger, forming a reverse peace sign, and with a double flick of his wrists, he flipped off his father. English-style.

———

With the same two fingers, he scooped the coagulated oatmeal stuck to his shirt and nibbled on it. He winced, slapping it back into the bowl on his nightstand. Finally, he hawked up a loogie and shot it across the room where the wall met the ceiling.

There was a constant chirping coming from outside. DJ opened the bedroom window, finding not the crowded bus stop he was accustomed to his whole childhood. Instead, an oak tree grew. Like Mary Poppins, a bird was perched on the branch outside his window.

"Piss off!" he said, waving it away with a shake of his fist.

Under the window, he pulled open the drawer to his nightstand, running his finger along the top of the small, bundled stacks of methodically folded magazine pages. He considered having a snort before heading out but decided against it—the little he had "sampled" had kept him up all night. When he finally did fall asleep, he'd had weird dreams of his father killing his mother, probably inspired by his new alphabetized mixed tape, which included AC/DC's "Back in Black" followed by Aerosmith's "Kings and Queens."

A mostly shy but sarcastic kid, DJ leaped from his bed, pulled his shirt off, and tossed it in the corner as he approached a box labeled "Ts" (for T-shirts, clever) and punched through the top of the box with all his might.

CARDBOARD – Making Weaklings Look Like Strongmen Since Its Inception!

———

Yanking out a jersey—Rainbow, "Straight Between the Eyes," (simply the top of a guitar crashing through a skull and set of eyes, what one famous guitarist in London said Jimi Hendrix's guitar playing did to him, 'hit him straight between the eyes'). He slid it on before grabbing his beloved white Fender Stratocaster from the bed where it rarely left his sight.

DJ looked down to find a strange beagle staring at him from the doorway and sneered at him. The dog's lip curled up, and they both stood motionless, sizing the other up.

He white-knuckled the door frame, thrusting himself past the dog and out of the room and down the hallway. DJ stopped at the top of the stairs long enough to sneak a listen. But, unfortunately, chatter from inside the bathroom was drowned out by running water.

"Get a hold of yourself," DJ heard his father say.

The bathroom door swung open, and Mr. Jones rolled to the doorway. The left side of his face was covered in shaving cream, his blond coiffed hair pointing straight up as if he had just stuck his finger in a socket. If it gave one the distinct impression he resembled singer Rod Stewart, which was purely by design—he had initially made a little dosh in the '70s as a Rod Stewart impersonator, with the ever-so-original moniker, Mod Stewart.

"Don't forget to say Goodbye to your Mum!" Mr. Jones barked, a twinge of melancholy in his voice. He reversed back in the bathroom, shut the door, and carried on where he had left off. Mostly just admiring himself.

DJ, however, said nothing as he bolted downstairs and into the kitchen in search of his father's Pall Malls to nick a couple. But, unfortunately, a couple was all he had. Gutted, DJ went to the bathroom and did his business in private, without a knock at the door, without interruption. All new view for you, he thought to himself. He then took the most incredible, hottest shower he ever had in his life. The loud staccato thumps coming from the stairs above the bathroom had little effect on him. He was on another planet.

When he finally emerged after preening and primping his dirty-blond curly hair and pencil mustache, he found the house empty. DJ returned to his room as if he had all the time in the world. He removed the record he had been playing for the last ten days straight, Black Sabbath's "Mob Rules" and one song in particular. He dropped the needle on song eight on the second side, "Falling Off The Edge of the World," and turned up the volume just as loud as it would go. He was never able to do it at his last place. He strapped on his guitar and put on the performance of a lifetime in front of the full-length mirror still leaning against the wall.

Singer Ronnie James Dio's voice was haunting, almost feminine, his lyrics thoughtful and mystic. Meanwhile, the build-up of the song, menacing in its approach, crescendoed into a face-melting extravaganza that left DJ quietly weeping while playing along to Tony Iommi's masterful guitar.

When the song came to its conclusion, DJ picked up the needle and placed it back in the groove, performing it three more times before turning it off and high tailing it downstairs.

Like a bull in a china shop, he barreled his way through the hastily furnished living room where more labeled boxes were piled, all the while avoiding the "elephant" in the room.

"*Goodbye t' your Mum,*" DJ muttered, mimicking his father. He opened the front door to spot a white couple out walking their Dalmatian. Probably named Spot. Not wanting to be seen by them or anyone for that matter, he slammed the door shut and leaned his back against it, plotting his next move.

What am I doing here? These m-fers want to f with me? By all means necessary, he thought, invoking the words of Malcolm X.

DJ slipstreamed through the kitchen and into the garage--he had a garage!--and felt around the wall until he found the light switch and flicked it on. It flickered for a moment as he stepped off the bottom step until he heard a pop sound. The bulb quickly dimmed out.

He scoffed and shrugged as he approached his red Vespa scooter (as much red from rust than its original coat of paint), clicking the garage door opener he had Velcroed to the gas tank —he had a garage door opener!

The sun, for the second time, blasted DJ in the face. Cool as a cucumber, he slid on his round, Lennon-Esque, mirrored sunglasses but struggled to get his helmet over his curls where his headphones were already stuffed.

After methodically preparing a new mixtape, compiled by title, subject, and song length just to fit everything on the same side, he listened to it while learning the streets of his new neighbourhood. His trusty black helmet stealthily concealed the high-yellow tone of his symmetric face. Not the first time in his short life where he'd felt the colour of his skin was an actual impediment.

Now, with his route all planned, he started the scooter with a turn of the key and revved it up. The Vespa leaped forward before sputtering out. DJ twisted the gas cap open and blew into the tank where only a hollow whistle emitted back.

Bone dry.

"F-f-f-f-f."

He climbed off the scooter, yanked his helmet off, and slammed it on the nearby workbench, cluttered with tools, before grabbing one of his two skateboards.

He was going to be late for sure but really could care less.

It was only fitting that the next song from the previous night's listen was "Young Lust" from Pink Floyd.

And with copyright laws being what they are, let's just say he definitely was a stranger in this new town.

DJ rode that skateboard like a man on a mission, his right leg raising high and coming down on the pavement with all his might. There was only one slight hitch: only the left side was audible when his right leg was down. However, when he raised his right leg to kick off the ground, the music would come through both ears.

Mono. Stereo. Mono. Stereo.

Having moved from the black concrete jungle off Thames Street, he was in a strange land amongst the green hedges and landscaped lawns of the white suburbia of Essex. This mixed-up, mixed-race kid felt far more conspicuous as he passed white folks walking their dogs or pushing baby prams, turning a head or two as he passed them.

The fact of the matter was that DJ liked one to think he was from the so-called ghetto, but he was literally from across the tracks of the actual projects, where most of his friends lived. He had been raised in a nearby middle-class apartment complex, the product of an extremely rare-for-the-area, and era, bi-racial marriage.

It was still a bit of a culture shock and a far cry from the neighbourhood where he was raised.

A far cry indeed.

What should have been one song turned out to be two and a half, with Queen's "Fat Bottomed Girls" and

Rainbow's "All Night Long" playing before finally arriving at his destination. The Rolling Stones' "Sympathy for the Devil" thumped, again only in his left ear.

DJ scoffed at what he was witnessing—a mecca for white teenagers. Essex High, a real-life "Breakfast Club."

He stopped his skateboard, flip-kicking it up into his hand just as the first bell rang. He was already perspiring but the enormity of change he was about to encounter had him sweating like a three-dollar-whore in church.

The loud chatter, laughter, and screams of students filled the hallways. DJ took note that even the smell was different than that of F.D. High—less activator, more hairspray. Most of the kids started making their way into school while others merely continued their conversations, or smoking their cigarettes, or both.

Pulling the schedule from his back pocket, DJ scanned it, looking for the number of his homeroom. He made his way inside, avoiding the stares and perplexed looks from other students. Surprisingly, he spotted a black girl coming his way and got overly excited, flashing her a toothy grin in a poor attempt to seek a little solidarity. It was far from the desired effect he was trying to achieve, coming across as more desperate and pathetic than cool. The second she saw him, she made like a magnet and repelled away, dropping around the corner and up a crowded stairwell.

The second and final bell rang, and most of the students picked up their pace in their last-ditch effort to get to class.

The ones that did not, the seniors, could probably care less, what with it being the last day before exam week.

Having found the room he was after, DJ reluctantly poked his head inside before fully entering. Cliques of students either stood around conversing or sat at their desks looking through notebooks or textbooks. Slowly easing through the room, his headphones still blasting the Stones through the left side, he tried to assess which seats were taken as opposed to those not.

He was unaware of the teacher as she came in, closing the door behind her and giving all those still standing the evil eye. Some begrudgingly moved to their seats. Others, not recognizing her, continued their conversations. Two guys formed goal posts with their fingers and thumb, plucking a folded-up paper back and forth across their desks.

DJ turned to see why some of the students had questioning looks on their faces only to find a small, rather handsome woman setting her briefcase and folder on the desk.

"Do you need a special invitation?" she asked rather caustically, clearly aimed at DJ. He removed his headphones, the 'Oooh ooohs' of Mick Jagger audible to those close enough, and looked for a definite empty seat. "Where's your desk?"

DJ struggled for just the right reply.

"I think he's new," a girl in the front row, probably the regular teacher's pet, informed.

She pointed to an empty desk next to a motor-head—one could conclude, due to the "Mopar" shirt he was sporting. Leaning his guitar against the side of the empty desk, DJ took a seat.

The teacher turned to spell out her name on the chalkboard in large block letters: MS. FINDLEMEYER.

"New?" one of the jocks whispered. "It's the last week of school!"

"Probably a narc," a long hair replied.

"You better watch yourself then," the jock retorted, snickering.

"Yeah, whatever," Long Hair replied before nervously adjusting something in his front pants pocket.

"That will be enough," Ms. Findlemeyer said sternly. "As you can see," she continued to the whole of the class, "Mrs. Cohen is out sick today. And as one of you has pointed out, despite this being the end of the school year, I intend to run a tight ship."

"Like the Titanic?" one kid whispered.

"You will get one warning and that is it. Think what you want using your inner voice. Now, let's take attendance."

She opened the folder. "I see that some of you are also in Mrs. Cohen's English class, so you can tell your other friends that I will not stand for any nonsense."

She began reading from the opened folder, "Adams?"

"Here."

A guy behind Adams, who clearly fancied himself a comedian, whispered the "Addams Family" theme: "Dun-nun-nun-nun," before snapping twice.

Adams turned and muttered, "Yeah that never gets old."

"It's new to the new kid," the Comedian whispered back.

Ms. Findlemeyer pointed at them as a warning before continuing. "Anselmo."

"Here."

"Eder?"

"I'd like to," the Comedian whispered.

"Here."

"Grodnitzky?"

"Here," one of the kids playing paper football said.

"Hamet?"

"To pee or not to pee," again the Comedian whispered.

"That's Hamlet," Ms. Hamet replied. "Here."

"Hoffman?"

"Here," the other kid playing football replied.

"Lilley?"

"You big, beautiful flower."

"Here," the kid with the Mopar shirt replied.

"Scherr?"

"Yes."

"Seidel." No answer. "No Seidel?"

"Here," Seidel the Comedian said, sounding annoyed.

"And Snyder."

"Here," a girl replied.

They got through attendance without calling DJ's name. Seidel pointed back in his direction. "What about Joe?"

The teacher's eyes looked from the folder to DJ. "Joe? Joe what?"

"Joe MAMA!" Seidel yelled, erupting into laughter.

"That's IT—OUT!"

"Hey, what about my warning?"

"NOW!" Seidel stood up, his chair scraping loudly across the floor as he gathered up his belongings. Then, proudly grinning from ear-to-ear, he waved to the class as he made his way to the front door where Ms. Findlemeyer already stood, her hand on the doorknob. She opened it up as Seidel changed directions and made his way to the room's back door.

Standing in the hallway, Ms. Findlemeyer found a heavy-set female holding a blue slip.

"Can I help you?" The student handed the masculine woman the pass, who read the name aloud. "David Jones?"

She scanned the room, her eyes landing on DJ, who pointed to himself. "Get your things, you're wanted in the office."

DJ did as he was told and headed to the front of the class. "Narc, fo sho," the long-hair muttered.

"They should've got a bigger narc," the one kid playing football whispered.

"They should've made a ni**er bark," his football-playing friend cracked.

Ushered from the commotion of the main office into a smaller inner office by one of the Guidance Counselors, Mrs. Williams, a small, portly, black woman, holding a stack of folders, guided DJ to a seat as she closed the door behind her. He leaned his guitar against the vinyl chair opposite the administrator's cluttered desk and had a seat. She set all but one folder down on her desk and sat down with a *whoosh* from its cushion.

Scanning the room while she read through the paperwork in what was presumably his file, DJ's gaze eventually landed on a poster to the right of him that had kids of various ethnicities with the word "DIVERSITY" on it. He scoffed, snorting softly through his nose.

She would have reminded him of his mum if not for one little peculiar habit she had: while reading, she would vigorously scratch her scalp. Lice? Then, taking it one step further, her eyes would shift from the folder to what she had captured in her fingernails, and after a brief examination, she would gnaw on it like a dog chewing on a soupbone. It seemed she was unaware she was doing it.

"Okay," she said, a bit posh, extending the word as one would a long sigh. "David Jones."

DJ nodded, unseen by the counselor.

Bad English
the III

"I want to commend you on the accomplishment of getting this far. The sheer amount of students dropping out, especially this time of year, is staggering. So, congratulations on your perseverance." She finally looked up at him. "However, I'm afraid your excessive absences, especially in one class in particular—English—leaves you exactly two credits shy of graduating. With this class, anyway. Summer school is going to be your last vestige..."

DJ watched her face zoom out in reverse, and even though her lips continued moving, he heard nothing further as he watched as his whole life passed before his big brown eyes.

"We'll be sending a letter by mail regarding summer school and, of course, upon completion, your diploma will be mailed to you," she said as a matter of fact.

Mrs. Williams stood up, leaving DJ in a literal state of shock. He reached out for his guitar, knocking it to the floor with a god-awful thunk. Mrs. Williams reared back like the cop in the infamous photograph transferring Lee Harvey Oswald to court when Jack Ruby snuffed him off.

She quickly composed herself as the school bell rang, partially bringing DJ back to Earth. He gathered up his guitar, clutched it to his chest like a baby, took one last look at the DIVERSITY poster and sneered.

DJ walked through the busy main office and its main door into the bustling hallway, nearly taking out two jocks in the process.

———

"Watch it dickhead!" the first jock barked.

"Christ, they lettin' in more...?" the other jock started to ask, showing some surprising restraint.

But DJ knew exactly what he wanted to say.

"What is that? A blond monkey?"

"Hey, nice hair, Chocolate Milk Boy," the First Jock said aggressively. "Ain't you gonna apologize?"

DJ continued walking down the chaotic hallway and outside through the double doors leading to the parking lot. The two jocks stopped just shy of the door closing in their faces.

"Told his black ass."

"Ran him right off campus." They laughed and low-fived each other.

DJ let out a huge sigh as he dropped his skateboard, spun around, and, with a quick adjustment of his guitar, machine-gunned the doors down.

In his mind.

At almost eighteen years of age, it was far from his first experience with bigotry. He had gotten the talk from his parents at six or seven. Not just about black-on-white racism but black versus light-skinned black, both of which he had plenty of experience. DJ just made a practice of turning the other cheek.

What would the Hitler youth there have said, he wondered, had they known he was half Jewish to boot?

Even the warmth of the sun was of little comfort to DJ as he legged it on his skateboard back home. Not the new house up on the hill, but the only home he truly knew. His 'hood.

His eyes quickly grew misty as he wondered what he was going to do. A single tear escaped from his eye down his cheek before taking a sharp turn back to his ear. Thoughts raced through his head as fast as his right foot pushed off the concrete with all its might.

The irony of it all was too much to fathom. The fact that, of all classes, English would be his downfall. He had probably said "English is my middle name" one too many times.

So, what, he rationalized, if he didn't cross the stage with a bunch of bloody strangers? White ones, at that. Being told by a black woman seemed almost the cherry on top. *That*, he would never get over. What would his black, English-teaching mother think?

Starving, DJ grabbed a slice from the first pizza place he passed that was open and plopped down on a bus bench to have a wee thought about the future.

He drew a complete blank.

Pizza dangling from his clenched teeth, DJ plugged his guitar into his Walkman, a modification made by his old neighbour, Stevie, an electronics genius.

All wired up and somewhere to go, DJ scoffed at the next song to play on his mixtape, "Working Man" from Rush. He guessed that's what he was as he strummed along with guitarist Alex Lifeson, cruising down the sidewalk, a makeshift concert on wheels.

———

All in his head.

Hiding behind his sunglasses, DJ weaved along the sidewalk, causing heads to turn but in a different way. He could see their remarks through clenched teeth and hostile looks.

Or so he thought. What he deemed had to be racist comments being thrown his way were nothing of the sort.

"Hey, look, it's Jimi Hendrix," said one of a pair of guys.

"I thought he was dead," his mate shot back.

One old rocker thought maybe DJ was too young to know who Jimi Hendrix even was. "You going to see Hendrix next week at The Civic Center?"

"Freebird!" his mate shouted.

It all went unheard by DJ, who was now lost in the music, the knot in his stomach replaced by the satisfaction of that piece of pizza.

Noticing passengers getting on and off a city bus, DJ saw a way to speed up his trip south and quickly picked up his pace. Just as he reached the bus's rear bumper, its exhaust expelled a massive plume of smoke into his face as it charged away from the curb. DJ stopped to cough up a lung.

Just then, a black '69 Chevy Chevelle screeched to a halt beside him. Out of the corner of his eye, DJ saw the passenger window lower. He lowered his sunglasses down the bridge of his nose to get a better look.

Inside the muscle car sat two teenage girls, one in a tank-top, the other in a halter top, both smiling at him. Fitting as it was, he couldn't hear the passenger over Santana's "Open Invitation" playing in his left ear, but he knew exactly what they were saying: "Do you want a ride?"

Without hesitation, DJ leaped towards the jacked-up hot rod as the brown-haired passenger swung the door open and pulled the front seat forward, mashing herself against the dashboard. DJ guided his guitar in, holding his skateboard against his back as he squeezed into the backseat.

With even less hesitation, the driver gunned it, sending DJ into his seat and the passenger and her seat back into place whilst slamming the door shut. Two things immediately struck him: the John Paul Jones bass line from Led Zeppelin's "Dazed and Confused," and the distinctive smell of marijuana. The passenger turned her body to face him as DJ's eyes lit up, spotting the lit doobie she had pinched between her thumb and forefinger.

Getting a sense that the worm was turning for him, DJ smiled as he leaned forward to take it from her, but to his surprise, she pulled it away. His smile dropped before she motioned for him to lean forward, and he did as she commanded. She turned the lit end into her mouth, cupped her hands ever so slightly against his face, and "shot-gunned" a long stream of smoke into his mouth.

———

DJ sat back and exhaled, coughing excessively. Five years of smoking cigarettes and weed, but you would never know it from this performance. The girls looked at one another and laughed as DJ's raspy, wheezing cough persisted.

The Driver turned the volume down. "You gonna be alright?"

"*Oh, yeah, yeah, 'ave eiva of you go' a fag? I mean a, a ci-ga-re',*" DJ inquired. "*I forgo', you don' call em 'at 'ere, do you?*"

There was a long pause as the passenger's eyes darted to the driver's, who looked at DJ in the rear-view mirror.

"Sounds like that's the last thing you need," the Driver said.

"Why are you talking like that?" the Passenger asked, her tone suspicious.

DJ shrugged. "*Dunno, I neve' been ahsk'd tha' before.*" The Passenger handed him a Marlboro red from her pack. "*Cheers, love.*"

"Are you really English or are you just messing with us?" the driver asked firmly, looking over her shoulder at him before returning to the road and mirror.

At Heathrow Airport, a father accompanied his son onto a British Airways flight bound for America. Mid-flight, the father began feeling poorly. By the time they reached US airspace, the father was writhing in his seat in excruciating pain. The co-pilot called ahead to Baltimore-Washington Airport and arranged for an ambulance to be waiting when they landed. The son accompanied his father to the hospital where paramedics, fearing he was experiencing cardiac arrest, raced against time and began administering life-saving CPR.

DJ lit his cigarette, exhaling smoke before nodding his head. *"Yeah, yeah, I am English."*

"From where?" Jill asked suspiciously, her mind on applying to be a cop.

"Norf' Ampton, in the Midlands, above Cambridge, bu' no' as far as Bumming'am." Just like his dear ole dad always said.

"Why are you here?"

"Yeah, why are you skateboarding in the streets of Baltimore?"

"Didn't anybody tell you how dangerous parts of Baltimore can be?"

"Well, i's a good fing you came along when you did then, innit?"

The girls both laughed as they exchanged names; DJ did his best to sneak peeks at their girlish figures. The bird driving, Jill, was top-heavy, leaving DJ to surmise she was probably "low-heavy," too. Lisa was the exact opposite, flat as a board. But they had cute faces and were very friendly.

They agreed to drive him to the Hyatt Regency hotel down in the Inner Harbor. He certainly could not ask them to take him to his neighbourhood.

"Are you staying at the Hyatt?" Lisa asked excitedly. "Show 'im the stash," she said to Jill, who opened up the cooler by DJ's foot. They had come prepared to party, as it was full of beer along with a pint of Southern Comfort; their plan was to sit up on top of nearby Federal Hill and have a few beers.

"*I wish*," DJ replied. "*Me cousin works there. He's a big CPA.*"

They pulled to the end of the driveway, farthest from the front door and DJ got out. "*Please don' piss off. Everyfink I love's in the back o' your car.*"

"We wouldn't do that."

Satisfied, DJ made his way over to the hotel entrance where he spotted Stan, his stocky, black, 19-year-old cousin, getting out of an olive-green SUV. DJ took note of how well-dressed he was, looking sharp in his hotel uniform as Stan handed the keys off to an older white businessman.

DJ waited just long enough for the man to get in and shut the door behind him to whistle. Stan quickly scanned the area until his eyes landed on his little cousin.

"Just in the nigga time," Stan said, a little louder than he probably should have.

"Did you say: 'nigga time'?" DJ asked with his raspy chuckle. "What are you, Superfly?"

"Just made that shit up," Stan said, taking a vogue stance. "And, yes, I *am* super-fly."

———

"White girls?" Stan replied, incredulous, after DJ's briefing. He drew close to his little cousin. "What do we know about white girls?"

"That's the best part--nothing." DJ continued slowly and salaciously, "Yet."

"Man, they just like black girls," Stan said high pitched to start, but his voice dipped down to a lower octave. "Just less pigmentation."

"Oh, there's one other thing..."

DJ advised him of the "hook," as it were.

"Ohh noo. Are you serious? Why can't you just be proud of who you are instead of where you're from? Well, let's hear it. If I'm going to go along with this, which I want to go on the record as saying I am opposed to, I at least must know if you any good, 'cause you ain't going to make me look stupid."

"Hip hip and cheerio and all that stuff," DJ said, purposefully unconvincing.

Stan reached out to strangle him. "It ain't no 'hip hip' it's 'pip pip'!"

"I'm joking," DJ said, trying to reassure him. Then, with a heavy accent, he said, *"Righ'! Wha's all this then? Bleedin' rubbish, tha's wha-tit-is, innit."*

"Did you even bring the 'yay yay'? You know, to sell to the white kids, just like we planned?

"What, to school?"

Stan rolled his eyes. "Let me go punch out before I punch you out."

———

"Ooh, I'm scared."

"Wait, I beg your pardon. David is American?" The Interviewer interrupted.

"DJ," Robbin corrected her. "Yes."

"*DJ*, yes. I wasn't expecting that. Forgive the interruption. Please, continue."

As Jill and Lisa stopped arguing over which one saw him first, DJ made his way across the driveway, strutting like a proud peacock.

"Let's just see who he goes for," Jill whispered.

"Yeah, we'll see. Ya never know, his cousin could be hot, too," Lisa added with a wink.

"Is your cousin coming?" Jill asked when DJ reached their car.

"*Yeah, yeah 'e'll be along inna shake of a lamb's tail,*" DJ said, immediately regretting how corny it sounded.

"So, you never told us why you're here," Lisa said as Jill sized DJ up head to toe.

"*There's no real easy way of put'in' it,*" DJ said after a lengthy pause.

"What?" Jill asked.

"Yeah, what?" Stan said, coming from another direction, taking them by surprise.

A bit of ambivalence was visible on the faces of Lisa and Jill. Maybe it was Stan's complexion, proudly a few degrees darker than that of his light-skinned cousin's. Or maybe it was his size, which conveyed a bit of plumpness, his stomach bulging out as he pulled his baggy pants up.

"Hey," Stan said in his usual effete manner, stretching the word out as if it was several syllables.

DJ took note of the girls' shoulders collectively dropping as if in practiced synchronicity.

"Hey," they repeated, exchanging a knowing glance when neither of the young men were looking.

"*M' paren's jus' died,*" DJ said before climbing into the backseat on Lisa's side. Jill and Lisa's jaws dropped as they shared a quick glance.

"Thank you," Stan said, ever so politely, her role in holding the seat back for them not lost on him. Jill mouthed to Lisa after Stan climbed in: *He's yours.*

"Let's go up the Hill," exclaimed Jill, not with a pail of water but a cooler of beer and a fifth of Southern Comfort chilling on ice. Lisa feigned a smile before climbing in, blasting the radio while Jill rolled another joint.

The Hill was Federal Hill, which carried historical significance for Baltimore and her part in the War of 1812. Baltimore is a big little city or a little big city in the small, mid-Atlantic state of Maryland, wedged under the Mason-Dixon Line and on the eastern seaboard. Stan and DJ were two very different cousins, but both Baltimore through and through.

"Why you say your father died, too? You gonna confuse yourself, man, I'm telling you," Stan whispered, a bit on the loud side.

"He's all but gone. It's like living with Dr. Strange-love," DJ replied in a low growl. Stan threw his head back in laughter. "It's a sprained ankle for f---sakes."

Lisa turned the radio down, asking, "What's so funny?"

Stan stopped laughing and looked to DJ for help.

"*I said t' Stan 'i' beats bein' inda back wif his bible fumpin' paren's,*" DJ said, laying on his thickest English accent yet.

Jill nodded, not understanding what he said before looking to Lisa for help.

Lisa looked back at him. "What?"

David slowly and methodically repeated, "*I said da', referring t' you two...dat dis,*" he drew a circle in the air pointing at them. "*Beats bein' back 'ere wif Stan's bible fumpin' mum and dad up front.*"

"Ohhh," Lisa and Jill said in stereo.

DJ pointed out the window. "*Tickle y'ass wif a fe'vah?*"

"What?" Jill asked, chuckling, at what she wasn't sure.

"*Particularly nice we'vah,*" DJ said, quickly winking at Stan.

"That is *not* what you said," Lisa laughed, checking him in the rear-view mirror as Jill turned to gauge his reaction.

Lisa hot-rodded them around the harbor, parking on the street adjacent to Federal Hill, where they scaled the west side steps to the top, spreading their blanket next to a two-hundred-year-old cannon that overlooked Rash Field and the surrounding harbor.

Stan stood back as the girls sat on the blanket; DJ sat on the other side of Jill on his skateboard, his guitar straddled across his lap.

"What's-her-name says you can drink on the streets in England? And the drinking age is sixteen?" Jill asked as she discreetly distributed beers from the cooler.

"What's-her-name,' Lisa cackled as she cracked the seal on the Southern Comfort.

"*Yes, tha's true,*" DJ figured.

"There's plenty of room on the blanket," Lisa said to Stan after swigging off the bottle and handing it to Jill.

"I'm good," Stan said as he cracked his beer.

"We don't bite," Lisa assured him.

"Speak for yourself," Jill cracked.

"So," Jill said, holding her beer out in front of her. "To your parents..." Stan hurried around the blanket to get in there, as they tipped their cans together.

"...may they rest in peace," Jill continued.

Stan shared a quick glance with DJ. Lisa took a big swig of Southern Comfort and passed it to DJ, who poured a bit on the grass before swigging some, and handed it to Stan.

"So, what happened?" Lisa asked. "I mean, can you talk about it?"

"Do you wanna talk about it?" Jill asked.

No one had asked him that all this time. He thought long and hard about what to say and exactly how to say it.

"Car crash," another half-truth he told with what was more of a Liverpudlian accent.

Although, with misty eyes, DJ gazed over at Stan and winked, a single tear escaped onto his right cheek, which he quickly wiped away. Stan merely rolled his eyes and took a swig from his beer.

As the alcohol further emboldened him, DJ clapped his hands. *"Righ'! Who's gonna f--- me then?"*

A long awkward pause ensued.

"Lisa?" Jill said, extending her hand towards her friend. "Care to answer?"

"No, no, I'm good," Lisa replied. "You?"

"No' big Sex Pistols fans, then, eh?"

A helicopter hovered over the harbor before coming to a landing atop the Hyatt Regency.

"Innat your 'otel, then?" DJ asked his cousin. Stan lowered his can, looked over his shoulder and nodded in the affirmative. *"Why d' they need an 'elicop'er?"*

Stan swallowed and looked at them, bleary-eyed. "It's actually a pretty cool story."

DJ puffed off a new joint, offering it to Stan, who dismissed it with the wave of his hand.

"Barry Levinson, you know, the guy that directed 'Rain Man' is from Baltimore. He did a bunch of movies here. From the way I heard it, he arranged it for Richard Dreyfuss—you know the guy from "Jaws"—when they were here shooting "Tin Men" so he could get to the airport to fly to New York to be in a play. Same helicopter used in '...And Justice for All' with Al Pacino, which Barry Levinson also wrote."

"That is cool, man," Jill proclaimed.

DJ yelled in Al Pacino's distinctive voice and Brooklyn accent. "This whole *court* is out of order!"

The other three froze and stared at DJ. Paranoia from the weed quickly set in and he wondered if they had caught on.

"*Is zat a true story, mate?*" DJ asked in what he deemed a quick save.

Stan knocked back another big swig, confirming with a nod that it was indeed true.

Staring out at the waters of the harbour, DJ let his mind wander. Finally, when speaking with an English accent, he noticed that you just butcher the words to shit. Cut off the middles and the ends, mostly, and you were speaking with an English accent.

"DJ?"

"Huh?"

I asked, have you ever seen the Cliffs of Dover?" Jill asked.

"*Wha's tha' then? Innit in Switz'rlan' or sumfin?*" DJ asked, honestly not knowing.

"The Cliffs of Dover. They're famous." Jill insisted.

Out of the corner of his left eye, DJ spotted Lisa's gaze shift from Jill to him. Out of his right eye, he could see Stan questioning him with his eyes.

"*Oh, the Cliffs of Dover. I fough' you said the Clips Up Do-*

ber. Tha's where they breed Doberman Pinschers, innit?"

Stan clapped. "Look at the time. I gotta get back."

DJ's eyes implored him not to go, but Stan was having no more as he stood up and straightened his pants.

"Oh no. Should we drive you back?" Jill asked.

"No, no, I can walk back. I come here for lunch all the time."

"D'ya wanna use me board?"

Stan finished his beer. "Actually, yes, I do."

DJ stood up and pushed the skateboard towards Stan. *"I'll walk wi' you',"* DJ said to Stan.

"No, no, stay with your new friends."

"No, no, I insis'," DJ said. *"B'sides, we need t' tal' abou' tea t'nigh'."*

"Do you guys wanna go to a party later?" Lisa asked.

"I can't tonight," Stan informed, wanting no more involvement in his younger cousin's sordid little schemes.

DJ, after contemplating it for a tick, said to Stan, *"Don' wai' up fo' me."* He gently laid his guitar on the blanket where Stan had been sitting. *"Guard i' wif your life, girls, I'll be righ' back, yeah?"*

"Why are you leaving?" DJ asked Stan when they got out of earshot.

"One lie begets another lie begets another lie. The Cliffs of Dover in Switzerland??"

"Okay, so I ain't good at geography."

"You ain't too good at English either," Stan said

through dramatically pursed lips as they reached the stairs. "You better hope they don't catch on, 'cause that one looks like she could put a hurtin' on you."

"She can put a hurtin' on me if she wants. Besides," DJ continued with his English accent. *"I got 'em just where I want 'em."*

"Rubbish," Stan replied with a pretty convincing accent of his own.

The phone rang at his father's garage, taking Mr. Jones, who was underneath a green 1971 XKE Jaguar up on jacks, by complete surprise. He jolted up, smacking his head on the oil pan with a loud and undoubtedly painful thud.

"Shit," he growled before grabbing the cordless phone from off the floor. Like flipping a switch, his phone etiquette came across as if he were a smarmy British disc jockey, "Exotic Auto." He rubbed his forehead, checking it for blood. There was a slight delay on the other end.

"I'm looking for the parents of David Jones. This is Mrs. Williams at Essex High School."

"That's me. I mean, there's just me. There something wrong?" Mr. Jones said, rolling out from under the car, extending the antenna of the once-white phone.

Mrs. Williams, not one to mince words, quickly got to the point. One might presume, still chowing down on her little scalp feeders.

"Not graduating, you say?" He then, this hardened man, made harder by the untimely passing of his one and only, dropped the phone, covered his face, and very uncharacteristically, burst into tears. We're talking full-on high-school girl sobbing.

"Mr. Jones? Mr. Jones? Are you alright? Mr. Jones? Are you alright?"

"I am, I certainly am," he assured her. And she would have been assured of that had she seen the smile beaming on his face, for the tears he shed were tears of pure joy.

Mr. Jones crawled his way up the Jaguar, favouring his left leg, slammed the car's bonnet shut with a resounding metallic thud and, leering sinisterly, wiped the oil off his hands with a dirty rag.

One thing was for sure: his father had won the "Car Wager."

"You just saved me a couple grand, mate," he could hear his father saying, regarding their little agreement at the start of the semester when he'd got a load of DJ's first report card.

"With grades like these, you can rest assured of a spot working at me garage," Mr. Jones predicted, pronouncing the final word like 'marriage.' "Because mark my words: you will not graduate. I'll even go one further. I am *so* sure you won't graduate that I'll put me money where me mouth is—I'll buy you a car. A *used* car," his father said with direct specificity. "That is how confident I am."

———

"*He's nice, innhe?*" DJ asked upon returning. Jill and Lisa nodded in agreement as DJ pointed out bulky Stan pushing that skateboard down the road below. "*Loo' at 'im go.*"

They both pointed and snickered.

"He's gettin' it," Lisa offered.

"*Dro'pin' trousers an' all.*" They laughed. "*Ja fink 'e's a bit of a poof?*"

Jill and Lisa share a smirk. "Who knows these days, right?" Lisa asked.

Lisa jutted her chest out. Jill looked down at her own, before stretching her legs out.

The competition between them was not lost on him.

And suddenly, DJ wasn't so paranoid.

The father abruptly got up from his gurney, declared himself feeling better, and, despite the protestations of hospital staff, casually walked out with his son. The experiment had gone smashing as they exited the hospital and went their separate ways. The older gentleman, carrying a suitcase, flagged a cab down outside the hospital, and away he went. His son, having nothing but the clothes on his back, scanned the area and began walking.

Chapter

II

"Of course, if you haven't figured it out yet, I am, obviously, the narrator of this story," Robbin continued.

Starling looked up from jotting copious notes with a questioning look on her face. "I beg your pardon."

"You'll see."

After consuming most of the beer, half the Southern Comfort, and a fair amount of weed, Jill, Lisa, and *I* headed back to Lisa's car where, after driving for a small amount of time, Lisa noticed in the rear-view mirror that I was passed out in the back.

Or was I?

Starling had an "aha" moment and continued writing.

Music from the radio covered their low-whispered debate on which one would get with me, but I was plotting to get them both! Eventually, I think I really *did* pass out. I was awakened to find us parked outside a carnival where all the sights and sounds were in full force.

"I was," I started to say before remembering to employ my accent. "*Wha's all this then?*"

"It's an American carnival. Thought it'd be fun for you," Lisa said.

As the three of us walked across the gravel parking lot, the sweet smell of cotton candy hung in the warm summer air; my attention zeroed in on the loveliest creature I had ever laid eyes on. A girl with curly blonde hair walked towards us, beaming with a smile of recognition. Then, as the gods would have it, she slowly waved in our direction. I pointed to myself, unclear where I knew her from.

"Been here long? I literally just got dropped off on the other side," Curly said, her eyes squarely on me.

Feeling impervious to pain, I swiftly spun my guitar up to my face and began playing it with my teeth like Jimi. And abruptly broke the E string!

I could still see her past the right side of the guitar when I guess she twisted her foot. Her expression changed from elegant to erratic as she suddenly lunged unexpectedly right at me! Lucky for her, and despite being drunk as a monk, I reacted fast enough, swinging my guitar behind my back, where the strap choked me around my throat, and she fell awkwardly into my arms! If I had not been there, I would not have believed it.

"*'Ello*," I said, not missing a beat.

Veronica expressed her embarrassment by pulling her curls down over her forehead and eyes. "Okay, that was, like, totally embarrassing," she said, mimicking a Valley Girl accent.

"Um, when you're done throwing yourself at our new friend," Jill cracked.

I lifted her back onto both feet. "*You all wight, love?*"

"Yes, thank you. That's what I get for not wearing flats to a carnival, I guess."

"You want to tell us what your name is this week?" Lisa interjected.

"Haha, still Veronica," she replied with a playful push of Lisa.

"*Plesha' to make your acquain 'ance. DJ.*"

"Pleasure to make your acquaintance," Veronica mimicked me with a straight face. "English?"

"*Yea, 'ow'd ya know?*"

Veronica scoffed. "Whereabouts? Let me guess: London."

"Veronica's been to London," Lisa said in a sing-songy voice.

"Just long enough to see Big Ben and Buckingham Palace," Veronica clarified.

"Tomatoes, *tomahtoes*," Jill said succinctly.

"*Actsh'ly, Norf 'Amp'on*," I said, wishing I had simply said London from the beginning.

Veronica's lip curled up. "What are you doing here of all places?"

"That's what we said," Jill said with a forceful laugh, frowning at Lisa as if to say, 'Game Over for us.'

Lisa leaned in to whisper in Veronica's ear.

"*D'ya mind?*" I said tersely. She nodded in understanding and moved away, leaving Veronica hanging.

"Like your friend," Lisa whispered not-so-discreetly, referring to the blemish in the middle of Veronica's forehead. She had done an excellent job in covering it up, as it now resembled the freckles that covered her cheeks.

"Thanks," Veronica said, now feeling self-conscious about it.

"Hey, y'all."

We all turned to find Rick, a big burly guy with a winning smile and biceps upon biceps, walking up to us.

"Hey, Rick, this is our new friend, DJ from England."

Rick heartily shook my hand. "DJ from England. You know The Beatles?"

"*D'ya know John Wayne?*"

Rick laughed a hearty laugh as if to say, *Touche*. To a guy passing: "Denny, check this out. This dude's from England."

"Oh yeah, whereabouts?" Denny asks.

"Place called Norf 'Amp'on, d'ya know it?"

"Is it near *Standing* Hampton?" Denny said, followed by a forced laugh and a snap of his fingers. "Sammy Hagar album. 'Standing Hampton.'"

"So, then you must know wha' a standin' 'ampton is, then?" I asked, starting to chuckle to myself. As much as using *then* twice because it just sounded better. And I was *pissed*. Piss drunk.

Denny laughed, and I laughed harder. Private joke with someone who got it.

Just keep cuttin' those words to shit, I reminded myself. *It's so easy and their hanging on my every word.*

"Well, is anyone going to tell us?" Lisa asked, slightly annoyed.

"I li'e 'er, she's very direc', i'nshe?" I replied, coming back to Earth.

"It's English slang for 'hard-on'!" Dennis erupted in laughter. I followed, but just so he didn't laugh alone. "I love British humor, Monty Python."

"Me too, mate."

That's where I learned 'John Thomas' means dick."

"He's righ'," I informed after sharing a snicker with him. *"'E knows his English stuff."*

"Yeah? Do you know The White Cliffs of Dover?" Jill cracked.

"Know them? I've seen them in. You know, in person," he said smugly.

I felt like I was quickly losing control of the conversation as the girls stepped back from the circle to admire Veronica's fingernails. I just needed to steer it back to myself.

"So, why are you here?"

There was a long pause with all eyes on me.

"*I've go' fam'ly 'ere then,*" I said, though it sounded more like a question. "*'Ere in th' colonies.*"

"Colonies," Rick repeated, followed by further laughter. "You guys going to Marshall's party?" Rick asked the crowd, who all confirmed they were. "Cool, we'll see you there!" he said before steering me away from the group.

"Let me show you around a bit before the party. Meet some women. You know what I'm saying?" Rick said as I looked back, wide-eyed, at Veronica, mouthing the word 'Help.' Veronica merely shrugged apologetically before turning to Jill and Lisa. "I mean, why play kiddie games? You know what I mean?"

I want her to love me, I thought, as Rick approached a convertible MG, directing me around to the passenger side

"*Nice car, mate.*"

"You smoke cigarettes?" Rick asked while removing a pack of Marlboro Lights and extending it towards me; I nodded, slipping one out. "What brand do you smoke?"

I tried to conjure up the name of cigarettes that would undoubtedly sound English. "*Crowns*" was the best I could come up with on such short notice.

"We'll have to find some for you," he said to me, holding a lighter out. "You know the National Anthem was written over there," Rick loudly mentioned, pointing in the direction of Fort McHenry. "When you bastards invaded us during The American Revolution." (Actually, it was The War of 1812, America's first declaration of war. Even I knew that but I had more of a pony in that race).

"Oh yeah?"

Rick briefly grabbed my shoulder. "That's all right, we forgive you," he said with a hearty laugh.

Before long, Rick and I were moving along the bars of the waterfront town of Fell's Point, where Rick seemed to know every doorman and bouncer.

"This is my friend from England," Rick would say, as if we had actually met in England, before leading me inside various bars and taverns. I tried my best to keep up with my energetic new host, weaving through the Friday night throng of patrons. The smell of cologne and perfume reminded me of school earlier but now combined with the smell of alcohol.

"Pahdon me, pahdon me, pahdon me," I said to every person I squeezed past, keeping up my guise, never knowing who I might be introduced to now or later.

Not even eighteen, I was handed my first beer in a bar. *I could get used to this*, I thought, as I took my first sip. Ironic. As my "old" neighborhood was less than a mile away, I'd walked down these very cobblestone streets all my life.

"Not bad, right?" Rick asked over the roar of the patrons. Uncertain whether he meant being in a bar, some birds nearby, or the beer itself, I approved of all by nodding and smiling. "Budweiser! Or would you prefer some English ale?" Rick yelled in my ear. I shook my head, drinking from the pint glass with an approving nod.

Rick then introduced me to some women standing nearby that I initially thought my host knew.

"This is my friend, DJ!" he was forced to shout over the music and clamoring of everyone inside. When he propositioned the ladies, who seemed wholly uninterested, it quickly became apparent that he was riding my proverbial coattails. Rick quaffed his beer quickly and indicated for me to do the same.

We made our way back outside, where Rick removed a cigarette and handed it to me before removing one for himself. Then, he addressed a question to his doorman friend. "Hey, where can he get his brand of cigarettes?"

To me: "What are they called again?"

"*Crowns?*"

The doorman replied, "Try the International Newsstand over at Harbor Place."

Rick snapped his fingers. "Yes, thanks. Hey, you know what they call cigarettes over in England? Fags! Isn't that hilarious?" The Doorman nodded, barely cracking a smile.

———

"*Cheers, ma'e,*" I said, patting him gently on the back.

"Don't touch me," the doorman replied. I held my hands up apologetically.

Outside of Harbor Place, Rick left his car idling as I stepped out.

"*Please don' leave. You've got my guitah in your boot,*" I reminded him.

"I'm not even wearing boots," Rick said, laughing that wholehearted laugh of his.

"*I mean,*" I started to say as I pointed to the trunk.

"The trunk, I know. Hurry up."

I quickly shuffled up the stairs to seek out my imaginary brand of cigarettes. Once inside, I approached the counter where a middle-aged man with Mediterranean features watched a mini-color TV.

"*D'ya have cigra'es called Crowns? Or any English cigare'es,*" I asked, of course, keeping up my accent just in case.

"Crown? Let me see..." The man scanned all the cigarettes above and behind him. "No, no Crown."

"*Or any cigare'es from Englan'.*"

"Well, I got these," he replied, removing a blue box and showing me. "They're French."

"*'Ow'd ya pronounce it?*"

"I'm not sure, "Gauloises" I guess," he said, pronouncing every letter and syllable as it was written. (Actually, they are pronounced 'Gawa.')

———

49

"I'll take 'em."

I paid and turned to leave when the shop owner said, "Where are you from?"

Looking around to make sure the coast was clear, I replied, "Just down here off Thames Street." I winked before pushing through the glass door.

"Did they have 'em?" Rick asked, rather excited to be of assistance.

"Nah, they jus' 'ad some French ones," I said, climbing back into the car.

"So, you found some French fags!" Rick said, laughing maniacally before shifting away from the curb. "Now we just need some broads and some blow!"

I locked eyes with Rick. *"I migh' know a bloke."*

"A bloke of coke?" Rick gleefully replied, uncertain what a bloke was.

"A bloke wif coke," I corrected him.

As quick as spit, I deftly guided Rick back to my new house and was running my fingers across the bindles as I had done earlier that morning. Taking two from the row of twenty and shutting the drawer, I turned to leave but thought, *What the hell.* I spun back to the nightstand and grabbed them all. And down the road we went.

Vying to get back to that girl, Veronica, I waited impatiently for Rick to retrieve my guitar from the trunk, or boot, as us Limeys say. The party was in full force. Kids were lined up on the front steps, nearly everyone holding a red Solo cup. I followed closely behind Rick as he threw a block for his new running back.

The music combined with all the chatter, laughing and screaming was deafening. *My first American party*, I thought to myself, chuckling. Well, at least, white American party.

Someone in the far corner nodded his head to get his friend to turn around. It was the two jocks from school that morning that I nearly flattened with the office door.

"What the—? You see what I see?" the jock said, looking over his shoulder.

"I see a UFO, an Unidentified Fa**ot...Oh!"

"That's the dude from school today."

The jocks looked confounded as I followed Rick, who clearly knew his way around, to the downstairs toilet.

Rick muscled his way to the front of a small line and twisted the doorknob. It opened, and Rick walked into an empty bathroom. He turned and looked at the line of teenage boys. "There's nobody in here."

"Nobody's waiting for it. We're just talking," one Dude said, a tad effeminately.

"Yeah, well, if it were an elevator, you'd just be *going down*," Rick said, waving me in before locking the door behind us.

After handing a twenty-dollar note to me, Rick instructed me to roll it up while he took a framed picture of a waterfront lounge chair wedged in beach sand and set it on the bathroom counter. Rick's muscles flexed to and fro as he proceeded to pour a healthy amount of cocaine from the folded Playboy cartoon onto the framed glass. Then, sliding his driving license out of his wallet, the burly bouncer proceeded to cut out four distinctive trails along the waves of sand.

Taking the rolled-up bill from me, Rick put it in his nostril as someone twisted hard at the doorknob before banging on the door.

Outside the door were those two Jocks.

"Hey motherf----r," Jock 1 shouted.

With the deepest, most gravel voice I had ever heard, Rick shouted, "I'm pissing in here!"

"Sorry!" the guy said, backing away from the door. Then, satisfied, Rick pulled up the wicker hamper to the sink before running the rolled-up twenty along one line and down the second.

"Whoa, Nellie," Rick declared within a long exhale, pushing on each nostril while taking a deep breath. He held up the makeshift straw for me.

Taking the bill in hand, I pulled the framed picture forward to get a better shot at the other two rows of blow. In doing so, I knocked a cup of abandoned beer off the counter into Rick's lap.

"You D--k!!"

I recoiled in terror. "Sorry," I said, trying to help, but as it was in Rick's lap, it left me little to attend to in response.

Rick grabbed a towel from the rack and patted his nether regions down. "Sorry, man, that was a bit uncalled for. Proceed."

I smiled, relieved, before snorting my two available lines, getting a whole new lease on life. We tidied up a bit before stepping out of the bathroom.

Before I knew it, Rick had helped sell all nineteen bindles; pictures and mirrors were coming off the walls at breakneck speed, and I was counting my money just as Stan and I had initially plotted.

"Could everyone stop leaving their drinks on the floor, please? My dog's getting wasted!" Marshall told the crowd.

Just then, Marshall's French bulldog staggered into the room, his tail wagging, knocking a cup over onto a framed picture of an abstract painting—Marshall screamed— and the beer rushed across the glass like a dam break, irrigating between the fine lines, without touching a single granule.

I followed Rick through the kitchen and out the kitchen door. Out back, people hovered in and around an above-ground pool. And it was no wonder, for inside were Jill, Lisa, and Veronica in their respective bathing suits.

Rick threw his arms up in the air, indicating he had indeed arrived. Finally, we approached the keg where some stoners handed Rick the valve, having just finished pouring beer for themselves.

"You guys getting in?" Jill shouted over the nearby boom-box.

"I'll skinny dip if you guys do" Rick informed with his hearty laugh.

"Okay," Lisa said, pretending to unstring her bikini top. Jill laughed and tried to give her a hand. Then they both turned on Veronica.

Rick handed me a beer and began pouring his own, laughing at the girls. "Now we're cooking with gas." He leaned closer to me and whispered, "Which one do you want?"

I took a long, hard look at each of them. All three, laughing, giggling & jiggling, looked even better undressed and wet. Finally, my eyes landed on Veronica, at which point I whispered to Rick, *"I like the girl wif the curly 'air."*

"F---, I knew it," he replied with his hearty laugh. "Bastard," he said as he dropped the hose down the side of the keg. "All's fair in love and war," he added ominously. "Undies, okay?" Rick asked, an odd choice of word for such a burly guy. All three girls whistled and cat-called.

"Last one in is a rotten egg!" Rick said, quickly setting his cup down and ripping his shirt over his head. *Jesus, this guy's an Adonis*, I thought.

They all laughed at my baby blue bikini briefs, but I was nothing if not filled to the hilt with liquid courage. Not to mention they were my favorite underpants.

Rick climbed into the pool by way of the ladder, with me following suit, and we were soon surrounding the three girls. Lisa immediately noticed my gold chain and pendants.

"You have a cross *and* a Star of David?"

I looked down before lifting them off my skinny little chest. "*Yeah, yeah. Don't wanna ge' lef' ou' on a, ya know, techni'cali'y,*" I said, followed by my stupid, wheezy laugh, which then led me to cough uncontrollably. The girls laughed at me, exchanging glances with each other.

"You okay, mate?" Rick asked, patting my back.

"*D'ya know 'ho said tha'? Elvis.*"

"Presley?" Jill asked.

"Costello?" Lisa said over Jill.

"*Bloody Abbo' an' Costello over 'ere,*" I said, indicating Jill and Lisa. Rick laughed, followed by Veronica, who exchanged a long look with me.

Jill and Lisa, however, were not laughing.

"*'Ow 'bout Elvis does Elvis?*" I sneered, taking an Elvis Presley stance. Wobbling my right foot under the chest-high water I parodied Elvis Costello, completely off the cuff. "What's so funny 'bout cheese, cloves and mustard sandwich, Oh-Oh-Oh."

Oh, how they laughed.

In my mind, I had them right where I wanted them.

It was about this time that a song came on the radio called "Hold On."

"Ya ever heard of these guys? Crack the Sky?" Rick asked.

"*No,*" I lied. "*Bloody good, though.*"

CTS was a West Virginia group that found immense success in the Baltimore-Washington area with their self-titled debut album and its follow-up, "White Music." So much so that the local radio stations played no less than seven of their songs in regular rotation along with bona fide international groups like The Cars and Styx.

The truth was I loved Crack The Sky and felt compelled to sing along but knew that would be a dead giveaway.

More teens arrived, more clothes shed, more bodies filled the pool. Lightning bugs blinked yellow in different areas of the yard.

"*Cor, wha's 'at?*" I asked, pointing at the bugs briefly flashing. I honestly did not know.

"Lightning bugs," Lisa said.

"Fireflies," Jill corrected her.

"Haven't you ever seen a lightning bug?" Lisa asked.

"Firefly," the others said, correcting Lisa.

I shook my head. It was true, I had never seen one before. Rick swatted at one, catching it in his hand, holding it open for me to get a better look at one. It lit up before flying away.

"Did someone say *fireworks?*" a long-haired guy outside the pool asked, holding up a fistful of bottle rockets that he pulled from a paper bag.

Everyone cheered. Long-hair walked to the corner of the yard, strategically inserted them into the soil, pointing away, and casually lit their wicks. The bottle rockets sparked up and whistled off until they exploded in the starry-filled night sky.

As I looked around, music blasting, fireworks exploding, bodies heaving in the pool, I declared in my mind that this was the most incredible night of my life!

"*I need to 'ave a slash. Where's the Costello?*" I discreetly asked Jill, obviously knowing where it was but wanting to use some more British slang.

"Oh, I wouldn't do that," she replied, flashing a look of confusion to the others.

"*A loo. Lou Costello,*" I explained, thinking I had just invented a Cockney rhyme (such as "Bubble and Squeak"--Greek, "four by two"--Jew). But, I would discover later, I had not.

"*Toile*," I said, making it easier for everyone involved.

"Ohh," Jill said, "there's one just inside by the kitchen, and there's another one upstairs."

"*I'll be back,*" I informed the group.

I excused myself, making my way out of the pool. I tried to make eye contact with Veronica as I slinked down the ladder dripping wet, but she was laughing and talking to Lisa and Rick. When my feet reached the grass, though, I was aware of her looking in my direction. Eyeing my guitar and clothes on the table, I scooped them up as they all stopped to watch me.

Looking sheepishly at them, I asked indirectly for their understanding. *"If I knew you betah?"*

"Fine!" Rick shouted. "You don't trust us. What is it? 'Cause, we're AMERICANS?!"

Hunched over, dripping wet, all my gear in my arms, I replied, *"Glad you understand, ma'e!"*

They laughed as they watched me, in my soaked baby blue bikini bottoms, shuffle up the back porch steps and go inside.

I slipped into my jeans and threw my shirt over my shoulder as I made my way through the raucous, crowded living room where dudes were doing beer bongs from a huge homemade device with the stereo blasting the same radio station as outside.

"WHOO!" one of the jocks shouted, having downed the whole funnel full of beer in a flash.

"Where the hell you think you're going?" the Jock from earlier in the day said, intercepting me at the banister.

"I was 'eaded upstairs for a slash."

"Slash?! You ain't slashing shit, homeboy," the other jock said, approaching from the other side.

The party's host, Marshall, must have seen me making my way through the living room; he stood up on the couch and began clapping. "I applaud the man that made it snow in June!"

"You remember us? From this morning? You almost knocked us into next week with that door, man," the second Jock reminded me.

"*Oh, wha' a small world. Was tha' you?*" I said, desperate for a piss.

The jocks pivoted their torsos towards each other and then back to me. "Why are you talking like that?"

"Where the hell you from??"

"*London. London, Englan',*" I lied to simplify things, confident that I could explain it away with ease. "*Could I jus',*" I said, pointing upstairs with a tilt of my head, desperation, I'm sure, in my eyes.

"HEY! This dude's from ENGLAND!" the first Jock shouted. "Craig! Give him a beer bong!" He turned back to me. "Why were you at our school?"

Why was I there? I thought. *Think. Think.*

I shrugged, "*Who knows, I migh' go there next semestah.*"

The jocks led me over to Craig, who was holding the beer bong, along with another jock who proceeded to fill up the massive industrial hose with four cans of self-proclaimed American-style lager, Budweiser, through an enormous funnel.

A much older guy stood nearby, drinking from a fifth of Jack Daniels. "A Brit, huh? That's cool." I nodded politely, nervous about the amount of beer they were adding. "What's the drinking age over there? Sixteen or something?" Jack Daniels asked. I nodded, though I was uncertain. "You can drink on the streets there, too. Just gotta be mindful of the bobbies, am I right?"

"*Th' wha'?*"

"Bobbies. You know, *police*," J.D. said.

After the last can was in, Craig lifted the beer bong high in the air to land the plastic valve up right on my lips.

"*We don't really call 'em tha' anymore,*"I said, trying to remember what my father called the police. "*We call 'em the Old Bill.*"

"You ready?" Craig asked his hand on the trigger.

"That's funny. My name's Bill. Well, Billy."

I feigned a polite smile as I opened wide for the valve. On the radio, the disk jockey was airing a conversation with a caller's song request.

Caller: "Hey, man, what's that song where it goes (mouths guitar sound like 'David').

"Three," Marshall counted out.

Disc Jockey: "Ya gotta give me more than that, man."

"Two!" I craned my neck in a vain attempt to see the pool and, more importantly, Veronica.

Caller: (mouths guitar to sound like 'What are you doing?') "That song, man!"

"One!" Craig released the valve, and the four cans of beer sat idle for a moment before disappearing down my throat with a whoosh. Everyone cheered!

Disc jockey: "Sounds like your talkin' about a 'Yankee Rose.'"

My eyes watered up as my throat contracted, and I swallowed the remaining beer, which filled my whole body with a cold rush, making me feel queasy at best. Now I desperately had to piss.

Caller: "Yeah, who does that song, man?"

"What kind of cigarettes do you smoke?" Billy asked me.

Disc Jockey: "David Lee Roth, man."

Catching my breath, I responded to Billy, "*Roth, mans.*" As soon as I uttered it, I realized it was a verifiable lie. I was going to need to keep Rick away from him.

"You alright, man? You not gonna puke, are you?" the first Jock asked, laughing.

"*No, but I go'a ta'e tha' slash,*" I said, pushing my way past and bee-lining up the stairs.

"That's a Cockney accent," Billy said to no one in particular.

"Who wants a beer bong?" Craig shouted.

I slammed the door behind me and lunged for the sink, my body rejecting everything I had partaken in the last twelve hours, if not my entire life. The whole sink was covered in yellow and red pizza muck, and I found myself to be damn near stone-cold sober but very woozy, as I tried my best to scoop everything into the toilet with a towel, which I buried in a laundry hamper. I washed my hands before splashing cold water on my pained, ghost-like face.

And like I'd seen in a million movies, I raised my head to catch my reflection in the mirror.

"*Blonde, James Blonde.*"

I was reminded of the 'faker' lyrics of David Bowie's "Changes."

After passing a river of water, I grabbed my guitar, swung it over my shoulder, and looked back, making sure I hadn't forgotten anything before grabbing the doorknob.

"Le's go ge' these birds," I said with the utmost confidence, firmly believing I'd get them all. I swung the door open and barreled right into someone's chest.

But this wasn't just anyone.

It was my oldest nemesis, Duke Warfield. What the hell was he doing here?

"What the hell are you doing here?"

"Duke," I said, feigning sincerity.

"You're the English guy with the guitar? I should have known. What are you doing way up here, Monkee Jones?" Duke asked with a look of disgust.

We had a history dating back to our pre-teen days. Duke was the only other black rock-and-roller in our neighbourhood. We had been on-again, off-again friends for as long as I could remember and were even in a heavy-metal band for a hot minute.

I tried to look past him, but Duke, being a rather big fellow, blocked most of my view.

"How you doin'?" I asked quietly without my adopted accent.

"Man, get the hell out of my way," Duke said, pushing by me and into the bathroom. "You learn how to play that thing yet?" Duke asked before slamming the door shut behind him. "How's your mom? Still got the hots for me?" Duke added with a shout.

That did it. I kicked the door in, grabbed Duke by the back of his collar as he stood over the toilet, and dragged him down, shoving his head in the piss-filled bowl.

Well, I thought about it anyway.

Duke had never got over the time when the other two guys in our short-lived band, Revelations, tried to get us to make up after a massive argument we had during practice. The drummer took us both by the hand and led us to shake, but, instead, I took a swing at Duke—and missed!

He, in turn, chased me all the way back to my apartment. Since my parents were both at work, I barricaded myself inside, watching through the peephole until Duke eventually gave up and went home.

Truth be told, I always fancied a bit of the chase.

Chapter

Bastard! Duke's here, time to leave, fun while it lasted, I thought as I booked downstairs, mumbling "F---" as my feet landed on each and every step. I white-knuckled it around the banister, hurtling myself towards the front door.

And that's when I was confronted by wide-eyed zombies, including the two jocks from earlier, all looking for more.

"You got any more of that..." the Long-Hair asked, tapping the side of his reddish nose.

"No, y'all wiped me out of business."

Jock 1 pushed his way through. "Bullshit, I know you're holding."

"Check his pockets, lyin' black bastard," Jock 2 said.

These guys are back to being dicks, I thought; that did not last long.

———

They all started to get aggressive. I looked over my shoulders and up the stairs, knowing when Duke came down, I was dead meat.

"Hey English!" a female voice said from behind the small crowd amassed in the living room around me. Veronica pushed her way through. "Mike, does your mother even know you're out?" she said, addressing the more aggressive of the Two Jocks from school. They made way for her, backing off to have a private discussion.

"*'Ello.*"

"Hello," Veronica said with a chuckle. "Leaving already?"

I searched for an excuse. "*I should prob'ly be gettin' back. I only wen' ou' to explore the neighbourhood, and that was ages ago.*"

"Do you wanna use the phone here? Or maybe Rick or Jill can drive you home?"

I tried to sneak a peek up the stairs. "*Strange ques'ion for ya, but d'ya wanna ge' ou' o' 'ere?*"

Veronica laughed. "And go where?"

"*Back to my, um, me uncle's 'ouse, I guess?*"

"You don't have the right to ask me that. This is America. You're the visitor. I ask *you* that! So, do you want to get out of here?"

"*And go where?*"

"I don't know, your uncle's house, I guess?" Veronica looked over her shoulder.

"*Sure, why not?*" I replied, taking one last peek up the stairs.

She held up her purse to indicate she was ready to go, and I practically pushed her out the door. *White chicks*, I mused.

I leaned in towards Long Hair and said on my way out, "*The black bloke upstairs has got all the stash.*"

"So where does your uncle live?" she asked me as we slipped out the front door without further incident.

"*I don' know th' exac' address. I jus' know i' overloo's a famous cowboy ea'ery.*"

"A famous cowboy what? Did you say 'eatery'?"

"*Yeah, ya know, the "Yippie-Kai-Ay" bloke.*"

Veronica wracked her brain before it finally dawned on her. "Ohh, you mean Roy Rogers?" she asked, laughing a laugh that went up several octave scales.

"*Precisely. I li'e your laff, by th' way.*"

"Thanks, I hate it," she replied, laughing the same exact way. "Roy Roger's a-ways up the road. We should probably catch a cab or take the bus." I followed her gaze as she craned her neck behind us. The road stretched out for miles and miles without a bus in sight.

"So, do you have a girlfriend back in England?"

"*Back in England? No.*"

"I'm just telling you now: I'm not gonna scrump you."

"*Wha's a scrump?*"

"It's a cross between screw and hump. Scrump."

___

"*Shit*, I thought, but said, "*Tha's a relief. T' be 'onest, I'm tired of tryin' t' ge' in a birds' knickers, I wanna ge' in a bird's 'eart for a change.*"

Veronica laughed so hard she doubled over, nearly losing her balance, and stomped her feet, attempting to regain her footing.

"I've never heard a guy say anything quite like that before. Must be an English thing."

We reached a bus bench that I knew all too well. Exotic Auto, my father's shop, overlooked it from a slope beyond the sidewalk. *Probably best I don't mention it*, I reckoned.

And then the lamppost overlooking the bus bench blinked dead.

"*Didya see that?*" I asked excitedly.

"No. What?" she asked, having not seen it herself.

"*Nuffin, really. Ligh's jus' seem to go--I dunno, OFF around me.*"

We sat down and again looked up the sprawling road—trucks and cars headed in both directions but still not a single bus in sight.

"*Wha' abou' you? You're qui'e a lov'ly bird, why don' you 'ave a boyfrien'?*"

"Who said I don't have a boyfriend?" She froze. "Hear that?"

I took a long, hard listen but heard nothing.

"Wait for it--"

I waited but still heard nothing, just random traffic

noises off in the distance. Finally, Veronica lifted her hand as if about to conduct a symphony and I thought I heard a rumble off in the distance getting louder as it neared—a Harley-Davidson softback turned onto the main road and a biker dude and his backseat babe blasted past us.

"*That's quite a talen' you go' there,*" I said, waiting a long beat for her to continue answering my question. "*So...?*"

Veronica laughed. "Oh, haha, just kidding. No boyfriend. My last boyfriend was a d---. We did an around-the-world trip after graduating, and the farther away we got from the U.S., the meaner he got. He's real conceited and thought everywhere we went, chicks were, in his words, 'diggin' me.' Got real old real fast. And then the teasing started, making fun of me and my name. Especially my middle name. By the time we got to Fiji, we were pretty much ah-finished."

"*Righ' is tha' why they said: 'What's your name this week?'*" Veronica nodded. "*So, <u>wha'</u> is your middle name?*"

"Okay, before I tell you, there's a bit of a backstory. My parents were kind of like hippies, you know, the long hair and the beads and the peace signs, all that. So, they were headed up to Woodstock, you know, the big festival?"

I flashed a proper peace sign and winked knowingly.

"Well, they got caught in all that traffic and got stuck out on the highway."

I flipped my peace sign to my flipping-the-bird gesture, English-style. "*Bloody traffic.*"

"Never made it to one day of the show. And I guess while they--you know, 'scrumped' on the side of the road, one of the songs playing was Jimi Hendrix. You *look* a little like Jimi Hendrix."

"Yeah, I get that a lot." (I didn't). *Hey, Little Wing. I mean, I can fink of worse songs. Could've been 'Purple People Ea'er or sumfink."*

Veronica laughed. "I guess better than Cross-Eyed Mary."

"Funny, Jefro Tull."

"Jefro," she said, laughing. "Say 'three.'"

"Free."

"Three," she stressed. "One, two, three."

"One, two, free."

"You can't say it, can you?"

"Say wha'?" I said, feigning ignorance, which came so easy. *"So, if I've go' me mafs corre'ly, you were born in... nineteen seventy?"* She nodded. *"Am I righ'?"*

"April 18th," she said, nodding.

"Oh, no way, I was born on the eighteenf. June eighteenf. Paul McCartney's birfday." Her eyes widened with anticipation. *"Nine'een Seven'y...one".*

"Younger man," Veronica said playfully.

"Oh yeah?" I acknowledged. Veronica chuckled as I stood up and whipped my guitar in front of me— *back to where it all began,* I recalled. I struggled momentarily at making a chord with my left hand but lightly began playing, singing a parody of sorts to

the tune of 'Little Wing': "Well, she's sit-ting on a bench."

"This guy ain't bothering you, is he, little lady?" said a gruff voice from behind us. We turned to the car behind us: a police car with two veteran cops inside.

White cops.

"No, no, we're just waiting for the bus," Veronica said, almost pleading.

The cop in the passenger seat looked at us disapprovingly as he rolled his window up before his partner steered the cruiser away from the curb.

I stepped back into the street and flipped them off English-style. "*Piss off, copper!*"

Veronica shook her head at the audacity of our lovely civil servants. Then, taking note of her green eyes drooping, I excused myself to have another piss.

Desperate times called for desperate measures, so rounding the corner out of sight, I climbed the chain-link fence and made my way across the lot of my father's garage. I stopped long enough to peer through the glass office door, checking to see if it was locked—it was. I could only make out the framed picture of my beaming father hanging on the wall inside. I flipped him off, as well, before making my way over to where a pair of 1970s-era XJE Jaguars were parked.

Opening the white Jaguar, hoping to find keys inside, I checked the visor, under the seat, and the console; nothing but a flat-head screwdriver.

Nevertheless, I tried it in the ignition with no success before I exited, looking through the fence to make sure Veronica was okay; she was holding her head up with her arm on the back of the bench.

I opened the next car door, the lime-green Jag my father, unbeknownst to me at the time, had been working on earlier in the day. I got in and again looked for the keys. None. I inserted the screwdriver into the ignition and gave it a turn, and much to my surprise, it not only turned but started up with only the roar a Jaguar's V8 engine could.

"Why are you doing this to me?" I asked no one in particular as I shifted the automatic gear on the floor into reverse and backed out of the spot. I then pointed the car towards the padlocked gate and paused before stomping my foot onto the gas pedal.

"Are we missing someone?" Rick asked Jill and Lisa.

All three looked around at all the partygoers. No DJ.

"Two people," Lisa was quick to point out to Jill.

The two girls ogled Rick as he climbed out and down the ladder.

"Dirty whore," Jill said of Veronica.

"Man, I ain't got nothing on me," Duke was imploring with the Two Jocks, who, it might be noted, were not calling him racist slurs.

Rick made this way through the house. Hilariously, all the sniffles made it sound as if everyone had the flu.

Unable to find DJ, Rick returned to the pool looking like a rejected puppy.

"He's gone," Rick said resignedly as he climbed back into the pool.

"Awwww," Jill and Lisa said as they welcomed him with open arms.

"You liked him, didn't you?"

He wrapped the monstrosities he called his arms around them, smiling the most priceless of smiles.

Marshall stood at the bottom of the basement stairs trying to encourage his drunk dog to come down, his limp little right legs dangling over the top step like wet noodles.

"Duke, can you help me? I'm trying to get him away from all this."

Without a word, Duke nudged the dog with his foot, sending him sliding sideways down the stairs before continuing.

The Jaguar shot across the pavement, and BAM! It was like hitting a brick wall without the front crumpling up; the car seemed to almost come off all four tires before coming to an abrupt stop.

How come it always works in the movies? I wondered. More importantly, though, I was concerned if Veronica had heard that.

I backed up for a second attempt and again charged the gate with the same result. As I sat idle, not wanting to give up after coming this far, I looked to the right of the gate where there was nothing but a fence between the adjacent poles. No cars, no curbs, there was nothing to impede my attempts at escape.

I backed up the Jaguar once more, as far as it would go without smashing through my old man's office. Instead, I paused for a moment before gunning it towards the chain-link fence; it raised and lowered with ease as if it were the hidden entrance to the Batcave. I made a quick right, followed by a second and third, pulling up right in front of Veronica, who was all but asleep.

"Fancy a lif'?"

Veronica's eyelids raised ever so slightly and then widened when she saw me behind the wheel of a Jaguar.

"Grab me guitar, would ya?"

I guided the stolen, well, "borrowed" car up the road, pretending not quite to know where I was. Veronica's long blond hair whipped frenetically in all directions. She attempted to hold and capture it with little success.

"So, where did you get this car?"

"Well, ya know bein' English and all, we've all go' the same key, innit?"

"Yeah, I can see that," she said, pointing to the screwdriver sticking out of the ignition. "All we need now is some Whitesnake," she said, referring to the now-famous Jaguar video from two years prior.

And with that, she climbed out of the window like Tawny Kitaen. I couldn't believe my eyes. Or my luck. I looked all around as she laughed hysterically, her hair whipping wildly. Then, nervous, I desperately pulled her back in.

Changing the subject, I offered, *"Ya go' a lo' o' air there."*

Veronica agreed, rolling up the window. "Yeah, maybe too much hair."

I laughed that stupid raspy laugh of mine. *"I meant air, not 'air."*

Veronica smiled, seeming to understand the slight disparity of the two words, as I stopped for a red light.

Asking her if she knew there were two versions of "Here I Go Again," I was astonished by her reply.

"Yeah, the 'drifter' version and the 'hobo' version. They were afraid Americans would change it to "homo," she said matter-of-factly. Of course, she didn't know it at the time, but with that one reply, that shit won my heart.

We drove up that new main road for a while, gazing at each other without saying a word. I could have driven forever had it not been for a light changing to red. But, instead, I braked and watched as the overhead streetlamps lit up Veronica's eyes, the greenest eyes I had ever seen. She looked at me, smiling slightly, and was quick to notice my sudden change of expression.

Don' loo' now, but those coppers jus' pulled up," I mumbled. Veronica froze. *"Slowly lean ova 'ere and give us a kiss."*

Veronica laughed, looking over her shoulder--there was no cop car. She turned and lunged at me. I closed my eyes to welcome her lips to mine. Instead, she merely kissed me on the cheek before sitting back and smiling.

"You're cute."

"*You're bloody lovely,*" I said as the light changed. Veronica smiled sincerely while straightening her skirt, pulling it down to her knees. I smiled and looked at the road ahead before proceeding through the intersection. "*My mum just died. And, as a result, my dad tried to kill 'imself.*" The first utterly true thing I had said all day.

"Oh my God. When? How?"

"*Ten days ago? She went in for what was supposed to be a simple procedure. Never came home.*"

Veronica moved closer in her bucket seat and ran her fingers around my right ear and neck before pointing out the Roy Rogers restaurant on our left.

"Yippie-kai-yay," Veronica said.

"Muttaf----," I said, like Hans in "Die Hard."

After two quick left turns, we cruised up the hill of my new street. Then, parking a few houses up so as not to be seen by my father in the morning, we stepped out, carrying on our conversation.

"You need to do something, something unique, to honor her memory, to keep her spirit alive." I slowly closed my door while Veronica slammed hers without a care in the world. I took her by the hand and led her down the street, passing what I could only assume was a neighbor sitting in the driver's seat reading the newspaper. It had to be near midnight. White people.

She gripped my arm tightly as we scaled the slight embankment and made our way through the six-foot-high privacy fence that surrounded the backyard—I had a backyard!

Light escaped from the living room windows.

"Gonna see who's still up," I said, guiding Veronica to a seat on a mechanical swing. We had a swing? She looked exhausted, and I wondered how this was all going to play out.

I slipped through the unlocked sliding glass door to see the dog merely lift his head and found my father slow dancing in his wheelchair with an imaginary partner as a commercial played on TV. The song, ironically, was Billy Paul's "Me and Mrs. Jones."

"Dad, wha' you doin'?" I asked, not realizing it was with an accent.

Surprised, Mr. Jones stopped in his tracks.

"Nothing. What are you doing?" Mr. Jones rolled over to the stereo and clicked off the music before reversing himself back to the recliner, where he switched seats with all the grace of a flopping fish. "Where you been?" he asked as he unmuted the television.

"Oh, you know me, just making friends everywhere I go." He sized me up with eyes as droopy as that dog sleeping beside us.

Bad English
the III

On TV, the commercial finished, leading back into "Late Night with David Letterman," who announced he was holding that night's Top Ten List: 'Top Ten Things We as Americans can be Proud of.'

Under the current circumstances, I could not help but smile, and upon the first couple of entries, I even found himself laughing aloud. Maybe too hard.

"What rubbish," Mr. Jones said, leaning forward. "You think this is funny?"

I turned my attention from the crack in the curtains back to my father. "Yeah," I laughed.

"Met all your teachers, know where to go to take your final exams?"

"Yup."

"Signed, sealed, and delivered?"

"Yup."

"Well, I guess that car is practically yours then, yeah?" he asked, grunting as he returned to the wheelchair.

"Looks that way," I said, overly confident.

Mr. Jones wheeled past me, then abruptly stopped. "Oh, that reminds me...your school called."

My heart sank into my stomach, and my pulse began to race like the show ponies at nearby Pimlico.

"You know that green Jaguar I have at the shop?" Dad asked, gripping my knee hard.

Do I? I thought. I nodded slowly. "Yeah?"

"Well, that was going to be yours. But you, mate, just saved me, oh, a few *thousand* dollars. So, you can start working at the shop Monday. In the meantime, I want you to take care of that lawn tomorrow. Front and back."

"Why me?!" I protested. "Why couldn't the owners cut the grass before they moved out?"

"It's our house, now!"

In the middle of our street? I thought, Madness being appropriate.

"And I let you live here. And don't forget to say good-night to your mum."

My eyes darted to the faux fireplace where the framed portrait of the three of us taken a week before her surgery leaned. My mother looked majestic and proud. Uncertainty existed in my father's eyes, contrasting with the painted-on smile on his face. I showed nearly no emotion at all. Though it was only about a month ago, it seemed like an eternity.

In front of the canvas, my mother resided in her new resting place, a black metallic urn with thick black, white, and gray stripes surrounding it.

I watched as my father stopped the chair at the bottom of the winding staircase, stood up on his left foot, and stepped on the bottom step before leaning back to grab the chair by the back. Step by step, he slowly ascended the stairs, dragging the wheelchair behind him. The dog, like him, climbed the steps behind one at a time.

"Need some help there, Dad?" I said, trying not to say it too loud.

"No, no, I've got to do this by myself."

This is going to take all night, I thought to myself. I looked back out the window at a slumped over Veronica.

After my father finally made it upstairs, I slipped back outside and took a seat on the swing next to Veronica.

"I am so sorry tha' too' so long," I whispered as Veronica opened her eyes, seemingly having forgotten where she was. *"Care to ta'e a ja—,"* I whispered, stopping myself as I wasn't sure how to pronounce jacuzzi in this accent. *"An 'ot tub?"* And, boy, was I glad I did.

We peeled off our clothes, me back to my briefs, Veronica back to her bikini, and climbed in. I wasted no time in sidling up in front of her and planted a long, slow kiss on her welcoming mouth. Our tongues playfully darted against each other's until we finally pulled apart; a long string of saliva dangled between our mouths, reminiscent of the spaghetti noodle shared between "Lady and the Tramp." We both swiped embarrassingly at it.

"'Ello," I whispered after the spit floated off across the steamy bubbling surface.

"Hello," she replied with a shorter version of her laugh. "It cracks me up every time you say that."

I strategically waited for the light to go out in my father's room before sneaking her into the house.

"Nigh' Mum," I whispered, pointing at Veronica and mouthed the words: 'This is Veronica.'

Weaving through the dark house, we made it up to the second floor and down the hallway to my room. Pulling her behind me, I stopped dead in my tracks, causing Veronica to plow into me, where I felt her breasts on my back. Probably the extent of any action I was going to get, I figured.

"*Wron' room,*" I whispered, realizing that my room, plastered with posters of rock groups, might be a dead giveaway.

I pushed past Veronica, leading her back to the room we just passed, the less-obvious study. She leaned against the wall while I quickly removed the cushions and pulled the hide-a-way bed out, lowering the far end's metal legs mere centimeters from the TV stand where a small color television sat. This fold-out bed had been used a ton. I could not begin to gauge how many bodies had slept on it over the years.

I retrieved a sheet, blanket, and a couple of pillows from the closet, and with Veronica's help, we made ourselves a cozy little love nest before climbing on from opposite sides.

Once settled in, I turned on the TV and flicked around until landing on a movie channel playing one of my favorite movies.

"'*Ighlander,' d'ya know it?*" I asked her excitedly. She shook her head, smiling with feigned interest. "*Oh, i's brillian', you'll love it. And i' jus' star'ed. So, these two blokes*

*are immor'al an' they've got to kill all the otha immor'als until
only one is left, and then he gets a Prize."*

"What's the Prize?"

"You'll see," I said, positive she would never make it
to the end.

On TV, two men fought with swords in the garage
under Madison Square Garden. Finally, when the Scot-
tish-born Highlander had the Polish Immortal Fasil
dead to rights, he swung his Japanese sword, cutting off
his adversary's head, and the garage exploded in magic
and electricity. After he ditched his sword, the camera
panned up, and I raised my hand as if I were a Conductor, looking over to see Veronica was out like a light. I
continued my faux-symphony as the camera rose into
the Scottish Highlands in the 17th Century.

An hour or two later, I awoke to find the movie was
long over, and another, an unrecognizable film had be-
gun. I adjusted my eyes; from the glow of the television, I could see her bikini bottoms on the floor. My
eyes traced down Veronica's back, and a lovely back it
was. It slowly expanded with each breath taken, a slight
snore emitting. My gaze continued down her denim
skirt. It was hiked all the way up past her waist; her ver-
tical smile tantalized and tortured me.

Don't do this to me.

I was quickly reminded of the scene with the passed-
out girl in "Animal House." And like the movie, I, too,
could see the proverbial Devil on my right shoulder

and Angel on my left. And though, theologically speaking, I struggled daily with the belief in any true higher power, I wondered if my mother was testing me from wherever her spirit roamed.

Nevertheless, I punched the Angel right in the nose, followed by the Devil. I wrestled with the button of my jeans before spooning up behind her, curving my toes alongside hers, melding my body along with her perfectly curvaceous female form.

The next time I woke up, it was daylight. I tried to shield my eyes behind Veronica's shoulder, nuzzling my nose in her curls. It tickled. My ears perked up at the buzz of dad's electric wheelchair as it passed the study in the hallway before bumping into my bedroom door.

"David, you—*now* where the hell is he?" Mr. Jones asked, incredulously.

I could hear the wheelchair along with a certain sniffing sound. My heart began pounding. So, was my head. I heard it stop and reverse, heading back my way. I quickly lunged over the side of the sofa bed, shoving Veronica's bathing suit and purse further under the bed and just barely at that. The study door slowly eased open as I flapped the blanket up and yanked it down, covering us both.

"Oy! What the hell are you doing in here? I need you to cut that lawn today. It's a bloody eyesore."

Mr. Jones' eyes focused on the long blond hair emerging from the top of the blanket. "Your hair's gettin' long now, innit?"

I can only assume he must have spotted the purse strap under the bed when he shouted: "OI! Get your arse out here." Mr. Jones rolled out of the study, scowling at me.

Climbing over Veronica, I slipped into my jeans, stumbling as I followed my father, who stopped at the top of the stairs, that damn dog by his side. "Walk down three steps and turn around."

"What?"

"You 'eard me. Walk down three steps and turn around." I walked down three steps, thinking of the Lynyrd Skynyrd song, "Gimme Three Steps," and turned around. Mr. Jones drove the wheelchair to the edge of the steps, bringing our faces mere inches apart. "What do you think you're doing? Don't you have any respect for your mother? For yourself?"

"Oh, *now* you wanna talk about mom. Let's talk about the elephant in the room for f--- sakes."

"What's there to say?"

"What's there to say? Oh, I've plenty to say."

"Yeah? Get that bird out of here. And then we'll talk."

I pointed at my father sternly as I headed back up the stairs, squeezing past him and making a quick beeline to my room. Then, grabbing a t-shirt, I slipped back into the study and leaned onto the bed where Veronica still lay sleeping on her side.

"Veronica...Veronica, you go' t' ge' up, ya go' a go, love." No reply. I leaned closer and began to nudge and shake her ever so gently but firmly. *"Veronica...Ronny."*

Ronny, I thought, *Sharonda, Veronica*. Holy crap. *Ronny.*

"Did you just say Ronny?" she said, opening her eyes with a smile. "I just had the weirdest dream about your uncle."

"*Yeah, you're gonna 'ave to tell me abou' tha' la'er.*" I reached under the bed to grab her bathing suit and purse. "*I just had a run-in wif me uncle. I'm so sorry. He's told me to ge' you ou' of 'ere. Arsehole.*"

Veronica looked a little punch-drunk and well groggy as she slithered out of bed, adjusting her now-wrinkled clothes. She straightened her hair the best she could and turned to pick up her purse and bikini. Because the bed stretched to the TV stand, she was forced to crawl across the bed, a vision I knew I would never forget as long as I lived. She swung her legs over the side where I had the shoes that caused her to fall into my arms, already lined up to step into.

"*Prob'ly shouldn't be seen in that Jag,*" I said as I led her to the front door. Veronica nodded as she accepted a kiss from me. She was still receptive, despite having been forced to beat it at eight o'clock in the morning. "*You alright? D'ya need any money or anyfing?*"

"I don't need anything," Veronica purred as I nearly forcibly pushed her out the door.

"*Can I call you la'er?*" I had the actual gall to ask under the circumstances.

"No. You *may* call me later." She relayed her telephone number to me, and I repeated it over and over to memorize it.

We kissed again before Veronica turned away from the house and made her way down the sidewalk.

A lot of firsts just occurred, I thought, as I then remembered something, running outside to catch up to Veronica to point out a shortcut: the steps that led back down to the Roy Rogers.

I patted myself on the back as I returned inside, quickly stripping the sofabed of its sheet and pillows, shoving them back into the closet. I began to close the sofa bed when I heard the front door close.

Where's he off to? I wondered.

I rolled over the sofabed, ran to the window, and watched as dad backed out of the driveway in his vintage nineteen seventy-eight Mercedes 240D. He turned the car to the right, meaning he wouldn't pass the Jag.

I knew I had to do something with the car and wondered whether I had enough time to try and slip it back into dad's garage or "carriage" with a "g." So I climbed into the driver's seat, put the screwdriver into the ignition, and it fired up at once. I quickly spun it around on the street and backed it into the driveway—I had a driveway!

Looking up and down the street, I rushed through the house and opened the garage door. After moving some of the boxes, I backed the Jaguar in. As I locked the garage door, I rationalized with myself that my father had yet to go inside the garage. I dragged the lawnmower out onto the front lawn before I locked it from the inside, trying to start it but quickly found myself looking down the hole of yet another rabbit hole. I seemed to recall a gas can inside, but I simply could not find it.

Can't fault me for that, I figured. I tried.

Just then, Dad pulled up along the front of the house and eased his Mercedes into the driveway. He opened the door, slid his left leg out, hopped on one foot, opened the back door, and yanked out the collapsible wheelchair.

"There's no gas," I informed him.

He dropped into the wheelchair and reversed it to the trunk, where he opened it and pulled out the gas can.

"My hero," I said sarcastically. "Thanks, Doc."

Chapter

IV

Before pulling into his modest one-bay garage, Exotic Auto, Mr. Jones, as he did every morning, unlocked the padlock and swung the gates open, pulling his car into his usual spot. Inside, as he also did every morning, he started the coffee maker while perusing the invoices on his desk with his typical pained wince.

As the coffee maker percolated, filling the room with the smell of fresh java, he looked out onto the lot where it occurred to him that something was out of place. He stood up and walked onto the small lot; cars in various stages of repair or signs in the windows of the ones for sale were parked on both sides.

Then it became clear: the green Jaguar was gone. He looked around the lot for it but to no avail. He walked over to where the lock still hung and checked and rechecked it a few times, concluding that it seemed to be

---

working correctly. Finally, with nothing else to go on, he looked up to the skies before quickly shuffling back inside to call the police.

Back at home, after falling back asleep, I woke up and had a bowl of cereal and, like a good son, set out to push the mower around the front yard—what the hell was I doing with a lawnmower?

As it was the first time I had ever mowed a lawn, I pushed it erratically and haphazardly, leaving patches of uncut grass across the entirety of the property. I was too focused on my music, occasionally stopping to play a drum fill or a guitar solo on my air instruments to give a good cahoot.

Once when I was about three or four, I had come out to the living room for a glass of water. It was late, I was groggy, Dad wasn't there, I recalled. Mom got up during a commercial break to fetch me a glass of Baltimore's finest when a man with a beard announced the next performer. I was mesmerized with this long-haired, wild-eyed madman and declared: "That's what I want to do, Mommy."

Despite making me chug an entire glass of water, the next day, and over his protestations, she gave me Dad's acoustic Yamaha guitar from under their bed. At first, I was scared to even touch it. Then, when I did, I quickly got intimidated by it; wouldn't pick it up for weeks at a time.

From that day forward, my mother proudly announced that I wanted to be a guitarist after seeing Jimi Hendrix. And I was the living embodiment of him. But no, the show was the Midnight Special. The man that introduced him: Wolfman Jack. The song was "Free For All."

The performer: Ted Nugent.

Exploring this third galaxy type of memory, I did not see the taxi pull up behind me.

While the taxi driver attended to the luggage in the trunk, a tall, very spry, elderly gentleman stepped out from the backseat. The older man, squinting from the sun, looked the house and neighborhood up and down. Finally, he paid the driver, but only after he had set his bags at the edge of the lawn.

As I backed the mower up, the old man pointed his walking stick in front of him, poking me in the ass. I leaped forward before spinning around to face my attacker.

Who is this old geezer? I wondered, and then I saw it—the hawkish nose and hooded eyes could only be one person: my family—the white English side.

To be exact, my father's father was the very man people from his old neighborhood thought had died during the war but, in reality, had simply never returned.

The old man opened his arms wide, but I couldn't take my eyes off the cane, even though there was nothing special about it, just a run-of-the-mill number with a gold inlay below the handle, not unlike the stripes on Mother's final resting place.

"What are you doing working on the Sabbath?" the old man said with a surprisingly thick English accent of his own, his arms still wide open, awaiting a response.

"Grandad?"

"There's only one."

"Well, I do have another one, you know. Like, what brings you here?"

"Trans World Airlines," Grandfather dryly replied. "They are no British Airways, let me tell you."

I waited a moment for a complete answer, but none seemed to be forthcoming, just a weird silence before he pulled me into his rumpled tweed overcoat. He smelled of strong aftershave, and his jacket scratched my nose.

"Came to see the first one in the family to finish school. Couldn't miss that, now, could I?"

There was a long pause until I felt his embrace loosen, and I pulled away to rub my itchy nose.

"You know, my mother graduated from college."

"Yeah, well, I didn't quite know her essence then, did I?" he said with a wink. "I *am* sorry about your mum, David."

I nodded, looking down across the unevenly cut grass.

"Last time I saw you, you were no bigger than a box of bananas. And green, as well. But look at you now. You look like a smart lad. I bet you got the world by the bol-locks, don't ya?"

I shrugged with uncertainty.

"Well, you do, don't you? Come on," Grandfather barked out as he nodded his head toward his suitcase and smaller kit bag, a valise, I think they're known as. It reminded me of the one carried by Jack the Ripper in the movie "Time After Time."

"Was that a true story, mommy?"

"A *time machine*?" my mother replied as we walked out of the cinema.

I picked them up as Grandfather practically pulled me across the lawn and up onto the porch--I even had a porch!

Inside, I led my grandfather through the house, giving him a less-than-stellar tour.

"Still unpacking as you can see...kitchen, living room, stairs up to the bedrooms," I said, pointing around the house. I guided him up to the spare room where the bed was still open, the sheets and pillows in a disheveled pile sticking out of the closet door.

"You were expecting me?" Grandfather inquired, with a twist back and forth of his torso.

I laughed. "Long story."

Returning to my room, I knew I was going to have to face all of this head-on. I was going to have to call her, and I knew she was going to be super-pissed at me.

Telephones, I hated them. I truly loathed calling people. Mostly because of the intrusion factor. Did the person you were calling truly want to hear from you? Or are they making faces and hand gestures the entire time? I much preferred getting calls to making them. And I was just as guilty of making those same gestures that I was worried about being done to me if I didn't want to speak to the person calling. Caller ID was just coming around, but it was kind of exciting when the phone rang, and you had no idea who was going to be on the other end.

The line trilled through the earpiece.

"Hello?" a girl answered.

"Hey, baby," I said.

"Don't you *baby* me? Why you ain't call me in three days? You up there wit' dem white bitches now?"

"Nah, baby."

"Playing that got-damn guitar, *I* got for you Christmas, ain't ya?"

"C'mon, baby, it ain't like that now." I said we were trying to get everything moved in as my eyes landed on all the unopened boxes in front of me. "You know, there are only two of us now. And you *know* how cheap my father is."

"Yeah, I bet.

"You know, you could be nice to me—MY MOM JUST DIED!" With a low intense roar, I said she was not getting the "two of us now" reference.

There was a long pause. "I'm sorry, Deji," Sharonda said, relenting sincerely.

She called me by one of the nicknames she picked up from my parents, originally DEJ, derived from my initials. But, depending on their mood, they were oft to call me Dej, Deji, or Deji Arnaz, a play off of Desi Arnaz from "I Love Lucy." Ironic, as my parents were like Ricky and Lucy Ricardo if you exchanged Cuban for English and white for black.

"You ok, baby?" she finally asked me with genuine sincerity.

"I'm ok. Hey, we still gonna go see that new Spike Lee movie?"

"Yeah, what's that called again?"

There was a pause as I resigned to say the words. "Do The Right Thing."

"Yeah. Do. The. Right. Thing."

I could not think of what to say next. "What's Tony up to?"

"Oh, now you wanna talk to Anthony."

"Hello?" a woman asked pleasantly on the other end of the line.

"*'Ello, may I speak to Veronica, please*," I said after having practiced it a few times for pure perfection.

———

"Hold on." I listened to the phone muffle as Veronica's mother shouted out, "RONNY! TELEPHONE." Into the phone, she asked, "May I tell her who's calling?"

"David Jones, but she migh' remember me as, uh, DJ."

The phone rustled again. " Are you calling radio stations in Australia? It sounds like Crocodile Dundee's on the phone!"

"That's his name, not his job and he's not from Australia, mom, he's from England." The phone ruffled yet again on the other end. "Hello?"

I took a deep breath, basking in the glow of the lovely tone of her voice.

"Hello?"

"'Ello..."

There was an excruciatingly long pause before Veronica finally replied. "I never get tired of hearing you say that."

"Crocodile Dundee, eh? Now that's a wife."

She laughed. I liked her laugh, it started low and rose one octave after the next. Voice was so important to me. Could even be, I reasoned, a make-or-break scenario. I mean, who wants to have to listen to an annoying voice? Who wants to be awakened by one?

"So you made it 'ome, al righ' then? I'm truly sorry abou' this mornin'."

"Yeah, the walk of shame at 8 o'clock in the morning. Thanks. You know, your uncle picked me up?"

My heart jumped in my chest. *"'E wha'?"*

"Yeah, he kept saying he was your father and that you were a bad, bad boy."

"Well, tha' par's true. I guess he finks he's me dad now."

"I love the way you say 'think'."

"Wha'? Fink?"

She chuckled, "Yea, 'fink. So, is he right?"

I contemplated not only the question but also how to best answer. *"Was he saying 'e's my dad, or was 'e sayin' 'my son'? 'Cause, that's an English fing: Alrigh' my son,"* I said, illustrating for her.

"You know, I'm not sure now. So, are you bad, English? He said I should be careful, should I be?"

"Whacthu fink?"

Another long pause.

"If whatever it was, last night or this morning, was any indication, I *"fink"* he's probably right."

"Can I come see you?" I asked, convincing her with little difficulty. Overjoyed, I hung the phone up and tossed it on the bed, not even caring that the receiver had fallen out of the cradle as I charged out of the room, grabbed the door frame, and swung out, stopping just short of slamming into my Grandfather in the hallway.

"Corr, watch out, lad, you coulda knocked me lungs out me back!"

"Sorry...sorry."

"I was looking for the toilet," he said, revealing yet still a bit of an English twang.

"Oh, it's down this way," I said, pointing him in the opposite direction.

"So, what's the plan, Stan?" Grandfather asked as he backed me into my room, stopping inside the doorway. I took note that he was dressed down in his tallit, a poncho-like piece of clothing with tassels that dangled called tzitzits. I emptied the last of the milk from my cereal bowl, puffing my right cheek out to store it temporarily,

"That reminds me, I've gotta call Stan, you know, my cousin?" I informed him after swallowing, setting the bowl inside the bowl of dried oatmeal that still sat on my nightstand from the previous morning.

I laughed that stupid, wheezy laugh of mine as I opened my box of t-shirts in search of a specific one.

"Did I say something funny?" Grandfather asked, a bit of an edge in his question.

"No, well, yeah. I just met this girl, and she thinks I'm from England. No idea why, and I was just telling her that the English say *'Alrigh' my son'.*"

I chortled, a little nervously knowing full well I would eventually have to come clean.

"A bird, eh?" I nodded. "Alright, my son," he said proudly. "Not bad, mate. May I hear some more, please?"

"Oh yeah? *Well, the truf is, I'm feelin' a bi' guil'y, she's really qui'e nice,*" I said as I withdrew the plain black T-shirt I was looking for.

"Ah, regrets, I've had a couple over the years. Truth be told, everything and nothing I've done in my life," Grandfather said, somewhat prophetically.

I stopped pulling the shirt over my head to momentarily ponder what he said, Since I knew little of my grandfather's life, I had no idea what to take away from the statement; likening it to a dirty pool, not being able to determine if it was terribly deep or extremely shallow.

Grandfather pointed to the Rolling Stones poster I'd hastily Scotch-taped to the wall the night we moved in. "Corr, ya know, I hope Mick Jagger never dies," he said rather solemnly.

I looked up as I pulled my head through my shirt. "What's that?"

"I hope Mick never dies," Grandfather reiterated, looking me squarely in the eyes before taking a step backward. "Yeah, as long Mick's alive, I'm the second ugliest man in the world."

With that, Grandfather tapped the wall beside the door frame and walked out of the room, leaving me to contemplate not only his surprising witticism but, to be honest, my entire existence. A big smile tore across my face as I tucked my t-shirt into my shorts. I got a look at myself in the mirror and yanked my shirt out as I looked ridiculous.

After a basic overview of the TV and the remote and cable TV, I left my Grandfather watching the baseball game and headed to Veronica's. I desperately wanted to take the Jaguar but didn't want to chance it in case my father had called the cops.

Instead, I filled the Vespa up with the remaining gas from the gas can and, leaving across the unfinished lawn, headed down to her house with the directions she had provided. Along the way, I practiced ways and scenarios in which to tell her the truth. I figured she would be upset, but how upset? I wondered. There was just no way of knowing.

Parking the scooter, I nervously climbed the steps to her front porch. At the front door, I took a deep breath and reached for the doorbell when, to my surprise, it swung open, revealing a little girl of about eleven, a mini-clone of Veronica.

"May I help you?" she asked, ever so politely.

"'Ello. Does Veronica live 'ere?"

Veronica's sister looked over her shoulder and yelled at the top of her lungs, "VERONICA! There's a black kid that talks funny at the door for you!"

"Dana! Rude," her mother snapped off in the distance. "Don't leave him standing on the porch. Invite him in!"

"Won't you come in?" Dana said as she opened the door, allowing me to step inside.

"Cheers, thank you?"

Closing the door behind her, and upon direction from her mother, Dana led me back to the TV room, giving me a makeshift tour that proved very deja vu-like.

"Our dining room."

"Nice."

"So, you're from England?"

"*Mmm,*" I offered, torn between continuing my deception and finding the right time to cease. *Clearly this is not the right time,* I concluded.

"Our bookshelves, books.

"*Very nice.*"

"That's our computer," Dana informed, before looking over her shoulder at me. "Do you have computers in England?"

"*Bu' o' course.*"

"Kitchen's through there."

"*'Ave one, as well.*"

The family dog, a small gray Shih Tzu, wandered out of the kitchen. "That's our dog. Do you have dogs in England?"

"*I'm only from across the A'lan'ic, not anuva planet,*" I said, chuckling, thinking about the new dog we had, some sort of weird replacement of my mother.

"Oh, and poet, too, I see," Dana shot back.

She led me into the television room, which was crammed with furniture and shelves upon shelves of books and knick-knacks. And of course, the man of the house, Veronica and Dana's father, sitting back in his recliner, wearing shorts and an old Ocean City tank-top. Baseball emanated from the TV where their father's attention was squarely focused.

———

"Daddy, this is DJ. He's from England." Their father barely acknowledged me. "You can have a seat on the sofa," Dana said, pointing to a dingy yellow sofa alongside the far wall.

I sat down and turned my attention to the game on TV. It was my beloved Orioles playing against the Milwaukee Brewers. The only sounds were the announcers, and the occasional roar of the crowd as the Orioles tried to take advantage of some throwing errors. I almost blew my cover, clapping for a base hit, and thought it best to sit on my hands.

After a long silence, Veronica's father finally spoke as he slid a TV tray out in front of him and sat up. "A Brit, eh?"

"*Yes, sir.*"

"I guess ya don't play too much baseball then, huh?"

"*No, bu' i' looks in'eres'ing.*" No reaction whatsoever from Veronica's father, making me a bit uncomfortable. "*More of a rugby man, meself,*" I added.

"You play?" her father asked incredulously, sizing up my boyish frame.

"*Not so much anymore, i's a bi' bru'al.*"

"I thought y'all played soccer."

"*Oh, you mean footy?*"

"Yeah, what's your team? Who do you support?"

"*Well, I'm from Norf Hamp'on, so it's the Cobblers.*" I then chanted: "*We are Th' Cobblers, We are Th' Cobblers.*" *Thanks, Dad*, I thought, *what would I do without you, ya pr---?*

When there was a close-up of The Orioles hat and its iconic logo, that of a Daffy-Duck-like bird, I decided to have a little fun.

"Oh, that hat's in the movie "Highlander, init?"

I thought I had this geezer completely fooled when something caught my attention out of the corner of my eye: Veronica stood in the doorway, wearing a Harley-Davidson t-shirt and Daisy Dukes.

"'Ello."

Veronica smiled. "Hi, ya ready?"

"Hey, look, remember that from Highlander last night? Same hat!" To Veronica's father: *"I 'ope your team wins."*

"Yeah, thanks," he replied before turning his attention to his daughter. "I thought you slept at Lisa or Jill's house last night."

Veronica's eyes bore imaginary lasers into my head as I approached. "Yeah, we watched a movie," she said nervously.

"Where are you two off to?"

"Just going to show him around and maybe go back to the carnival since we didn't stay very long last time."

"Not in our car, I hope."

"Daddy, you already said I could," Veronica said pleadingly while waving at me to hurry up.

Veronica's mother approached from behind us, carrying two paper plates with the most oversized sandwiches I had ever seen.

"*Good ahftanoon,*" I said, trying to get in good with the mother, feeling I had just failed with the father. And maybe Veronica, too.

"Hello," she said warmly to DJ, "if I can just squeeze by."

"*Oh, of course,*" I said, making room for her to pass. Veronica smiled at me as her mother placed one plate on the TV tray in front of her husband before taking a seat in the other recliner, where she placed her plate on her thighs.

"Eleven o'clock," Veronica's father said without looking from the TV.

"Eleven? How about my usual curfew?"

"You have a usual curfew?" he responded, punctuating it with a sharp laugh.

"Midnight," her mother offers.

"*I' was nice mee'in' you bof.*"

With both of their mouths full, they each acknowledged me with a grunt as Veronica pulled me out of the room.

Swallowing, Veronica's mother said to her husband, "He seems nice."

Veronica's father took a big swig of beer from a bottle on the table between them. "He thinks he's got me fooled, he's about as English as my left nut." His wife laughed, almost spitting food out of her mouth.

"Why do you say that?"

"That skinny little bag of bones tried to tell me he plays rugby," her father said before shouting at the television. "Come on, what was that?!"

Back at the Jones house, Mr. Jones arrived at home, tired, spent, and frustrated. The police had come to investigate the "missing" Jaguar from his lot and all but accused him of some sort of fraud. It was beyond them that the car had disappeared through a padlocked gate, and Mr. Jones was at a loss for a logical explanation. Nevertheless, they filed a report.

So it came as a surprise, to say the least, to walk into his new house, not to find his son, but his father.

"Dad, what are you—?" Mr. Jones whimpered as he fell into his father's arms.

"There, there, son," Grandfather said, holding Mr. Jones.

Finally pulling back after a good cry, Mr. Jones wiped his eyes. "What are you doing here?"

"I told you wild horses weren't gonna keep me away." Grandfather's accent seemed to differ ever so slightly with his son than with DJ, almost unnoticeable to the untrained ear.

"Yea, but I truly didn't think you were going to come," Mr. Jones admitted, leading his father to the sofa. "You remember the last time you said that."

"Look, I want to say again how sorry I am about Polly," Grandfather said, ignoring his son's last comment. "Wish I could have been here for the, what do you call it, it's not a funeral. So, what's it called, "the burning"?"

Five minutes in and his father had already said something that he knew was said to perturb him. "It's just a regular service. We did sit Shiva."

"Yeah, but she wasn't Jewish."

"That's what she wanted, that was part of her wishes."

"Fair play, I guess. You all right?"

"As good as I can be, I suppose."

"And the kid?"

"Well, I'm guessing you saw him, that's how you got in, yeah? What did you think?"

"Seemed normal, but teenagers, you know?"

Mr. Jones nodded. "While I'm happy you're here, your trip may have been all for naught." Grandfather tilted his head slightly.

"Shall we take mine?" I asked, pointing to the Vespa.

Veronica shifted her little heart out from gear to gear in the family car, an old Orange Datsun, weaving in and out of traffic with ease. With the music playing loud from the radio, and the wind whipping our hair about as it did the night before, it reminded me of the "date" scene with Dustin Hoffman and Katherine Ross's characters in "The Graduate."

We ended up in a seafood restaurant on the bay on what had to have been the outskirts of town. Veronica and I were seated at a picnic table set up family-style along the entire length of the room. I tried unsuccessfully to order a beer, but after being shot down by the cocky waiter, I followed Veronica's lead and ordered an iced tea.

From the music to the chatter to the fans yelling at the Orioles game on several of the TVs, it made for a difficult conversation, which, I was starting to gather, was probably her intention all along.

When our food arrived—a dozen steamed crabs that they ceremoniously splayed across the table in front of us—I decided to have some fun.

"Well, what's this then? We s'pposed to eat these?"

"Yes, I'm going to show you. Take one of the crabs like this. She held the crab up by the backfins, the claws facing me.

"What's all the brown lumpy stuff?" I asked as I hesitated to even touch it.

"That's the second-best part, Old Bay seasoning. We Baltimoreans eat it on our corn flakes," she exaggerated. *No, we do not,* I thought.

"We gonna eat 'em or send 'em into battle?" I said, attacking her crab with mine. She finally laughed, as did I.

She "showed" me her special technique on how to open crabs and I faked my way through with beginner's luck.

We made our way back to the carnival where we walked through the throngs of crowds, and the more we seemed to hit it off, the deeper a hole I dug for myself. It seemed it was easier to continue my ruse than it was to garner the courage to tell her the truth. Plus, I rationalized, it was more fun being someone else, something I was not. Was she really getting to know the real DJ or just an imposter? These things ran through my head as she revealed details about her and her life thus far.

She led me to the Ferris wheel where, after standing in line for a long silence, we finally stepped up on the platform to await our car. The carny operator raised the bar for us to climb aboard, both feeling the nervous jitters of being so close. However, after being locked in, the Ferris wheel began to rise off the ground to accommodate the others in line, and my stomach churned as I white-knuckled the carriage.

"*I prob'ly shoulda mentioned, I'm afraid of 'eights.*"

Veronica chuckled, taking my hand in hers.

"I should probably have mentioned...I'm bisexual," Veronica offered a bit sheepishly.

"*You WHA*?!" I yelled in mock deference, jumping to my feet only to slam my head on the steel cover above us. "Ow, shit," I said, grabbing my head as I sat back down, noticeably without my accent.

"Careful," Veronica said, trying to assess my reaction. "You sounded American when you said that.

"As a matter of fact, I *am American,*" I should have said.

"Does that really bother you?"

I snickered. "*No, no' at all. I am, too.*"

"You're bi too? Have you ever been with a guy?"

"*No, I mean, I believe everyone is bisexual to a cer'ain degree, and I, on occasion, DO fin' some men attrac'ive an' all.*"

"Like Rick?"

"*Rick? Ha. I mean, yes, he is a perfect specimen, in-nit?*" Veronica laughed. "*Bu' when it comes t' an 'airy dick and arse...eww-hoo-hoo.*"

Shit, I thought, I should have seized the opportunity a second before to tell her the truth when I almost blew my cover. My foot slid across the metal floor, rubbing my hairy leg across the soft skin of her smooth, shapely leg. Our eyes connected and we both moved in for a kiss. Probably not the best time to tell her with our lips locked. Even more awkward than what I was about to reveal after our lips peeled apart in all their wet bliss.

"*I wan'ed to apologise for this morning.*"

"Oh yeah, which part?"

"*Well, you know, the kickin' ya ou' part, 'specially after, ya know.*"

Veronica's eyes darted left to right and up and down, eager to see where I was going with this.

"*I mean, technically I,*" I swallowed before continuing in a whisper. "*I took advantage of you.*"

Veronica's eyes stopped their movement, her eyebrows furrowed. "Yes. You. Did." There was a long palpable pause as I looked out over the carnival and wondered how far the drop was. "That doesn't mean you won't do it again, I hope."

I let out a long sigh of relief.

"What, you think my skirt just hiked up like that on its own?" she said dismissively before leaning in and kissing me, a mischievous smile on her naughty face.

By the way, I'm not really English, I thought, as her tongue flicked across mine.

Now. I should tell Veronica right now as we sat in front of her house—she had a home!—but I could not think of the right words, the appropriate words under the circumstances. And what circumstances they were. What had I got myself into? I could see her lips moving, but the thoughts that were swirling around in my head were overwhelming, so I heard nothing. I kissed her again before climbing out, not saying the things that needed to be said.

The same could be said about my mother. It was over so quickly, so unexpectedly.

In fact, how could I reveal my true self when I didn't know who my true self was anymore? Things were changing so fast.

I rode the scooter back home and stealthily squeezed through a squeaky front door. The main level was dark, all the lights were on, upstairs and downstairs. I tiptoed upstairs and made my way down the hall towards my room, acknowledging the light on in the spare room, the door slightly ajar. I made my way into my room and, without turning on the light, closed the bedroom door quietly behind me, leaving roughly the same gap as the spare room's.

Stripping down to my skivvies, I made a makeshift bed on the far side of my bed so as not to be seen from the doorway of my room. I hoped against all odds that my father had not noticed the Jaguar missing off the lot, and with the next day being Sunday, I could slip it right back in, so to speak, as easily as I got it out. It should be a piece of cake.

And speaking of discreetly slipping it in, I reveled in the fact of how cool Veronica was. I licked my lips, getting one last taste of her lip gloss.

Making the difficult decision to get up to brush my teeth, I crawled around the bed, stood up, and listened at my door for any sign of my father. Then, feeling the coast was clear, I swung my door open, grasped the door frame, and swung out of the room—and this time, right into Grandfather, barreling into his chest like a linebacker, knocking him awkwardly to the floor.

"Jesus!" I yelled out, startled, trying to grab the elderly man's hand on the way down. "Are you ok?"

"No, and, Christ, don't call me Jesus!"

I fumbled for the light switch on the wall, nearly stepping on him to reach it. As the hallway illuminated, I found my Grandfather grabbing his chest in excruciating pain. "You alright?" I asked, dropping to my knees beside him.

"Do I look alright?" he managed to utter.

"What's going on up there?" Mr. Jones shouted from downstairs.

"Dad! Call 9-1-1!"

Grandfather shook his head, staring at me intently. I could hear the sound of my father's footsteps approaching as he reached the landing.

"No, no hospital. Get my nitroglycerin. It's in my room."

"What's happened?" Dad asked again, locking eyes with me as I stopped in the doorway of the study.

"I bumped into him," I said as I rushed into the room and flicked on the light. "Where, Granddad?!"

"By the telly," he muttered, still in pain as Dad dropped to his knees alongside his father.

"BY THE TELLY!" my father shouted.

I returned, twisting the lid off of the small glass bottle. "Here, here," I said, pouring the entire bottle into my palm.

Both men reached into my hand and grabbed a pill. Dad administered the nitrate to his father's gaping mouth, dropping it onto his dry tongue. I watched as Grandfather greedily accepted it, his face changing from blue to white and finally to an off-pink hue.

"Should we call an ambulance?" I asked.

"With what they charge?" Grandfather lamented with a breathy whisper. "Just help me to my bed."

With an arm over each of our shoulders, we helped him shakily to his feet, easing him gently down the few feet of the hallway as best we could, and lowered him gently on the sofa bed.

"He can't sleep on this. He's sixty-five years old," Dad said as his dad sat back rather awkwardly.

"Sixty-seven," Grandfather corrected him.

"You sure you don't want to go to the hospital?" I asked, seriously concerned.

"When I've got the NHS?"

Well, I'm going to phone my physician," Dad pointed to the desk on the other side of the opened sofa-bed. "See if my address book is in the top drawer."

I made my way delicately over Grandfather's legs and opened the drawer only to find it was empty. "Blast, it's in a box in the garage," he recalled.

"I'll get it!" I barked, knowing full well I had to keep my father from entering the garage, and began to maneuver my way back over the sofa bed.

"No, no, I'll do it. You'll never find it. Just keep an eye on him."

"David, don't go to any trouble."

"It's no trouble, Dad," he said, scurrying off and mumbling "F---, f---, f---," as he darted downstairs, unaware I was muttering the same thing.

Resigned, I had a seat beside my grandfather, who must have read the panicked look on his young grandson's face. "I, uh, borrowed a car off Dad's lot last night and stupid me hid it in the garage. Well, my life is over."

Grandfather breathed deep and heavily.

"When David was about your age, he snuck out of the house. Took my car in the middle of the night. It ended

up breaking down somewhere, probably hot-rodding."
I laughed at the phrase more than the situation. "Anyway, he came home and confessed. So instead of punishing him, I made him tow it home and fix it himself.
So, don't you worry about him."

From down in the garage, and probably throughout
the neighborhood, Mr. Jones could be heard screaming, "DAAAVIIID!"

Grandfather slowly winked at me.

Chapter

V

"I need to go back to Old Blighty, Davey, my boy."

I woke up groggy on the sofa-bed in the study and tried to gather not only my thoughts but my bearings, as well, seeing as this was the third day in a row waking up in new surroundings.

Grandfather stood in the doorway, looking like a shell of the spry man that had arrived only the day before.

"You talking to me? You just got here."

"I need to see my doctor. Can you take me?"

"To England?" I gave it a lengthy consideration. "Ok, who drives?"

"I've already bought you a ticket. We leave tonight."

"What? For how long? Have you talked to Dad about this because after last night he might have something to say."

"A week. Why? What's he going to say?"

"Um, 'No', for starters."

Grandfather puffed his lips out, waving dismissively. "Start packing. Leave the rest to me." He gingerly eased out of the room. I rubbed my eyes with my right hand and adjusted myself in my jockeys with the left.

This is one hell of a week, I thought.

"No, no, absolutely not. It's as if he's being rewarded for bad behaviour,"

"What do you want from him?? I mean, you going to take me?"

"Yeah, leave David here for a week? By himself? In a new house. You don't even know how long it's going to be. What if they recommend surgery? What if, you know?" With that, Mr. Jones paused, he held his hands up and shrugged. "He'd be devastated. What's he supposed to do then? Why can't we just put you on a plane and have Thom meet you at the airport?"

"Thom? I wouldn't trust Thom to wipe his own arse" Grandfather said without a hint of facetiousness. "It'll be fine."

I thought it best to make my entrance. I felt powerful. Grandfather was sitting at the table piled with small boxes, stacks of papers, boxes and cans, and the like. Dad rolled back and forth in his wheelchair. He stopped long enough to direct his attention, and his ire, towards me.

"This is just crazy. He's supposed to start at the garage tomorrow."

"Alright, so he starts next week. What's the difference?"

"You do realize your trip here was for nothing," Mr. Jones pointed out, though it was becoming clear that he was losing the argument.

"Maybe *not* nothing after all," Grandfather reasoned.

He stopped pacing, brushing at some imaginary crumbs on the counter while Grandfather directed me out of the room through a not-so-subtle head nod. Understanding, I quietly backed out.

"I'm sure he could use a change of scenery."

Mr. Jones threw his arms up as if to say 'Look around.' "I don't even know where his passport is."

"I do," I called out.

I peeked around the corner to see Grandfather flashing an expression of 'There you have it,' before winking in my direction.

Hopping on my Vespa, I headed towards Veronica's house, finally deciding that it was *absolutely* the time to tell her the truth, express my true feelings for her, get down on my knees and apologize for my deception and for allowing things to get so out of hand. Then promise her, if she forgives me, the sun and the moon and the stars above. Or some shit like that.

As I turned onto her street, her house in my sights, I noticed two people standing on the porch. I quickly braked and maneuvered my scooter behind a battered station wagon adjacent to her house. My heart sank while I watched her stand up on her tippy-toes to hug the tall male she was talking to and then my stomach did a double-flip when the man turned around.

Of all f------ people—Duke Warfield.

What was he doing there? And why was she hugging him? How did they even know each other?

Devastated, I backed the Vespa up, spun it around, and puttered off. My stomach clenched ever so tight.

When I arrived home, I found my father and Grandfather standing outside my father's Mercedes in the driveway.

"Well, look who decided to show up?" Grandfather sarcastically said.

"You're going to miss your flight!" Mr. Jones barked.

"Ok, ok, let me just go pack real fast."

"You haven't packed yet?"

"T-shirts and jeans, socks and underwear. It ain't no fashion show. Just transfer from box to bag. *Shan't be a minute,*" I added with an accent. *Nice touch,* I thought before running inside, leaving my scooter on the sidewalk.

Mr. Jones pointed that detail out to his father, who in turn pointed out his suitcase sitting idly next to his son. Mr. Jones transferred it to the boot, shaking his head about the both of them.

Stuffing the very duffel bag my father had brought to America 20-odd years ago, I looked around the room before focusing my attention on my guitar. Should I or shouldn't I? This might be my chance, my *destiny*, I thought as I made a futile effort in shoving my guitar into an already overstuffed bag. I finally relented, pouring out all my clothes, sliding the guitar in, and haphazardly stuffing them all back in. I slid on my denim jacket, stuffing the pockets with cassette tapes like detectives stuff theirs with gun cartridges.

Clothes – check.

Guitar – check.

Money – half of this was Stan's share of our proceeds. I grabbed it all. I'll get him a souvenir.

Passport – garage.

Shit.

I picked up the duffel bag—it weighed a ton—and bolted downstairs to the occasional beeping of my father's car horn. In the garage, I punched into the box labeled "Important Documents" and rummaged through it, retrieving my passport.

Lastly, I waved goodbye to the Jaguar. "Would've been nice."

As I turned to leave, something in the corner caught my eye.

A chainsaw—we had a chainsaw!

That gave me an idea.

I peeked through a slat between the garage door and the wall. I could see my father and grandfather still sitting in the car. I pulled the starter cord of the chainsaw, the metallic growl of the killing machine roared to life.

I cringed as I peered through the slat a second time, but they both appeared unfazed by the sound. It helped that the patriotic redneck in an American flag T-shirt across the street was mowing the lawn.

Having rolled the car's windows down, I lowered the safety goggles on my face before lowering the boom on the roof. Metal against metal screeched out and sparks flew everywhere.

For about two seconds before the motor cut off.

I took another gander outside before starting it up again. This time I came in underneath the roof and pushed the tool up, only to be met with incredible resistance through the Jaguar's "side-burn" that ran down the passenger side's windshield. Moving onto the rear part of the roof, I further struggled, but eventually, after several grueling minutes, had completely severed the roof from the Jaguar's sleek body. It was a gnarled mess, irreversibly damaged.

Maybe I'll get it to keep it, after all, I thought with a snort through my nostrils.

By the time I exited the house, my father had pulled the brown German bomber out onto the street and was just sitting on the horn.

"Come on!"

I chucked my bag in and slipped inside. My father had not even fully lifted his foot off the brake when I remembered I forgot one thing.

"STOP THE CAR!"

Mr. Jones slammed on the brakes. Both men turned around, quizzical looks on their old mugs.

"I forgot something," I insisted.

Inside, I approached the mantle and took the urn in both hands, gently placing my head against the cool pewter texture and held it for a moment. "I won't let you down," I promised before fast-footing out of the house.

"Bet he forgot his passport," Grandfather mumbled.

I slipped back into the car and shut the door behind me.

"Passport?" Grandfather asked.

"Say goodbye to your Mum."

They both stared at me before turning to stare at each other.

"Well, what are you waiting for? Let's go," I insisted.

Because we were so pressed for time, we were only left with an awkward good-bye at the curb beside Departures. Grandfather and I checked in while I discussed my concerns regarding leaving my father alone to fend for himself, something he had never done before.

"Just what the doctor ordered," Grandfather said with a ring of irony. "That's my old army-issued," he said, referring to my duffel bag. He turned the handle inside out and there, scrawled in black ink, was JONES, D.

We eventually boarded the plane, where we were greeted by an overly enthusiastic Stewardess. We had not taken two steps into First Class when Grandfather, upon rechecking his ticket, stopped at 4A.

"Well, this is me," he casually claimed.

I stopped and checked my ticket. 34B. That put, I figured, thirty rows between us as Grandfather moved into the row, setting his carry-on bag on the seat. People began to form a line behind me.

"Sir," said the Stewardess, "please keep moving."

Carrying my duffel bag over my shoulder, I looked back at Grandfather, who had all but forgotten about me as he took his seat. Resigned to the fact that I would be sitting alone and *not* enjoying the various amenities of First Class, I continued up the aisle towards Coach. In doing so, the handle on my duffel bag (or Grandfather's, as I just learned) got caught on one of the armrests.

Sitting in the last aisle seat of First Class, I could hear the passenger, dressed all in black, including a turtleneck (in June), commiserating to an older gentleman sitting across the aisle from him.

"Bloody humid, bloody boring, poxy place."

His attention was immediately drawn to me for some reason as I wrestled with my tangled-up bag, finally wrangling it from its captured state.

"Look at this prat, coming to muck up ole Blighty, are you?" he muttered, as I maneuvered my bag from behind me, clutching it into a sort of bear hug.

It was because of this shift that I did not see the man slip his foot out into the aisle.

Right on cue, I tripped over it, falling onto the floor of the cabin, smacking my face on my guitar's tuning pegs.

"Sorry about that, mate," the all-in-black Brit muttered unconvincingly, his cheeks puffing in and out in not-so-contained laughter.

I struggled to my feet and turned to find the rude man chuckling; the man across the aisle, embarrassed by the man's behavior, began flipping through the In-Flight magazine.

"*Why you bahstad!*" I shouted as I threw the bag back over my shoulder and scowled at the evil little man. *"I've come to expec' this sor' o' fing from these bleedin' Americans, bu' t' ge' this from one of me own...!"*

I looked over my shoulder to spot Grandfather, looking back in my direction, a glint of satisfaction in his eye.

Leaving the little man in black, too, turned his attention to the In-Flight magazine. I continued into the Coach section of the airplane while avoiding the stares of other passersby.

What the hell was that all about, I wondered as I shoved my duffel bag in the overhead compartment, nearly taking up all of the available space. I was excited to turn and find a single young woman of Indian descent reading a book in the seat next to mine.

Things are looking up, I thought to myself as I slid in beside her and locked in. She flashed a solemn but invitingly warm smile.

Bad English
the III

I dug through the cassettes in my pockets, pulling out a particular favorite I especially wanted to hear. As much as I loved CDs, I was late to jump on the bandwagon. There was nothing quite like making a mixed tape, something you could never do with a CD.

As this was my first plane trip since I was a baby, I was nervous and excited as I sat back, waiting for us to get going.

Once the pilot announced they were preparing for take-off, I pressed Play on my Walkman and waited; as the plane headed off full force into the skies, Traffic's "Low Spark of High Heel Boys" slowly built. Through the left ear only. It occurred to me that I must look like the Memorex ad of the guy sitting in front of a huge speaker.

I spun my headphones around so my left ear would be available to the girl beside me, should she want to converse.

As the plane took off it occurred to me that I should have told Sharonda I was going to England. But when the music roared in my right ear the thought quickly escaped my mind. I worried my fear of heights might overwhelm me, but surprisingly, I handled it like a pro.

After the plane had leveled off and the co-pilot announced that passengers could move about the cabin, the stewardesses slowly made their way up the aisles with beverage carts.

It seemed to take forever, but when they finally reached our aisle, I sat up in an attempt to appear more adult-like while the girl beside me ordered an orange juice.

"And you, sir?" the flight attendant asked.

"*I'd like a Budweiser please,*" I said, reverting to me ole accent just to be on the safe, legal side when I noticed another stewardess coming up the aisle holding a bottle of champagne. "*I'd ratha 'ave tha' though,*" I said, smiling at the sight of champagne.

"This is, in fact, for you," said the second Stewardess. "From the gentleman in first class."

"*Tell my grandfather 'Fank You',*" I said, feeling as if I was finally getting some respect.

"This is from a gentleman who sends his apologies," the Stewardess corrected me. I took the bottle from her with both hands and examined it closely, as if it were a trophy of sorts.

Having already opened the can of Budweiser, the first Stewardess asked, "Will you still be requiring this, sir?"

"*I's a lon' fligh', why not?*"

She opened the seat tray and placed the beer on it along with two cups. I handed her a 5 dollar bill and told her to keep the change. Last of the big spenders.

"Care for a mimosa?" I asked the girl beside me after the beverage cart continued past.

"No, thank you, I don't drink," she replied demurely.

While we had dinner, we spoke about ourselves and she was surprised to find out I was American. "You should be proud of who you are," she offered, giving me pause.

"Yeah, that's what my cousin, Stan, keeps telling me."

"Well, then, you should listen to him. He sounds like a wise man."

Her name was Anna and she was a lovely, insightful girl. She expressed her dissatisfaction at the feature film that was playing, the anti-Apartheid film, "Cry Freedom."

What she took issue with was the fact that, even though the film was about Steven Biko, the focus was, according to her, regrettably, on the white South African reporter, Donald Woods.

Anna further informed me that the reason she was overly sensitive about it was that even though she was from India, she had been raised in Soweto, South Africa, since her parents had moved there when she was a child. Steven Biko was, it turned out, her godfather; a remarkable revelation, if true.

(Author's Note: With the advent of the World Wide Web, the author tried to research the validity of her claim, yet found no truth to it whatsoever).

Anna went to sleep before the film was over while I kept that stewardess on her toes for the duration of the flight, using the overhead dispatch button to order up beer after beer. I continued drinking until I eventually nodded off.

A few hours later, the sun shone through Anna's window when she raised the shutter after an announcement from the pilot that we were making our final descent into England, waking me from my drunken slumber.

I squinted, peering out at the miles of green grass and pastures.

"I'm never going to want to leave here," I confessed, before promptly passing out again.

After exchanging numbers and wishing each other well, I watched as Anna made her way up the aisle on her way to disembark. I stayed back to manipulate my duffel bag from the overhead bin while not holding up the few rows behind me. By the time I reached Grandfather's seat, it was empty.

I questioningly pointed that out to the nearby Stewardess, who initially greeted us.

"David, yes?" she said, approaching as she held out a folded-up piece of paper. I nodded, obviously confused.

"Your Grandfather was experiencing some discomfort, so the pilot called ahead and had an ambulance waiting for him. He wanted me to give you this."

Reading the paper, it only included the following: Cousin, Ian - 424 Blackfriars Lane, along with the word "Hostels."

I looked up at the stewardess, who appeared impatient. "And no one thought to tell me?"

"We tried, love, but you were dead to the world. He's been taken to the Surrey and Sussex Heart Centre."

"Sorry?"

"Surrey and Sussex Heart Centre." She removed a ballpoint pen, clicked it with her thumb, and handed it to me. "That's in East Surrey Hospital on Canada Avenue."

"Canada Avenue?"

"Now, you need to get the train, it's on the way to London."

I departed the plane expecting it to be a joke of some sort. Loved ones embraced one another, but no one was awaiting me. Because I had not checked a bag, I bypassed Baggage Claim and found myself in the Departures wing of Gatwick Airport. It occurred to me I was in quite a bind as I only had the few hundred dollars of my own "savings" plus the couple hundred dollars that my father had given me.

Spotting a Bureau de Change, with several people of different ethnicities sitting behind bulletproof glass. I scanned the signs hanging over each window with various flags from around the world and their respective exchange rates.

The US flag had $1.76 beside it and I shoved all but $20 through the small opening thinking I was going to be rich. The man, who looked to be Middle Eastern, punched away on a calculator, printed out the exchange rate, and spun it towards me to view through the glass.

I was gobsmacked to find out it was a fraction of what I thought it was going to be. "Well, I came to seek my fortune and it looks to be just under four hundred pounds," I muttered under my breath.

What choice did I have? I figured as the man counted out the paper money and coins, pushing it all through the small slot, leaving me wildly perplexed. Especially when it came to the coins. I was still examining them as I side-stepped over to the adjacent counter, a miniature pub.

"*Pin' of Lowenbrau, please,*" I said, taking my cue from the gentleman before me. *Might as well not come off as a tourist*, I concluded.

"Coming right up," the barman said, as he adeptly went about pouring a lager. "How are you today?"

I jammed my pinkie into my ear, trying to alleviate the pressure. *"I cahn' 'ear a fing, I jus' go' off th' plane."*

"Did you? Just now?" he asked, somewhat incredulously. I nodded as the barman placed the full pint glass on the bar. "Two pound fifty, please, sir."

Rifling through the paper currency, I found a five in the middle of the wad and laid it on the bar. "Out of five." The barman tapped a couple of buttons on the register, removing a handful of coins, which he placed on a plastic tray, and set it on the bar.

"Cheers, mate, welcome home."

I turned with my lager in one hand, change in the other, while completely forgetting my bag was on the floor and stumbled over it.

"Crap," I said while deftly managing to neither spill a single drop of beer or a solitary coin.

———

Bad English
the III

The change was so foreign to me that I was compelled to ask a nearby woman what each of the coins was. She was kind enough to explain not only what each was but, most importantly, how much they were worth. After she was done, she made a recommendation: "If you can find the time, you must go see Stonehenge."

Everyone was so prim and proper, much different than America.

I had a seat at a table and continued my pint of lager, mesmerized by the comings and goings of passers-by. I found myself laughing every time at a pre-recorded announcement that played every few minutes over the loudspeakers: "Unattended baggage will be taken out and destroyed."

I was unsure why it was so funny, maybe it was the woman's choice of words or the matter-of-fact manner in which she said it. Or maybe it was simply the alcohol, but it made me laugh. I looked over at the older couple that I was sharing the table with for their reaction, which, was non-existent. They merely looked at me oddly but must have concluded I was harmless enough. It did not occur to me at the time, but I must have been coming across a bit like Dudley Moore in "Arthur."

After the length of time that it took to knock back a couple of pints, I figured it was time to get a move on. I stood up and reached out for my duffel bag but found myself extremely dizzy and dropped back down into my seat until the cloudy vision passed. When it finally did, I picked up my bag, which seemed to be even heavier than I remembered, and looked for an exit to no avail. I paused for a moment by the telephone kiosk and came to the sad conclusion that I needed to call home, but I had to have just the right explanation on *why* I was calling home.

"David?"

Why don't nobody never call me DJ, I wondered. "*Veronica? Can you hear me?*"

"I can hear you! Where are you?"

"*I'm in England.*" I found myself shouting. "*I'm sorry I didn't say goodbye. I had an emergency!*"

"So, I'm never going to see you again?"

"*Do you want to see me again?*"

"Do *you*?"

"*You haven't found a boyfriend yet, then?*" I asked, clearly fishing.

"Oh, I've got them lined up around the corner."

"*'Ave someone 'old me a place, I'll be back on Monday. Can I call you again?*

"Of course."

"*Wonderful. By the way, miss you too. Bye.*"

"Bye." I began to lower the receiver back to its cradle when I heard: "David!"

I quickly lifted the phone back to my ear. "*Yes?*"

"Instead of goodbye, can you say 'Hello'?" A smile tore across my face.

———

"'Ello."

I hung up with a new lease on life. I was so elated that I wanted no one or nothing to bring me back down to Earth, so I decided against calling home. Instead, I stopped a middle-aged woman stuffed into a uniform, wearing an airport badge, and inquired how to get out of the airport. She showed legitimate confusion as to how I was able to exit an inbound plane and find myself in Departures. She quickly whisked me away through an unmarked door, down a small stairway and into the Customs Inspection area.

"Good morning," the Customs Inspector said when it was finally my turn. "Passport and ticket, please."

"Morning," I said, handing him my passport, before making a mad search for my ticket, finally finding it bent in half in my back pocket.

"What is your purpose in England?"

It suddenly seemed odd that the real reason I was here was for my grandfather, yet we were not even together. "Vacation," I offered instead. *"'Oliday."*

"And what do you plan to do when you leave?"

"Probably cry."

The Inspector peered over his glasses, sizing me up before stamping my passport with a KACHUNK. He handed me and my ticket. "Enjoy your *'oliday.*"

In other words, he meant, *Come on in, ya cry baby.*

And with that, I officially crossed into England.

Now what? I wondered.

———

Stopping at an information booth, I inquired how to get to East Surrey. The woman in the booth suggested I buy a British Rail ticket, taking the nearby shuttle to the train station, and from there taking the train to East Surrey. I bought a British rail ticket and headed for the shuttle.

Following her implicit instructions, I found my way to the shuttle which, as luck would have it, had just arrived, nameless, faceless travelers pouring out through its doors. As soon they had all exited, I stepped inside, dragging my bag behind me, and took a seat.

The shuttle remained empty for what seemed like an eternity, but in reality, it was just a long five minutes. When, finally, the doors shut and the shuttle proceeded to its next destination, it drove less than half a kilometer when it came to another stop and just sat idle while no one either entered or departed.

I had the sneaking suspicion that it was the end of the line. The wrong end. Spotting the wall through the windows of the front-facing doors was a dead giveaway.

Finally, a few passengers stepped on and I got the idea that I was now on my way. The shuttle set itself in motion, coming back to the stop where I initially boarded and stopped and opened its doors, allowing more passengers on before departing again. I decided I was going to scream out loud if it went back to the same stop I had just come from. Luckily for me—and my fellow passengers—it continued in the right direction, eventually arriving at the train station where I boarded a train bound for London, with East Surrey as one of its stops.

Ticket in hand, bag over my shoulder, I entered the First Class car, full of confidence from the alcohol I had been consuming all night. The plan was to feign ignorance if or when I was confronted about being there.

Until then, I would take a seat and enjoy the view. After chucking my bag on the overhead rack, I acknowledged the businessman that took a seat across the aisle from me. Setting his briefcase down on the table, the businessman gave me a polite nod and dove into some work that he pulled from his case.

As the train resumed to Victoria Station, I rested my chin in the palm of my hand and watched the scenery as it whooshed past. English homes, English cars on the opposite sides of the English roads, combined with green trees, green fields, green parks, and green football pitches all passed me by like a movie montage in fast forward. Such a turn of events from the past few days and weeks. I felt myself getting rather emotional.

An older black man in a flawlessly pressed white jacket and black trousers pushed a beverage cart into the car from the adjoining car. I felt like a gin and tonic would be fitting and ordered one. The businessman looked up from his work and sized up the young man ordering mixed drinks on a weekday morn.

"Would you like one?" I asked him. He declined by shaking his head in a polite but "not a chance" assertion.

Paying for my drink, I sat back, taking a large swig of the elixir. *Mmmm, quenching.*

With my buzz, along with my emotions, getting the best of me, I addressed the gentleman across the aisle. "Did you ever just stop and take a long look outside?" I asked, my words slurring more and more. "I mean it's really breathtaking, wouldn't you agree?"

The businessman peered over his glasses at me, his pen drooping slightly in his hand before following my cue by looking out the window beside him.

"Right?"

The gentleman continued to look at the scenery outside while occasionally peering at me out of the corner of his eye. "It is quite nice, isn't it?" he politely admitted, more likely in a subtle attempt to pacify the intoxicated little American. He eventually returned to the work at hand.

The gin and tonic went down with ease while the charms outside turned into equal parts wonder and disappointment.

The wonder of finding England, with all its historical proportions, combined with the disappointment of seeing everything from buildings to billboards riddled with graffiti. I was gutted that a small fraction of the English population was taking their phenomenal surroundings for granted.

British graffiti.

Who did they think they were? Americans?

With the steady rhythm of the train on the tracks, I soon fell back asleep, or passed out, with my chin awkwardly on my chest.

The Business Man proved kind enough to wake me up when the train pulled into the station.

"Victoria Station, mate."

"Victoria Station?" I asked, jumping to my feet, groggy and confused. "Is that near East Surrey?"

The Business Man scoffed. "No, I'm afraid we stopped there thirty minutes ago."

"Thirty minutes?" I repeated, thinking about going back to sleep, but decided against it as I could not contain my excitement, completely forgetting why I had come to England in the first place. I yanked my bag down, haphazardly slinging it over my shoulder, nearly taking the businessman's eye out with my guitar's pesky tuning pegs.

Needless to say, I was feeling little pain when I exited the train and quickly dropped my bag to the ground. Dragging it across the concrete platform and into the bustling station, people either dodged the bag or found themselves having to quickly jump over it to avoid tripping altogether.

One thing was for certain—I, David English Jones, had arrived.

———

Chapter
VI

"Nice to see you London, been waiting long?" Just a couple of Centuries is all.

Into the hustle and bustle of London I went, as I took one small step out of Victoria station to find it overcast and extremely muggy; the sky was gray with patches of blue breaking through the dark, hanging clouds, giving it an ominous feel. Swarms of black cabs, mini cabs, cars, lorries, motorbikes, and red double-decker busses all jockeyed for position within the narrow driveway.

And the noise. Unlike anything I had ever heard outside of a movie: English ambulance sirens in the distance, motorcycle messengers screaming through the carport with their Kawasakis and Suzukis buzzing like swarms of bees, people politely, and not so politely, shouting.

Taking a deep breath of fresh British air, I gagged from the exhaust fumes mixed with women's perfumes, which made complete sense to me because women were milling about everywhere. *What this must have been like in the Sixties*, I thought, disappointed I was born so late.

One of the destinations on a bus idling nearby caught my eye: Piccadilly Circus. I knew that name. Or was I confusing it with Monty Python's Flying Circus? I guessed the English had an affinity for circuses. But for me, it seemed the center most part of London and a great place to do a quick once over. Like Veronica, Big Ben and The Palace worked for me.

The bus began slowly pulling away from the curb and I watched in awe as a businessman hopped on the bus platform, grabbed the pole, and made his way to the front of the bus with all the grace of a dancer out of "The Umbrellas of Cherbourg."

Hell, I can do that, I thought as I held my bag's strap tight across my shoulder, ran across the pavement, and leaped upon the back step, grabbing for that pole on the platform only to find it just out of my reach. My bag, which was much heavier than I anticipated, pulled me backward off of the bus, where I watched my short life pass before my eyes. Luckily, I came to a shocking but safe, cushioned landing in the middle of the street.

"Duffel bag breaks young American tourist's fall, news at eleven."

Off in the not-too-far distance, my eyes landed on an upside-down word: UNDERGROUND.

I pulled myself together and made my way towards the tube station, my first concern being for my guitar and camera inside. Just under an ad for the musical, "BUDDY," I noticed a pub and considered nipping in for a quick tinkle but felt I should prod on. Or at the very least, call the hospital about old Grandad, make sure he's ok.

But then I thought, *Well, if he isn't, going there's not going to do me much good. Why did they even let him leave without me?*

Upon quick examination, I was relieved to find my camera and guitar unscathed. I, on the other hand, am practically a bleeding casualty. I almost made several Brits show actual human emotions by having broken their steady gate to urgent places unknown as I did this in the middle of the station.

I figured Piccadilly Circus was close enough. No harm in seeing a little of London before I was holed up in a hospital for the rest of my brief stay.

Descending the escalator, I was engrossed by the framed ads on the walls advertising theater productions, shops such as Harrod's, lagers and films ("Batman" with Michael Keaton and "Licensed to Kill" with Timothy Dalton were everywhere, leading one to believe those were the only two summer movies being released). The station itself was filled with the music of Beethoven's "Ninth Symphony." I knew it was the Ninth because it was forever immortalized on the Rainbow album, "Difficult to Cure." I found where the lilting music was coming from when the escalator dropped me by a skinny little gal effortlessly playing violin, an open case at her feet with various coins inside.

I reached into my pocket, withdrew a coin, and flipped it into the air. As soon as it left my fingers, as if in slow motion, I watched as the thickest of all the coins, the pound coin—in effect, a dollar—spun cinematically to its destination: her coin-filled case. Sadly, all I could do was wave goodbye to it. I was happy I could help her out financially.

Like I always say: "In for a penny, in for a pound."

As soon as I got on the train, I traced my finger along the Underground map above the door, realizing, yet again, I was heading in the wrong direction the second they announced the next station, Pimlico – I was headed back to Baltimore!

I looked around for help, but no one paid me any mind, something I would soon become accustomed to. And sort of revel in, as well.

At the next stop, I quickly merged with the mob of passengers exiting the train, and followed the signs to the correct platform, managing my way onto the proper train to Piccadilly, after switching trains at Green Park station.

I was overcome with emotional jitters of some sort.

This was London! Really real London. I half expected everyone to break into song and dance!

I took it all in with a deep breath, again the smell of exhaust combined with perfumes made my eyes water and my nose curl.

The hustle and bustle of Piccadilly made Victoria Station look like a parking lot. Sidewalks were crowded with smartly dressed, ugly bastards in well-tailored suits; the women all seemed to be wearing silk blouses & miniskirts with fishnet stockings! All moving and grooving, not all good-looking, not by a long shot. But for many of them, I'd give it a shot. I just made that up.

SONY and FOSTER LAGER was all you needed to know according to the company that sells the advertising over the Piccadilly Circus round-a-bout. I recognized the Fountain in the center, from which movie, I was not sure, but I knew every movie that took place in this city featured Piccadilly as exemplifying London, England. Having worked at a video store for nearly two years, it was like a crash course in film exploration.

I had to see it up close and, as I had done a million times before, instinctively looked to my right to cross the street. Finding the coast was clear, I stepped off the curb onto the crosswalk. A bicyclist to my left screeched to a halt mere inches from me; my shoulders, along with my entire face, scrunched up as I waited for the impact. Instead, the bicyclist stopped on a dime, nearly flipping over his handlebars. By the skin of both our teeth, no less.

Bad English
the III

Mouthing the word 'Sorry,' I stepped back over the painted sign on the street reading 'Look Left' that I'd previously missed and stood as still as a mouse on the curb. *Everything* was the opposite in England, I quickly remembered.

Behind me, I spotted a Tower Records mega-store and safely slipped inside, still anxious but quickly felt right at home as I perused the CD section from A to Zed.

I had been a late bloomer when it came to CDs, firmly believing that nothing could or would surpass vinyl records. I had so many records and just could not see myself re-purchasing everything in its new digital format. So, I held off as long as I could until I got my first boom box for Christmas a few years earlier, and since you cannot play records at the beach or wherever, I broke down and bought my first CD, "The Blues Brothers" soundtrack. I never looked back.

Looking at the prices of CDs in London was confusing but ultimately disappointing. While I found lots of CDs I wanted to purchase, the price of 10 pounds only looked appealing, until one figured that with the conversion it was almost twenty dollars. On no planet was I paying twenty dollars for a CD, no matter how bad I wanted it. I did, however, find a Whitesnake cassette of "Live in the Heart of the City" I had been searching for years, for a fraction of the price, and happily bought it, the mother-lode with more songs than the CD could hold.

I liked Whitesnake before I had ever heard a single song, becoming aware of them in several of my rock magazines. Deep Purple was probably my favorite group of all time. When they broke up, they split into two different camps: Rainbow and Whitesnake. Rainbow had found success early. Whitesnake, however, with its members including keyboardist Jon Lord, drummer Ian Pace, and Deep Purple's third and final singer David Coverdale, who together made up three-fifths of Whitesnake, remained an England, Europe and Japan-only band.

That all changed in 1984, when my local rock station, 98 Rock, did their nightly feature, New Music Phone-in Poll, where they played Whitesnake's latest release, the title song from their album, "Slide It In." With its suggestive lyrics, it was an instant hit for me. Suddenly, album and cassette bins started carrying all of their previous releases and they quickly became my "new" favorite band.

Ironically, Rainbow's first singer, Ronnie James Dio, left to join Black Sabbath when they fired their first singer, Ozzy Osbourne. And when Dio left Sabbath to go solo, Black Sabbath brought in Deep Purple's second singer, Ian Gillian for one record and tour. That was the tour my mother took me to see. Now, that I recall, that was the last rock concert we ever went to together.

I had to find my grandfather, or this cousin, Ian, or even just a place to lay my head and, more importantly, store my bag, if for nothing else to free up my arms. I approached a weathered, old man in a weathered, old jacket and hat, holding up Evening Standard newspapers in both hands. "Tiananmen Square Showdown" was the headline with a picture of a lone man standing in front of a tank, plastered on the front page of every copy.

"Evening Standard! Get your Evening Standard!"

"Excuse me, sir, are there any lockers around? Someplace I can store my bag for a few hours?"

"Evening Standard," he said earnestly, ignoring me.

"Just need a locker, do you know if there are any around?"

"Evening Standard," he continued, shaking his head, waving me off.

"Thanks. Thanks a lot," I said in frustration.

Exhaustion and jet lag starting to take their toll, I dragged my bag down the sidewalk where I waved down a black cab and ran to the end of the street where it pulled over and waited for me.

"Where to, mate?" the grizzled driver asked after I awkwardly approached the lowered window, huffing and puffing. I pulled the paper out of my pocket and pondered whether I should go to the hospital or try my cousin.

"Which is closer?" I asked, holding up the paper through the plexiglass divider.

"Black Friars Lane," the Driver said without hesitation.

"Blackfriars Lane it is, then."

The driver reached out the window behind him and opened the back door for me; I felt a sense of relief rush over me as I dropped into the back seat before the driver took off, maneuvering that cab through the narrow London streets like the bullish vessel it was. It did not help my equilibrium, not one iota, by being on the opposite side of the road, which I felt was blurring my perspective.

Every corner turned, I cringed and prepared for the worst, believing the cab was not going to make it without taking out a parked car or bus turning from the opposite direction, but the driver guided that black, battlecruiser like a ship on the open waters as I slid back and forth across the vinyl seat.

This afforded me the time to enjoy the scenery, the centuries-old architecture, with its blend of old stores and modern shops and just the fact that this was London, England. It was like a dream I knew I was going to wake from any minute.

The cab finally came to a stop outside of a large but dingy pub, the once-white walls now black from the soot and pollution of modern-day London.

"Here we are, mate," the driver said, chewing madly on a piece of gum. "Seven pounds eighty."

"This is it?" I asked.

"Four twenty-four Blackfriars Lane," he confirmed as I dug in my pocket. I had already amassed quite a pocket of change but opted for another ten-pound note, handing it to him, and in return receiving more coins as change.

Man, you really got to carry some weight in England, I thought, paraphrasing The Beatles' song.

Looking up at the sign hanging above the door, it read: The Royal Coat of Arms. It was a pub, clearly, but I was unsure whether my cousin worked there. I knew I had a cousin a few years older, but that was about all I knew; my father always seemed to hold that side of the family at arm's length for reasons that were not always clear to me.

Sure, I knew the "official" story, but I always thought there was more to it.

Isn't there always?

I smiled to myself after making way for a mum and her two sons dressed in their little school uniforms, like mini Angus Youngs, complete with matching hats and short pants.

I entered the pub through one of two doors on opposite sides of a nondescript wall. I half expected to find the inside as dingy as the outside, but rather than an antiquated hole in the wall, I found it was the picture of modernity. Well, modern for Central London in 1989.

Color TVs hung from metal brackets throughout, along with a rather high-tech for its time digital jukebox on the wall. Dartboards and a pool table could be barely seen through the smoky haze, a cigarette in nearly every hand, mouth, or ashtray. The only thing inside that was truly old was the bar, the red velvet booths, and the clientele.

Besides myself, the youngest person in the pub was the barman, who looked to be in his forties, if a day. And, I observed, not a woman in sight.

I approached an open space at the bar, leaning my bag against it, trying to get the attention of the barman, who was having a conversation with an older man with deep lines on his face. Without looking directly at me, he held up his index finger, indicating he was aware of my presence. He waited for the old man to finish his anecdote and they both laughed before backing away and approaching my end of the bar.

"What can I get for you, laddie?" the barman asked with a heavy Scottish brogue. *Highlander again*, I thought.

Checking the paper again, I looked up and asked rather innocently, "Is there an Ian Jones here?"

"Is there an Ian Jones here?" he repeated before laughing what seemed too hard a laugh for such a question.

"Why, his name's Ian Jones," he said, pointing to the old man with whom he'd just been speaking. "And that's Ian Jones," he said, indicating a man in his fifties throwing darts with a mate. "And that's Ian Jones as well," he laughed, referring to a man limping into the pub.

I lowered my head onto my fist which was firmly placed atop the bar. "You wouldn't happen to know if any of these Ians are my cousin, would you?" I asked, already knowing the answer. When I heard no reply, I raised my head as my bleary eyes tried to focus on the barman, who was all smiles and head shakes.

"'Ere, Sammy!" a burly boozer at the far end of the bar said, getting the attention of the barman, who left to attend to him.

Taking one last scan of the room, I figured if Ian was around the same age as me, none of these old geezers fit the bill. The barman approached the beer taps to pour a couple of pints.

"I do have a young scalawag who stays upstairs," the barman said, taking a quick second from pouring to direct his comment at me. "When he doesn't owe me money."

He delivered the fresh pints of lager to the unkempt burly Brit.

"Oh," I said, a renewed sense of interest, "is he here?"

The barman spun to the cash register to ring up the drinks. Over his shoulder, he replied rather dryly, "No, he owes me money."

I dropped my head back down on my fist.

"You look like you need a drink, mate," the barman said to me.

That's the last thing I need, I thought, shaking my head before thanking him and leaving. The Scottish barman laughed with the punter closest to him at the bar as I dragged myself out.

———

"That was funny, lots of Ian Joneses in tonight." The Punter nodded as he took a long drag off his cigarette.

Hungry and exhausted, I knew if I didn't sleep soon, they were going to find me passed out in a London gutter somewhere so I continued walking for about a half-block, question after question running through my mind:

Should I just go to the hospital? If I did, did that get me any closer to sleep? Unless my cousin was there and then he might have a place to stay. But what if he wasn't there, I wondered, is there a chair next to Grandfather's bed? Maybe I could stay at his house. I mean, why am I not there already?

I stopped and flagged down a taxi.

"I need to find a hostel," I told the driver through the halfway-lowered window.

"You mean the one on Carter Lane?"

"Yeah, that's the one," I lied.

"It's right around the corner, mate. You're practically there."

I pepped up upon hearing that news and tried unsuccessfully to talk the taxi driver into taking me, but he insisted it was more trouble than it was worth.

The cab driver drove off, leaving me standing on the corner trying to decipher the directions I was given. I walked up and down Queen Victoria Street looking at the sides of buildings where the street signs were but never spotting one that read Carter Lane. I asked a stocky businessman with ginger hair, and as it turned out, I had been walking parallel to it the whole time—it was one street over.

Hostel Headquarters was stenciled on the windows of a one-story storefront. I stepped inside and found racks of clothes and shelves of books, coffee mugs, and various other souvenirs; I wondered, most importantly, where they housed everyone.

Nevertheless, I made my way through the racks to a glass counter where a somewhat unkempt young lady with glasses stood. She proceeded to give me the run-down of how the Youth Hostels Association membership worked with all the energy and enthusiasm of a mortician; a mere eight pounds would buy me not only a membership card but the all-important list of hostels throughout England. Blah blah blah take my money.

She directed me to the nearby photo booth where I dropped a pound coin into the slot before stepping in, pulling the curtains shut, and having a seat. I looked at my reflection surrounding the lens, laughing that I looked like nothing short of death warmed over.

Then came the four consecutive blinding flashes in two-second increments. I stepped out and awaited my photos when, after a minute or three, they dropped into the slot. The order of the pictures brilliantly captured the four stages of my jet lag and utter exhaustion; from the surprise of the first flash, to the settling of the other three, the final photograph revealed me to be on my last leg, metaphorically speaking. Decimated.

After checking my passport, the girl showed her only ounce of emotion when she smirked at the photographs, cutting the second picture out, deeming it the best, and stapling it to my new YHA membership card. She handed it to me along with the other three pictures, two still attached, along with a brochure with the list of hostels. It was official, I was now able to find a place to rest my head. If I had not been completely wrecked, I would have jumped for joy.

I then spent the next two hours taking cabs to hostel after hostel, finding them all to be completely booked. Of course, they were, this was the start of summer and, as I was quickly finding, I was not the only one traveling on the cheap. Admittedly, I *was* seeing some of the finest hostels in London, but what good were they if I could not check-in and get myself some sleep? I was quickly growing frustrated with this membership.

It was in a hostel in Catherine Street where I was once again told they had no beds, that a French bird with long, raven-colored hair in braids told me of a hostel called Tent City in East Acton. She jotted the number down on a piece of paper and handed it to me; I got so excited that I nearly knocked over a German backpacker that had been standing behind me.

───

"You may want to call first!" she called out. *Solid advice*, I thought, as I had already spent nearly twenty pounds on taxis with no success.

I slipped into a nearby pub that had a payphone inside the front door. The phone trilled on the other end with double brp-brp sounds, but I was unsure whether that meant it was ringing or engaged, so I stopped a bloke who walked in for confirmation. I held the receiver to his ear and asked if it was ringing. The man took a quick listen and confirmed with a laugh that it was.

"'Allo? Tent City," the woman said with a strong accent.

"Do you have a room?" I asked.

"Room? Oui, we have room," she said, clearly French.

"I can come now, yes? Oui?"

"Yes, oui."

Finally, pay-dirt. Sleep was close, I could feel it. With a new lease on life, I effortlessly swung my bag up over my shoulder, rushed back outside, and quickly hailed a cab. Once inside, I closed the door and proudly announced, "Tent City, East Acton, please."

The driver, a more grizzled cab driver than the last one, slowly looked over his shoulder at me. "Mate? D'you 'ave any idea where East Ac'on is? It'll cost you at least thirty quid. You need to take the tube, mate. It's just around the corner."

Yeah, everything's always around the corner to these guys, I thought, feeling defeated and a bit thrown by the man's pronunciation of 'tube' as I exited the taxi and headed to play my new favorite game show: "Where's The Chube Station?" Feeling a sense of deja vu, I roamed around looking yet for another "landmark" I could not seem to find and felt like kicking myself for allowing the taxi driver to talk me out of a ride to Tent City.

Still not being able to wrap my head around my fate, my gaze came to rest upon one thing in particular—a Meter Maid walking away from slapping a ticket under some poor sod's window wiper.

"Excuse me, can you tell me where the tube station is?" I thought, remembering the end of Oliver Stone's "Talk Radio" when the crazy white supremacist approaches the controversial Jewish talk radio host, asking for him his autograph before pulling his gun out to assassinate him. The funny things that go through one's head, BAM BAM BAM!

She paused for a second, looking up from her ticket book, a smile spreading across her pasty, white face that bore a certain resemblance to actress Tracey Ullman. "You're American, aren't you?"

"Not only that but it's nearly my birthday, as well," I threw in for good measure.

"Well, Happy early Birthday," she said, ripping a ticket from her book. "I've always wanted to go to America." She placed the ticket on the windscreen of a Ford something or other. "Just to see if it's like it is in the movies, ya know?"

She stepped up on the curb, gently taking my arm, and led me along the sidewalk. I assumed she was leading me to the tube station, so I reveled in answering her onslaught of questions:

"What are you doing in England by yourself?"

"How is your grandfather? You haven't seen him yet?"

"Will you go back to the pub and try and find your cousin?"

She told me her name was Loretta and she showed genuine concern and care for me and my unusual predicament.

Instead of leading me to the tube station, however, she led me back to the police station with offers to use the phone at her nearby flat. As I sat on a small vinyl loveseat in the lobby, I overheard an older Constable talking to two young Meter Men, sounding a lot like something straight out of a Benny Hill sketch:

"So Halloran and I are on patrol down in Grosvenor Street when we hear this bird screaming at the top of her lungs. 'Help! Help! Someone call 9-9-9! Someone! Please call 9-9-9!' from what looked to be a third-floor window of some council flats. So, we bust in and find this bird tied to the bed." He paused to laugh a hearty belly laugh; the younger man snickered, though visibly uneasy. He whispered, "And she's as naked as the day she came into the world. Ooh, and what a lovely set, too." He cupped his hands in front of him indicating she was apparently busty. "It's at this point we find this little dwarf lying face down on the floor, naked as well, except for a cape around his neck and, we would soon find, a mask over his eyes. A dwarf Batman! She says, 'Are you gonna stand there all day gawkin' at us, or are you gonna help us?' Halloran tended to the bloke, and I," he said, smirking sinisterly, "well, I took me time untying her."

"What happened, as if I have to ask?" asked one of the young men.

"I'm getting to it, I'm getting to it," the older constable continued. "Apparently, during their little 'bat-ca-pades', the bloke climbed up on the wardrobe and was about to dive down on this beauty when he slipped, fell, and smacked his head on the edge of the bed!"

All three men laughed.

Ow, that's smarts, I thought to myself.

The Constable made a joke that I could not make out but the three men laughed even harder.

"Alright, Loretta," the Constable said as she reemerged, now in her street clothes (jeans, blouse, and her hair down from its tight bun). Less officious, more attractive.

She raised her arm straight in the air and twisted her hand in a royal wave.

My gaze slowly dropped from her hair, down her body (not bad) to her bright white tennis shoes.

"Oh, you like my new trainers?" she asked. I nodded. "I just got them. Ready?"

Loretta and I walked to a nearby bus stop while she did most of the talking. I concluded that she was lonely and probably liked having someone to talk to.

Another interesting turn of events. The film, "An American Werewolf in London" sprung to mind, and while Loretta was clearly not a nurse like Jenny Agutter (in fact, there was no one quite like Jenny Agutter), I kind of wondered whether I was going to get lucky like David, the main character in the movie (hopefully minus the werewolf attack).

After a short bus ride (I loved the red double-decker busses when I wasn't falling off the back of them!) where I watched Loretta deftly purchase our tickets, taking note for future reference, it was a quick jaunt until our stop. I followed her off the bus and up a quaint little residential street.

We passed an older woman walking her dog who gave Loretta a look of sheer disgust, but she was completely oblivious to it as she blathered on. I, however, was not and wondered what the look signified.

Loretta came to a stop in front of a building and ascended the steps towards the front door, which she opened without a key. Stepping inside, she unlocked the door to the left revealing that this was a house with a series of flats within.

She slowly opened the door to reveal a small foyer with a leather loveseat just inside. Her flat was a modest one, to say the least, with the prevalent color being black; a black sofa, a matching black chair, black coffee, and matching end tables, even the shelves and bookcases and wood paneling were black. The only colors that distinguished themselves from the motif were the bright, vibrant ones of two framed movie posters, both from 1939, "The Wizard of Oz" and "Gone with the Wind," that hung on the wall above the sofa.

"Whatcha think?" Loretta asked with obvious pride as she locked the door behind us.

"It's nice." I then added with an accent, *"Me first flat."*

"I like it," she offered, dropping her purse on the chair as she crossed the room. "Make yourself at home. There's the blower, you should call the hospital and check on your grandfather. I'm going to put the kettle on. Do you fancy a cup of tea? Or do you prefer coffee? You Americans love coffee, don't you?"

"No, no, tea would be lovely."

That seemed to make her happy as she bounded off around the corner to what could only be the kitchen. I leaned my bag against the chair and took a seat on the couch. It was lumpy, as if it had been sat on a great deal, but I did not care, I was just overjoyed to be inside somewhere as my exhaustion was reaching its zenith. I could hear Loretta moving about, water running, mugs being placed on the counter.

Something in the corner caught my eye and I slinked off the couch and crossed the room to get a closer look.

The leather apparatus was shaped like a wooden horse with buckled straps on each side. As I ran my hand across the leather, it reminded me of one of those bull machines you find in country bars like in the movie, "Urban Cowboy."

"David?" Loretta called out from the kitchen. I jumped up, as if I had been caught doing something illicit but was not completely sure why. "If you want, you can lie on my bed and watch telly. It's just down the hall. There's a phone in there, as well."

Telly, I thought to myself with a smile. *That is what the room is missing*—a television.

"Ok." I walked down the hall, stopping at the kitchen to smile at Loretta. She smiled back and again I wondered where this all might be leading.

"Hello?"

"Mr. Jones?"

"Yes?"

"Mr. Jones, this is Vice-Principal Cassidy from Essex High."

"Yes."

"Mr. Jones, it's been brought to my attention that, I don't quite know how to say this, but an error seems to have been made by one of our office staff."

"Oh?"

"Your son's name is David *English* Jones, is that correct? Transferred from Frederick Douglass High this week?"

"Go on."

"English. Of course," she said to herself, putting it together.

"What's all this, then?" Mr. Jones asked, looking out through his window at the still-empty spot where the green Jaguar had been sitting.

"Well, apparently, one of my staff erred with regards to the school records of another David Jones. David Englebert Jones."

"What exactly are you saying?" he asked softly.

"Well, it's rather embarrassing really, but when Mrs. Williams informed you both that David didn't have enough credits to pass this semester, she was reading the file of David Englebert, not David English."

"What *exactly* are you saying?" he asked, this time more forcefully.

"Yes, Mr. Jones, David *is* eligible to attend graduation ceremonies on the 17th, which I noticed is the day before his birthday. I think you'll agree, that's the best birthday present one could hope for."

Mr. Jones shook his head, still staring at that vacant spot. "I'll be damned."

"Provided he passes all his exams next week, of course."

"Oh, yes, of course," he said, shaking his head and laughing.

"I don't understand."

"What's the matter?" Loretta asked, as she handed me a hot cup of tea. I lowered the phone back into its cradle and sat on the side of her bed.

"The hospital said they have no record of any David Arthur Jones having been admitted today."

"What? Are you sure you have the right hospital, lovey?"

"Surrey and Sussex Heart Centre," I said, tingling from being called "lovey." I showed her the paper. "Jesus, they'd still have a record if he was brought in dead, wouldn't they?"

"Oh, of course they would. You don't think?"

"I don't know what to think," I said as I blew on the tea before burning my lip on the edge of the teacup; my stomach let out an enormous growl.

"Well, let's try some other…was that your stomach, darling?"

I nodded. *Darling.* "I haven't eaten anything today."

Loretta stepped back and turned the television on. The screen blinked on, exhibiting a darts match in progress. "Have a lie down and I'll make us something to eat. And then we'll call around to every hospital in England, if need be. Have you tried calling his house?"

"I don't have his number, I didn't plan on us being separated."

She nodded, understanding, and winked at me before backing out. I switched through the four channels, and returned to the third offering, an old back and white film with Ingrid Bergman. "Gaslight" possibly?

Crawling back on the bed, I wondered where my grandfather could be. Looking around, this room, it proved much brighter than the living room, with its pastel-colored pillowcases and duvet on a big brass bed.

"So, David?" Loretta called out from the kitchen. "Tell me about America."

"What would you like to know?" I said, running my finger along her extensive record collection, which was a spectrum of musicology, all alphabetized and sectioned by genre, not unlike my mother's collection. I was well impressed and then my finger came to rest on one album in particular. I slipped the album out, examining it closely, front and back and all points in between. *The mother-lode*, I thought before returning it to its proper place.

"Is it as brilliant as it looks on TV?"

"What? America? Well, you know," I said, before letting out a yawn so huge, it nearly dislocated my jaw from my skull. "Don't believe everything you see on TV, you know?"

"Yeah, I know, but I just really want to go. Every place seems to be so different from the next. Just look at all the different landscapes, climates, weathers, cities, towns, accents. I've always wanted to go to America. America and Hong Kong. It looks so brilliant there, too. I mean, nearly everyone's Chinese but it's an English colony so everyone speaks English. I want to go before we give it back to China," she added matter-of-factly.

I nodded, as in off.

A few moments later, Loretta must have walked into the bedroom carrying a plate of cucumber sandwiches with the crusts meticulously removed. I was deep asleep, my mouth agape, unbeknownst to me a dribble of drool had run down my chin and onto the pillow.

Loretta smiled, motherly, but with a certain devilish gleam in her eye.

Waking up either ten minutes or ten hours later, I found myself in a completely dark room where it took me a second to gather my thoughts and remember where exactly I was. Lying on my stomach, with my arms outstretched, I tried to roll onto my back but could not, due to the simple fact that I was handcuffed to the bedpost, I just couldn't.

"What the—?"

I then heard a match strike and saw my shadow on the wall as the room temporarily illuminated from the glow of the tiny flame. Paying me no mind, Loretta, now dressed in a button-down shirt, fishnet stockings and, what could only be described as hump-me-pumps (or 'scrump-me-pumps', as Veronica might say), lit a candle and closed the bedroom door.

"Hey, what's with the..." I started to say until I got a glimpse of what she was wearing.

"Oh, hello."

I turned my head over my right shoulder to get a better look at her as Loretta lowered the needle onto her phonograph player with a scratch, missing her intended target, catching instead the end of "Julia", the Beatles song about John Lennon's Mum on their often-referred to White Album.

Having never known a Julia, my focus was not on The Beatles song fading (Lennon repeating Julia in succession) but Loretta's shadow as she raised something over her head. I twisted my neck and saw beyond the cat o' nine tails she was wielding, my eyes narrowing in on the dimly lit rack of whips and chains on the back of her bedroom door.

"This is a joke, right?" I asked with a nervous chuckle.

Suddenly, the song held some importance as I racked my brain trying to think of the next song on The White Album by quickly humming the ending.

I arrived at the same moment, immediately remembering the next song was "Birthday."

"Didn't you say something about your birthday? So how many lashes is it? Eighteen?"

"Wait! Wait! Wait!" I yelled, struggling and writhing to no avail. "IT'S NOT TODAY!!"

I then watched in horror as her shadow moved on the wall above the bedpost where my hands were turning red from struggling. Her arm raised over her head as I grit my teeth and prepared myself for what was coming, hoping against all hope she was just playing a funny on me.

"Don't worry, it's gratis," Loretta said in a comforting manner, before laying it onto my partially bare butt with a mind-numbingly loud THWAP!

"OWW! What's gratis??"

"It's free, silly," she said before laying another one on me; my flesh grew as blood-red as my wrists.

"OW GODDAMNIT!! STOP!! STOP! STOP! STOP!"

I could not believe this was happening to me as Loretta laughed maniacally, continuing for sixteen more lashes.

When she finally relented, she hopped on the bed straddling my back, and unlocked the cuffs. I pushed her off me, falling on the floor in the process. She continued laughing, not maniacally, as before, but now more demure-like.

"Every boy needs a good lashing every once in a while," Loretta informed me, way too matter-of-factly.

"What the hell is the matter with you?!" I yelled through gritted teeth, pulling my pants up and buttoning them at a frenzied pace. "You seemed so normal!" I said, grabbing my shoes and running out of the room and down the hall. I ran right past the living room and comically had to double-back to grab my bag, where I grabbed one of the sandwiches, shoving it into my mouth before wrestling with the locks until I finally escaped the mad woman's flat.

———

A few moments passed before there was a knock at her door. Loretta, tying her robe shut, crossed the living room and without hesitation, swung the door open.

"You don't know where you are, do you?" she asked as she found not me, but the man I had interacted with on the plane. "Sorry, love, I'm not open right now."

The man made his way inside. "I intend to persuade you to be very open with me, love," he said menacingly.

"Hey, what's all this then?" she said, backing up. "I'm going to call 9-9-9."

"I just need to know what you and that curly-haired boy discussed," he said, closing the door behind him.

"I invited him here to use the phone, that's all. What's this all about?."

Spotting the bondage bull in the corner, his eyes narrowed in on hers. "Not to your lovely flat, I mean here. In England."

"He just said he was accompanying his grandfather and they got separated."

"What else? What else?" he asked impatiently, taking a step towards her.

"That's all, I swear. I swear."

She opened her mouth to scream but he lunged forward, covering her mouth with his gloved hand.

I ran halfway up the street, vigorously rubbing my chafed, red and swollen ass. I eventually stopped and tried to sit down on a small set of steps to put my sneakers back on, but due to the obvious pain, chose to crouch down instead.

Now I knew why that woman looked at Loretta with such contempt. *What other possible reason could it be?* I wondered.

As luck would have it, for the first time all day, I accidentally happened upon a tube station.

First time for everything, I thought as I headed inside.

Chapter
VII

Going it alone in a foreign country that, luckily, spoke English...*because English is my middle name,* I thought, hating myself forever saying that, was less than ideal.

With the help of a polite, old geezer, or bloke, or whatever, I sussed out my route, transfers and all, and descended into the belly of the tube station to wait for the first of two trains. Jovial businessmen combined with more gals in mini-skirts slowly filled up the platform, some unashamedly drunk and loud. Two especially sloshed chicks held each other up as they passed, one taking notice of me.

"WHOO!" the first girl yelled.

"WHOO!" I yelled back.

"WHOO!" she yelled again as she staggered down to the end of the platform where an empty bench awaited them.

———

When the train finally screeched into the station, the whoosh of the breeze felt amazing, literally giving me a second wind. Not that Loretta's London Welcoming Committee failed to achieve that, but the long wait combined with the lengthy, dramatic day was undoubtedly taking its toll.

Copping a few zzz's proved difficult as my head rolled back and forth on the window, leaving me little to do but read the opposite sides of newspapers being read by various passengers, and when I finished reading them, I turned to the adverts posted inside the carriage and read them, Tiananmen Square being the talk of the town. Well, the world. Once finished, I picked up a tattered newspaper from the floor and, after perusing the tabloid-like headlines, turned to the next page to find a topless model aptly titled Page 3 Girl. *American newspapers need more of these*, I thought.

It took what seemed like a hundred stops to get to the transfer station, and after boarding the next train, I continued for what seemed like another hundred stops, finally arriving in East Acton.

I came out of the station and it was not lost on me that there was neither a turnstile nor anyone checking tickets as I moved along with countless others, essentially having gotten a free ride. I could get used to that.

As I stepped outside, the sun was disappearing behind the buildings. Fitting, as I, too, was fading fast. I walked for a bit, not knowing exactly where I was going, and decided to hail yet another taxi when I spotted a blond rocker girl up ahead. I picked up my pace to catch up to her; as I drew closer, the first thing I noticed was a picture of Sid Vicious stitched to the back of her denim jacket with safety pins.

"Excuse me," I said softly, trying not to scare her. "Do you know where Tent City is around here?"

"Tent City. I go to Tent City now," she said with a heavy French accent. "I will take you."

We walked through the lower-class, two-story home neighborhood for a few minutes until I finally asked her. "So, have you seen the movie 'Sid and Nancy'?"

She went on to complain that so much of the movie was untrue, it did not happen that way, and that she did not particularly care for it or its portrayal. I was gutted but conceded I knew little of the punk movement or its portrayal of the ill-crossed lovers.

I couldn't get her to stop talking as she continued that the Sex Pistols music in the film was, in her words, "too clean," not the raw sound that made The Sex Pistols the great punk band they were. Those were all the reasons I loved it. At the time, when I first saw it (it changed my life) I wanted to be the Pistol's guitarist, Steve Jones. I loved rock and roll. Especially guitarists. I must have played air guitar to all the greats: Hendrix, Page, Nugent, Stevie Ray, and Ritchie B. Loved my singers: Dio, Coverdale, Plant, and Paul Rodgers. And drummers, forget about it. John and Keith, Mitch and Ginger.

She continued to talk about punk rock music with her sexy French accent, which was starting to grow on me, while my mind wandered off as I began recapping the day's events:

Lost my grandfather, can't find my cousin, roaming the streets of London with a bag that now felt like I was carrying one of the Time Bandits, all the while gaining the same international advice from ladies from different parts of the world: 'Don't believe everything you see in movies.'

Tough lesson for a teenager who educated himself working in a crummy little video store where nobody ever returned the VHS tapes; a kid who would set his alarm clock to two or four in the morning to watch old gangster movies with James Cagney or Paul Muni. But it was the video store and all their films on tape that taught me about life and love and music and history. Everything from "All the President's Men" to "Krush Groove" to Costas Gravas' "Z."

After about a 10 minute stroll, we shuffled up an asphalt walkway towards a medium-sized, concrete building with an aged, yellow sign nailed to it: TENT CITY. Not exactly a city, I noticed, but more of a compound.

Inside, the French punk girl walked right up to a tall, intimidating, pink-haired, French punk in red spandex, wearing spiked wristbands and a hot-pink choker. After a look of pure disdain he shot in my direction, they kissed hard, intensely deliberate.

So much for that, I thought as I made my way over to a large counter proudly flashing my YHA Membership card with my goofy photo stapled to it. A different French punk girl informed me that they were not affiliated with the YHA.

F-f-f-f, I thought, all for nothing.

I paid for two days at 3 pounds a day, just to be on the safe side. I did not, however, like having to relinquish my passport as a deposit, but what choice did I have? All I cared about was sleep, as it beckoned me, and I was now oh so close.

She issued me a blanket and an oversized parachute bag with a combination lock while directing me to the men's changing room where I locked up my duffel bag inside the parachute bag, chaining it to a large wooden divider alongside dozens of others.

Having everything I needed, my blanket and guitar, I was already counting the proverbial sheep.

"Pillow?"

"It's on the bed."

I nodded, satisfied.

"Excuse me," I said as I tried to pass two young French men speaking in their native tongue, engaged in a most passionate conversation while completely ignoring me. "Excuse me," I repeated with no success.

Frustrated as they continued talking with their accents that I now deemed anything but sexy, I forcefully pushed through them. They responded with scowls and some likely choice French words.

"Merci, merci me," I thanked them in French, paraphrasing the late, great Marvin Gaye song, a favorite of my dearly departed mama, before walking outside to find four massive, green Army tents. "Things *definitely* ain't what they used to be," I said, paraphrasing the next line in the song.

All of a sudden I'm on an episode on M*A*S*H*, I thought as it began drizzling; I tilted my head back, welcoming the cool rain on my face.

I reached the "B" tent and slowly poked my head inside. It was pitch black as there was no lighting whatsoever, but I could see enough to know that only a few of the beds were occupied. I sought out my bunk, "B23," according to the card I was issued, and finding it was a top bunk, I chucked my guitar and blanket on the flattest mat and pillow I had ever experienced and hopped up.

It mattered little, in a mere matter of minutes, with the torrential rain pouring now, I was dead to the world, my guitar strap wrapped tightly around my arm, the blanket pulled up to my eyes. I was out like a light.

And I slept. Until well past dawn.

Just kidding.

I woke up about an hour later, again discombobulated, in a dark room, the only light creeping in from an outside lamp post. The rain had stopped, and I needn't have questioned whether I had dreamt the meter maid situation as my still-stinging buttocks could attest.

I made my way back into the main building, waving to the French girl that brought me there, now behind the counter where a sign for phone cards was taped.

"How do the phone cards work?" I asked her.

"We have five, ten, and twenty-pound phone cards," she said with her sexy foreign accent.

I contemplated it for a moment. "I better just take a five-pound one, I don't want to be lugging a twenty-pound phone card all over London," I said, pausing for her to laugh. She didn't. "Too heavy."

She continued staring at me expressionlessly. I waited a further moment before shaking my head while I dug into my pocket.

Inside the kiosk, after several minutes of studying the phone card for complete instructions, I took out the number of the hospital I had jotted down on the paper provided to me by the First Class stewardess. The female nurse on the other end searched her records but could find no David Jones admitted in the last week.

After explaining in detail how we had been separated at the airport, she showed genuine concern, assuring me that she would call around to the other hospitals in the area, and if I called back at a later time, she would leave any information at the desk.

Is this a joke? I wondered as I decided to head back into the city.

———

The Hospital, no grandfather.

The Royal Coat of Whatever, no cousin.

"This's becoming a righ' Royal Coat of F--- Up," I muttered aloud. The older fella (wasn't everyone?) I passed, paused to size me up.

I had managed the tube, now I needed to manage the tube platforms, I decided with all the optimism I could muster.

Still holding onto the only ticket I had bought that day, I headed back to the East Acton station and, again, passed the empty ticket booth to face yet another platform snafu, where a mousy woman pointed me in the right direction, towards the city center and not, as the platform we were on indicated, away from it.

I contemplated jumping the tracks, but with the luck I'd been having, I wisely decided against getting charred into black-eyed piss. Reaching the opposite platform, I waved my appreciation to her, but she merely ignored me, without so much as a look in my direction.

I strongly felt I was more determined than ever to take this town when I arrived at Oxford Circus station. I was genuinely surprised it was as busy at ten o'clock at night as it was at 10 a.m.

Street musicians played for change by the escalators as I ascended up and out, sheepishly following the other cattle as they narrowed into a single line passing the inspector booth.

Taking their lead, I held my ticket up towards an Inspector whose neck was working at actual breakneck speed in checking the validity of everyone's tickets. So, it came as a welcome surprise when the inspector failed to stop me as I slipped through and fast-footed it outside onto Oxford Street.

True nighttime city action like nothing I had ever seen before, outside of a movie. I passed a disheveled gray-haired old man wearing a large sandwich board with the word REPENT on it. Martin Scorsese's "The Last Temptation of Christ" was playing inside.

At half ten (or as they say in the U.K., less than an hour before "last orders"), I arrived back at The Royal Coat of Arms, finding a spot at the bar. When the Scottish barman approached, he smiled at me with recognition.

"Any sign of him?"

"Ah, Ian Jones? No," he said loudly but sincerely over the crowd noise. "Fancy something to drink?"

"Um, yeah, sure why not? A pint of lager, please," I said with aplomb while my eyes perused the menu board on the wall behind him.

"What kind?" the barman asked, grabbing a pint glass and pointing to the taps. "Carling?"

"Sure. And can I get a ham and cheese sandwich?"

"Salad?"

I considered it; I would never have eaten one if my mother offered it but thought a salad might be swell. "Sure."

After the barman placed a pint of Carling on the bar for me, I took it to the phone kiosk. Inside, I dialed my house and was told that it would be ten pounds for the first three minutes.

"Too rich for my blood," I muttered under my breath, a favorite phrase of my old man's.

"Oh, doctor, I'm calling to see if my Grandfather was admitted," I said upon hearing a man's voice.

"First off, I'm not a doctor, love, I'm the head nurse and secondly, I've got three bloody football supporters that just walked in, you're going to have to wait a tic, taa. Have a seat," he shouted before placing me on hold. Odd the hold music playing was a muzak version of "A Hard Day's Night."

"I bet you're the head nurse," I mumbled as I quaffed half my pint in two huge gulps.

"Thank you for holding. Right. So, what's your grandfather's name, love?" he asked when he finally returned.

"David Jones. David Arthur Jones."

The nurse went on to inform me that one of his colleagues called every hospital around Gatwick Airport but no one had either admitted or heard of him. "Probably just went home, love. Haven't you his number?"

"Didn't think I'd need it," I said before hanging up and returning to the bar where my sandwich was waiting, with lettuce and tomato (*tomahto*) on it. Hence "salad."

After destroying it and the accompanying potato chips (or crisps, as they're called there), I ordered one more pint as reality started to set in. I lit up a fag from the pack of Gauloises I bought with Rick, which now, in light of everything, seemed like a lifetime ago, and enjoyed the for-its-time liberty of smoking. In public. In a bar. Well, pub.

Feeling more than a little buzzed after my third lager, I handed over ten pounds, telling the barman to keep the change; the barman responded with a look of confusion as I stumbled off the barstool, grabbed my guitar, and staggered out through the closest of the pub's two entrances.

Exhaling and looking up into the starry night, I heard a car door shut nearby, and out of the corner of my eye, spotted a tall, wiry young man walk briskly from a red VW Beetle into the pub's furthest door.

Could *that*?

I shrugged and started back towards the tube station but found myself beelining back into the pub, an air of deja vu as I approached the bar while I again scanned the room just as I had earlier.

"I know this is a long shot but did that Ian you were referring to just come in by any chance?" I asked the barman, who was counting a small fortune of paper currency.

"Did you not see him, mate?" he replied in a heavy Scottish brogue, holding up the money before sliding it into his front pants pocket.

_____

"I'm sorry, what?"

"Yeah, he just went upstairs," pointing towards a nondescript door beside the bar with a PRIVATE sign on it. "First landing, first door on the left."

"Can I? I mean, may I?" I asked, to which the barman nodded, giving me the go-ahead.

On the second-floor landing, I urgently approached the first door on the left as the barman had directed me. I slung the guitar off my shoulder and leaned towards the door to have a listen. Hearing nothing inside, I lightly knocked. Not a peep.

I was just about to knock again when loud footsteps approached the other side of the door before it swung open. It was the same guy from outside and was, despite the punk rock hair-do that seemed to be growing out and the droopy, hooded eyes, a dead-ringer for my father when he was younger. I was drawn immediately to his "BOLLOCKS TO THE POLL TAX" t-shirt. We sized each other head to toe, both stopping to take in each other's identical stone-washed jeans

"Yeah? Whatchu want?"

"Are you Ian Jones?"

"Who's asking?"

"I think we're cousins," I said, smiling with a big toothy grin, relieved.

"I ain't got no bl—cousins," he said, clearly stopping himself before slamming the door in my face.

My jaw slowly dropped to the floor. What the hell

was that? I felt compelled to knock again and explain myself but as I was standing just inches from the stairs, I sure as shit did not want to go ass over teacup down them.

Then there *would* be a David Jones in hospital.

I reluctantly trudged down the stairs without getting any of the answers I was after. I reached the bottom and turned the doorknob, cracking it open ever so slightly, enough to hear someone say: "'Ere, give us two pints, Tommy, or I'll kill ya" followed by roars of laughter.

Upstairs, I heard a door close and, feeling relieved, turned with a smile, hoping my cousin had come to his senses. There was no one there. *I've come too far*, I thought as I pulled the door shut and made my way back upstairs.

I eased my ear onto Ian's door, listening for any movement inside but could only hear the punters down in the pub. A toilet flushed nearby and turning to see where the sound came from, I found Ian stepping into the hallway. Ian's long, blank face turned menacing; his teeth bared, revealing a missing third tooth while his feet practically came off the floor.

"WHO THE F--- ARE YOU?!" Ian roared as he lunged for me, grabbing the collar of my t-shirt with both clenched fists and tackled me into the door, which went flying open. We both landed on the floor, Ian crushing me under his substantially heavier weight class, knocking the wind out of me.

I struggled to catch my breath but with just enough gusto to groan, "I'm a Jones," before desperately gasping for air.

Ian slowly rolled off me and with that, removed his knee from my stomach, which I immediately grasped, wincing in pain.

"I lost Grandpa," I said, clearly still in pain, yet wondering where *Grandpa* came from.

Ian extended his hand, which I reluctantly grabbed, and he swiftly lifted me to my feet.

"David, yeah?" I nodded, still holding my stomach. "Whatcha mean lost him? I thought he went to America to see you. You're the one graduating, innit? First in the family, I'm told."

"Well, technically that would be my cousin, Stan. Lookit, Grandad was having some heart things, I don't know, and asked if I would bring him back here to his doctor. But when we got here, he disappeared. Do you have his number?"

Ian peeled his t-shirt off, revealing a muscular back and a couple of tattoos, one of the Grim Reaper, the other of The Rolling Stones lips and tongue logo.

"Whatchu mean, *disappeared*?" He walked to the wardrobe and chucked it inside, pulling a clean shirt from a dresser drawer—a Blues Brothers t-shirt.

"Just that. When we went to get off the plane, he was already gone. They told me he was taken to the hospital as soon as we landed."

"What hospital? I thought you were supposed to be watching him."

"Yeah, well..." I said, shrugging, not wanting to get into the reason. Ian mocked me with a shrug of his own.

"Well, truth be told, it doesn't look like I'll be graduating. Not next week, anyway."

"Cor, you gave him a heart attack, ya bastard?" Ian declared.

"No, no. He doesn't know that part. But yeah, it's kind of my fault," I vaguely offered.

Ian nodded, pivoting on his right foot as he took a last look around the room. "Your mum just died, yeah?"

"Care for a cup of Rosey Lee?"

Robbin stared for a moment without so much as a blink. Starling returned her narrow focus with a discerning look of her own. Britt relented first, blinking.

"Yeah, I'd love a *cuppa*," Robbin said. "If it's not too much trouble."

Starling smiled behind her N-95. "Not at all, we have a *lecky*." She stood up and crossed the room where an electric kettle sat on the marble counter, advertised by the hotel as a European breakfast bar.

"I had started the kettle, but, for whatever reason, I completely forgot." She poured out two cups, put them on a silver tray, along with the sweeteners and cream, and approached Robbin. She set one cup on the table to the right of her most interesting Subject.

Robbin reached into her purse on the floor and removed a silver flask.

"Might need a little boost," Robbin said, withdrawing a silver flask. "D'ya mind?"

"No, no, not at all. Please."

Robbin adeptly spun the lid off and it hovered momentarily above in the air before she caught the lid in the palm of her hand.

"I didn't know it was going to do *that*. That's a bit of magic, innit?"

She poured a healthy amount into her teacup before holding it up in an offer to Starling.

"Oh, no," she said, with a nervous chuckle. "Enjoy."

"Slainte."

Robbin unashamedly slipped the end of the flask under her mask and took a big swig. Just as swiftly she capped it and dropped it inside her purse beside the chair.

The Interviewer returned the silver Russell Hobbs teapot to its cradle. "Just out of curiosity, what exactly *did* DJ's mother die from?"

"If you were to ask the catty black women of our complex they'd probably say she talked herself to death. Grandmom said she was born talking and never stopped, never at a loss for words. And she was *opinionated*. She would tell you this is how it is and that's how it was. But no, she actually died from a big heart. An enlarged heart. Went into the hospital for surgery, came out of it fine. Then she just up and...."

I tensed up as Ian walked determinedly towards me.

"Sorry, mate," Ian said, gripping my shoulder as he switched off the light and yanked the door open. "Come on."

We trudged down a dark back stairway together, me not completely unaware I was copying his every move.

"Didn't you have a brother, too?" Ian asked as I followed him down and out to a nearby work van whose sliding doors were both open. He instructed me to get in.

"Kind of. A tractor-trailer ran my mother off the road when she was eight months pregnant, had a miscarriage."

There was no passenger seat, so I leaned back against the massive dashboard, my back to the windshield, which, along with the floor, was filled with trash. *Rubbish*, as Dad was apt to say. I was literally standing on fast-food wrappers and empty cigarette packs. Ian slid his door shut and started it up with a low rumble while struggling with the shifter to get into first gear.

Loud crunching metal.

"Gri-nder," I sang, parodying a heavy metal growl. "Looking for geaarrss."

Ian's eyes darted to the left before slowly turning his head to size me up with a look of disgust and maybe even disappointment. He finally wrestled it into first gear and jerked the van away from the curb with a strong lurch while my feet slipped on the wrappers like a rug was pulled out from under me. I got my hands up just in time to stop myself from slamming face-first into the heavy-duty aluminum wall in front of me. I quickly gained my balance back jamming my feet on the floor, legs stiff as a board.

We drove for a while, neither of us saying a thing. Sitting backward, as the old joke goes, I could not see where we were going, only where I had been.

Ian steered the van through lefts and rights until we eventually hit a freeway. As the sky slowly darkened it looked as if he was taking us out of the city. Far, far away. Ian opened it up, switching into a higher gear while I watched the white stripes pass on the road outside. Suddenly something caught my eye.

"Check this out" I called out, trying to get Ian's attention over the hollow sound of the wind. I desperately needed to make a connection with him.

With someone.

Anyone.

It seemed like all my contact had been with either taxi drivers or rude French people.

And seemingly caring women that eventually just wanted to punish me.

What did I ever do to you, Mommy?

———

Ian continued looking straight ahead.

"Come on man, turn the light on," I begged. "Ian."

Ian switched the light on and reluctantly gazed over to find my arms outstretched, fingers wagging. Under my hands, the trash was whipping itself into a cyclonic frenzy.

"It's a kind of magic," I said, quoting the "Highlander" and followed it with Christopher Lambert's little snicker. "Hee hee hee."

Ian rolled his eyes before switching the light back off. "I haven't seen it."

Haven't seen what? I wanted to ask.

My attention turned to Jake and Elwood Blues on Ian's shirt. I began vibrating my lips to the TV theme, "The Peter Gunn Theme," a song featured prominently in "The Blues Brothers."

"Dun dun donna dun dun donna"

At the appropriate time in the song, Ian vibrated his lips to the trumpet bit:

"Waah wahh. Waaaah waaah wah."

We both simultaneously lip-vibrated the next horn bit:

"Wah wah wah waah waah waah waah waah wah wah."

Ian pulled the bottom of his t-shirt out to get a better look at the washed-away image of the Blues Brothers.

"F---in' dog's bollocks, they were," Ian said.

The British. They loved the blues. I don't know what it was. They took *our* blues and sold it back to us. And here I was. Stuck in the middle of the Atlantic Ocean.

Eventually, Ian slowed the van down, weaving it through some intricate turns in a posh little area, God knows where.

"D'ya ever drive, English?" Ian asked, as he turned the headlights off and slowly pulled onto the left of the narrow road, leaving the truck running. I shook my head, not sure what he meant.

"I gotta pick somefin' up, d'ya wanna 'ave a go?" he said, indicating his seat as he stepped out onto the street. "I may need you to—" Ian said mysteriously as he pointed out through the windshield.

"Oh. Ok," I said, shrugging. I did as Ian requested and moved over to the driver's seat, getting a li'l nervous.

Satisfied, Ian tapped lightly on the outside of the van and turned and walked back past where we had driven. I picked up his trail in the outside mirror, making a slight adjustment to follow his movements. Ian shuffled up the sidewalk of a rather house far fancier than my new one, yet like mine, surrounded by tall shrubs. And then I could see him no more.

"I gotta pick somefin up, d'ya wanna 'ave a seat?" I mimicked my cousin, over and over, turning it into a song while I drummed aggressively on the steering wheel. "The f---in' dog's bollocks, watch him eat the meat. Eat the meat, eat the meat."

With the light from a nearby lamppost, I spied a

wrinkled-up newspaper on the floor with what looked to be Princess Diana in a not-so-flattering beach photo. I snatched it up and began flipping through the pages looking for the Page 3 girl. No such luck, different newspaper.

"Psst!" came from behind the van. I looked in the mirror to see Ian running my way before ballet-jumping in the air. "Go! Go! Go!" he barked at a low whisper.

I tried to shift the truck into first gear, but it made that horrible grinding noise again. I looked over my shoulder to find Ian disappeared again only for him to reappear on the passenger side. He lifted a small collie into the truck, the last thing in the world I expected, and set it down between us. Standing at the dashboard like the captain of a ship he pointed towards the horizon as I finally shoved it into first gear. Pulling away from the side of the road, I looked back to see what was chasing us but there was no one there.

"Other side, other side," Ian barked, a little louder now, as he pushed the steering wheel sending us across the narrow road.

"I know, I know."

"You got to stop there, mate" Ian pointed out through the window while keeping the dog from flying forward with his leg. "Maybe I better drive."

"I got it, I got it," I assured him, looking down at the collie who was huffing and puffing, tongue out, tail wagging. "Um, that's not Granddad."

"Come to get Sir Drops-a-Lot."

"Sorry? Surrey! Let's go to Surrey and look for him. Wait, what?"

"My dog. Sir Drops-a-Lot."

I erupted into laughter as Ian reached into his once-white painter's pants and pulled out a pack of cigarettes. He stuck one between his lips and clenched it with his teeth.

"Then why were you running?"

Ian turned to look me up and down, before extending the pack in my direction. I gladly took the pack and grabbed a cigarette for myself before handing it back. "What are these? Roth-mans? Roth-mans??"

"Yeah, wha' of it?" he asked with near-contempt.

"Oh, nothing. Stupid, really. A sort of PRE-moni-tion, I guess."

Ian scrutinized me before continuing. "I 'ad this bird watching him for me, thought she might not give him back."

Makes sense, I thought.

Ian shoved the pack back in his pocket, withdrew a Zippo lighter, sparking it up with a snap of his middle finger, lighting his cigarette before extending it to the tip of my cig.

"So I just rescued him. Back," he said, snapping the lighter shut.

"What, were they abusing him or something?"

"Not really. Well, sort of. These silly sods changed his name. To Oyster. The stupidest name I ever fuc-in' heard. You believe that?"

I mean, I'd heard worse.

"Me and my ex, we got him together, when he was just a pup. Named him Sir *Drops*-A-Lot because whenever I caught him pissing or havin' a shit in our flat, I'd scream 'OY! SIR!'"

"Why Sir Drops-A-Lot?" I laughed.

"Cause he's fu—in' dropping turds and whiz everywhere, innit."

I erupted into my wheezing, raspy laugher. "That's the funniest fu—in' shit I've ever heard in my whole life."

"You see why I had to get him outta there."

I nodded. "I thought the whole time we were going to see Grandpapa."

"Grandpapa! Now, that's the funniest shit *I've* ever heard."

"I don't know what to call him, I'm trying different ones out. What do you call him?"

"I'm sure he's fine. I gotta get this back to the worksite," he said, leaving, it seemed to me, open for interpretation.

"Is this not your truck?" Ian shrugged, not answering. "So...you just borrowed it for a dog-napping?"

Ian seemed to roll it around his huge head before

nodding matter-of-factly. "Yeah."

We parked up at a magnificent high-rise, the architecture alone clearly gave one pause. Sir and I watched as Ian locked up the van and followed him. "Show you sumfin'," Ian said, leading us around the back of a building where some modifications and upkeep were underway.

"Stay," Ian told us both.

I sat down on the marble steps that overlooked a sprawling tree-lined park and scratched Oyster, or Sir Drops-A-Lot, behind his ears. Ian disappeared around the building, returning minutes later hauling a ladder. He casually walked past us, swinging it over our heads, and made his way up the steps towards the building.

Give me that ladder and step on it, I felt compelled to say.

Does Granddad stay here? I wondered as we followed Ian to the building. He carefully leaned the ladder against the wall between the first and second-floor balconies and their adjacent windows.

Lights were on in all the rooms on the first and second floors. Unfazed, Ian turned and waved me over.

"Stay," I said to the dog and amazingly he did just that.

"Hold this," Ian said, referring to the ladder as he put his foot on the bottom rung. I grasped the right and left sides as he started climbing up slowly and stealthily until he reached his intended destination, a second-floor window.

Sir approached, wagging his tail. My attention turned from the dog to the sliding door of the first-floor patio where I could see an older woman watching a tennis match.

Wimbledon? I wondered, it was the only remotely tennis-related thing I knew.

Whatever it was, my heart was pumping so hard, I could see it outside of my chest cavity, pumping like 'Mr. Creosote' from "Monty Python's The Meaning of Life."

I watched Ian cautiously peek in the window where, after a few seconds, he seemed to be smiling. Peering under his arm, he waved me up. With more than just some reluctance on my part, I slowly climbed up as Ian shifted over, standing only on his left foot to make room for me. When I reached the same rung, Ian goaded me to have a look. I was too short to see so I climbed up one more rung to see what all the fuss was.

Expecting to see my grandfather reading a book, or spinning yarn, I was surprised to find the side profile of a twenty-ish young lady with long, chestnut-brown hair sitting at a desk. A large textbook propped up against the wall before her, it appeared she was studying. *In June?* It was abundantly clear, even from just her profile, that she was nothing less than stunning.

"F---in' beautiful, yeah?" Ian whispered. I leaned to the left, nodding.

"I see her every day. Whatcha fink? Nineteen? Twenty?"

I shrugged, took another peek, and nodded in agreement. She pushed herself away from the desk, stood up, and stretched, her white robe falling open just a bit. I tried to pull back but could not take my eyes off her. She turned towards the window, revealing the shortest of T-shirts and shorts before we locked eyes.

Shit! Too late!

She raced to the window, where she let out a blood-curdling scream with such force that it sent the two of us along with the ladder flailing away from the wall and hurtling towards the ground. I couldn't speak for Ian, but I braced myself as we fell back towards the cold, hard ground, my whole stupid life, a series of embarrassments and naïve fuck-ups, passed before my eyes.

The ladder came up off the ground, locking under the iron rungs that protected the first-floor windows. The top end of the ladder slammed against the thick marble atrium surrounding the grand terrace that overlooked the park. The bird's screams of bloody murder continued; Sir proceeded to howl at the girl's shrieks.

I lost my grip and found myself holding onto the ladder with one hand while Ian let go completely, falling to the ground. He stood up and tapped me on my leg, my feet dangled mere inches from the ground. I let go, took a small drop, and found myself standing below the terrace while her screaming continued. Lights began blinking on in nearly every window as she caught her breath and screeched again. Luckily, the patio shielded us as Sir stood up on his hind legs and copied her again.

"OY SIR!" Ian whispered forcefully, pointing out our escape route, as her infinite screams of terror filled the London air like a World War Two civil defense siren. Sir Drops-a-Lot finally stopped, quickly catching up with us as we ran full-on "Chariots of Fire" across the park, successfully eluding capture.

Ian and I parted ways at the Tottenham tube station but not before getting somewhat of an assurance from Ian that he would do all he could to track down our El Padre Grande.

"Where's he live?"

"Birming'am."

"Is that far?"

Ian scoffed. "It's a wee bit north of here."

I wondered why he seemed less concerned with the whereabouts of our oldest living Jones than I did. True, I knew so little of both men and their relationship that I could not say one way or the other. Maybe I was just being overly dramatic. Or maybe there was bad blood between them.

"Dad? It's me! Hey, do you have Grandad's phone number? Yeah, I know, I lost him! What do you mean, what do I mean? He was off the plane and into an ambulance before I woke up."

Bad English
the III

Yeah, that wasn't going to work, I figured. Best not to call home. Not yet, anyway. I walked around the corner and right into British funny man, Rowan Atkinson. Well, sort of.

Polly Jones loved British humour almost as much as her husband, maybe more so. PBS, The Public Broadcasting System would play British sitcoms, such as "To The Manor Born" with Penelope Keith and "Are You Being Served?" would play every Friday, and for a while, Saturdays would show "Monty Python's Flying Circus" followed by "Fawlty Towers" starring Monty Python's John Cleese. She would gather family and friends together as if it was a big weekly event.

Most of the neighbours would bore easily at the dry British humour and would excuse themselves, but Mom loved it as much as Mr. Jones. She, however, did not care much for Benny Hill, saying his humour was stupid, childish, and misogynist. But occasionally you could find her laughing at Benny's silliness, looking over from doing the dishes or some odd task. With cable, came more channels like Arts & Entertainment, which aired comedies like "Alas Smith and Jones" and me and Mum's favourite, "Black Adder" with Rowan Atkinson, who would go on to star in "Mr. Bean" and the charity concert where we were first introduced to his rubber-faced antics, "The Secret Policeman's Other Ball."

"I'm home," Mr. Jones called out as he swung the door open in a desperate attempt to feign some semblance of normalcy. He closed the door slowly and sullenly limped through his new house, having ditched the wheelchair. No one was around to afford him the sympathy he so desperately sought.

The house was a palace in comparison to where he had lived his entire twenty-two years in America, not to mention his childhood home in North Hampton. He concluded that it merely lacked design. (Well out of character, "Polly wants a Cracker" popped into his psyche).

Intending to put more things in place, making him and DJ feel more like they had a home, Jones hopped through the kitchen on his way to the garage where the movers had stored their lifetime of accumulations.

He quickly changed his tune when he found his guitar case leaning against the wall. He heaved it up on the counter and for the first time since retiring his Mod Stewart persona, he slowly opened it, revealing his old acoustic Yamaha guitar. Now he felt compelled to play dress up and put on a rock show in his new home.

All his old rock clothes were in a trunk in the garage. He swung open the door and fumbled for the light switch, flicking it on. The room remained mostly dark, rays of light streaming in from around the garage door.

"Oy vey, for f---sake."

He stepped down into the garage and spotted a flashlight on the cluttered workbench near DJ's helmet. He switched it on and waved the light around the room.

It abruptly died on him. Mr. Jones smacked it in the palm of his hand. It leaped back to a steady ray of light.

DJ's father spotted it immediately and gasped as it took his breath away—the green Jaguar, mangled to bits. What was left of its roof had been placed haphazardly jutting out of the top of its current makeshift convertible state. He fell back against the workbench, slamming the helmet hard on the table, as DJ had just done days earlier.

"DAAAAAAAVIIIIIIIIID!!!!!" he yelled, clenching his fists. He scoffed and shook his head as he reached over his shoulder and switched the light off. "Well played, ya c---."

After roaming the London streets of Convent Garden and the West End Theatre District, I wondered why in the coolest city in the world all the pubs and taverns closed at 11 p.m. I quickly found out that the tube stations don't stay open much longer, as I kept finding them padlocked shut. So I took a seat outside the station and plunked on the strings of my guitar.

As I sat with my legs crossed, playing quietly to myself, two scruffy teenagers, a boy, and a girl sat down facing me, making me feel self-conscious enough to stop tinkering. Their fingers, toes, and hair were filthy, leaving me with the impression that they were homeless.

"You're really good," the girl said.

"Um," I said, cocking my head as if to indicate I wasn't even playing. "Thanks?"

"Are you squatting nearby?" the boy asked.

"You mean, where am I staying?"

They both nodded, and I detected a sense of urgency on their parts.

"I'm staying at Tent City in East Acton."

Dirty English Hippies. Got up and f-cked off without so much as a by-your-leave!

"Safe to assume that he doesn't know how to use that phrase," Starling mumbled.

Robbin continued, without so much as a by-your-leave.

After what seemed like days walking across the Greater London region, the sky showing its first rays of orange sunrise, I found a taxi idling next to an as-yet unopened tube station.

"*Tent City, East Acton, please,*" I said, desperation in my English accent, which I employed so as not to be denied a ride by an Englishman.

A brief snooze later, the driver announced we had reached our destination. Those tents had never looked more beautiful. It was nearly five a.m.

"Eight pound sixty, please."

I counted out the change, placing them through the window and the driver's awaiting palm, who counted them faster than I. "*Cheers, mate,*" I mumbled as I started to crawl out with what little energy I had left to muster.

"That's only eight pounds fifty. It's understandable, they are small.

So much for him thinking I was English, I thought as I fished out another 10p coin. *What would a Brit be doing staying at a youth hostel in London anyway?* I mused as I made my way across the field, skipping the main building altogether.

Chapter
VIII

It was 5 a.m. when my head finally hit the vinyl lump in the mattress they dared to call a pillow.

Someone poked their head into the tent. "Jean-Paul!"

I squinted at my watch, it was now six a.m.

The guy continued calling out for his friend, "Jean-Paul!"

I vigorously scratched my inner thigh and crotch as it was now literally starting to get under my skin. *Great, now I'm developing some psychosomatic crap*, I thought before rolling over and pulling the blanket over my head, my preferred method of sleeping.

Jean-Paul finally awakened on the other side of the tent while I continued scratching away, each scratch giving way to an itch somewhere else on my body.

"David. Wake up. David."

I woke up to find Grandfather standing above me. When did I move to the lower bunk?

"Get up, my son."

My heart began pounding and my breathing became erratic. I opened my right eye expecting my Grandfather, but all I found was an empty tent. Thinking it was ten or eleven in the morning, my heart skipped a beat when I opened my left eye to check my watch. It was nearly five o'clock at night! I had accidentally let the day slip away.

As I gathered my gear and bolted into the main building of Tent City, I grabbed a t-shirt and headed into the men's restroom where I brushed my teeth while various Frenchies played grab-ass, flicking towels at each other and such. Teeth clean, I stepped into a toilet stall. I was confounded to find an old–fashioned water tank with the pull-chain. As I sat there, I found myself chuckling at the graffiti etched in the walls and door. Things such as "God is Dead – Rimbaud, Rimbaud is Dead Meat – God".

Unbeknownst to me, what I can bet was a hairy hand reached out on the sink and nicked my toothpaste. Taking a shower with a bunch of random Europeans, with their uncut sausages dangling between their hairy legs, I was glad I was circumcised. While I soaped up and washed my frizzy hair, I decided I was going to have to call home and began compiling excuses.

As I headed back to the tube station, a pair of women in housecoats blocked the sidewalk talking to a middle-aged woman in a second-floor window. I stopped to take in the view, her low-cut shirt revealed a rack so big it looked like an ass sitting on the sill.

"Whatchu looking at?" she yelled at me. I came back to earth and pushed past the Housecoats. Shuffled my arse just a little faster to the station.

I bought what would become my staple for the week, a banana and chocolate milk, at the little market outside the tube station and headed inside. Without buying a ticket. Again.

While the train screeched and rattled, sending us passengers rocking back and forth, I found myself growing concerned by the posters placed prominently throughout the carriage focusing on "FARE DODGING." Their campaign consisted of "DIVERSE" (I was reminded of that poster back in the Guidance Counselor's office). People in various careers, all in handcuffs, with their testimonials of why they did what they did. The ultimate result? Fines, jail, and police records. I decided then I should probably start buying tickets.

Exiting at Piccadilly, I walked along a busy curved road of fancy clothes shops and expensive salons, where, along the way, I acted like I was David Hemmings in "Blow-Up," taking pictures all over London. Spotting signs for Buckingham Palace, I headed in that direction. The Queen was probably expecting me for lunch, I reckoned.

———

I descended a set of marble stairs and found myself by a tree-filled park where people were scattered everywhere. People of all shapes, ages, and sizes sat in identical white and green striped lounge chairs, others were stretched out on blankets, some having picnics. I walked for what felt like hours, but the Palace simply seemed to escape me.

Taking a much-needed load off on an available park bench, I pulled my guitar across my lap and strummed a few chords, finding it wildly out of tune. Tuning my guitar was not exactly my forte, so I got up and continued walking. I felt like I was close, but it seemed like I was just going around in circles. I wanted to ask but feared people's reactions.

"Buy a map, ya bloody Yank. What do I look like, Traveller's Aid?" That could be a feasible response to an inquiring American, if one forgot how bloody polite everyone was. I did.

And if I asked with an English accent? "What? You don't know where your Queen lives?"

It was quite a conundrum.

If it had been a movie, the camera would have done a crane-shot straight up, high above the trees, revealing Buckingham Palace just on the other side of Hyde Park. But this was real life.

I made my way back the way I came, ascending the marble steps and landing not on Regent Street but the street parallel, Haymarket Street, until I found an outdoor sandwich sign on the sidewalk advertising "Spaghetti Bolognese 4.99."

I ventured inside the quirky little pub and had a seat at the bar where I ordered a pint and a plate of spaghetti Bolognese, but only after I confirmed it was meat sauce and not bologna. Just short of putting my lip under the dish and inhaling, I destroyed it and headed out.

Getting the hang of the Underground, maneuvering from one station to the next, sometimes even getting on the right platform, I made my way back to Leicester Square. The massive cinemas that surrounded it advertised the latest summer releases (several, like "Nightmare On Elm Street 4" had played in the US months before). It was still light out, so the street performers were scarce. Instead, tourists stood in long lines in hopes of getting tickets to huge West End productions such as "Miss Saigon."

Maybe I should get things going, I thought to myself.

I crossed the square to the arcade next to the massive Hippodrome nightclub. I had tried to get in the previous evening, mostly just because it was open, only to be told: "You're dressed too casual, mate."

After exchanging a few pound coins into smaller denominations, I proceeded to sink ten and twenty-pound coins into the coin-pushing arcades, the ones layered with coins that nudge forward (in theory) upon more coins being dropped in, hopefully landing in just the right place forcing the dangling coins to drop out.

On a four-pound investment, I made a whopping seventy-five pence. All it did was convince me that I was not a gambler. Lesson learned. Again.

I made my way to Charing Cross, where the previous night I found myself roaming the streets of the West End theatre district and Covent Garden. Eventually, I found myself standing again in front of The Spice of Life, a bar that briefly appears in the background of "Sid and Nancy."

This time it was open, so I eagerly ventured inside, finding the interior to be very rock and roll. Several punks sat at one table, rockers at another, and ordinary patrons scattered throughout. I approached the empty bar, setting the camera case down to set the camera back in. I ordered a pint from the black barman with a very posh accent.

Pint glass in hand, I kept to myself as I walked around the room, checking out the pictures and posters that adorned the walls. Punk and rock icons, every picture proved cooler than the last. I felt like I was really at a place that the Sex Pistols, or at least Sid Vicious, had hung out in, which made it even more awesome. Until I remembered what the French punk girl had said, and the wind got sucked out of my sails.

Polishing off my pint with ease and wanting to try as many new things as possible, I decided to be a little adventurous and ordered a pint of bitter. The barman pumped the dark fluid three times from an old-fashioned tap into a fancy glass mug that recalled the "Is she a goer?" sketch from Monty Python's Flying Circus. I knew upon the first sip that I had made a terrible mistake. It was horrible, earning every bit of its name. An understatement if ever there was one. I scanned the room and when I deemed it safe, I poured it down the front of the carpet-lined bar until the glass was empty.

"Another pint of bitter?" the barman asked when a mere minute later I placed the empty glass on the bar.

"Could I have another lager, please?" I sneered.

"Sure, just figured since you drank that one so fast."

I shook my head as the barman poured me a fresh pint. I picked up my glass and proceeded to scope out the photographs on the other side of the room.

Nearing the men's toilets, I ducked inside and relieved myself. Upon exiting, my eyes landed on my camera case as it headed for the door! I screamed, tossing the contents of my nearly full pint glass at him.

The man turned around wide-eyed, the back of his head and shirt now drenched. "What the HELL'S that all aboot?!" he shouted with a Canadian accent.

My eyes darted to the bar where my identical camera case was still sitting. As I started to apologize, I felt a firm grip on my shoulder and half-expected to see Rick the Bouncer. No such luck as the barman took the empty glass from me and told me I had to leave amongst the laughs and jeers from some punks at a table.

I made my way to Ian's pub and had a few pints while waiting for him to return home, but he never did. So, after leaving a note for Ian, I headed over to the West End district where the previous evening I had discovered a show that I thought I must see. My mother would have demanded I go.

Finding the Aldwych Theatre, I purchased a ticket for that night's performance, the last ticket they had. Thanks, Mom. As I turned from the Box Office, ticket in hand, my eyes locked with a lovely black girl walking past, drawing on a cigarette.

"Fancy attending the *theatah?*" I mumbled under my breath.

Figuring I had enough time to take in dinner before the show, I sat in one of the many pubs in the busy area, where I realized I was running desperately low on cash, under a hundred pounds, which at the rate I was going was not going to last me until Monday. I made the executive decision to switch to rum and cokes. You know, to be cost-effective.

As I sat waiting for the fish and chips I had ordered, the following exchange occurred behind me:

"All right, John."

"Hello, Jack, how ya keepin'?"

"Not bad, not bad, you ready for one?"

"Go on then."

"Two pints, Stevie McQueen,' when you get a chance."

"I see they've brought Benny Hill back on the box."

"He's brilliant, isn't he?"

I chuckled to myself upon hearing this, as that was the British import show I liked to watch late on Saturday nights when I was thirteen years old in the hopes of seeing a bare breast. I was reminded of my mother laughing at some of Benny's antics, despite always saying he wasn't funny.

It should have come as no surprise that Rowan Atkinson was an absolute scream in "The Sneeze." Appearing in eight out of the ten one-act plays by Russian playwright, Anton Checkov, the comedian spared no laugh, no mere glance; never had one made the simple act of sneezing so hilarious. I never would have guessed how enthralling the theater was had I not seen it for myself. I, along with the entire audience, laughed and howled at the funny faces, delivery of lines, and on-cue pratfalls that left the audience itching for more.

There was another itch going on. This one, in my pants. It grew from slightly annoying to an all-out assault on my senses that I could not seem to just scratch away. Luckily the people sitting on either side of me were so mesmerized with what was going on onstage that I was able to discreetly slide my hand in to get at it with a little more vigor. I scratched away, convincing myself the itching was subsiding, and withdrew my hand but no sooner was it out than I was forced to dive back in. Had those French f---ers gotten to my soap with itching powder?

Emerging from the Aldwych after the show along with everyone else, I was buzzing from the comedy, as well as the drinking ritual before and during. I so wanted to share my experience with someone, I slipped into a red telephone kiosk outside the theatre. It was plastered with sex cards with their specialties along with their phone numbers.

"You have one minute remaining on this card," the automated voice informed me.

"Hello?" Veronica said through the phone.

"*'Ello. I can almost 'ear you smiling,*" I said, slipping my hand back down the front of my pants to better get at yet another itch. "*You alrigh'?*"

"What are you doing? Are you coming back?"

I withdrew my hand, having gripped something foreign between my fingertips, my attention turned to the microscopic object as I held it up to get a better look.

IT WAS ALIVE!

"I think I got crabs!" I announced in a sudden panic.

The phone disengaged, leaving a distant beeping sound, a sound like that of a foghorn of an offshore ship. I flicked the critter against the window, hung the phone up, and stepped out into the moist night, noticing among the sex ads, a scantily clad woman wielding a whip overhead that, despite the blacked-out eyes, was a dead ringer for Loretta, the Meter Maid.

Upon exiting the kiosk, I found Ian pacing back and forth, carrying what appeared to be a small amplifier. Pointing to my guitar, Ian asked, "You a player or a poser?"

"Well, I--"

"Come on," Ian said, cutting me off before leading us down the street, past the congregating theatergoers, to the nearby Aldwych Tube Station. "We're going to go busk for some coin."

"What's busk? I've seen signs all over the place, 'No busking'."

"Cor, you are green," Ian shot back, perturbed as he bought me a ticket inside the station. "Best places to play are Piccadilly, Leicester Square, a bit crowded usually, Soho, some parts of Charing Cross."

We got on the tube for a quick jaunt to Charing Cross and made our way up to Leicester Square. As usual, it was booming. Most of the faces were familiar to me from the night before: the magician with his fire juggling unicyclist partner, the girl playing saxophone to pre-recorded music at the other end of the square.

Ian went on to talk about his countless days and nights spent here when he had no money and no place to live. "If I could marry an inanimate object, I would marry Leicester Square."

"That's deep, man," I replied as I followed him in his hurried pace across the square towards Piccadilly.

"F---in' ay, mate."

When we reached the saxophone girl, who had a modest crowd surrounding her, including a homeless man who made signs of the holy cross in the air, I quickly whipped my camera around and snapped off a few pictures before jogging to catch up to Ian. He was passing the Swiss Air Building at now breakneck speed up the same darkened street I had found myself on the previous evening. Or was it the night before last? It was all running together, making it hard to keep track. We passed the gateway to Chinatown with its red and yellow lanterns. I, again, slowed to take a picture.

"Soho," Ian informed, holding his arms out like Moses parting the Red Sea. "The closest we have to a red-light district.

The song "Roxanne" sprung to mind as we came upon the Raymond Revue Bar. I lifted my camera to take a picture of the hot bird sitting at a table outside the front door. She spotted me pointing my camera in her direction, stood up, and walked behind the adjacent wall to shield herself. I lowered the camera and ran after Ian as the woman came out from hiding, returning to her seat. This gave me another chance for a photo. She pivoted on her heels like a duck at a shooting gallery and broke for the wall again.

"Put that f---ing camera away!" she yelled at me, shaking her fist from her hiding place.

"What's the problem, baby?" I shouted back before Ian grabbed me by my shoulder and pulled me away.

"Piss off!" she yelled as she reluctantly slithered back into view, flipping me off English-style.

We descended into Oxford Circus station, me trying desperately to keep up with Ian, as he weaved through several people on the down escalator. Hopping off, he veered towards the Victoria line, me in close pursuit. I made my way off and broke into a run to catch up with him as he disappeared down the hallway. I rounded the corner only to find him leaning against a poster of the Prince soundtrack for "Batman."

"You ready?" Ian asked.

"What? Right here?"

"No, at the bottom of the escalator. People going both ways?"

"You mean 'bi'?" I replied with a snicker.

Ian glared at me as he pulled out a microphone and cord with a splitter to plug into the amp.

Genius, I thought.

"Wild Thing, ya know it?"

"Hendrix, of course. But I should probably tell you something, I'm not very good."

"It's 3 bloody chords. A-D-E. Surely you can play 3 bloody chords," Ian said, pulling me by the elbow over to the escalators.

"There's something else," I said, beginning to turn beet-red. "I get stage fright. Like bad."

"D'ya want me to play? You can sing," Ian said, plugging the amp into a socket between the escalators. "Can you sing?"

I shook my head as I awkwardly fumbled with the three chords, leaving Ian to roll his eyes before flicking the switch to the amplifier. Feedback squelched loudly from the amp, bouncing off the walls of the station.

"Check one-one," Ian said, his voice booming through the amplifier. His eyebrows raised, he nodded as if to ask if I was ready. I shrugged, uncertain if I was ready but relented upon Ian's grimaces. "Right! ONE-TWO-FREE-FOUR!"

And so it began, a raw awkward impromptu version of "Wild Thing."

Ian took his jacket off, tossing it on the floor between the up and down escalators, and threw whatever change he had in his pocket inside as an incentive to others, I supposed, to donate to the cause.

Genius.

When it came time to start singing, Ian began crooning in true, gravelly-voiced, punk rock form. He then started getting into it, stomping his work boots, clapping. At first, looking at the floor but then, as his confidence started building, began looking right into the eyes of the onlookers and passersby as he belted out the song with all his powers.

People came and went—stodgy old men with grimaces painted on their pusses, young people who rushed by, some even stopping long enough to watch. It all eventually blurred together for me, like one long rock video. And with that, came the occasional coin tossed our way into Ian's jacket.

My eyesight began to dim, getting misty, and it occurred to me I was crying. Overcome by emotions: my mother, Veronica, Grandfather, my new relationship with my cousin, everything came flooding out.

I saw Sharonda's face. Smiling. Angry. Sad.

When it came time for the solo, I, in all my glory, tried with all my heart but failed miserably. I just hit a high note and stretched the string, plucked the note, bending it, before jumping back into the three chords.

Nevertheless, we came to the end of our 3-plus minute extravaganza and approached the jacket finding we had amassed quite a small fortune of coins in all denominations. Ian kneeled and counted our booty.

"Did you see me connecting with those American birds?"

"Yeah," I lied, I saw nothing through the misty haze. "How do you know they were American?"

"Their college jumpers." Ian detected my confusion. "Sweaters. How did you convince anyone you're from England when you don't know the simplest of f---ing terms, mate?"

"Well, no one said Americans were smart," I countered.

Ian cocked his head as if I had proved his point.

"Now what?" I asked.

"Gimme 'at," Ian said, referring to the guitar. I slid it off my shoulder and handed it to him, who, in return, passed me the mic. Ian sat on the amplifier and after properly tuning it began masterfully playing "Amie," of all tunes, by Pure Prairie League. I was wowed not only by the choice of song but by the pure prairie gentleness of it. At the appropriate time, Ian cocked his head indicating to me to hold the mic for him to sing into.

More coins followed. I was in awe.

"That was awesome! What should we do now? Let's do Wild Thing again!"

"We could," Ian said, his focus averting to something on the escalators. "OR, we leave now!" he said urgently, scrambling to unplug the amp and grab his jacket.

"What? Why?" I asked, trying to gauge Ian's urgent demeanor. I followed his perspective up the escalator and spotted two coppers making their way down. Fast.

"This ain't exactly legal, ya know?" Ian replied, pulling me down the hall behind him.

We scurried down the hallway and as luck would have it, reached the platform on the Bakerloo Line where a train was waiting with all its doors open.

We hopped on, making our way through the carriage, peering through the window to see if the cops were zeroing in on us. The two officers, one male, one female, reached the platform just as the doors shut. While the male cop was blowing his whistle, I whipped my camera around took a picture of them just as they put their hands on their hips and shook their respective heads in resignation. The train left the station, leaving the pair to turn and walk back the way they came.

"Four-pound twenty-two," Ian said after counting the money, placing half in my hand as we sat at a table, waiting for our drinks.

"My first paid gig."

I told my cousin what had been happening, from the thrashing I got my first day to the French-run Tent City, to my discovery in the kiosk earlier.

Ian laughed hysterically; he had a similar raspy laugh to me.

"And you think it's from the American bird? It's probably those nasty bunk beds or that traffic warden! You need to get to a chemist, mate. Get yourself some crab killer."

I nodded; the waitress approached from behind Ian. I discreetly pushed on my crotch under the table before flashing Ian a 'Shut up, here she comes' look. She set down a pitcher of lager and two frosty mugs on the table between us.

"Did you decide what you want?"

After looking at me for confirmation, Ian replied, "Large pepperoni and sausage pizza?"

Ian poured beer into the two mugs and slid them over as the waitress walked away, writing down our order on a small pad of paper. I lifted the glass up to take a sip, stopping at the last second when I noticed a sizable shard of glass missing at the rim. I set it down and rotated the glass to avoid cutting my lip.

"So, you never answered my question about Grandad."

"What are you doing? What is it, chipped?"

"Yeah, it's no big deal."

"Grab her and have her take it back."

"Naah, it's no biggie, really."

"Bust your lip and tell her."

"Noooo."

"Come here, let me tell you something." I leaned forward to hear what Ian was going to say. He raised his fist. "I'll do it for ya."

"Get the f--- outta here," I replied, jerking my head back out of his range.

"F--k it, I'll do it meself," Ian said, leaning close to the table where he proceeded to knuckle his lip until blood began dribbling between his two front teeth. I laughed at the preposterousness of Ian's act as he switched mugs across the table before dabbing his finger with blood; he waved the waitress over.

"I'll evoke sympathy, you push for another pitcher," Ian plotted. I nodded, agreeing to my role in the scheme.

———

"Whatcha need, lovey?"

"I need some serviettes and another mug. This one just did a number on me."

Spotting the blood, she said with concern, "Oh, it certainly did, you poor thing. Back in a flash," she said with sincerity, scampering off.

Ian winked at me; I shook my head as he gulped on his beer. The waitress returned with packages of wet wipes and a new full mug while retrieving the damaged one.

"Shouldn't he get a free pitcher or something?" I asked.

"Oh no, no," Ian countered, laying it on thick.

"Well, how about a couple of bottles?" the waitress generously offered.

"Holsten's?" Ian quickly countered.

"Holsten's it is," she said, walking away. "There goes my poker money," she grumbled, thinking she was out of earshot.

Ian watched her over his shoulder. "Double bagger, but nice arse. I'd do her. From be'ind."

"Man, I think she's paying out of her own pocket."

"Poker?" Ian asked, taking the pitcher in both hands and pouring it directly into his mouth, beer running down both sides of his cheeks. Ian belched an earth-shattering BRAAAAP. "I'll poke 'er." We both laughed, our similar wheezy laughs reverberating in our booth and off the shop window. "I'll poker!" Ian said, louder than he probably should have. "I'll get her with a red-hot poker!"

I tried to warn Ian that the waitress was coming up behind him, but we were both laughing so hard I simply could not get the words out. She placed two bottles of Holsten's on the table.

"Are you two brothers?" she asked.

"You think I look like him?!" Ian asked, roaring.

"Cousins," I told her, as she nodded and backed away, leaving us both continuing in our hysterical laughter. Could we pass for blood brothers? He wasn't the only one to not think so.

"Has she fucked off?" Ian dropped his head on the table, still wheezing. "Why didn't you tell me she was coming?"

"I couldn't catch my breath," I said, still trying to. I fell over in the booth. There I looked across the aisle where an Indian family was enjoying dinner, spotting an indescribable object in the lap of the sari-wearing matron. "What's in that woman's lap?

Ian followed my gaze. "Her stomach!!" We both roared uncontrollably.

Eventually, the pizza came, and we calmed down long enough to stuff our faces and drink more beer. Ian prevented the waitress from clearing the table leaving empty pitchers and beer mugs all over it. Both full and buzzing from the beers, I headed to the bathroom; Ian informed me he would take care of the bill and meet me outside.

We wandered through the London streets, making utter fools of ourselves. Upon reaching the Marble Arch something occurred to me.

"My camera!"

"What about it?"

"I think I left it back at the restaurant."

Between the two of us, we could only remember the name of the pizza place, Pizza Express, but not its location. We stepped into a phone booth and called two different locations before finding the right one.

"*Did you find a camera?*"

"Yes, we have it here."

"*Can you tell me where you're located?*"

"Shouldn't you know that?"

I looked at Ian, who sat outside on the curb, yawning as he held out his hand to dismissive passersby. "*You would fink, wouldn't you?*" I replied more to myself than the woman on the other end.

She rattled off the address and we managed our way back. The restaurant was closed, most of the lights inside were off and no staff was present. I approached the door and it pushed open with ease, making my way to the cashier stand, peering behind it.

On the floor was my camera bag with the cheque poking out. I pushed through the little door, which squeaked ever so slightly, picked up my bag, and walked out, meeting Ian across the street.

"Did you not pay the check?" I asked Ian.

"After what happened to my lip? It didn't seem right."

"*You* did that to your lip?"

"Principal, mate," Ian said, grabbing the cheque, balling it up, and tossing it over his shoulder.

We parted ways and I made it back to Tent City before the tube stations closed.

Sleep, oh glorious, sleep, I thought as I climbed onto my bed, wrapped my camera case and guitar strap in a complex fashion around my wrist and arms, and lay back ready for slumber to consume me.

"Jean-Paul!"

Chapter

Something was weighing down on my chest as I slept. My breathing grew heavy and strained. Who was doing this to me? Where was I? Oh, yeah, in London.

I woke from one of those deep sleep dreams but could not remember what I had dreamt for the life of me. I lifted my watch to my face and squinted; it was five o'clock at night! Again! I could not believe I had let the entire day slip away again.

I recalled bits of the dream I was having just before waking, panicked and sweating, seeing the old man in various places I could only assume was London. Calling out for him, he conveniently seemed to elude me, always just outside of my reach.

Except for one other person, the tent was empty. Another day, another bed. How far I've come from the 'hood in just a week.

———

Rummaging through my bag, I could find neither my toothbrush nor my tube of toothpaste. So I walked back to the bathroom, where there sat only my toothbrush. Bastards.

I found my way back to Ian's pub. Walking through the door for the third time in two days (if one did not count going back in the other door), I decided that if I could not get any further information about Grandfather, I would call home collect at 11 pm, which would be 6 o'clock back in Baltimore. But, of course, there was the distinct possibility that he called and, no matter how cryptic, left a message for me, leaving my old man either worried or seething.

At the Royal Coat of Arms, I had a few pints while waiting for Ian to return. When he did arrive, he seemed a bit annoyed that I was waiting for him, as if he had to babysit me again.

The two of us made our way to Piccadilly Circus as night was now upon us. I took pictures of the Foster's Lager sign, passing black cabs, and the red, double-decker busses.

"I want to get some different angles, I'm-a cross over to the fountain, get a picture of Cupid."

"It's not Cupid, stupid."

"Yeah, whatever."

I shrugged before carefully crossing the street, this time looking right, even though the crosswalk light had changed. I merely followed the crowd. Once on the tiny island, I sprawled myself out on the concrete in front of the fountain with what *looked* to be Cupid, a diapered baby holding a bow and arrow atop it. I continued snapping pictures, having to take two of the Foster's Lager signs to fit it all in.

Over my shoulder, my gaze landed on a group of male and female punks sitting on the steps of the fountain in what I concluded was some sort of hierarchy. *What a great photo that would make*, I thought. I twisted my body awkwardly and tried to squeeze off a shot discreetly.

As I squared up the camera, I took notice of the fat punk girl with green hair on the lowest rung looking directly at me. Not wanting to raise the ire of her or *anyone* in the group, I stood up and approached them.

"Pahdon me, could I ge' a picsha of you all for me magazine?" I asked the girl, who, sitting on the lowest step, was still staring at me.

"Ask him," she replied, pointing to the black punk on the top step, who was looking off to his left as if captaining a ship.

I took two steps to the right. *"Pahdon me, mate, can I ge' a picture of you guys for me magazine?"*

The black punk slowly turned his head to size up who was asking.

"Three quid, mate."

Uncertain how much quid was compared to pounds, but figuring it must be a lot, I replied, *"Will you be 'ere tomorrow nigh'? I'll 'ave to get me magazine to forward me the money.*

"Where you from, then? Australia?"

"No, Norf...Ireland," I answered. North Ireland??

"Bollocks," the black punk replied aggressively.

Why, after all the North Hamptons, did I say that? I chuckled uncomfortably before turning and walking away.

"Oy! Come back 'ere!"

I looked back to see the black punk standing up and directing the other punks to follow suit. I picked up the pace, going from a sprint to a fierce jog.

The punks descended the steps and began to give chase.

"Grab him!" the black punk yelled.

"Grab his guitar!" another yelled.

"Smash his camera!" the girl with green hair yelled.

I pointed the camera over my shoulder as I ran down Haymarket Street, passing under the balcony of the Rock and Roll Wax Museum with Mick, Elton, and Bowie in their iconic poses above, the punks hot on my trail.

Where is Ian? Where is Ian? Where is Ian?

"Why you running?!" the black punk said, grabbing my guitar. "I just want to ask you something!"

"Give me that f---in' guitar!" the skinny, zitty punk shouted.

To my complete surprise, the black punk spun me around as they all converged on me, trying to take my shit.

"OY!" a voice shouted from behind me. "Leave 'im be."

We all turned to see Ian step out from the passenger side of a white VW bug.

The black punk immediately let go of my guitar.

"Clive," Ian said as he shut the car door. "Wha's all this, then?"

"This doesn't involve you, JT."

JT? Who the hell is JT?

"It's between me and Norf Ireland, here."

"Yeah, well, that's my cousin, so it sort of does involve me."

My hero, I thought as I noticed a majestic sort of aura surrounding my cousin.

Clive's eyes darted from Ian to me, looking us both up and down. "You know this wanker?"

"Yeah," Ian and I both said simultaneously.

Clive stepped back and scoffed. "Well, there *is* a resemblance."

"See ya, Clive," Ian said somewhat cordially.

The other punks were already heading back up the street. However, one girl, a cute but chunky punk rocker with purple hair and caked-on make-up, walked backward rather slowly, smiling at Ian. I looked as if I was watching a tennis match as I observed the weird connection between them.

"Give my love to Oyster," she said rather demurely.

"Yea, alright," Ian stoically replied before turning back to the VW.

I liked her ripped-up fishnet stockings as she took one more step back before turning and rushing to catch up with her mates.

"Who was that?"

"Ha. If you can believe it, I used to run wif 'em a bit." Ian opened the door, taking a seat inside.

"No, I meant the girl. So you were a punk??"

"That's the bird that was watching Sir. Yeah, I was. Got f---in' boring."

"Oh. Ohhhh."

Ian messed about inside the car. "What'd you say to make them go mental, anyway?"

"Nothing. I just asked, *'Can I ge' your picsha for me magazine?'*"

Ian laughed. "What'd they say?"

Mimicking Clive, "*'Free quid.'* How much is quid anyway? I mean, how many pounds."

The VW roared to life as only a Volkswagen can, sounding like an electric tin opener.

"Whatchu mean 'ow much is quid? Quid's just an-otha' word for pounds, innit?"

"So, three quid is just three pounds? Shit, I had that. I could've got the picture I wanted and avoided all that."

Ian pulled his right leg in, closed the door, and rolled the window down. "Getting in?"

"Is this yours?" Ian merely winked. "No?"

"No, you can always get a loaner in Piccadilly. You coming?"

I reluctantly walked around to the other side of the car while scanning the area, but for what? I was not sure. I climbed in, and Ian began pulling away from the curb.

"Where'd ya wanna go?"

"Liverpool!"

"Within f---ing reason."

The VW putt-putted down Haymarket Street while I rattled off a litany of pictures I wanted to take: Buckingham Place, London Bridge, Big Ben. St. Paul's Cathedral.

"St. Paul's Cathedral??" Ian flipped a quick U-turn.

"I was on a tour there today. Hey, why did that one punk call you JT?"

"Whatcha writing a book?"

"No, I—"

"The bird that had me dog named me JT for John Thomas."

"Cause you're a dick?"

"Yeah, with a big one, so they say," Ian said, his eyebrows bouncing. "And she would know. She's seen enough of 'em," Ian replied with a goofy smirk. Then, pointing through the windscreen, "Trafalgar Square."

I pointed my camera at the passenger window and squeezed one off. Unfortunately, the flash bounced off the window, nearly blinding us both.

"Might wanna roll that down, or this'll be a big f--king waste of time, yeah?"

Eventually, Ian pointed out St. Paul's Cathedral. It was majestic, bathed in white lights, a half-moon hovering above the dome. Ian pulled over to allow me to take a few holiday snaps.

I checked my watch. "Oh, it's almost midnight. I want a picture of Big Ben at midnight."

"Bloody tourists," Ian mumbled, shaking his head.

We parked up, about a block from London's towering timepiece, England's most famous landmark, maybe of all the UK. It proved a perfect place to land. If he had parked any closer, I would probably have had to walk backward a block or three just to fit it all in. So now we just had to wait.

Ian stepped out, rounding the Beetle, first having a seat on the hood, trunk, boot, or whatever before sitting in the passenger seat. I looked back to see him closing his eyes while waiting on me to take one bloody well-timed snap.

At eleven fifty-five, Big Ben went completely dark. What was it doing, recharging? I looked over my shoulder again at Ian, who appeared to be sleeping; I continued to wait. Finally, at nearly midnight, as the two hands of the clock converged together, the bells started chiming—twelve deafening BONGS. The lights never came back on, defeating my intentions entirely.

"Well, that was a big bloody waste of time," I said as I approached the passenger side.

Without opening his eyes, Ian said, "Did you even take one?"

I lifted the camera haphazardly over my shoulder and shot one off behind me. "Happy?"

"Ecstatic. Get a shot of Westminster Bridge 'cause this is as close as we're going to get to it. We'll swing 'round the Palace, and that's it for the night. Well past me bedtime."

Ian climbed over the stick shift, and I dropped into the passenger seat. I fiddled with my camera, checking to see how many pictures I had left on the roll, while Ian swung a wide u-turn.

"Would you look at that? Hold on!" Ian said, something grabbing his attention ahead of us as he jammed his foot on the accelerator. At the intersection, a red VW Beetle with its left blinker on was about to turn left, while a blue VW Beetle, with its right blinker on, was about to turn right, all while the traffic light was blinking yellow. Again, I was reminded of the fireflies back at the party.

Picking up what Ian was putting down, I squeezed a shot off through the windshield as he gunned the VW even harder right up the middle. The VW Bugs making a nifty little spectrum of red, white, and blue as the traffic light turned red.

I spotted it immediately--the police car at the intersection.

The white cop car rounded the corner. Overhead yellow and white lights began flashing.

"F--k!" Ian shouted, the police lights splaying off his face from the rearview mirror.

"What do we do? What do we do? Make a run for it?" I asked, panicked, running scenarios through my head of collect calls from jail to my father.

"Jus' be cool," Ian said, steering the VW to the side of the road.

Ian and I watched from our respective side mirrors as the copper methodically exited the police car and approached tight-assed up to the driver's side window, which Ian was already rolling down.

"Evening."

"That was reckless and stupid what you did just then," he said before bending down and putting his forearms on the car door, a scowl on his officious puss. Then, to our surprise, a smile stretched across his face. "But a brilliant effect."

"Dedicated it to the Queen Mum herself," Ian replied, a bit smarmy.

"Did he now?" he asked, his eyes shifting over to me; I smiled and nodded nervously. Then, finally, his eyes shifted back to Ian. "Yeah, well, no more amateur effects, eh? You want to be patriotic? Join the R.A.F." With that, he stood up and tapped the roof of the Beetle. "Have a good night. Drive safe."

The copper turned and swaggered back to his car while we both simultaneously let out a sigh of relief.

"Well, that's us for the night," Ian said, pulling away from the curb or whatever stupid name they surely have for it.

"I can't believe how cool the bobbies are in England. If this were America, they'd have us spread-eagled out on the pavement. But here, the bobbies, they just—"

"Stop callin' em that, sounds stupid. 'Bobbies,'" Ian said in mocking deference.

I jerked my head back as if Ian had just cold-cocked me.

"You can call 'em 'coppers' or 'cozzers' or 'The Ole Bill' or what I call 'em: 'c—ts.' But nobody calls 'em bloody bobbies. Ever."

Ian drove us to the nearest tube station, Embankment, where we ditched the car and walked inside the station. Ian directed me to the platform I needed. Just after we said goodbye and began to head in our separate directions, Ian looked back.

"Ya wanna go to the fair tomorrow night?" Ian asked.

"The fair?"

"Ya know, a carnival?"

I shrugged, "Sure."

"Meet me at the pub around six."

"Okay."

"An' leave the guitar," he said before turning and stepping onto the escalator, shrinking in his descent into the Underground.

Spotting a double-decker idling by a bus stop and knowing the tube stations would be closed at this hour,

I hopped on the rear (successfully) and sidled up to the driver, protected in a hermetically sealed booth. I informed him I was heading to East Acton. He told me the amount, I happily paid, and informed me he would announce my transfer spot. I made my way up the stairs to the second level, where I knew they had a smoking section.

Beautiful people blended with uglier ones, all sitting in various rows; one black dude with twists sat alone on the back seat. I had a seat about halfway back and lit up one of my fancy French cigarettes. The guy in the back had just rolled his own and took a large and loud drag, too large and loud to be just a cigarette. I peered over my shoulder and flashed him a knowing smile, to which he responded by holding his tightly twisted "fag" up as an offering. I leaped to my feet and, with my hands, rolled them like the wheels of a train as I shuffled back and plopped down in the seat beside him.

"I could use some of this right now," I said, pinching the joint between my thumb and forefinger, taking a big hit. I coughed my head off like a madman.

"Good, eh?" this British brother asked me with a deep voice. "Never 'ad nothin' like this before, 'ave ya?" He waved his hand upward, suggesting I have some more, which I was only happy to oblige, inhaling more before handing it back.

"American, yeah?" I nodded before exhaling a tremendous amount of smoke that made the upper deck appear like a dream sequence. "You know why?" I shook my head, coughing a bit more. "Hash from Afghanistan, man, that's why. The Russians bring it in. Your government don't let too many Russians into America."

"It's good," I lied, tasting the tobacco blended in. "That's interesting," I mumbled, not minding the tobacco too terribly as I took the joint for yet another ride. The tobacco, I found, made me a wee bit dizzy before the stoned part kicked in.

And boy, did it kick in.

"First time in London?" I noticed the bass guitar wedged in behind the seat under the window before nodding. "Whatcha think?"

I exhaled, wheezing as I coughed. "It's brilliant. It's like mini-skirt Hell," I blobbed. "If I could just get rid of all the annoying sods."

The black guy laughed, exhaling smoke through his nostrils. "That wouldn't leave too many people."

"That'd be alright." We both laughed.

"Ya thinkin' about staying, then?"

"In London? I'd love to. The thing is, though, my passport's only good for six months and work is prohibited. It's stamped on my passport in big bloody letters."

The black guy shrugged that off. "There's ways around that, mate. You can do what I did when I moved down 'ere. Get a barman job in a pub. You can pour beer, yeah?"

"Can't be too difficult."

"Ya live upstairs, they pay ya, feed ya."

"What do I do? Go to every pub in London?"

"It's easier than that," he assured me. He told me that there was a consulate in Piccadilly called The New Zealand House where, in the alley behind it, a small shop that sold job lists for eighty pence. "Just pub jobs, both live-in, which is what you want, and live-out. You pour beer for a few hours, off for tea, come back for a few more hours, and you're off by eleven," he said with a proud smile as if he had invented the process.

I began to have an epiphany. Why couldn't I stay? I wondered. Nothing was keeping me from staying.

I was handed the joint again, took another enormous hit, coughed, and sat back to think a bit further through a hazy cloud.

Lawrence, my *new* hero, eventually reached his stop. We shook hands, and he told me the name of his local pub, which I could not quite make out. Not that it mattered as I had no idea where I was, but through the window, I thought it might be Trafalgar Square.

The bus quickly filled, leaving me to wonder: *Where are all these people coming from so late at night?* It was now pouring down rain outside, so everyone was soaking wet. I found myself in the backseat, wedged tightly between two couples. Feeling a tad awkward, I bailed, taking a seat next to a thirtyish woman wearing a see-through slicker and mac. She paid me no mind as she continued to stare at the scenery passing us by through the window. I leaned back and closed my eyes.

"Could you move over, mate? You're all over me!" someone shouted from the back of the bus.

I opened my eyes and turned, along with most everyone else, to see what the commotion was. The bloke of one of the two couples that I had moments before abandoned was taking issue with the fellow that had taken my seat. A cross between Paul Schaffer and Elton John (not that there was much of a contrast between the two piano-playing legends), balding with big campy glasses and flamboyant attire, a Cheshire grin that seemed forcibly painted from ear to ear.

"A little gay tonight, are we?" the man asked with amusement, though the campy guy found it just as funny. I looked forward, relieved I had switched seats, sharing a fleeting glance with the woman beside me as she returned to staring out the window.

At the next stop, a large portion of the passengers stood up and clumsily made their way off the bus, including the woman next to me. I slid over to take her place by the window. The man, again, loudly directed a question to the campy man, "There's a lot of empty seats now, ya catch my meaning?"

He did catch his meaning, standing up and walking up the aisle, passing row after empty row before having a seat, as if you had to guess, right beside me. Reluctantly, I squinted out of the corner of my eye to see the man smiling at me like a cat eyeing up a canary.

"You know, there are a lot of seats, and I'm getting," I said, stopping myself for obvious reasons. "I'm exiting just up here."

"Oh, at the Holiday Inn? I am, as well," he countered enthusiastically. I nodded, letting him think what he wanted to believe.

The bus stopped a few feet past the Holiday Inn, and we both stood up and made our way down the stairs, where the campy fellow got off the bus. I stepped back and plopped down in a vacant seat, waving at the frowning fellow as the bus door closed and pulled away.

"The young man going to Acton? This is where you transfer!" The driver announced at the next stop.

I disembarked and soon found myself sitting on an empty bench, on a desolate street, in a seeming ghost town. Coming down from my buzz, I knew if I didn't keep moving, I was going to climb under the bench and pass the hell out.

With no bus in sight, I got up, gathered my gear, and began to head in what I hoped was the direction to East Acton. I would give anything to see the dome of one of those tents right now.

A sleek silver convertible Jaguar with the top up (and intact) pulled alongside me. The window lowered with a slight automated sound, and sitting in the driver's seat was the most beautiful woman I had ever seen.

Her halter top and mini skirt glistened with the flicker of tiny jewels.

"You look as if you could use a lift," she said in the sultriest voice I had ever heard. With her mouth reduced to a perpetual pout, she opened the door for me. I lifted my right foot to enter, but it was an elevator shaft. It was too late to turn back, but my bag weighed me down as I fell backward. My leg jerked--and I woke up from a brief nap, still sitting on the bench. This time I did get up and start walking.

And walked.

And walked.

And walked.

I would never see a bus in either direction, but occasionally I *would* see or hear a random car or truck; some would pass by, others could be heard nearby. Finally, I happened upon one of those futuristic spot-a-pots, and I could not have come across one at a better time, as I was in desperate need of one to unload all my bodily functions. I dropped in the required 20p coin, and the cylinder-shaped door rotated open with a Star Trek-like WOOSH.

Stepping inside, it had all the comforts of home with a toilet, sink, mirror, soap dispenser, and towel dispenser. Not only was it spic-and-span clean, but it smelled fresher than any bathroom I had ever encountered. I dragged my gear into the cleanest public toilet in the world as the revolving door WHOOSHED shut.

As I sat on the toilet, my head propped up on my two palms and my knees turning bright red from my elbows, I heard the one sound I feared over all others—an approaching large automobile of some sort. I stretched forward and pressed the OPEN button, and jumped to my feet. A giant petrol lorry rumbled past in my direction on the road. My relief was short-lived, as a bus, *my* bus, was close on its mudflaps.

"Shit!" I yelled, my pants still around my ankles. I ran out of the loo, pulling my drawers and pants up in one complete jerk of my waistband.

"WAIT!" I shouted as it came to a stop at the traffic light a few hundred feet past where I stood.

WHOOSH as the door to the toilet closed behind me, followed by a motorized rumbling and spraying as the loo began its self-cleaning process. I fished in my pockets and withdrew another 20p coin (never a shortage of change in London pants pockets) and waited for the sounds of cleaning to subside before dropping another coin in the slot. There was a lengthy heart-stopping delay before the door WHOOSHED open. The first thing to catch my eyes was my guitar, now wet and glistening from the overhead lighting. I dropped my drawers and returned to the unfinished business at hand, knowing I now had all the time in the world.

All cleaned up, and I set out for what seemed like the longest walk of my life. I crossed tiny footbridges, train tracks through parks and playgrounds. My exhaustion was at loggerheads, but I pushed on, seeing this dark little corner of England one small step at a time.

"Trouble, oh, trouble, can't you see? I am completely lost, now won't you leave me in my misery-y-y...."

After what seemed like days across the outskirts of East London, I found a taxi idling next to an as-yet unopened tube station, the sky showing its first rays of orange sunrise. By the time I reached Tent City and hit my bed, I cared not if I ever woke up again.

"Jean-Paul!"

Ugh.

Chapter

Deliberating about what I should do, having woken up again having missed most of the day, I did my daily routine and headed out, buying my usual banana and chocolate milk at the market outside the tube station I frequented daily. My crotch was on fire, so I inquired where the closest chemist; about a ten-minute walk.

I noted that whenever I asked for directions to someplace, it was politely given not in miles, or in England's case, kilometers or meters, but how many minutes it would take to get there.

As I walked past all the shops along the way, I began singing an absurd song about my current situation and destination.

"I come from the Land of the Hot Steamed Crabs," I sang in my head while I marched like the leader of a parade, pretending to involve the shopkeepers and random people I passed. "But these ain't the type you eat. They're the kind you get off a toilet seat!" I continued singing. "Got crustaceans in my pants that are bothering me. Gotta get to the chemist before they overrun me. GOOD MORNING!"

Ten minutes later, I was amongst family, I joked to myself, as I stepped inside Marcus Jones Chemist.

Roaming the aisles, not entirely sure of the product I was after, I had to swallow my pride and approach the counter. There was no question I would use my English accent in this instance and whispered to the pharmacist, a kindly old gentleman, who came around the counter, leading me up the aisle to where it sat on a shelf. My face turned red as a *tomahto* as the pharmacist explained how to treat my condition.

Wasting no time, I nipped into the bathroom at the tube station and in the privacy of one of the bathroom stalls. With the dipper attached inside the lid, I applied the reddish-brown substance to my pubes, where the carpet did *not* match the drapes.

If things were not weird enough, as I stood there with my pants around my ankles, a furious knock on the stall door jostled me.

"PISS OFF!" I shouted in the most resounding voice I could conjure up, taking my cue from that night with Rick.

"I beg your pardon, sir," the near intruder answered back in a high-pitched tone before shuffling away.

So, humiliating, I thought, as I closed the lid ever so tightly and slid the bottle into my backpack. I fanned my crotch before pulling my pants back up. And I was off.

Piddling about most of the day, I roamed the London streets. When I spotted one of those soldiers with the big fuzzy hats, I decided to make a second attempt at locating Buckingham Palace. Truthfully, I wound up being too fearful of asking anyone in either accent about where it was. I considered asking with an Italian accent but decided against it for a multitude of reasons.

Giving up again, I ducked into a pub, having a seat back at a corner table where I ordered a cola and packet of crisps, as I was nearly busted.

I wished someone had told me earlier that I could buy an all-day pass to ride not only the tube but the busses as well. *Too little, too late*, I mused. I thought I was doing the sensible thing the day before when I'd paid the rest of my week at Tent City. So I was excited, yet disappointed, when Ian invited me to the fair in Canterbury before parting ways the night before, suggesting we probably would not return until the following day.

As I sat at the table, marking my time, one crisp at a time, a well-dressed man walked into the pub, waving and shaking hands with some of the men sitting on stools at the bar. The sun coming in from the windows and open doors momentarily shielded the man's face from me; only when he turned and waved in my direction did I finally get a good look at him.

It was John Merrick back from the grave. Okay, maybe it was not the Elephant Man, but there was a striking resemblance. His face looked like a candle holder had been tilted to allow the hot liquid to harden down the outside. His nose fared no better; it also favored that side of his countenance; his eyes were heavy and impenetrable.

I felt my hand lift, as if by an unseen specter, and waved; the crumbs from my crisps dropped like tiny grains of salt onto the table. Despite not finding the Queen's residence, I had now truly seen it all. I feared because I was alone at the table that the man might take a seat at it and quickly poured the chips straight from the bag into my open mouth and sipped the last of my cola through the straw, which was mostly water from the long-melted ice cubes. I awkwardly pushed the chair away from the table with a scraping sound. Then, grabbing my guitar and camera case, I made my way towards the door. Passing the man, he mumbled or grunted what must have been a Goodbye, waving to me as I walked outside.

By the time Ian arrived at the Royal Coat of Arms, I was drinking the only thing I could truly afford, ice water.

"I thought I told you last night to leave the guitar," Ian said as he led me up the stairs.

"With those crab-infested French punks? Ha, not a chance, mate."

"Well, I wasn't planning to pay for my room until Sunday night, so I got one of the micks here to watch the dog."

I felt terrible but not as bad as my imagination had conjured of what the French might do with my guitar if I had left it there. I imagined a cross between Jimi Hendrix at Monterey Pop and Richie Blackmore and Pete Townsend at the end of nearly all their gigs. Total destruction

"Two tickets to Canterb'ry," Ian informed the ticket counter person when we arrived at Victoria Station. It immediately reminded me of the Eddie Money song, with Canterbury in place of Paradise.

"Round trip, sir?"

"Returning tomorrow." Ian paid for both tickets, handing one to me as we turned and made our way across the busy station. As usual, I rushed to keep pace with him.

"So, where are we staying again?"

"We'll see," Ian replied, keeping things a bit mysterious. I did not mind terribly in the least—anything to be away from those rude, smelly, snail-eating frogs.

Ian quickly nodded off on the train, leaving me to watch the world whisk by through the windows just like the day I arrived. Sober this time, however. As the train rolled on and darkness settled in, my focus turned to the passengers sitting nearby and walking past. A strange lot, I concluded, making up funny little backstories for each of them. When I got bored with that, I returned my attention outside, focusing on anything illuminated we passed, such as pubs or headlights of cars waiting for the train track lights to change. Finally, we stopped at stations with funny names like Sittingbourne and Bapchild. *Where did they come up with these names?*

Canterbury. What was associated with Canterbury? I tried to recall. Was it a ghost? The Canterbury Ghost? The Ghosts of Canterbury? I was compelled to ask Ian and was sort of relieved that he was asleep for fear he might eviscerate me for my continued lack of knowledge. Eventually, with the CHUGA CHUGA of the train on the tracks as my soundtrack, I, too, nodded off, my head rolling to and fro on the cold hard window. Something to which I seemed to be adjusting.

As we were both deep in sleep, the Conductor, or Guard, like the patch on his uniform proclaimed, came through to punch our tickets. Ian raised his ticket in the air with neither a flinch nor a bat of his closed eyes. The Guard gave it a quick once over, punched it, and returned to Ian's open hand resting idly on the seat. I smiled as I handed him mine, holding my hand out for its return, trying to get comfortable again, though conceding that I had never been relaxed for a moment.

———

An announcement bellowed over the intercom was not quite conducive for the ideal nap at each station we arrived.

Ian nearly leaped out of his seat when they finally announced Canterbury Station. He shook me awake, as if I needed it, what with the barrage of station announcements, which, admittedly did decrease ever so slightly the farther we made our way from London. It had only been an hour-long journey, but it seemed longer as the train pulled into the station. The 'Canterbury' sign greeted us as we stepped off the train and onto the platform. I stopped to take a picture. Ian, as was becoming his modus operandi, did not stop and wait for me. Instead, he ascended the steps into the station with a seemingly new lease on life. He quickly disappeared out of sight as I hurried once again to catch up to this man-on-a-mission.

Architecturally speaking, the station itself was bland and uninspiring. However, I quickly concluded Ian knew precisely where he was going; odd, as I didn't really see my cousin as the carnival type. It then occurred to me that a week ago, I wasn't one either, but through a minor act of deception that blossomed into something far more than I ever could have imagined, it made me a believer.

I needed to call Veronica and straighten out our last call if only I had a few extra pounds.

***

"No. Don't. Stop. No. Don't. Stop. No, don't stop. No, don't stop. Just don't cum inside me."

"No, you didn't say that," Jill said. Veronica tilted her head as if to suggest otherwise.

"What, you don't believe me? He's so frickin' cute," she said before affecting her own English accent. "*Technically, I took advantage of you,* she mimicked, before laughing. "No, hon, technically, I took advantage of *you.*"

"You dirty bitch," Lisa said. Lisa and Jill both laughed.

"So, *do* you?"

"Do I what?" Veronica asked. Now it was Jill who tilted her head. "No, I don't have *f---in'* crabs!" Veronica insisted.

"You sure?" Lisa pressed.

"I'm sure!" Veronica said through gritted teeth.

Lisa, Jill, and Veronica were sitting out on Veronica's back deck in their bikinis, taking advantage of the afternoon rays.

"And then he just hung up? What a dick," Jill said, leaning over to pick up her Big Gulp spiked with, what else? Southern Comfort.

"I think we just got cut off. It sounded like he was calling from a payphone."

"That makes no sense. Unless he's married. You know, had to go out to call you. I just don't get the crabs part," Lisa said.

"Why did he go back suddenly? I mean, who does that?" Jill asked, putting her drink back down.

"Maybe he went back for the reading of the will. I mean, both of your parents die, you're bound to be getting some bank," Veronica said rather calculatingly.

"Not both his parents, just his mom," Veronica clarified. Lisa leaned forward to lock eyes with Jill on the other side of Veronica. "No, he told us both his parents," Lisa said.

"No," Veronica insisted, "just his mother died."

"Yo-ho," came a voice from behind their 6-foot fence, followed by an elbow. None other than that of Duke's. He thrust a large brown paper bag atop it with his other hand. Veronica moved her hand as if petting an invisible dog.

"Anybody hungry? I got crabs."

"Veronica—" Lisa started to say before Veronica silenced her with a look that could kill. She struggled to get up from her lounge chair and let Duke in. He entered the backyard with a George Jefferson strut and placed two brown paper bags on the picnic table, pulling a beer out of one of them.

"Did you see the black guy with the guitar at Marshall's party last week?" Jill asked as Veronica looked at her with the same look she gave Lisa.

"Who? David Jones?"

"How do you know his name?" Veronica asked.

"Man, I been knowing him since elementary school. Little punk ass bitch."

The three girls all shot glances at each other.

———

"I don't think we're talking about the same guy. This dude's from England," Lisa protested.

Taking another swig, Duke almost choked from laughing. "Man, he's from Frederick Douglass High. He do the accent?"

All three shook their heads; a shared look of being duped tore across their faces.

"His father's English."

"Is he dead?" Lisa asked.

"Hell no."

Veronica pointed to Lisa and Jill as if to say, *Told you so*.

"I knew there was something fishy when he didn't know what The Cliffs of Dover were," Lisa said.

Duke approached Veronica, who was staring off into space. "Hey, where you at, Little Ding-a-ling? Hearing Harleys off in the distance?" Faking a smile, she took hold of his wrists to prevent him from slipping his arms around her waist. At six foot three, he towered over her. She finally relented and placed her hands behind his broad shoulders, making her feel further diminutive. He bent down and kissed her lips; she was slow to reciprocate.

"What about your mother? I can't remember anybody ever talking about her."

"She abandoned us when I was a kid. Only just started talking to her a couple of years ago," Ian reported. We had been walking for about fifteen minutes—first

passing bed and breakfasts, followed by several churches with graveyards. It made for a rather eerie stroll.

"Sorry, but I guess that's better than nothing. What
about Uncle Thom?" I snickered at the literary character, not even knowing why.

"Look," Ian said, nodding off into the distance.

A massive white tent appeared on the outskirts of
a large green field, lit up by the moon and stars. As we
drew closer, it proved to be not a carnival at all, as I was
expecting, but an actual traveling circus. It seemed to
be concluding as attendees poured outside the tent and
made their way in all directions. Probably on their way
to deluge the pub for last orders.

We weaved through and around the exiting mass-
es, all these British faces coming at us simultaneously, finally reaching a narrow dirt path that cut through
a small swatch of trees and bushes. We entered what
could only be the carny village. Trailer upon trailer
stood crammed into one another as close as they possibly could. I remembered the Elephant Man I had seen
and wondered if he might be here among them as I
followed Ian to the farthest corner of the make-shift
community, convincing myself he had to be here.

Finally, spotting circus performers and animals being led to their cages by their minders or trainers or
whatever, I knew we were in carney village.

"PSST" came from a blood-red trailer. Ian made a
sharp right, with me close on his heels. There, beside

the trailer door, we found a tall clown smoking a cigarette. I fell back and stopped as Ian approached him.

Despite the painted-on smile, the clown ominously opened the door for Ian, who climbed the three metal steps before ducking down. He turned and waved for me to follow him. Ian stepped inside while I nervously nodded at what I assumed was a man behind the mask. He paid me little mind as he flicked his lit cigarette butt to the ground and followed us both in, closing the door behind him.

The trailer was smaller inside than it appeared. An unkempt cot sat along the far side of the wall, pushed flush against a tall wardrobe closet, and smelled nothing short of death. Or failure. Ian took a seat on the bench by the front of the trailer, kicking the suit box jutting out from underneath to make room for his feet. I sat beside Ian on the opposite end, a good inch between us. Turning my body towards Ian, I gave the clown enough room to squeak by with his big floppy shoes; the ball atop his hat slid comically across the low corrugated ceiling.

"How much does he know?" the clown asked, with what appeared to be an American accent. The first I had heard in England.

"Nothin', you told me to wait," Ian assured him as the clown picked a towel up off the cot before sitting down.

I wondered if they were talking about me. *Where do I know that voice from?* was the next question that popped in my head. I shot a quizzical look at Ian, who shook his head and returned his gaze to the clown.

Opening the left door of the wardrobe, the clown looked at me, but I found myself staring at my reflection in the mirror on the inside of the cabinet door.

As Ian had made no formal introductions, I was not sure what to say. "So, how long have you been a clown?"

Wiping the make-up from his face, the clown answered matter-of-factly, "Oh, about a month." The U-shaped smile was disappearing, the blue circles around his eyes were lessening. As the towel increasingly got soiled from the make-up, the face became more apparent. My eyes shifted from my reflection back to the clown. The resemblance, though decades in age between us, was the same despite the difference in complexion.

My jaw dropped to the floor. "GRANDAD?! Where the hell have you been?"

Grandfather pulled the jester hat down the side of his head along with the blue wig, with the horseshoe track of gray hair surrounding his shiny crown.

"You alright, my son?" he asked, flashing that Jones smile.

Chapter

As my eyes darted back and forth from Grandfather to Ian and back to Grandfather, I kept waiting for them to tell me it was all an elaborate prank. Landing back on Ian, he merely raised his eyebrows; his expression remained as poker-faced as ever. Feeling eerily similar as I did in the Guidance Counselor's a week prior, a certain clarity manifested itself. Had they been?

"Sorry about all the cloak and dagger, but we felt it necessary to take certain...precautions if you will," Grandfather said. Ian leaned forward, resting his beefy arms on his knees. "We think you can help us, Davey," he continued.

I peered out of the corner of my eye at Ian, who was unaware of me doing so, his focus being on Grandfather.

"You see, we've got a little scheme we're putting into motion and think you could play an integral part in it.

———

Ian tells me you're a pretty good driver. And you handle yourself pretty well under pressure. Well, we need a driver. What do you think?"

I took a long think to ponder the question.

And my answer: "Sure, why not? In for a penny, in for a pound."

Grandfather looked relieved to hear that. "I'm relieved to hear that." Yeah, right, they weren't getting off that easy.

"What do I think?!" I said, slowly standing up to confront them both. "I think you're both crazy! Have you guys been like watching me this whole time? Was the entire heart thing bullshit? What were those pills anyway?"

"Heartburn. I *did* have heartburn."

"Yeah, well, I'm getting heartburn. I probably lost the girl of my dreams because of all this!"

"Sit down!" Grandfather barked menacingly. Ian tugged on my shirt, pulling me back down to the bench. I practically sat on his knee.

Grandfather stood up and unzipped his rainbow-colored jumpsuit, revealing a tank top and boxers and, of course, his tallit, before slowly stepping out of it.

It suddenly occurred to me. "You don't even have an accent."

"Look, I understand you're upset, you're confused, you're thinking, I don't know what you're thinking, but Ian and I need to pick something up, and we need a driver."

"It's not Ian's dog, is it? 'Cause, we picked him up the other night." I knew it came off sarcastic, but I didn't know if this was all real or not. They both shook their heads. "What, another dog? Two dogs?"

"More like dags," Ian said.

"Dags? What're dags?"

Grandfather slipped into his pajama pants. The same pajama pants I noticed he was wearing when I knocked his ass out in the hallway. *Guess I didn't even do that.*

"Diamonds and gold and silver."

"That's DAGAS," Ian and I said simultaneously. Ian laughed; I cracked my first smile.

"Wasn't that a painter?" I asked.

"That's DEGAS, with an E," Ian retorted.

"OI!" Grandfather barked. "Oy vey. Look, lads, I need you two to be serious for a moment," he continued, buttoning up his pajama shirt. "Everything depends on it."

We both nodded.

"What exactly am I driving us from?"

"I think," Grandfather said, sitting down. "I feel, at this point, the less you know, the better."

"But I don't know nothing. Don't seem fair."

"Doesn't seem fair," Ian corrected me. "And 'don't know nothing' is a double negative."

Grandfather dropped his head into his hands,

"Might as well tell him now. He's going to need to know anyway," Ian reasoned.

"Look, kid. David. I'm dying."

"Well, we're all dying, innit?"

"I hate when people say that," Grandfather said with venom. "I haven't got long to live, and I would like to spend my final days secure, without worry."

"What do you mean secure? You going to rob some-one?"

Grandfather's eyes darted to Ian; mine followed.

"I didn't tell him nothing," Ian assured Grandfather.

"Speakin' of double negatives," Grandfather mumbled. Was he referring to Ian's statement? Or me and Ian? I scoffed as I looked back at Ian. From the look on his face, it seemed as if he was pondering the same question.

"Look at ya, two peas in a bloody pod," Grandfather added.

"Wait, are you guys planning on robbing someone?" I said, followed by a nervous chuckle. This time I avoided looking at either one of them. "Why me? Like, when did you think of me? You guys were just sitting around one day, and somebody said, 'Hey, let's rob someone and get DJ from the US to help us?'"

I leaped to my feet, banging my head on the ceiling with a loud thump, similar in both action and pain as with Veronica on the Ferris wheel. "Why? Why me? Why?" I asked in a high-pitch groan.

"Sit down!"

Rubbing my head, I tried to sit down, this time waiting for Ian to move his leg.

"We're not robbing anyone," Grandad clarified.

"We're just gonna make it *look* like a robbery," Ian said gleefully.

"You wha'?"

"*That* is why we thought of *you*," Grandfather said, pointing at me.

"But why me again?"

"Cause you do a hell of an English accent."

"Yeah, but you didn't know I could speak English."

"You can't," Ian quickly countered.

"I mean with an accent," correcting Ian.

"Yeah, me, too, mate."

"Ya cock." We both laughed. Then we saw the scowl on Grandfather's mug.

"Eighteen years with your father, I suspected you'd be sounding like him. And we wanted to, sort of, keep it in the family, you know," Grandfather said. "Look, you want in or what?"

"Do I want in on what?"

"Look, it's as simple as Satan," Ian said. "We've anonymously submitted some rare gems to be auctioned. So, on Monday, we're going to walk into that shop, where our man on the inside has overvalued them for insurance purposes, and take them."

"Back," Grandfather added.

"Monday? But we're going back on Monday," I said, forgetting what home even was anymore.

"I've already taken the liberty of changing our tickets to Tuesday."

I sat silently, contemplating what to say, what to do. Then, finally, I clapped my hands and rubbed them together.

"How much we gonna make?"

"*We*, he says," Grandfather said. "Plenty, pal, plenty. You need any stake money?"

Ian stood up, bending slightly so as not to hit his head; I followed suit, though I need not make the same effort.

"Steak sounds good. I'm broke," I said, pulling my pockets out.

"Not that kind of stake," Grandfather said, opening his wallet and handing me two ten-pound notes. "Now go on, leave me be."

"Let's leave ole Grumps to his beauty sleep," Ian said, leading me out of the trailer. Neither of us even said goodbye to the old man. Instead, I watched him lay back on his bed as I shut the door, forcing it to close entirely.

I tried to keep pace with Ian but was intrigued by the carnival folk milling about their tiny village. While it was not backstage at Ringling Brothers and Barnum Bailey Circus, more like Todd Browning's "Freaks," there were some that were noteworthy: such as the hunchbacked man walking a monkey on a leash with a bandaged tail and devouring a stick of candy floss. Another, the silhouette of a woman on horseback that I silently pleaded with the gods for her to turn her head; when, as bad luck would have it, she did, I wished she hadn't. Shielded by her long wavy cascades of hair, she had a face as big and round as that of a soccer ball. She smiled at one of the carnies, which made her face appear even more prominent.

Eventually, we passed through the thicket from where we first arrived, finding the lights around the tent all but extinguished. A few men pulled at ropes to dismantle it. So much was going through my head that I failed to notice Ian had stopped to light a cigarette; I plowed right into his back.

"Watch it," Ian mumbled through clenched teeth.

"It's kind of how it all started," I aptly surmised.

"How what started?"

"Bumping into Granddad in my house. I guess that was all fake, too."

"Come on," Ian said, leading me by the arm across the field.

"How long has he been working as a clown?"

"Couple of weeks, setting himself up for an alibi," Ian explained.

We arrived at an unassuming Bed & Breakfast in the center of town where we waited to check-in, or whatever you do at a B&B. I could not help but think of Basil Fawlty, the John Cleese character from "Fawlty Towers."

Bad English
the III

The owner, a petite older woman, made no mention of the fact that two young men with nothing but a backpack between them required a room, with only a double bed no less, a pretense I assumed was all part and parcel with the plan. She gave us a small tour of the sitting lounge, where two old monocle-wearing goats playing chess looked as if they had passed onto the other side, and the breakfast quarters, where, admittedly, I looked forward to brekkie. As she began to lead us upstairs, Ian took a chivalrous position and assured her we could find the room on our own.

"It's late, and there's no need for you to make the pilgrimage upstairs."

"Bathroom is down the hall on the right."

The room itself was what one might assume an English bed and breakfast might be: antique-style furnishings and floral linens.

"I'm knackered," Ian said as he plopped down on the pretty bed cover with bright pink roses.

"So, are you ever going to tell me your guys' big scheme, or what?" I asked, having a seat on a small plush Victorian love seat that faced the fake fireplace.

Ian went on to tell me that his father, Uncle Thom, was part owner of a jewelry broker in London. Unbeknownst to his partner, he had over-insured some jewelry Grandfather had acquired during the war, mostly smuggled out of Africa.

There's Africa again, I thought.

"Gramps says, and I happen to agree, that communism and apartheid are both on their last legs. In a few years, they'll be footnotes in history books. You know why?" I shook my head. "I'll give you a hint... Three letters, three letters are going to topple it all. You know what those three letters are?"

"Um, HIV?"

"How the hell would HIV bring down—? No. C-N-N."

"CNN? What, The Cable News Network?"

"Yeah, you see, it's everywhere now, beaming pictures off satellites from all over the globe. It's already changing the way we see other parts of the world. People aren't going to stand for outdated rubbish forms of government oppression any longer. They're bound to crumble. So, these gems from Africa and Russia are going to be worth a lot less. So there's going to be a surge, a real black market for them."

First, I'm hearing of Russia. This had to be, by far, *the strangest thing I had ever heard.* And a little revealing, as hard as that was to believe.

"So," I said, changing the subject. "How is this all going to work?"

"It's really quite simple. Monday is a bank 'oliday, so—"

"What's a bank *oliday*?"

"It's an 'oliday where banks and offices are closed."

"What's the holiday?"

"I dunno, summer or sumfin', it's hardly the point," Ian said, frustration growing in his voice. "So, with the banks and such closed, the streets won't be as busy. We have an appointment, so we'll be buzzed inside. We go in, put masks on, show some firepower and—"

"Wait, what do you mean firepower?"

"Ya know, shotguns."

"Shotguns?"

"Yeah, they don't even work. It's all for the cameras. So, we get our loot, high-tail it out of the store, and you drive us away."

"And no one gets hurt," I mumbled to myself. *Famous last words*. I stood up and pulled the blanket back before modestly turning away to pull my shirt over my head.

"What the f--- is that?!" Ian shouted. I spun, expecting to see a spider or something rabid in the room.

"What?!"

"All over your back! What *are* those? Bites?"

I craned my neck in a way that I could see what the fuss was all about. Ian pointed to the free-standing antique mirror. I approached it, twisting my body to see the reflection; there were little red spots that led up and down my back like some erratic game of connect-the-dots.

"You haven't got crabs, ya f---in' nutter. Those look like bed bug bites!"

"Are you serious?? Those f---in' frogs!"

Ian kicked a pillow off the bed onto the floor.

"You ain't havin' no kip in *this* bed, mate."

I yanked the blanket off the bed after Ian rolled up off it and curled up half on the hardwood floor, half on the rug.

Eventually, when the excitement died down, and we were lying quietly in the dark, Ian was the first to break the silence.

"You like The Beatles, yeah?"

"Yeah, of course. They were my first favorite band, after KISS." Ian snickered like Scooby-Doo.

"Did you know the entire phenomenon of The Beatles was a well-executed experiment?"

"I beg your pardon."

"Yeah, it's true. Brian Epstein planned everything from as far back as Hamburg up to their break-up in 1970. All that Paul is dead stuff, yeah?"

"Yeah."

"All thought out as far back as 1959."

"Huh." I took back what I had previously thought. *That* was the strangest thing I had ever heard in my whole life. I mean, everyone knows that John Lennon came up with the Paul is Dead stuff the first time he smoked weed with Bob Dylan.

I farted; Ian returned the compliment. We erupted in hysterics. Nervous tension, I figured.

In a smoke-filled room, three generations of men sat discussing their plan.

"What about Jimmy Nichols?" the eldest asked.

"He can't see three feet in front of his face," the youngest replied.

"That's far enough to see through the windscreen," the father to one, son to the other, reasoned.

"What about that, uh, Trevor, whats-his-name?"

"Trevor, the fish market bloke? He's banged up on a tenstretch."

"F---in' ell."

"I can't believe I didn't think of this sooner! What about David?" the youngest proudly proclaimed.

"His wife just died," the eldest said, shooting it down.

"No, the kid," Ian countered.

"His mum just died!" Grandfather stressed.

"Yeah? Might be nice for him to get away," Thomas pointed out.

"We can control him," Ian said.

All three men dragged on their cigarettes as they contemplated it.

"How d'ya like your tea?" Ian asked me, though I was still sleeping. I squinted out of my left eye at Ian, who was standing at the in-room electric kettle.

"Whi' an' swee', li' my women," I said.

"Oh, god," Ian uttered as he prepared us two cups of tea.

I was in good spirits after the best night's sleep I'd had in weeks, maybe months, despite waking up in the middle of the night with an epiphany: there was no way that this heist thing was real. It all had to be a big set-up. I, therefore, concluded this was going to be the best surprise party London had ever seen. I was so sure of it that I fell back asleep with ease. Twice.

When I woke up again, about an hour later, the room was quiet. I sat up and noticed the now-cold cup of tea sitting on my nightstand. I climbed out of bed and poked my head into the hallway. Seeing the coast was clear, I put my shirt on and went to the bathroom before making my way downstairs, thinking maybe Ian had gone from the bed part to the breakfast part.

"Good morning, sir. Will you and Mr. McCartney be joining us for breakfast?" the owner inquired. "We have a lovely window table that overlooks the garden."

"Um, yes, I'll be right back," I replied, chuckling at the McCartney reference.

"Wonderful, I'll have you all set up."

I returned to the room to find the room key sitting by the kettle. *You have got to be kidding me*, I thought, grabbing it along with my backpack, and rushed downstairs to the counter where we had checked in. Dropping the key on the register, I noticed the name Ian used to check-in: James McCartney, as in James Paul McCartney. *Nice touch*, I thought as I passed the dining room where the owner arranged flowers in a tiny glass vase on the table she prepared for us.

Making my way back to the fair, I again crossed the field, taking the dirt path through the thicket of trees to find that, except for some strewn trash, the carny village was long gone.

"Whaaaa?"

Chapter
XII

Venturing back to Tent City, I mucked about in the main building, not wanting to lie down on my bed if it genuinely was infested but wanting no contact with the staff either. They *knew*. How could they not?

The punks were listening to some weird music, part electronica, part smooth jazz. I liked it, but I sure as hell wasn't going to tell them. I considered going to The Royal Coat of Arms to seek out Ian but, *been there, done that.*

Instead, I went through all the things I had accumulated in the last week, making two piles: one for trash, one for keeping. Souvenirs and the like: it's of papers, adverts, subway tickets, my hilarious YHA pictures from my first day, my airline ticket.

Airline ticket. That was something I could do: call to confirm if my flight was leaving on Tuesday.

Bad English
the III

Taking the two piles I had made, I put one pile back into the parachute bag and locked it up, dropping the second pile in the small trash bin attached eye-level where all the bags were attached.

In the phone kiosk, I called Directory Services and obtained the toll-free number for TWA, confirming my flight for Tuesday evening. True to his word, Grandfather had changed our flight until Tuesday. I tried to be cheeky and upgrade my seat to First Class and was shocked to find that one was already reserved in our names.

Things are looking up. I decided to grab a cheap bite to eat and ventured out into East Acton to find a fast-food joint.

Returning to tent city after buying the worst chicken sandwich I had ever eaten at a place named Wimpy's, based on the hamburger-loving Popeye character, I returned to the bench by my parachute bag. As I sat there contemplating what to do for the day, something on the bulletin board across the room caught my eye; I stood up and crossed the room.

Someone had pinned my YHA pictures to the cork-board: 'DORK' was written in blue ballpoint pen on the top picture; on the lower image, it had a patch over one eye, one of my teeth blacked out, the word 'COOL' on it.

I yanked it down and looked around the room to see if I could determine who the culprit was. Different groups of people were in conversations, some laughing. All seemed French. Then one broke into a song as the others followed suit, all singing what must have been the French National Anthem, measured by their patriotic enthusiasm.

They finished with a roar, all laughing and cheering, quite happy with themselves.

At my wit's end, I erupted into my own patriotic song, "Born in the USA." Bruce Springsteen, an artist I was not even that crazy about but was well-suited for the moment. Repeating those four words over and over, I strummed on the guitar, stomped on the floor with my jaw jutted out.

All the Frenchies stopped their conversations and looked at me like I was the scum of the earth until I finished. Then, they resumed their talks but had a new warm feeling about me.

The pictures had not been for the trash pile but rather to be saved; I rushed to the bin and fished out the various souvenirs that were in there, including my plane ticket!

That was bloody close, I thought. I returned to my bag, where I switched out the piles, throwing away the *correct* stack of trash.

As darkness settled in with no word from Ian or Grandfather, I resigned to the fact that I would have to go to sleep in what I was now referring to as Bed Bug City. And I slept.

"David Jones!"

Bad English
the III

I opened my left eye. It was already morning. Had I just heard my name?

"David Jones?!"

I rolled over to see Ian poking his head in the tent. "Yeah, I'm here."

"Let's go," Ian said.

Someone complained in French from one of the beds.

"Piss off, Pierre," Ian said. "Come on, my son. It's on!"

I leaped from the bed and yanked my army blanket behind me. Ian's appearance surprised me—he was wearing a suit and tie, and his usually unkempt hair was matted down. He looked like a proper businessman. We crossed the walkway on a foggy and misty morning and went into the main building, where I unlocked my bag.

"Should I bring everything?"

"NO. *Leave* everything."

I quickly switched out my last t-shirt, stuffed my blanket into the bag, and securely fastened it. Ian led us outside, where a blue Volkswagen camper van was still running. *Of course, it is*, I thought. *All part of the test, innit?*

Ian slid the door open, locking eyes with me. He tilted his head for me to get in. I froze.

Is this all a joke?

Ian's hooded eyes narrowed, and he tilted his head again, but more insistent. Once inside, I looked for any clues that might answer the questions swirling around in my coconut. Like, where do I sit? Ian silently responded to my question by taking the driver's seat, leaving the other for me.

"Here, put this on," Ian said, throwing a black knit cap in my lap.

As I stuffed all my curls up inside that way-too-small hat, Ian ground the gear into first. I felt compelled to sing the Judas Priest song as I had the last time, but with the look of consternation on his face, I decided to keep it to myself.

The van leaped forward, careening towards a small concrete dividing wall in front of us before braking to a stop. He veered right and made an awkward 3-point turn, heading in the opposite direction.

"Keep in mind, it pulls slightly to the right."

If this is a surprise party, I thought, *Ian's undoubtedly not breaking character.* He popped a tape into the cassette player; The Who's "Who Are You" jammed from the dashboard speakers.

Nice touch, I thought as Ian weaved us through the foggy, desolate streets until we finally made our way to Victoria Station.

It was now eight-thirty, and there was little in the way of traffic, either auto or foot. I liked this station because it sat opposite the giant sign for the "Buddy" musical, and I regretted not getting a ticket when I'd had the money to see it.

Maybe next time, I rationalized. I did not know it yet, but there were many more of those to come, and not for such trivial things as missing London musicals.

I checked my watch and looked out the window to-wards a set of the station's glass doors. Then, like clock-work, Grandfather emerged. He, too, was wearing a suit and tie while carrying a suitcase. He walked around to my side of the camper while I tried to open the door, but it would not budge.

"Unlock the bloody thing, would ya?" Ian insisted. In an aha moment, I pulled up the weathered lock but-ton, the plastic piece long gone, and again tried to open the door. Grandfather, growing ever impatient, was do-ing his part outside. "F---in' 'ell, move back," Ian said as he raised his leg and kicked at the door. It swung open with a loud ka thunk.

"Sit on the floor," Grandfather said as he climbed in. I did as he told me; he pulled the door shut, setting the suitcase behind me. I crossed my legs and looked up and back and forth from Grandfather to Ian. "Victoria to Whitehall to Charing—" Grandfather said to Ian be-fore being cut off.

"I know, I know," Ian said, sounding a lot like me on *our* night in that work van.

We pressed forth, Ian driving, Grandfather navigat-ing, me sitting on the floor unable to see f—k-all from my perspective, just the buildings passing by with the street signs high on the walls.

"You'll be fine," Grandfather said, gripping my shoulder. I nodded, still not sure whether this was re-ally a thing or not. "It's all just a show, anyway—little thing for the cameras. Think of yourself as a driver for a couple of actors after the theater," Grandfather said, his American accent showing hints of English.

"Sorry about earlier, you know, with the door," I offered in return. Grandfather winked at me as he reached back and pulled the suitcase forward, opening it up.

"One standard disguise," he said, pulling out two Groucho Marx combo glasses, nose, and mustache. He handed one to Ian, who set it on the seat between his legs; Grandfather slid his on. "The Secret word of the day is Insurance Fraud," he said in the style of Groucho Marx from his TV show, "You Bet Your Life," imaginary cigar in hand and all.

Whether real or not, I reasoned, I was getting my money's worth as Grandfather pulled out two rubber masks, handing one to Ian and keeping the other for himself; but, unfortunately, I could not make out exactly what the faces were.

Lastly, he pulled out a plaid valise. I was suddenly struck by the bag, as it was similar to the ones that caused all the commotion in "What's Up, Doc?"

"Turning on Whitehall," Ian said as he turned right. That's what the sign said.

"Houses of Parliament," Grandfather pointed them out through the windscreen. I stood up on my knees to see them and the upcoming Westminster Bridge. Then, I sat back down, banging my head on the wall behind me.

Grandfather began to whistle a familiar tune. It took a few moments before I realized what it was. "I'm Reviewing the Situation," from the movie "Oliver!" I wondered if a villain *could* be a villain all his life.

Ian remained focused on driving, not saying a word. I recognized the Hippodrome out Ian's window. Leicester Square. So, if memory served, we were nearing Oxford Street. Almost there.

"Here." Grandfather handed me a hand-drawn map. "Get a good look at it. This is our route out. Read it aloud, so I know you understand it."

"First left, Great Chapel," I started before being cut off.

"Where we shall pray," Grandfather said, injecting a bit of levity.

"Right on Noel, pass one, two, three streets, where it turns into Great Marlborough Street, which is what I'm going to need, a great big Marlboro. Right on Argyle," I smirked, thinking of Argyle, the driver from "Die Hard." I chose not to elaborate on my amusement.

"Park behind the Palladium," Grandfather said.

"The London Palladium?"

"Right where I borrowed it from," Ian injected.

"The stage manager's an old drinking mate of mine. He's boozed-up through every night's performance and usually passes out as soon as he locks the doors for the night," Grandfather informed.

Ian turned the corner onto Oxford Street and pulled along the curb. He kicked the parking brake into position with his foot; Grandfather reached into the bag and removed two sawed-off shotguns. He handed Ian a shotgun shell. Ian cracked open the gun and slid it inside.

"Holy shit," I muttered, not realizing it was aloud.

"Just a starter's gun," Grandfather assured me. *Not like any starter's gun I've ever seen*, I thought, but then again, I never saw one before.

Lastly, Grandfather removed two modified umbrellas, with the handles cut off, handing one to Ian. *They're going to have their hands full with all that*, I thought.

Ian slid the plastic Groucho glasses on, which made him look equally absurd as Grandfather. He then put the rubber mask on the back of his head. Finally, they slid the umbrellas, with their handles removed, into the ends of the shotguns. Ian pointed the driver's seat out to me.

Hunching over, Ian approached the sliding door on the driver's side behind me, speaking comically like Igor: *"Walk this way."* He thrust it open with all his might and jumped out, helping Grandfather by taking his elbow. They reached inside, retrieving their "umbrellas."

With me in the driver's seat, we three Joneses looked ready for business.

I *still* wasn't convinced that this was a thing.

Looking every bit like the two legitimate businessmen their plan called for, I chewed on my fingernail as I watched my grandfather and cousin, their modified umbrellas and weirdly fitting suits bouncing up and down upon their every step. Then, finally, they approached the building with Y & T Goldbroker's - Established 1968, embossed in gold on the window.

My heart pounded as fiercely as the wind blowing outside. Sitting in yet another stolen auto, I watched through the window as the two men disappeared behind an alcove, the only storefront on the entire block whose door did not face the street. I took notice of the sign underneath: Bank Holiday Precious Gems Auction - Today at Noon.

"Won't they be surprised?" I muttered under my breath.

I tried to get a better view inside but could not see through the thickening fog. It reminded me of the Talking Heads lyric from "Once in a Lifetime": "How *did* I get here?" I had no idea as I sat there how ironic that song and its lyrics would eventually play out. But it was big.

Suddenly a newspaper whipped violently back and forth through the air in front of me, and for a brief, fleeting moment, it took my mind off what must be occurring inside if I was to believe it, of course.

Prince Charles emerged from the shop about the same time that newspaper slapped me right in the face with a muffled POP! Ian told me later: "You got bill-posted with a Page 3 bird!" I pulled at the paper, ripping her head off, her boobs under my panicked face.

"Nice tits, love!" Prince Charles shouted, clearly Ian, as he ripped the headless and topless girl off my face.

"GO! GO!" from under the rubber mask approaching behind Ian. The Iron Lady herself, Margaret Thatcher.

"Get in!" I found myself yelling as I pounced like a cat into the passenger seat awkwardly on my left forearm, forgetting I was already in the driver's seat. I hoped no one saw that.

"Fuck are you doing?" Ian asked, throwing his umbrella inside, where it separated from the thick shotgun and landed on the floor behind us. He turned to help Grandfather but had his hand swiped away as he hopped in with ease. Ian followed him and barked.

"GO!" he slammed the door shut, but Grandfather's shotgun was sticking out; the umbrella top fell off into the street.

I proceeded to turn the ignition. Metal against metal screeched out, making all three of our spines shiver. I forgot. It was still running.

"It's ALREADY RUNNING! GO!" they both shouted.

Checking the right-view mirror, I observed the umbrella spinning wildly, like a dreidel. I drove straight along the curb. My eyes shifted back to the windshield and momentarily forgot on what side of the street I was meant to be driving. *I could never do this stoned.*

As I veered to the left, my eyes landed on the rearview just as they removed their rubber numbers, only to find ski masks, their eyes visible. One set, Ian's, excited, Grandfather's weary and worrisome.

"Other side, other side," they both yelled, pointing through the windshield.

"Truth be told... I always fancied a bit of the chase..." Robbin's eyes connected with Starling's.

Before I had settled on being called DJ, which, in part, stemmed from the rise of rap, like Run DMC with Jam Master Jay, I had been walking through my apartment complex with my next-door neighbor, Terence. We came across two older dudes, feverishly shaking a lamppost. Twelve years old at the time, I used some salty language for my age, in effect, telling the older boys where to go and how to get there.

And the chase was on.

Terence and I got a good lead on them as the older boys chased us out of the horseshoe-shaped low-income apartment complex and into the tree-lined single-story homes nearby. We took refuge at the front of one house, in particular, wedging ourselves tightly and quietly between the outside wall and its four-foot-high bushes. We watched in terror as the two teens, in full force, ran past us, merely a few feet away.

Finally, after the appropriate amount of time, Terence and I emerged from our hiding place and stealthily made our way back to his apartment, where we played games and listened to the radio until it was time for me to go home.

Walking in my front door, I moved down the hallway, hearing voices coming from the living room. My mother stood up from the couch and faced me, scowling at me as I entered the room just in time to see one of the teens that had been chasing us.

"I think you know Duke," she said.

(Yes, that Duke!)

"He's been telling me the most interesting story about how you two met."

I could not believe my eyes; my own mother had betrayed me.

Duke stood up and, even at 14, was already pushing 6-feet. "Well, I've taken up enough of your time," he said, reminding me of Eddie Haskel from the TV show "Leave It To Beaver."

To me: "Walk me out?"

He put his arm around me as we walked down the hall.

"Now I know where you live," Duke whispered in my ear.

I shuddered as I unlocked the top lock to the apartment and opened it for Duke.

Stepping out into the hallway, "I'll be seeing you."

I watched him lumber down the stairs before closing the door, leaning with my back against it, and let out a huge sigh.

———

Oddly enough, we would eventually become friends. Okay, maybe friend was too strong a word. Let's say friendly. And it wouldn't last. We came to learn that, despite being black and living in a black neighborhood, we both loved rock and roll. So we started a band we could not even agree on a name for: I wanted Revelation 13 after the Bible passage, giving it a more demonic slant. Duke wanted Revelations, which I despised.

During practice one day, we had a massive row, which resulted in me quitting the band. When the other band members, two white kids that Duke had recruited because they had houses where we could practice, called for a truce and got the two of us together to kiss and make-up. Well, instead of shaking Duke's hand, I took a swing at him. And missed. Duke chased me all the way home. We never spoke again until the party.

"Can I stop you for a moment?" The Interviewer asked.

"Sure," she said, though visually perturbed again.

"You said, 'Truth be told, I always fancied a bit of the chase.'"

"Did I?"

"Yeah, I mean, I can play it back for you if you like."

"Whatchu mean play it back?!" Robbin nearly shouted as she retrieved her handbag from the floor and abruptly leaped to her feet. "I was *implicit* in my instructions, no recording devices of any kind," she furiously reiterated as she picked up her handbag and stormed to the hotel door.

The Interviewer lifted the Time Out magazine from the table and picked up the mini tape recorder, clicking it off. "If you leave now, you risk losing the reward money."

"It's not about the reward money. Never was."

"Robbin, I'm sorry, it's just common practice for reporters. We're only human," she said, clicking the tape recorder off. "We can't remember every word, every nuance."

Robbin gripped the doorknob so hard her knuckles were turning white. "For the record, I was picturing it in me mind, you know. These, again, were his exact words."

"Right, sorry, of course, they were." Starling pointed towards the chair. "Won't you, please?"

Removing a cigarette from a Silk Cut Silver package, Robbin lifted her mask, lit it and inhaled deeply.

"Oh, what the hell? We've come this far, right?" Robbin said, exhaling a long stream of smoke, relenting as she slowly made her way back to the sofa. "Might as well keep recording. Actually, might I hear a bit?" The Interviewer rewound a bit and played it back:

"Can I stop you for a moment?"

"Sure."

"You said, 'Truth be told, I always fancied a bit of the chase.'

"Did I?"

"Yeah, I mean, I can play it back for you if you like."

"Whatchu mean play it back?!"

Robbin cringed, stubbing her cigarette out in the ashtray. "Your voice never sounds on tape the way you imagine it in your head, does it?"

The Interviewer nodded as she stopped the tape, pressed Record, and set it back down on the table.

Chapter
XIII

I an shouted: "The brake! You gotta release the brake!"

"How do I do that?!"

"Step on the regular brake, it'll release it!"

I did as I was told, and by Jove, it released the brake; it felt different, more agreeable. I gunned it, and we sputtered up Oxford Street, the two men swaying back and forth as they removed their shirts and ties. They were now whispering, but I was too focused on driving.

"Right! Right!" Ian yelled at me, pointing right, so I knew it was me he was addressing.

I made the right turn but struggled with what lane to turn into out of habit. *Opposite, think opposite*, I told myself as the steering veered again to the right.

"Scam go off as planned?" I asked, thinking that was pretty funny. But then, it occurred to me that maybe this was not the surprise party I thought it was after all.

"Smashing," Grandfather reported before scowling at Ian.

My stomach tightened into a knot as I could sense something was wrong. Not having my daily routine of washing my banana back with chocolate milk was not helping the situation.

"Could you drive any faster, please?!" Ian barked.

I looked over my shoulder at Ian. He stopped whispering, followed by Grandfather. I took note of the t-shirt Ian had stripped down to: "Sid Vicious I Did It MY WAY."

"Watch the road," Ian said.

Returning my attention to the matter at hand, I stomped my foot harder on the gas. The speed gauge rose from fifteen to twenty to twenty-five. I felt I was too close to the parked cars on my right, so I eased over to the left a wee bit. An oncoming motorcycle honked at us as I was veering over the line, so I eased back over when—THWACK!—the VW's mirror knocked off the side mirror of a parked car.

"What was that?" Grandfather asked.

"Nothing, just nothing," I said.

I recognized we were now in or near Soho when I spotted that novelty shop I quite liked. *When we get our money*, I thought, *I might go back to that shop and buy that poster collage of all those people I like*. Then, remembering what was at stake, I looked in the rear-view mirror to see the two of them in a heated conversation, at which point Ian locked eyes with me.

———

"The road?"

I did as I was told.

Passing Poland Street, I was aware that my next turn was coming up. I started feeling a bit queasy. I wished that's all it was. I got that weird, back-of-the-throat feeling and knew what was coming. Up, that is.

I tried to roll the window down, but the handle came off in my hand. I pushed open the triangular vent and could now taste it as it made its way up. I shoved my mouth into the small opening, and like an erupting volcano, I puked up what little was in my stomach. I moved my foot to the brake, then dry heaved. And again.

The van slowed as I focused on throwing up. Having a weak stomach himself, Ian gagged, looking around for something in which to throw up; nothing at his fingertips, he threw up into them. Now, if only Grandfather would ralph, we'd have had the perfect hat-trick. But it was not to be.

"Could you both stop throwing up! What's gotten into you two?"

I sat back and wiped my mouth only to realize I was passing Argyle Street, our next turn.

I slammed on the brakes, but they locked up trying to make the last-minute turn. Instead, the van went into a slide across the wet asphalt.

"Ian! Ian!" I shouted for no apparent reason as my eyes laser-focused on the red post box on the corner that we were headed towards in what seemed like slow-motion. We careened up onto the sidewalk, missing it by inches. Ian fell into our grandfather's lap, covering his crotch with the contents of his stomach.

"Well, what are you waiting for?!" Ian shouted.

"Get going!" Grandfather added.

I desperately tried to get the gear back into first, but it was having none of that. Ian crawled over between the seats as Grandfather deftly removed his pants, revealing coveralls underneath. Trying to roll the muck in the folds of them, like the childhood baseball game he had as a kid. With subtle tilts of the wrist of the handheld game, the player rolls tiny silver pellets into small holes marked "SINGLE," "DOUBLE," "TRIPLE," and "HOMERUN."

"Let's leg it," Grandfather said. "This won't surprise anyone that knows ole Martin. Including ole Martin."

"Especially Martin," Ian piped in as we all scrambled about the van.

The three of us climbed out as a police Jag, lights and sirens on, screamed towards us. We all froze. The Jaguar passed and turned the corner despite a camper van up on the sidewalk. Not your typical getaway car.

Grandfather briskly walked away to a trash can. Looking in all directions while transferring something from the valise into his pockets, he ditched the bag. Pulling a painter's cap down below his eyes, he turned and casually walked away, suitcase swinging by his side.

"Come on," Ian said, grabbing yet another suitcase from behind the seat and pulling me in the opposite direction. "Ditch that hat," Ian said. At the next bin, I peeled it off my head and did just that.

The two of us made it unscathed to Oxford Circus Station, where Ian casually approached the ticket machine and bought us two tickets to Victoria Station.

"What do we do now?" I asked.

"Walk this way," Ian said. I felt compelled to reply with the old punchline: 'If I could walk that way,' but sensed now was not the time. So instead, I sang the Aerosmith song. In my head.

As we headed down into yet another of the countless tube stations, a few random people in front and behind, I felt a bit more at ease. That is until two coppers ran past us, practically skipping steps on the escalator down.

"Armed robbery and shooting in Oxford Street, two or more suspects," squelched out of one of their radios.

Shooting? I looked over my shoulder to make sure no one was on the step behind me before backing up on the next step, further distancing myself from Ian.

What have they gotten me into? I thought as I wiped the sweat from my forehead. *If we get away with whatever this is*, I thought, *I ain't never going to do another bad thing again as long as I live.*

Allowing more space between us as we skipped steps down the sinking stairs to the tube platform. Ian turned left, me right. *What I would do for either right now*, I thought as I stared at the ads for Jack Daniels and Foster's Lager on the wall of the opposite side of the tracks.

I took a seat on a small bench with an ad for "Bigfoot and the Hendersons" on VHS and wondered why they changed the name from "Harry and the Hendersons."

Hearing the train approach, I felt some sense of relief as I stood up and basked in the rush of wind as the tube whistled into the station. I spied around to gather where exactly Ian was on the platform, but my view was blocked by people running for the arriving train—including two police constables.

"Mind the gap," came the recorded announcement over the intercom. Why would I mind?

The train doors opened; passengers got on and off. The police separated, checking everyone.

What exactly *were* they looking for? I mean, what do jewel robbers look like? And do they typically take the tube?

I stepped into the nearest carriage, grabbing a seat at the end by a smelly unkempt hobo drifting in and out of consciousness while, ultimately, keeping an eye on the cops still on the platform. Ian entered the opposite end of the carriage and, without acknowledging me, had a seat.

The bell chimed with a BING-BONG while I licked the sweat off my upper lip. The female cop talked to someone I could not see, but I assumed it was the Conductor. The doors remained open for longer than usual. They seemed to be holding the train, but *why*?

I was now drenched in sweat; I discreetly fanned myself by pulling the collar of my t-shirt in and out. The smell of my armpits reeked of desperation.

Finally, the constables stepped onboard through both carriage doors before they closed behind them. The train proceeded while the cops met each other in the middle, where they whispered into each other's ears while scanning the passengers in the carriage. I avoided looking at them or Ian and figured he was doing the same. Instead, I looked at the numerous adverts above the windows as the subway whooshed through the dark tunnels.

Out of the corner of my eye, I could see the two constables making their way over in Ian's direction. The train came to a sudden unexpected stop. This was not uncommon, as it had done it more times than I could count over my week there. They often stopped to allow another train to pass or, more often than not, something mechanical. But why now of all times?

Either way, the carriage became mind-numbingly quiet. That is until the lights went out. Screams and loud whoops of excitement followed gasps. It was then that I realized I was solely responsible for all the noises. Then, just as fast, the lights blinked back on.

"You know what I got 'ere!?" someone unexpectedly shouted. I, along with several other passengers, looked up and over to see what the commotion was. Ian, suitcase across his lap, was staring in my direction; I pointed to myself questioningly. "Just some things that are going to make me a very wealthy man!"

Had he lost his ever-loving mind? I shrugged, not knowing how else to react. The cops looked back and forth at us and each other.

Ian's outburst piqued Cagney and Lacey's interest. I swallowed hard in anticipation of where he was headed with that—going for the looney angle?

"Three hundred and thirty-three songs," Ian shouted. He tapped on the case as if a proud father. "All I got to do is record them! That's where I'm 'headed now, mate!"

I nodded, displaying what I could only describe as a sort of feigned interest as the train lurched forward into motion.

"Excuse me, sir," the female constable said. "Do you mind if I have a look at your case?"

Ian gripped the case protectively. "Why would I want to do that? So you can steal me songs and get all me future earnings?"

"Sir, we have reports of an armed robbery no more than thirty minutes ago and—"

"What's that gotta do wif me, then?"

"Please, sir, we don't want any trouble. Just permit us --"

"PerMISSION?!" Ian yelled.

The male officer stepped forward. "D'ya wanna get banged up?"

"BANGED UP?! For WHAT?!" Ian yelled at a higher octave than the last.

"Hey," I shouted, not sure what, if any, accent to employ. "He hasn't done anything!"

The male constable turned and pointed at me. "Shut it, or you'll be next!"

Various male and female passengers also piped up: "Leave 'im alone. He hasn't done anything!"

"I repeat," the female constable said. "Will you grant us permission?"

Shrugging, desperation in his eyes, Ian scanned the carriage for help, but none was forthcoming.

Ian popped the locks open and reluctantly turned the case around to face them. I tried to gauge some sort of signal from him, but none was forthcoming. Finally, he slowly started to open it when the train screeched around a tight bend. All the passengers swayed to their left as if synchronized while sending the cops off their balance, only remaining upright by grabbing the closest pole.

I lurched forward, intrigued, trying to get a better look, as did a few of the other riders. The male constable rifled through the case, which, from my vantage point, seemed to be nothing but papers. Seemingly, he reached the same conclusion, finding nothing remotely nefarious. Instead, the male officer raised a stack of documents, warped and yellowing, to get a better look at Ian's self-proclaimed lyrics.

"You call this...dribble songwriting?" he asked, before proceeding to read the lyrics off the top page in hand: "'When the day turns to night, And my feelings turn to blight.'"

"You sure you're using that word properly, mate?"

One could see the steam rising off Ian as he looked defiantly about the carriage.

"'I soon get the itch, To turn you into my bitch?'" Laughing, the constable looked to his partner, who was sizing up Ian. "'I am the Witchmaker, You are the witch, I am the Bitchmaker.'"

To the carriage: "Everyone? You got it... 'And you are my Bitch.'"

There were scattered laughs throughout the train, including one pretty fit gal who seemed to be taking a shine to Ian. She winked at him; he, in turn, feigned an apparent fake smile in reply.

He tossed the papers back in Ian's suitcase. "Charming. I got five words for you, mate: don't quit your bloody day job."

"That's six words. What's a copper know about music anyway?" Ian replied, shutting the case and spinning it back around to lock it.

"Yeah, well, Elton John's hasn't got a thing to worry about, now does he?" the constable fired back.

"You just proved me point! Who the hell is Elton John?!"

The two constables moved to the door closest to Ian as the train pulled into the Green Park station. The doors opened, and they stepped off, laughing.

At the next stop, I followed Ian's cue off the train and out of the station.

"Did you really write that song?"

"Yeah, when I was like fifteen or sumfin'. Black Sabbath could've done themselves a favour."

Out of the frying pan and back up into the fire, we soon hopped on a bus with Oxford Circus as one of its stops, and I followed Ian upstairs to the top deck. After a few minutes of silence, which, internally, was killing me, it soon became crystal clear what he was doing. He was leading us back to the scene of the crime.

And this, Ladies and Gentlemen, was how they got caught.

Traffic was at a near standstill, but we could see far enough ahead that the street was cordoned off; police directing traffic, with fire engines and police cars parked everywhere. Including where I was parked just moments ago. The bus eventually inched past the shop where this all began.

I noticed him right away, standing outside, wrapped in a blanket drinking a cup of coffee, or maybe, tea--the rude little man from the plane.

Thunderstruck, it all became clear. *That has to be Uncle Thomas.*

———

Bad English
the III

He was speaking to a constable and what looked to be a detective in a rumpled blazer and trousers. I nudged Ian, who simply nodded.

What is Ian doing pressing the bell to stop at the next bus stop? I followed him off and could not fathom why we were making our way back towards the scene of the crime. Was this not how criminals ended up getting caught?

"What's all the excitement?" Ian asked a newsagent as he paid for a newspaper.

"Robbery apparently," the newsagent replied enthusiastically. "I think one of 'em was killed."

"Dead?!" Ian asked, obviously shaken but not stirred.

"'Ad is 'ead nearly blown off. Ever heard of one that wasn't?"

"Christ on a cracker, d'ya see it?" The newsagent shook his head as he turned to a young couple buying 'Modern Bride' magazine.

My head reeled. Everything I had thought had been a lie. Ian pulled me away.

"Shouldn't we have, like, alibis or something?"

"*You* are my alibi," Ian whispered.

"Who's mine?"

In the meantime, Grandfather made his way back to Victoria Station, where he slipped into a phone kiosk, faked a brief phone call, and jetted, leaving the suitcase behind to spread the police force thin with a mysterious package alert (a common IRA tactic). He then boarded a train for Dover, where the fair's caravan had arrived the previous afternoon and set up for a week's celebration. Being his day off, he could choose to either sleep in his trailer or have a wander in whatever town they arrived. So, it would not be uncommon for the crew to have zero contact with him.

Nevertheless, Grandfather made it back without further incident, but with a dark sense of dread over his entire being. However, he should not have been surprised.

Grandfather dropped down on the cot in his trailer, the weight of the world on his shoulders, and removed the satchel containing the loot he had put up for auction. Diamonds, gold, and silver glistened despite the crummy light that streamed through the window of the door as he sunk deeper in the indentation of the overused mattress.

After forty years of menial jobs, the oldest David Jones thought this was his ticket out, his one-way ride into the big time. He needed to know what happened in his son's little shop, which was now becoming a little shop of horrors. It mattered naught, and he realized he should not have been the least bit surprised.

Grandfather rolled it back in his mind: he was behind Ian when the shot rang out. *Had one of them shot at me?* Or was it something more nefarious? The suspense was killing him, and he knew his time on earth was waning. His biggest concern now was whether Thom could hold up under pressure.

You bastard, he thought. *What have you done, my son?*

The eldest Jones *should* have known better:

Twenty-two years earlier, in the summer of 1967, his sons, David and Thom, found modest success with their little three-piece country trio, The Car Parkers Band. An homage to their hero Carl Perkins. (Original, right?) Their English country and western song, "Come Out to the Country," found airplay on BBC 1 Radio.

What? You never heard of the English country and western sound? That's because, thankfully, it died a quick death.

Grandfather, though, recognized an opportunity and quickly jumped into the act as their manager. But instead of booking them on a tour of the UK, he got them on an east coast tour with, of all groups, The Monkees, after reading their opening act, Jimi Hendrix, had just bailed their tour in July.

Two months earlier, The Beatles had released their masterpiece, "Sgt. Pepper's Lonely Hearts Club Band," and the musical landscape was changed forever. CPB had performed two shows on their way up the east coast, though it was Davey Jones of The Monkees, not David Jones of The Car Parkers Band that the audiences wanted to see.

By the time they reached Baltimore, which was supposed to be a momentous occasion—Grandfather's return to his hometown since leaving to fight in the war—it had all come to a screeching halt backstage at the Civic Center. Specifically, when Thom accused his younger brother of sleeping with his girlfriend back in England, of all things. Something the 18-year-old David Jones emphatically denied.

They got into a knock-down, all-out brawl, Thom punching one of David's front teeth literally down his throat (if you look closely, Mr. Jones's right front tooth is a shade darker than the rest). Albeit reluctantly, Grandfather took his eldest son's side in the kerfuffle. The two jetted back to England, breaking up the band and leaving David and their drummer, Nigel, to fend for themselves.

It was outside, sitting on a bus stop, nearly skint, that Mr. Jones would meet his future wife, Polly Parker. Polly and David hit it off, seeing it as a sign from God. She had bought her ticket to see, not The Monkees, but up-and-coming Jimi Hendrix. So instead of getting a refund, she opted to see The Monkees with their new opening act.

The three ended up in a White Castle restaurant where, of course, Polly characteristically did most of the talking. He joked later that he met his Nubian Queen outside a castle, and she, in turn, brought home an English King. Not as lucky, Nigel would have money wired to him on Sunday and returned to the UK the following day.

The following year, 1968, one of the most tumultu-ous years in America's history, Polly and David would marry, something far more acceptable in black circles than in white ones. Practically unheard of at that time. But they were more widely accepted in the black com-munity, at least to their faces, with people treating Mr. Jones as if he was one of The Beatles than they would have been in a white neighborhood.

Ian and I made our way back to The Royal Coat of Arms, where he gave me precise instructions before slipping through the back entrance to the pub. I went around and entered through the front door. A mid-dle-aged woman was behind the bar, talking to the only person in the pub, as I made my way to the upstairs door.

"Morning," the barmaid said. "Can I help you?"

"I was just going to see if Ian was here?"

"Well, he would be at work at this time," she said.

"Oh," I said, surprised by her reaction. "Even with the holiday?"

She considered that for a moment. "I suppose. Where are you from, love? Canada?"

"Um, yeah," I lied.

"Yeah, I've seen him a few times this week," the old geezer informed, flashing a toothless smile as he point-ed his cigarette-holding hand towards me. Ian Jones, I presume.

"May I check?"

"Sure, but you're probably wasting your time."

"Thanks," I said, waving my hand to them before slipping upstairs. I knocked on the door before going inside, where Sir immediately greeted me with a lick and a furiously wagging tail. Ian, having changed into new clothes, was switching through the channels on the TV. Finding nothing, he left it on with the volume down. I ran over and grabbed my guitar, practically embracing it as if it were Veronica. *Rather wish it was.*

"So what happened?" I asked.

"Looks like my dear ole dad fucked us royal," Ian said, having a seat on the edge of the bed, rubbing his temples as he tried to think. I had a seat in the not-so comfy chair, tightly clutching my shield of armor by Fender Stratocaster.

"Let me ask you something," I said. Ian rolled his eyes, clearly not wanting to talk, let alone answer any of my stupid questions. He had too many of his own that needed answering.

"Why me? Like, when did you guys come up with me as part of this plan?"

"Dunno, a few weeks ago. Needed someone we could trust."

"Someone you could trust? You guys don't even know me."

"We do now. Come on, let's show our faces downstairs."

Ian leaped from the bed and grabbed the doorknob; I slowly made my way out of the chair when I heard a crinkling in my pocket. Knowing there was no way it was money, I reached in and pulled it out. It was Grandfather's handwritten getaway directions. *Don't need that,* I thought, as I balled it up and threw it into the plastic bin by the wall.

"Hey, when something like this happens, don't they watch the airports and train stations for 48 hours?" I asked.

"That's only in the movies," Ian replied as he turned the doorknob. "But. you know, you may be right."

We headed downstairs to the pub, where we ordered some pints and sandwiches. It was exactly noon, and the bar had a substantial lunch crowd.

It was then that nearly all the televisions in the pub switched over to a Breaking News Story:

"An Oxford Street jeweler clings to life this afternoon after a robbery by two masked men this morning of Y&T Gold Brokers. Police are looking for at least two, possibly three, men in connection with the brazen early morning robbery. The Flying Squad is investigating. Authorities are also looking into a Volkswagen camper van found abandoned a few kilometers away to determine whether it was involved. If anyone has any information, they are asked to call Scotland Yard. In other news, a Traffic Warden was found—"

The Flying Squad conjured up images of cops with their arms outstretched, soaring through the London skies like giant birds.

"Right! Where were you two this morning?" Katie, the barmaid, asked Ian and me.

"I was probably rolling over and farting at that time of the morning," Ian said with a forced laugh.

"And you saw me," I said, nervously smiling.

"And you two?" she asked two blokes at the other end of the bar. "You have anyone that can vouch where you were this morning?"

"Look, if I made off with a bunch of loot, d'ya fink I'd be getting pissed in here of all places?"

A few of the punters laughed and proceeded to bark over one another, making it one big hodge-podge of whimsical bulls---.

"I just want a cut of the action, love," Katie said, laughing; the cigarette she was lighting bounced like a diving board between her lips.

The kitchen chef, a young guy with a cigarette dangling from his mouth, placed our sandwiches on the bar. Not a moment too soon, as I was bloody starving.

"Cheers," Ian said. He grabbed his plate and, with a tilt of his head, indicated for me to follow him to a nearby table. We sat down, and Ian proceeded to devour his sandwich like it was a defenseless animal. Despite how hungry I was, I could not bring myself to eat.

So instead, I just nibbled at it. I had no problem, however, finishing off my pint. Nor did Ian.

"Suppose we had better lay low today," Ian mumbled.

"I never got to see Buckingham Palace."

"Are you 'avin' a bubble, mate? Wha' wif all that's going on, that's your main concern?"

"What's a bubble?"

"Bubble. Bubble bath. A laugh. Are you 'avin' a laugh?" Ian finished his pint and took note of my empty glass. "It's your shout, mate?"

I considered the phrase, and with the day's events, I did just that. Screamed. "AAHHHHH!"

All the "punters," probably the first English slang I ever remembered, turned and scrutinized me for my sudden outburst. Ian eyed me with such disdain that I could see the steam coming off his head. "It's your round, mate."

"Oh, I've only got about four or five pounds," I admitted.

After Ian finished taking me to task, I approached the bar and ordered a pair of pints.

"Three pounds, love," she said, plopping two pints on the bar. I handed her my last four pounds; she held up the fourth coin, flashing a perplexed smile my way.

"Keep it," I said.

"Ta?" she replied with a shrug, setting it on the side of the register.

Returning to the pool table with our pints in each hand, I asked Ian why the barmaid gave me such a weird reaction. "Pound's an insult? It's almost two bucks."

"You don't tip barmen in England, stupid git," Ian said, snatching one of the pint glasses. I jerked my head back as if hit. Again. "You buy 'em a drink," he said, softer.

"Oh."

We spent the entire day drinking and playing billiards. Ian, not surprisingly, excelled at the game. Me, not so much. We kept our conversation to a minimum as our respective minds reeled at the day's events. Our only conversation was when Ian won another game.

"You ever hustle for money?" I asked him, getting Ian's only smirk of the day. A smug one at that.

At one point, I nipped off to the loo where, just before entering the stall, I snatched a newspaper from atop the bin and took it in with me.

On the front page: "BRAZEN MORNING JEWELRY HEIST"

They apparently love the word 'brazen' in England, I thought, as I scanned the article, which contained scarce new information. 'Examining CCTV footage... partner distraught' (*yeah, right*).

Or were they lying to me? I wondered.

'Owner mistook robbers for security hired for auction.' *Nice touch. Jesus, they might get away with it, after all*, I thought. *We*, I reminded myself.

Ian proved he was a hustler by playing a couple of sad sacks, winning a few pints, and eventually pocketing some cold, hard cash. I was well impressed.

In what turned out to be the highlight of my day, maybe even of my week, Ian nipped off to take care of something, and a bloke approached me, asking me if I wanted to play since we had been on one of the two tables all day. He asked if I wanted to play for money which I quickly rejected, but after some prodding, I reluctantly agreed to play for a beer, hoping, if I lost, Ian would "shout it out."

As it was my table, I got the break. And what a break it was, sinking the 8-ball and winning the game.

"You know you just won, mate."

"I know," I replied, a smile tearing across my face.

"Double or nothing?"

"No, thank you, I'll just take the beer."

"Should we at least finish out the game?"

"Sure."

He bought me a pint, and we played the remainder of the game with the 9-ball acting as the eight-ball. On the very last shot, I hit the cue ball with such force that it clipped the nine, which, in turn, bounced off the sides three times. Ian casually strolled back in just as the nine rolled into the side pocket.

"What's that look all about?" Ian asked me.

"I just won this game. Twice!" The geezer nodded, confirming what I said.

"LAST ORDERS!"

A pair of Holsten Pils in hand, we headed upstairs to Ian's room, where we were greeted again by Sir Drops-A-Lot, who had kept true to his name, leaving several piles for Ian to clean up.

Not much of a life for a dog, I thought as I reached for the drawstring to the overhead light. Ian grabbed my wrist.

"Let's leave it off, mate. For the time being." I nodded in understanding, sitting on the edge of the bed.

Ian switched on the television and flicked through the four channels. Eventually, he found what he was looking for—a news report.

"Closed-Circuit Television Video was released this evening, showing the brazen robbery today (*there's that word 'brazen' again*, I thought) of Y&T Pawn Brokers in Oxford Street where the robbers made off—

"Pardon the interruption, but you keep saying Y&T Brokers? This is about the Smarte-Bixby robbery, is it not?" the Interviewer inquired.

"Well, I think he changed the name. You know, for obvious reasons," Robbin offered.

The Interviewer nodded with pursed lips. "But not *Ian's* name. Interesting."

"If I'm not mistaken, Y&T is an American rock group."

"Thieves made off with an undisclosed amount of jewels," the female newsreader announced from the papers in her hands before the footage enlarged on the screen. "The two masked robbers enter the store waving guns. As one can see, the owners' hands immediately go up in the air, clearly complying. One of them smashes a case, removing what the owner identified as a sizeable 3-strand pearl necklace, while the other holds a satchel that one of the owners fills from a display tray.

"We must warn you: the following footage is graphic—the robbers force the men onto the floor and, as you can see, turn to leave when the owner manages to get to his feet." One of the robbers appeared on the left side of the screen; a flash from his gun could be seen emitting before the robber backed out of view.

"The owner, Irving Tannenbaum, was rushed to hospital in critical condition. His partner, Thomas Jones, seen here, is assisting with the investigation."

"Look at the old queen," Ian said with contempt.

"Witnesses say that a camper van was seen driving off and was later found abandoned a few miles away. Police are seeking the public's help.

"In other news, The Bomb Squad was dispatched to Victoria Station after a mysterious suitcase was found unattended in a telephone kiosk. Police do not believe the two incidents are related but are continuing their investigation. A Traffic Warden in Knightsbridge was found--"

Ian turned to me, blocking the TV. "You know that wasn't us, right? I mean, you can tell by the footage that wasn't us, right?"

I shrugged and tried to speak, but no words came out.

"Oh for fuck sakes, mate, that's not us!" Ian walked out of the room into the hallway, leaving the door open. Then, spotting another resident, he did a 180° and returned inside the room, closing the door. Next, he walked vigorously towards the window, his muscles flexing as he shoved it open.

"So, you're saying your father did that," I said more than asked.

"Well, I doubt the old man did it to himself!" he yelled a little too loud, pausing to take a deep breath. "That was *not* us."

"And I suppose that wasn't one of you that smashed the case and took that necklace, either."

"I didn't want to make it *too* obvious." Ian reached into his pocket and withdrew the necklace. "*You* want it?!" Ian said, tossing it in my direction.

"No, thank you." I karate-chopped it away in midair. It landed in front of Ian's pillow. "I got to be honest. Up until you guys came running out, I thought you were throwing me a surprise party."

"You wha'??" Ian erupted into maniacal laughter. "Rather wish we had. We are so fucked."

"I can't go to prison. Look at me!"

Sir began sniffing at the gap under the door to the room.

"Oy, Sir, you can't have to shit again," Ian barked at Sir. "Should I take him out?"

"No, I'll take him."

Ian grabbed a lead, attaching it to his collar as a thunderclap made us both jolt, followed by the sound of falling rain.

"Of course," Ian said, leading Sir out for a walk. I got up and grabbed my guitar to noodle on as I began pacing back and forth.

Thinking I heard a click from the door, I spun around.

"That was quick," I said, though I could see no one was there.

A bright streak of lightning preceded another thunderclap, revealing a silhouetted figure in the reflection of the window.

I lunged for the drawstring, pulling it; the light quickly flickered out.

"What is with me and lights?" I mumbled.

"I don't know, what is it with you and lights?" the familiar-sounding voice asked from the shadows.

The light came on. I was in mid-turn when I found a man with his hand on the light switch on the wall. Under the country gentleman's hat, the man slowly lifted his head, revealing himself to be none other than Uncle Thomas!

I stopped dead in my tracks. My only recourse was to pull down on the string, still in my hand. The light turned off.

"Hey, turn that back on," Thomas retorted, flicking on and off the light switch.

I pulled on the string, but it didn't work. Thomas lifted the switch, and the light blinked back on before I pulled it again. The room went dark.

"Cut that out!" Thomas said before the light came back on.

I felt my wrist grabbed as Thom pulled it down, bringing the light back to life before I yanked it away and backed towards the window.

"Well, well, well, look what ran out of the end of my little brother's cock," Uncle Thomas said warmly with just a dash of menace.

I was beside myself as he folded a T-shirt of Ian's then ran his white-gloved finger across the TV stand. "Waiter! There's a blonde pube in my blood pudding. Come here and give your Uncle Thom a kiss."

I stood frozen.

"I'd first like to welcome you onboard the Jonestown Express. You've got an interesting family, kiddo."

Oh, Ian, oh Ian, oh Ian, please come back, was all that kept running through my mind.

"I said," he lunged, grabbing me in a massive bear hug. "Give us a kiss!"

I struggled to escape his grasp, but Thomas was too strong. We slammed against the window, shattering it. Pieces of glass glistened in the moonlight.

"HELP! IAN!"

"Speaking of bastards, where is that son of mine?"

"He'll be back any second," I said urgently. "And if he finds you here, he'll--"

"He'll what?"

"I don't know, but it won't be pretty."

"I'm shakin' in my shoes." Uncle Thomas let go long enough to spin me around, clasping my mouth with his gloved hand. "See, you're coming with me to the hospital. There's a little plug I need UNplugging."

I pulled his hand away. "Look, I don't know what you want from me. I just thought maybe I could meet a nice nurse, maybe get shagged."

"Stop me if you've heard this: A young boy runs up to his father and says, 'Daddy! There are two people making love in the bushes!' The father says, 'It is Paris. The City of Love. It's au natural!' 'Yes, but Daddy, the woman, she is dead.' 'What?' The father runs to the bushes and finds the man shagging away. He runs down a police officer. 'Officer! Officer! There are two people making love in the bushes!' The policeman says, 'It is Paris. The City of Love, it's au natural.' The father says, 'Yes, but the woman, she is dead!' 'What?' He runs to the bushes and finds the man shagging away. 'Sir, you are making love in the bushes!' The man looks over his shoulder and says, 'It is Paris. The City of Love. It's au natural! 'Yes, but the woman, she is dead!' The man says, 'No, she is not dead. She is *English*!'"

I scoffed just as Sir entered the room, still on his lead, followed by Ian to find the ensuing commotion. I was never so happy to see anyone.

———

"Ian!"

"What are you doing, Dad?!" Sir began growling and barking.

"We made a real mess of it today, didn't we?"

"No, Dad, that was all you. Now could you let go of David before he wets his Y-fronts?"

"Oh, he's all right, Jack," he said before speaking loudly into my ear. "We're just getting ourselves acquainted, aren't we Davey boy?"

Ian followed his father's gaze over the bed and the glistening necklace. "Nobody said anything about smashing cases."

"Yeah, well, nobody said anything about attempted murder either!"

"Touchy touchy. I could have had it ALL! Guess I just got a little too greedy," he replied, each word raising one octave after another, not unlike Veronica's laugh.

"D'ya think?"

Sir charged at Thom, yanking the lead from Ian's grasp, and clenched his jaw onto Thom's foot; he screamed, letting go of me to fend off the dog. Ian gave him a rugby tackle while pulling my shirt. Thomas fell backward into the window, smashing out the glass, Sir's teeth embedded into the bone. Ian grabbed the dog's tail and yanked him back with a yelp, releasing Thom's foot, sending him flailing out the window with a scream that sounded all too familiar. A cry I knew all too well. My father.

Ian and I rushed to the window to find Thomas lying spread-eagled on the pavement.

"Jesus," we both said in unison.

"Stay here," Ian said.

Ian left me with Sir, both of us badly shaken.

"You ok, Oyster?" I said, crouching down to pet him.

Outside, Thomas rolled over with a grimace and a grunt and apparently made his way to his feet. Then, what must have looked like a reanimated corpse, Thomas limped around the pub where he had to have been gasping for air and hailed a passing mini-cab.

"Where to, sir?" the driver asked. The passenger awkwardly climbed in, closing the door, and sat in silence. Blood was reportedly expelling from his nostrils.

The cab driver, a man of Sikh descent, eyed him impatiently in the rear-view mirror. "Sir?" He repeated, turning to get a better view of his passenger whose eyes were lifeless, vacant. "You alright, cunt?"

Ian ran around the corner to find his father gone. He kicked at a couple of shards of glass and looked up at the broken window. He continued around the rest of the pub, not seeing hide nor hair of him, just a black cab passing by.

The driver arrived at hospital and ran inside to get help, returning moments later with two hospital attendants pushing a gurney with the utmost urgency. "He just got in my taxi, and I don't know!" They opened the back door and began testing him for alertness and checking his vitals.

"Can you hear me, sir? Do you know your name?"

To her partner: "I am getting a pulse. Non-responsive. Let's get him inside."

They maneuvered him out of the back seat and onto the gurney with the utmost care, rolling him into hospital.

"I doubt that's the last we'll be seeing of him tonight. You might as well sleep here," Ian told me, indicating the chair. "Just don't get any ideas. I'm likely to kill."

"Sleep? Yeah, right. I don't see that happening any time soon."

Ian finished the last of his beer and set the bottle down. He pulled the chain to the light and dropped back onto the bed.

"Ian? Are we in big trouble?"

Ian merely chortled, dismissing me, or so I thought until I detected light snoring coming from him. I sat back in the chair, clutching my guitar as if it were an assault rifle, feeling I was on all-night watch.

Chapter
XIV

Delirium kicked in for the most terrifying situation of my short life on this planet: The Flying Squad burst into the room through the windows and doors to find me and Ian naked in each other's arms.

It jolted me awake, where I looked over to find that I was alone in the empty bed. *When did I move here?*

No maniacal uncle had murdered us in our sleep. And, of course, Ian was nowhere to be found. Or did he get Ian and was now waiting for me somewhere? I checked all around the room. No note. Just Sir Drops-A-Lot, who was thrilled to see me, licking my face, wagging his tail.

I slid on my jeans, which seemed baggier than the day before; granted, I had hardly eaten, couldn't even remember the last thing I had (was it a bag of crisps?). I then found a 10-pound note in my front pocket! Was it meant for me? I convinced myself it was before slipping it back in my pocket. Next, I went to the bathroom down the hall, did my business, splashed some water on my face, and tried to run my fingers through my tangled bush.

My last day in England; my first as a not-as-of-yet wanted man.

I looked through Ian's wardrobe for a change of shirts and found a tattered old punk shirt and studded belt and couldn't resist. Slipping the shirt on and pulling the belt strap through the loops of my jeans, I gave a Sid Vicious-like sneer in the mirror before flipping myself off.

Having a few hours to kill before returning to Tent City to grab my gear and catch my flight, I decided to have one last go at finding the Palace. I slung my guitar over my shoulder and gave Sir a good scratch behind the ear.

"Be a good boy," I told him. 'You too,' I thought he might say back to me; it certainly applied, I felt, before sneaking down the back stairs of the pub.

As I was walking across Westminster Bridge, whistling "London Bridge is Falling Down" and waving good-bye to Big Ben, Ian had made his way over to the hospital after not finding his father at home. He first had to slip in through a second-story window to avoid the police car sitting out front. There, Ian switched into some more respectable clothes left behind over a year ago. Knowing he was risking everything by being so bold, Ian was determined to get to the bottom of things. He made his way to the nursing station, where things were bustling.

I stopped to view a statue of Oliver Cromwell. I knew the name, but I could not pinpoint his place in history. Little did I know it was the name of a street exit on Baltimore's 6-95.

"Can I help you?" Cromwell asked.

"I'm looking for my dad," Ian said morosely. "He's probably here visiting his partner, Irving Tannenbaum. Brought in yesterday? Gunshot wound?"

She looked down a roster of patients, her finger stopping on Tannenbaum, Irving. "Yes, he's in room 310, but no one can go up right now."

"Do you know if his partner is upstairs? Thomas Jones?" She again ran her fingers down the roster. "He wouldn't be a patient. He'd be a visitor."

"No, we have a Jones, Thomas. Brought in early this morning."

"You're 'avin' a b—. You're joking. What's happened? No one ever said *he* was hurt, as well."

"You said you're family, yeah?" the nurse asked, her eyebrows furrowing up as she did.

"I can help you with that, sir," said a voice from behind Ian. He recognized the portly old man immediately.

"Would you mind stepping over here, please?" He led Ian aside to a waiting area. "I'm Detective Brompton of Scotland Yard," he informed as he withdrew a small notepad. "And you are?"

"Liam Jones."

"Only child, is that correct?"

"Liam Jones?" Starling again interjected.

"He goes by his middle name. Liam Ian Jones. His full name is Liam Ian Arthur Jones."

"I find it amusing that he used their real names."

"Ian was not amused. He felt he grassed him up."

Starling slowly nodded.

"What's happened to my dad?" Ian urgently asked. To the trained ear, Ian was speaking in an octave slightly higher than his usual speaking voice. It lent itself to a more innocent demeanor, almost naive if you will.

"Your father was brought in by a mini-cab driver a little after midnight last night. He was non-responsive, having contusions about the head and back as if he had taken quite a fall."

"Is he ok? Can I see him?"

"Let's walk and talk," Detective Brompton said. Then, indicating the vending machines they were passing, "Would you like a coffee or tea?"

"No, no, I just want to see my dad. How did he end up in the same hospital? Where did they find him?"

"The cab driver, a nice man from India, was so distraught that he cannot exactly remember. But that's not important now," Brompton replied.

Ian, though not showing it, was pleased to hear that. "You *do* know about the robbery of their shop yesterday?"

"Yeah, I couldn't believe it was their shop. How is Mr. Irving?"

They reached the lift where Detective Brompton pressed the UP button. "They think he may never walk again. Or see again."

"Oh my lord," Ian said, genuinely surprised, as the doors opened. They waited for an elderly couple to make their way off before stepping on. Brompton touched the button for the third floor before the door closed. Ian hated the smell of hospitals.

"Now, Mr. Jones, forgive me for my next question, but I do have to ask." Ian watched the numbers above the door as they illuminated, first the two, then the three. "Where were you yesterday around 9 a.m.?"

"I was home, well, I mean, I live above a pub. The Royal Court of Arms. Was there all day. You certainly don't think I had something to do with this?"

The bell rang, and the elevator door opened. Brompton was still writing in his notepad as he followed Ian out. "And someone there can verify that?"

"Absolutely," Ian said, stopping to wait for Brompton to lead the way.

Brompton finished his notes and said, "Good. And no, I do not think you had anything to do with this." He put his hand on Ian's shoulder as he led Ian down the hallway to room 320.

Inside, Ian's father was lying motionless in bed, tubes in his nose and mouth, EKG rhythmically beeping.

"Now, doctors say that he did come to, briefly, and was talking, but Ian, prepare yourself for what I am about to tell you."

Ian turned to give his first proper up and down look of the detective. His eyes darted back and forth with nervous anticipation.

"It appears your father has no recollection as to what happened to him at all yesterday. In fact, he has no memory of who he is," Brompton informed him.

Ian desperately refrained from not smiling. If this were true, he thought to himself. We might just get away with it. Karma, eh?

"Rubbish," Ian said. He approached the side of the bed and drew his face close to his father's. Then, with his voice still that one octave higher, he shouted, "DAD!"

His father remained motionless.

"No cause for worry. He's heavily sedated," the detective informed Ian.

Ian lowered his head onto his father's chest, wiping away an imaginary tear.

"I'll be back, ya bastard," he whispered in his father's ear.

Next, Detective Brompton led Ian to Mr. Tannenbaum's room. If he had not been told it was him, Ian would have never known it was the seventy-year-old man. Like his father, he too was hooked to various machines, blinking and beeping. His bald head was wrapped down to his neck, with another bandage wrapped around his chest. The nurse attending to him barely paid the two men any mind.

"Jesus," Ian muttered.

"Are you a religious man, Mr. Jones?"

"I'm Jewish, but I don't pay it much mind."

"Well, if you do pray, include him in your prayers. He's going to need it."

Ian lowered his head and stared at his feet. There was a long silence.

Standing up straight, he asked, "Can I make a special request?"

Three times I set out for the Palace, three times I failed; three-time loser. I had no idea how close I had gotten. Again. If I had just followed the path around Hyde Park, I could have seen Buckingham Palace with all that so-called pomp and majesty, but I had given up. So I found a pub, instead, called "The Spread Eagle" on Great Peter Street. Accident? I think not.

I remembered the chance meeting with the Rasta bass player on the bus the other night and knew one thing for sure: I could undoubtedly find The New Zealand House. I remembered passing it so many times on my way in and out of Piccadilly Circus and Leicester Square.

On Haymarket Street, I passed a newspaper stand where every headline was about the robbery. I was thankful money was scarce because I would have bought them all—best souvenir EVER!

I hope I keep my sense of humor in English jail.

I was not only able to find the Embassy of the Kiwis but walking through the massive lobby, I found the little alley behind it, with its expensive-looking antique stores and such. A wealthy couple passed by, the young woman showed off her ring to the older man in the pinstriped suit. In the shop window, the Rasta must have been referring to was a computer-generated job list. I slipped inside and purchased one for 80p, or about a buck and a half.

Perusing the list of Live-In jobs while I walked, I found there was plenty. After I landed at a bus stop, I determined which would take me back to Tent City with one transfer. As I waited, I took note of the little video shop behind me.

A bell rang above my head as I entered and wandered the aisles until I found what I was looking for, a video box for the movie "Highlander." The same film I watched with Veronica on our fateful night together.

The art design on the UK version depicted the cast in various scenes from the movie. It was a far cry from the US release, which merely showed the Highlander, Christopher Lambert, in a trench coat holding a sword out in front of him.

I had initially seen "Highlander" at The Downtown 6 by my house on a weekday afternoon. With maybe two other people in the entire cinema, I took a seat in the back row, not knowing what to expect. But I was so blown away by the opening scene, along with that pulsing Queen soundtrack, I made my way up to the center row and plopped down, knowing I was in store for something special. And, boy was I right.

When it was released on video the next year, I bought a copy on VHS, but I never liked the cover. So, when I was certain no one was looking, I slipped the empty box under my shirt and casually walked out of the store. It would have been fun to see when they finally figured it was missing: "There can be only one box."

Bypassing the bus stop for fear of being caught, I rushed through a bustling Chinatown where the shop windows were filled with the carcasses of various animals and mock-ups of different dishes that the respective restaurants served. I eventually made my way into Soho.

I was reminded that Soho was a bit sleazy, and that suited me fine. I stopped at a food cart and bought myself a gyro (pronounced "year-o," not "gyro", as most people call it).

Inhaling it as if it was the last meal on earth, and there was no saying it wasn't, the most horrific woman approached me. Wearing a ratty fake fur coat and high heels, her hair looked as if it had been hacked with a butter knife. She reminded me of a joke my father often repeated: There goes one of the Lee sisters, Beastly. Or, in this case, Ghastly.

"Juwannagoround, love?" she incoherently asked as she leaned against the kebab cart before jumping forward. "Oh, hot."

"Huh?" I did not understand what she said but thinking she might be asking me for the time, I checked my watch. "One o'clock," I said, tzatziki sauce running down the side of my mouth. I wiped it off with the back of my hand and walked around the corner into a small alley where I leaned against a brick wall and continued eating.

As I stood there stuffing my ever-fattening face, I noticed two hard-bitten blokes standing a few feet away. They stood silently, and I wondered what they might be up to.

"You waitin' for a prozzie, too?" the one asked, directing the question to me. "They're a bit scarce today."

"Tha's *alrigh'. I'm in no 'urry*," I responded for a bit of a laugh.

Ghastly came around the corner, eyeing me up again. *Here's one, fellas*, I thought to myself.

"Yachangeyourmind, love?" she asked, this time a bit more coherent.

"Sorry?" *Why are people always chatting me up?*

This time she spoke her slowest and clearest: "I asked you earlier if you wanted to go 'round."

Swallowing my last bite, I finally understood what she was getting at.

"*Whatchu mean?*" I asked, now just trying to get a rise out of her.

Just then, a police Jag rolled around the corner and stopped beside us. Two coppers were inside as the driver rolled his window down.

"You," the cop said. I pointed to myself in question, thinking, *Oh shit*. "Yeah, you. Up against the wall." I thought of Pink Floyd as I turned to face The Wall.

My heart began pounding as I scanned the area for a place to escape, but not much in the way of options. Finally, I looked over my shoulder at "Miss Lee" approaching the police car. "Didn't I tell you the other night I didn't want to see you around here anymore?" the cop forcefully suggested.

"Oh, yeah," she said. "I remember you."

"Good, now get a move on, ya old tart."

"I'm going," she oozed as she turned and awkwardly hobbled away in her big, white scrump-me pumps. The Jag followed closely behind her until she turned right and disappeared around the corner. The cops watched her for a bit before turning left. I nearly buckled to my knees.

"*Wha' a fuckin' cow,*" I said to the two blokes, whose attention was now diverted down towards the other end of the alley.

———

Bad English
the III

"Is that her?" the second bloke asked his mate.

"Wouldn't *shag that slag wif my dog's dick*," I continued. *"I mean, I'd 'ave to get a dog first."* I recalled I *had* a dog.

At home.

Home. I've been in London longer. I knew as much about home as I did the gender of that dog. The first bloke turned to size me up. "Where ya from, mate?"

In light of my reply to the punk rockers, I surprisingly exclaimed, "The States."

"The States? Why you talkin' like that, then?"

"Dunno, bored, I guess," I admitted, with the emphasis on 'bored.'

The two blokes laughed.

"American Wanker in London," the second bloke said with a chuckle. A scantily dressed black prozzie with a straight blonde wig gained the men's attention by waving him down. "I'm up. Wish me luck."

The second bloke slapped his mate on the back and shuffled off down the alley, leaving his pal standing idle beside me. We both stepped back and leaned against the brick wall. I looked up the road where The Raymond Revue Bar stood aglow, in its pink and red neon lights. I asked the bloke if he'd like to go in and have a drink. He shrugged, which I assumed meant 'Why not?'

"Yea? Cool, let's go."

We both walked up the alley towards the club and the small steps that preceded it, where a woman sat behind a small make-shift desk.

"Six pounds, two-drink minimum," the woman said matter-of-factly before pointing to the camera under my arm. "And no pictures."

"No problem," I assured her as I pulled that ten-pound note out of my pocket and handed it to her. She pulled out a drawer and quickly replaced it with four one-pound coins, dropping them in my sweaty palm and waved me past. I looked over my shoulder, waiting for my new-found drinking buddy to plunk down his six pounds, but he remained motionless, only looking over his shoulder.

"You coming?" The bloke slowly shook his head. "But I just...are you serious?" Resigned, I turned and began down the small hallway that led to a winding staircase with multi-colored walls of pink and purple.

When I reached the bottom landing, I passed through a doorway of hanging floor-length hippie beads (like those that hung in the entrance of our kitchen my entire childhood) into a sublimely dark, medium-sized room. Music played loudly but not enough that one could not hear the buzz of conversations coming from the few tables in the middle, all but one occupied by men who all seemed to be from various European countries.

One fold-up card table consisted of four scantily dressed women talking amongst themselves. At the far end of the room was a small bar. To get to it, you either had to pass through the tables or along the right side, lined with booths with drapes that were either open or closed for privacy.

I especially took note of the folded-up, roll-away bed that sat along the left side of the room as I made my way to the bar and spun a menu around to read. The barman flat-out ignored me. Instead, one of the negligeed women, a dirty-blonde-haired gal with decent enough curves, approached my left, picked up the menu, and led me to one of the booths, laying it on the table without saying a word. I sat down, sliding in to accommodate her as she made it clear by her movements that she would be joining me. I opened the fancy leather-like menu and could not believe the prices: A six-pound lager, an eight-pound lager, or a ten-pound glass of Champagne.

"What can I get you, love?"

"I'll have a lager," I said, specifically pointing at the cheapest drink on the menu.

She grimaced, slamming it shut as she stepped out from the booth and made her way back over the bar. I scanned the room, unimpressed by what my six-pound entry was getting me. Finally, the hostess returned with a small plastic cup of lager, the same I used on the plane, and set it on the table in front of me. *Six pounds for that?!*

"Buy me a drink, love?" the hostess asked me, grabbing the table with a bit of a wiggle of her hips. *Is that supposed to turn me on?* I wondered as I fished another two pounds from my pocket to combine the four still in my hand and placed them on the table.

"Maybe later," I quipped. Then, taking a sip before following it with a purposely obnoxious: "Aaaah."

"Cheap bastard," she mumbled as she scooped up the coins, pushing herself back away from the table before clickety-clopping in her heels back to her table of hostesses, probably all collectively groaning at the poor excuses for men that afternoon.

I slid on my Lennon shades and decided to nurse my six-pound beer for every penny it was worth, trying not to dwell on the UK to US conversion. Waiting for the upcoming show, I figured the tiny stage and the roll-away bed were not there for nothing. *Bring on the showgirls*, I thought salaciously.

It was then that one of the two men at the table closest to the hostesses leaned over and asked with an accent that was anything but English, "When's the next show, love?"

"Sorry, love," she replied with all the pleasantness of a prison guard. "No shows in the afternoons."

That does it, I thought, having reached my zenith of disgust. I slammed my beer, about two tablespoons worth, climbed out, and at a furious pace, made my way to the illuminated EXIT sign opposite the stairs that led into this shithole.

"See ya, ya poxy prat!" my charming hostess shouted as I pushed my way through the exit door.

Oh yeah? I thought, *I'll fix your trolley, baby.* I stopped the door from shutting entirely and whipped my camera out, switching it on. Then, I pushed my specs up into my hair and swung the door back open.

Taking notice of the table of men that asked about the show, his friend pointed me out as I snapped a photo with a bright, blinding flash in the otherwise dark room. One of the Negligees had followed the man's pointing finger and had covered her face in time. The other women, including my mouthy hostess, jumped up and ran in opposite directions, like rats on a sinking ship. Finally, the one who had covered her face ran towards me. The two guys clapped and laughed, high-fiving each other.

As I tried to gather my gear, I let the door go; it caught the side of my head, knocking my sunglasses to the floor in the gap of the door. The hostess grabbed the door as I backed off, looking back over my shoulder. She stomped on my specs, grinding them into the ground as if putting out a fag. I was as crushed as my glasses. One of the last things I could remember my mother ever giving me.

I ran up the steps at a hurried pace as I ran around another corner, briefly spotting the two prozzie blokes, their arms briefly patting each other on their backs, implying, to the keen eye, two satisfied customers. Then, spotting a double-decker idling by a bus stop, I hopped on without even looking at its destinations.

It had taken several hours, but the staff finally adhered to Ian's request that his father's bed be moved into the same room as his partner's.

"They're partners in every sense of the word, if you know what I mean," Ian had told one of the more sympathetic nurses. In reality, however, he just wanted to be able to keep a better eye on them. Worst case scenario, Ian rationalized in his mind, maybe they'll off each other.

I returned to Tent City with enough time to shower, change and grab my gear to head back to Gatwick Airport. As I sat on the bench to get dressed, shoving everything in my bag, including my ill-gotten "Highlander" video case, a couple of Frenchies were standing nearby. A fat one and a tall, thin one.

The Fat one watched and listened as the Slender one spoke in French with such aplomb that I could not help but look up to see if he was expressing his anger towards the Fat one. Slender put a piece of paper up against the wall and dramatically slapped it repeatedly before letting it fall to the floor and walking out of the room. My eyes connected with Fat's, and we shared a little chuckle between us. Just then, Slender walked back into the room and saw the smirks on both of our faces, directing a question to me in French.

"What's that?" I replied, pulling my duffel bag out of the parachute bag.

Slender repeated the question in his native tongue.

"I'm sorry," I said, my eyes darting from Slender to Fat Frenchie for help. He was utterly useless.

"Do you speak French?" he asked.

"No, I don't."

Slender threw his arms up in the air as if to say to his friend, 'My point exactly!' Or something to that effect.

I opened one of the new cassettes I bought at Tower Records in Piccadilly, took the one I listened to on my way here out of the Walkman, and slid it in, figuring at least I could drown out the rest of the world on my way home. I pressed play and could hear it starting to roll. And then came the worst sound known to man, a high-pitched scribbly sound. I quickly stopped the tape, opened it up, and pulled the cassette out, along with three feet of tape!

Noooooooooo, I screamed in my head. *I need a pencil.* I wrapped the tape around the cassette and discreetly chucked it into my bag. *That'll fix it right up.*

I grabbed the parachute bag and its lock, squeezed past the two Frenchmen, and plopped them up on the counter. The French girl behind it looked at the number on the bag, leaned underneath, and returned my passport. Two blonde Aussie backpackers had just walked in, and so I grew a little bold as I put my passport in my pocket before unleashing on the Slender Frenchman standing in the doorway of the men's restroom/ changing area.

"OH YEAH? I'M SORRY I DON'T SPEAK YOUR STUPID FUCKING LANGUAGE! YOU PEOPLE ARE RUDE! YOU STOLE MY TOOTHPASTE!! AND YOU ALL SMELL EVEN AFTER YOU TAKE A SHOWER!!!"

Slender turned and shrugged at the fat Frenchman. The Aussies broke out into laughter.

"You tell 'em, mate!" one of the Aussies said. The French girl's eyes widened as she lit a cigarette.

I made my way out of the building, feeling victorious.

"So you can confirm he was here?"

"Yeah, all day," Katie, the barmaid, said, leaning against the cold shelves. "Drank lagers and played pool."

"So, other people saw him, as well?" Detective Brompton asked.

"Oh, yeah, lots of my regulars."

"By himself?"

"No, he was with a bloke, his cousin, I think he said. Canadian, if I recall. He tried to tip me a pound coin. Gave me a chuckle."

"A Canadian, eh?" Brompton asked, his comic attempt at sounding Canadian. Ian had not mentioned that.

"Maybe American?" she offered.

"And these are the only stairs up?" he asked, indicating the stairway behind the adjacent door.

"No, there's a back stairway, as well."

"Right, cheers," Brompton said, closing his notepad.

"You don't really think he had something to do with that robbery, do you?" she asked.

He slipped his notepad into the inside pocket of his gray blazer. "My primary function is to work my way from the inside out. Elimination without discrimination, love," the detective offered. "Keep my visit here, mum, if you would, please." Katie nodded as the detective made his way out the door.

Katie, however, could not wait. Instead, she ran back into the kitchen to tell the cook of the latest developments.

To the English, a secret is something they tell everyone in confidence. They cannot keep a single solitary secret to save their souls. Likely from watching all "Eastenders" and "Neighbours" rubbish their whole lives.

Outside, Brompton walked around the pub. He pulled on the back door and found it locked. When he reached the far side of the building, he brushed some rather large shards of glass on the far end of the cement with his less than shiny shoes. Looking up, he squinted, not from the sun but to get a sharper look, taking note of the broken window. Ian's window, to be exact. He withdrew his notepad and wrote in it before returning it and the pen to his pocket.

After a transfer on the tube, I arrived at Victoria Station, not weirdly familiar but almost second-hand to me as I made my way through the bustling thoroughfare. Something caught my eye, something I had expected to see more of, but to the best of my recollection, I had not seen once—a typical bowler hat-wearing Englishman swinging an umbrella by his side. It made me chuckle as I approached the ticket machine to purchase my ticket, pressing the Gatwick Airport button for it. Nine pounds twenty. I checked my pockets, knowing full well that I had probably about three pounds in coins. I could try to board the train and play stupid. Not a hard thing to do, I reckoned.

What other choice did I have?

I checked the giant sign for the correct platform and made my way to it, where people were already boarding. I got on, purposefully avoiding the First Class carriage. *Maybe if I just shuck and jive*, I figured, I could get away with it.

The train was surprisingly crowded, so I considered myself more than lucky to find a seat next to an attractive brunette about my age, sitting across from a thirty-something couple. She smiled politely, her big oval eyes widening as she did. I heaved the bag up onto the overhead steel rack, and like a spider, I sat down beside her.

After a few moments, they made a last 'All Aboard' announcement, and the train lurched forward, then jerked to the right, nearly sending me into the lap of my newfound traveling companion. Not that I minded, mind you.

Settling in, the couple across from us engaged me and her in conversation. They asked me what I was doing in England, how I liked it, and my name. It turned out that the woman was the older sister of the girl beside me, Karen, who had just finished her A-levels (whatever that meant). Her sister and her American husband had come from Seattle to attend her graduation.

"Oh, I graduate next week, too," I lied, unaware I was telling the truth.

"From University, as well?" Karen asked.

"Well, no, but my birthday is the 18th."

Karen laughed, as well as her sister. "Mine, too!"

I smiled as we simultaneously both said, "Paul McCartney! Jinx!"

We all shared a good chuckle, looking at each other with pure joy in our eyes.

"How would you like to come to live with me in my flat," I heard her say. In my head.

I looked down. Unbeknownst to her, her hand was pressing down on my leg just above my left knee. She looked out the window with anticipation for something.

"There it is," she said, pointing out the window with excitement. "Pink Floyd, Animals."

Outside, the train passed a rather dilapidated factory featured on one of the classic psychedelic group's album covers--without the giant pig.

She looked from her brother-in-law to me. "You like Pink—"

"Floyd," I said in awe.

She looked down, and spotting her hand on my leg, quickly pulled it away, mortified.

"I've been leaning on his leg for about the past five minutes thinking it was the seat!"

To me: "Why didn't you say anything?"

"What was I going to say? Excuse me, would you mind taking your hand off my knee, please?"

We all chattered again. I connected with Karen's eyes, as we were at the same eye level.

I looked up the aisle at a newspaper someone was reading: "Hunt on for Jewel Robbers." My eyes shifted to the couple across from me. I must have looked as if I had seen a ghost.

"Tickets, please," the Conductor said as he approached.

Chapter
XV

Just when I finally met a girl that did not want to hate me or spank me, I parted ways with the three from the train, all wishing each other well. I insisted on paying them back for the train ticket, a suggestion at which they, thankfully, scoffed.

As was par for the course, I found the TWA ticket counter and got in line, bypassing a security checkpoint. When the oblivious agent finally discovered it, I was re-routed to the front of the queue, where I was asked the three crucial security questions.

"And lastly, has your bag been in your possession the entire time?"

"Yes."

"Right, there you are," the agent said, returning my ticket and passport and directing me to my departure gate. I heaved my bag over my shoulder and whistled while I walked.

"Excuse me, sir, could you come this way, please?" a deep, gravelly voice from behind me said, pulling on my arm. My stomach locked tight as I turned to find Ian with a big Cheshire grin on that ugly mug of his.

"You almost gave me a bloody heart attack," I mumbled, looking all around the terminal—just ordinary travelers going about their day.

"Oh, hey," I said, reaching into my bag and pulling out Ian's t-shirt. "I borrowed these." I pulled the studded belt off and thought my jeans would drop to my knees.

"Ach, keep 'em, my punk days are well behind me," Ian said. I started to shove them back into my bag. "Actually," Ian said, reaching inside the bag, "I'll take the belt." He removed it and slung it over his shoulder, as he was already wearing a belt, though his pants seemed tight enough not to need them.

We continued to walk, me holding my pants up until we reached the final gates of the North Terminal.

"Not counting yesterday, what did you think of England?"

"Ha, yeah, no, I mean, I like it a lot. Never did find that palace, though. What's it called Lindsey? Like Lindsey Buckingham, Buckingham Palace? That's a Cockney rhyme, right?"

"Haha, no. So, how did you manage that one, Connor MacLeod?" Ian said, quoting "Highlander."

"So, you *have* seen it!" Ian smirked, raised his eyebrows, anticipating an answer to his question. "Well, this is gonna sound stupid," I said, explaining my fears of which accent to use and the responses I thought they might elicit.

Ian stopped and laughed, all but the missing tooth showing.

A "psst" sound came from our left; we turned to find Grandfather facing the same direction.

"What are you doing sitting over here?" I asked, pointing to the actual gate.

"Put your bloody hand down," Grandfather whispered through gritted teeth. I slowly did, quickly remembering what was at stake. Grandfather cocked his head to the left, indicating the empty seats beside him. I set my bag down and took a seat next to Grandfather. Something in my back pocket was jabbing me in the butt. Ian, in turn, took a seat behind us, facing in the opposite direction.

"Any news?" Grandfather said, looking at me but directing it at Ian. I started to speak.

"They're both in hospital," Ian said, his head slightly turned to hear and be heard.

"Whatchu mean *both*?" Grandfather whispered.

Ian went on to explain what had happened the night before. "He fell out the window, innit?" Showed up at the pub last night, almost made Davey here piss his tighty-whiteys."

Grandfather looked to me for confirmation. *My Jewy blueys.* I nodded.

"Well, they haven't much to go on," Grandfather said with slight twinges of an English accent mixed throughout, I noticed. "Needless to say, your father is the spawn of Satan."

"Guess that makes you Satan, then, eh?" I chuckled nervously.

"Suppose it does," Grandfather mused, looking at me; my smile dropped.

"Well, I gotta go. Gotta get to hospital, in case he comes out of it or whatever," Ian said, standing. "See if he's having us on."

"*If?* Yeah, right," Grandfather scoffed. "Keep us updated, yeah?"

Ian nodded, putting his hands on each of our shoulders. "Godspeed, lads," he said before pulling his right hand from Grandfather's shoulder as if it burned, giving it a little shake.

"Very funny," Grandfather said.

"I ain't going to take this ride, so I guess I'll see you on the other side," Ian said mysteriously. *Was that one of his songs?*

"Are you coming over on a later flight?" I asked.

"Haha, no."

Without another word, Ian turned and walked back through the terminal. "Pardon me!" Ian said to no one in particular. "Can you tell me where the bleedin' palace is?" he said with a laugh before disappearing out of sight.

I smiled and thought *I'll miss that twat,* before turning to witness Grandfather's disapproving countenance. However, my smile quickly faded when I reached into my back pocket and withdrew the mystery item—a pack of Rothmans. And the necklace!

"Ah, shit, my pants," I said way too loud as I shoved it back in my pocket.

Some travelers stopped and scrutinized me with equal looks of disgust and horror.

The TWA Representative picked up the microphone.

"This'll be us," Grandfather said matter-of-factly.

Just as Grandfather said, the Rep announced pre-boarding would begin for anyone with small children and other needs. I watched as he slowly made his way to his feet, transforming right before my very eyes. Now hunched over, putting all his weight on the walking cane, he slowly hobbled over to get in line for boarding. Of course, I jumped and followed him.

Beside the TWA agent was what appeared to be a young rookie detective checking passports while the airline agent checked tickets. Some he asked questions; others, he silently confirmed his approval. Finally, Grandfather and I approached the counter, where I gently took his arm to enhance our guise.

"Tickets and passports, please," the TWA agent said.

We handed them to him as the agent took a perfunctory gaze at them, passing the passports to the detective as he typed away on the computer.

"So what brought you to England, gentlemen?"

Il Maestro spoke softly and slowly. "Just wanted to show my grandson this amazing city I fell in love with during the war."

"And what did you think, young man?"

Unbeknownst to him or me, I took a page directly from Ian's handbook, speaking in an octave higher than my usual voice. "Gee, it was swell," I said, sounding like one of The Bowery Boys. *Where the hell did that come from*, I wondered?

"What was your favourite part, then?" he asked, looking up from examining our passports.

Suddenly, a wave rushed over me, and everything English passed before me, all the things I forgot about England: Jack the Ripper, Abbey Road, Liverpool, and, of course, Stonehenge.

"If I had to choose just one, I'd have to say Buckingham Palace."

"We're very proud of it," he replied with a warm smile. He handed our passports to the agent, who, in turn, gave them to me. "Have a nice flight."

I led Grandfather down the jetway, waiting for the detective to scream, 'Wait! Just one thing!' as if the end of an episode of Columbo, but it never happened. We continued, each step bigger than the last, feeling like Billy from "Midnight Express" as he walked out of that Turkish prison.

"Good evening," said a lovely American stewardess.

First Class, I thought, *this is going to be awesome.*

She checked our tickets and pointed down the aisle. "Last row on your left."

"I'm with him," I said, beaming. The Stewardess nodded before looking past me at the pregnant passenger stepping in behind us.

Grandfather started straightening up as he made his way through First Class. I stopped at the last row of First Class as he continued into Coach. Confused as to why he was not taking a seat, I scanned my ticket: 37A. Gutted, I continued back to the last row of coach, where he stood back, making room for me to chuck my duffel bag into the overhead bin, not caring one lick about the guitar's tuning pegs as I shoved it in. I gave Grandfather a confused look as I crouched and crab-walked sideways over to the window seat. Grandfather took the aisle seat, focused straight ahead for any last-minute surprises that might arise.

"I thought we had first-class seats," I whispered.

Grandfather gave a slight head shake, the realization of why they were switched becoming perfectly clear.

"I really shouldn't be doing this," Katie told Detective Brompton as she unlocked the door to Ian's room. Sir was sniffing at the gap under the door. He backed up as Katie slowly opened the door into the room. "Lock it up when you're done, yeah?"

"I shan't be long," he assured her.

Satisfied, she withdrew the key from the doorknob and dashed back down the stairs to the pub. Brompton eased in, leaving the door slightly ajar as he scanned the dark, dusty room.

"Good dog," he said, giving Sir a couple of friendly pats on the head. Then, he moved about the room, looking for anything that would either confirm his suspicions or alleviate them. He could hear the voices of the punters below but not clear enough to decipher their exact conversations.

He opened the drawers to the dresser, carefully rifling through the minimal amount of clothes Ian had to his name. Next, he opened the wardrobe, found a couple of shirts hanging, dirty clothes in a ball at the bottom. Sir stood wagging his tail, hoping for a scratch or another pat on the head.

Brompton checked under the mattress before dropping to the floor for a peek under the bed. Nothing but dust bunnies. He stood up and turned to the window he had observed earlier, running his finger across the broken glass that remained. It seemed freshly broken, but how could one make a positive determination? He did, however, take note of a few pieces inside the window sill. He turned and noticed the squished dog turd and checked the bottom of his shoe. It was him.

"Bugger."

Downstairs, Ian walked into the pub, which was

hopping, not unusual for a Tuesday night or any night in a London pub. He approached the bar closest to the door upstairs, where Katie was chatting up a pair of old slappers. *So rare for this place*, Ian thought.

With Sir sniffing at the crack under the door, Brompton took a seat on the end of the bed and lifted his shoe to get a better look. He craned his neck over the top of the waste bin, seeing nothing but a couple of empty beer bottles. He ripped a paper from his notepad and scraped the excrement off the sole of his shoe.

"Don't they ever let you out?" He carefully folded and tossed it into the bin, but no sooner had it circled the inside, he decided against it. There could be no reasonable explanation if discovered; he reached in and retrieved it when something caught his eye—another larger crumpled-up piece of paper.

"Give us a bottle of Tennant's Super, would ya?" Ian asked as Katie's head was down. She looked up and turned pale at the sight of him.

"You look like you've seen a ghost."

"Goin' for the 'ard stuff?" Katie asked, forcing a smile as she tried to compose herself.

Ian smiled. "Yeah, you know, gotta catch up to this lot," he said, tilting his head in the direction of the rabble-rousers.

Detective Brompton stretched the paper out. Hand-written street directions. He set it on the table and removed his notepad.

Katie popped the top and set it on the bar. "Two-pound ten, please, Liam."

"Ian," he said, correcting her. She nodded, picking up the three coins from the bar.

"Ian. What did I say?"

Brompton knew most of the streets but needed to check a map to confirm what he thought they might be. Sir nosed the door open and started to squeeze out the door. "Whoa, boy, whoa," the detective said, balling the paper back up and chucking it back into the bin. It swirled around inside like a basketball rounding a hoop before stopping between the two bottles. The detective pulled Sir back in and closed the door.

Ian placed two two-pound atop two ten-p coins on the bar. "Ta," he said in gratitude before turning towards the upstairs door.

"Ian!" Katie shouted.

Brompton looked up.

"Have a good night!"

"Yea, you too, darlin," Ian replied before slowly turning a little puzzled and heading through the door upstairs.

Hearing the noise from the pub increase tenfold, Detective Brompton turned and bee-lined down the hall towards the back stairway just as Ian charged up, missing each other by a short hair.

Ian entered his room and was greeted by an over-joyed Sir.

"Who's a good boy?" Then, spotting the poo stepped on, as well as a smaller glob by the door, Ian pushed Sir off. "You got shit on your paws?"

Ian looked suspiciously around the room. Sir Drops A Lot followed suit.

"Preparing for take-off. Cross-check," the pilot announced over the p.a. system.

And take-off we did. After the drinks had been distributed throughout the cabin at thirty-thousand feet, a whiskey on the rocks for Mr. Jones, me opting for Sprite, the back row became a confessional of sorts. I acted as a priest, or rabbi, in Old Man Jones' (just came up with that) version of 'This Was My Life.'

"Pond-hoppers."

"Pond hoppers?" I genuinely laughed, curious. "What the hell is that? Cockney for pill poppers."

"Haven't you not noticed, Grandbaby?"

I covered my mouth. *Grandbaby.* I had to stop myself from laughing. *I'll let him have that one. It might be the only one he gets.*

"The son always tires of the father. It's the grandfather and grandson that have to start looking after each other. You know this family."

I think I do a little bit more now.

"Unfortunately, we come from a long line of jesters and thieves."

Bad English
the III

He grew up in Baltimore, that much we shared. The old man sitting beside me grew up during the Great Depression, which according to him, was not that great at all. Forced to work at an early age, he carefully cherry-picked what he did to get something, anything, on the table. Sometimes aboveboard, like re-selling newspapers, but more often dubious things.

"I maneuvered through the darkest recesses of the Baltimore underground."

Underground.

When the Second World War broke out, he was far from quick to enlist. He bucked around for two years until his 23rd birthday. He had never been out of the state, let alone the country. He then blathered on and on about campaigns in France ("the French women were *especially tickled*"), Italy ("Italian women, what can I say?"), and finally, Germany ("Ah, ze frauleins"). He finished his whiskey with a solemn gulp and pressed the attendant call button to order another.

"I don't know if I was good or just plain lucky," Grandfather said as the Stewardess placed another miniature whiskey bottle on his tray. "Cheers, love," he said with no hint of an English accent. "Or if it was the man upstairs, but I got through it all with the only scratch being a case of the crotch rot."

Me too, I laughed inside my head. But it would be short-lived.

Grandfather went on to tell me the horrors of liberating the German concentration camp, Dachau. Something I just could not fathom.

"It was there, I..." Grandfather quaffed another whiskey down and again hit the call button. Then, when the Stewardess didn't come fast enough, he hit it again.

Eventually bringing another miniature from the galley behind us, Grandfather watched her hips swishing and swaying, as she maneuvered herself down the aisle towards another flashing overhead call light. After she was out of sight, he closed his eyes; I listened as the speed of his breathing increased.

"Let's just say I carry...little fragments of my brief time there," Grandfather said resignedly, placing his hand over his heart.

After a painfully long pause, I asked, "What was Grandmom like?"

Grandfather, whose eyes seemed to glaze over, took a deep breath. The lines on his face almost disappeared altogether as he recounted his memories of his former wife.

"Ah, your Bubbe. Lizzie, what a woman she was. Biggest brownest eyes you've ever seen. She was the reason I converted to Judaism. She had this, I don't know if you'd call it a trait, but she always curled her hair behind her ear as she spoke, which I absolutely loved. I don't even think she was aware she was doing it. I continued loving her even long after she left me. Ironic, she left me for my drinking habit and eventually drank herself to death. She was a good woman, though. Took pity on a childish fool like me, who only really knew war and destruction and sorrow."

"Wait, we're not really Jewish?"

"Our last name is Jones. We're from Wales."

"What? They don't have Jews in Wales?"

"Just Jonah, that I'm aware of," Grandfather said, rubbing his eyes as he chuckled.

"The Outlaw Jewsy Wales," I blurted out as it popped into my head.

"I guess if it weren't for your Uncle Thom and me, you and I wouldn't be sitting here right now," the old man said, ignoring my whimsical outburst.

"Yeah, what was all that about?" I asked, knowing the version I had heard, but I wanted a different perspective.

"It was my chance to shine, back in my hometown, managing a music group. But, unfortunately, my two sons were in it. Now that's what I call bad management."

I snorted, partly understanding, partly sympathizing, before excusing myself to use the bathroom. Grandfather, seemingly annoyed, slowly got to his feet, allowing me to pass. The man sitting alone across the aisle looked over from watching the movie playing and solemnly nodded. Grandfather reciprocated with the same.

When the man's attention returned to the movie screen ahead of him, Grandfather opened the overhead compartment and fished through my duffel bag. He found the Highlander case and shook it before opening it, confirming it was empty. Then, discreetly, he transferred an unseen object from his inside jacket pocket into the case, closed it shut, and shoved it deep inside the bag before closing the compartment with a gentle click.

"I'm sorry, visiting hours are now over," the nurse informed Ian, who sat on a small fold-out chair between the hospital beds of his father and Mr. Tannenbaum. He lifted his head up and solemnly nodded, standing up. "Thank you."

She backed out to attend to her other patients. Ian folded up the chair and leaned it against the wall by the door. He walked to the far side of the room and, after unlocking the wheels of his father's bed, pushed it as close as the machines in between would allow. Then, satisfied, he took both men's hands in his and appeared to make a small prayer before leaving.

With both of their hands left dangling over the side of their respective beds, Thomas's hand stretched out further, taking Irving's hand in his and held it.

After a few seconds, Mr. Tannenbaum yanked his hand away.

"Everything come out okay?" Grandfather joked as I returned from the bathroom. I took notice of the new mini whiskey bottle on Grandfather's tray as I eased past him and back into my seat.

"Oh, yeah, just like my favorite book, "The Yellow River by I.P. Long," I joked.

"Very funny," Grandfather replied, though he seemed far from cheerful.

There was a long pause as we both sipped from our respective drinks.

"I'm sorry I didn't get to know your mum very well."

I pondered the statement and my feelings before I finally answered. "That's all right. She was a great big pain in the ass."

Grandfather nearly choked on his drink. "Easy now."

"No, I'm serious. For the last five years, she did nothing but bust my balls. Nothing I ever did was right, I—"

"You never heard the phrase: 'If you have nothing nice to say?' Wait, do you mean since your bar mitzvah?"

"Yeah, how did you know?"

"I insisted you have one."

"You did? You're the reason behind me having to learn Hebrew?"

"Guess she wasn't too keen on the idea."

"No, *she* was well into it. It was *Dad* that was against it."

"You don't say. Well, maybe she just expected you to be a man after that."

"I didn't even have pubes yet!" I said, recalling the bizarre comment of Uncle Thomas.

Grandfather chuckled. "I'm sure she just wanted what was best for you."

"I guess. She sure had a funny way of showing it. It's like right when I started getting into rock and roll, she stopped liking it."

"Is it possible it was something else?"

I thought long and hard, rolling scenario after scenario through my feeble mind. Finally, I pressed the button on the armrest and tried to push my seat back, but it barely moved as it was against the wall already. *Just like everything else in my life*, I thought, *nothing fucking works proper.*

"So, how did you scrape your knee?" she asked as she applied mercurochrome to his bloody scrape.

"I fell."

"Well, obviously, silly."

"He shouldn't have said that about her."

"Who shouldn't have said what about whom?"

"Joey called Lisa a hairy beast."

"You walked five miles on a sidewalk-less street to defend some girl's honor? I think that's lovely, David," pangs of English peppered throughout her Baltimore accent.

He looked up into her eyes as only an innocent child of five can.

"What's an honor, mommy?"

"It's when you—"

Bad English
the III

I was suddenly yanked from my daydream of my mother abruptly waking up in a stupor, pulling indiscriminately on the tubes inserted in her arms, nose, and mouth. Dad did not stand a chance as he grappled with her flailing arms, trying the best he could to pin them down to her sides.

"Go get a nurse!" he shouted.

I gasped, my eyes welling up as I turned to find, through the myriad of tears, Grandfather in full snore mode. I covered my face with my hands and lowered my head onto the seat back tray, hiding my sudden emotional outburst.

When the plane finally descended into Baltimore, I wiped my eyes to look through the window, reflecting on the times as a kid fishing and crabbing on that same body of water, The Chesapeake Bay. Then, I would be in the boat with Stan and Uncle LeRoy and my Aunt Nola, watching the planes passing overhead, wondering where they were coming and going.

Now I know.

Grandfather and I were some of the first to be led off and headed down to baggage claim to await Grandfather's luggage. He brought two suitcases and two huge boxes, sealed tightly with cello tape. *Was he moving home? Won't Dad be surprised?*

We queued up at Customs, where I got in one line and Grandfather in another, longer one. I waved him over, but he merely shook his head, not wanting to be a bother.

What is he up to? Surely, no one can be looking for us on this end, I told myself. Or could they?

Inching closer and closer to the gate back into the U.S.A., my stomach began to churn. I was uncertain if it was the chicken I ate on the plane or if it was just my nerves, figuring it was a combination of the two. I watched as the Customs Inspector, a grizzled, middle-aged man, went through suitcase after suitcase, rifling through people's personal belongings with neither discretion nor a care in the world.

I stopped at the blue line on the floor, awaiting my turn, and looked back over my shoulder to see Grandfather, who had a few people still ahead of him.

The passenger at the inspection table was shoving his things haphazardly back into his suitcase as the Inspector returned his ticket and passport, waving me over before the man had completely walked away. I dragged my bag across the floor and approached the metallic table.

"Passport and ticket." I checked my pockets, forgetting which pocket I had stuffed them in.

"Coming back from Barbados?"

Pulling the ticket and passport from my back pocket, I handed them to the Inspector. "No, England. London, England."

Bad English
the III

The Inspector confirmed what I was saying by looking at the two items. "London, England, ay?" His Baltimore accent was extremely thick, I noted, kind of like an American Cockney accent. "And what were you doing there?"

I thought for a moment, *definitely not involved in any robberies*. "Getting in touch with my roots."

"Is that a fact?" he asked, sizing me up for the first time. "Do you have that green card you should have filled out on the plane?"

"Oh, yeah," I said, reaching into my front pocket and pulling it out. It was slightly bent and wrinkled, *like my Uncle Thom*, I thought with an internal chuckle. I was sure to keep that to myself, along with a lot of other secrets.

"So, nothing to declare," he said after perusing the card.

"I probably came back with less than I went with," I said. "Especially money."

"Well, it is one of the most expensive cities in the world," the Inspector offered before reaching into the duffel bag. "The guitar was yours before?"

"Yes, sir."

"Musician, ay?"

"That's debatable."

He then pulled out the "Highlander" video box. Should I have declared that? He rattled it; did it make a sound?

"You know European movies don't work over here. It's a different conversion," he informed.

"Yeah, I know." Odd, I thought, as it was empty. "I just liked the artwork."

The Inspector turned the box right side up and gave it a good once-over.

"Not bad." He shoved the video case back into the bag and pulled the drawstring tight. "Welcome back, Mr. Jones."

I looked back to the next line only to *not* see Grandfather.

Again? Like having a pair of Houdinis in the family.

I made my way to the double doors with the sign that declared EXIT - NO RETURN BEYOND THIS POINT, taking one last look back at all the Customs lines before turning and pushing through the doors. I was immediately hit in the face by what seemed like a gang of paparazzi with their flashes, but in reality, it was just the setting sun blasting through the terminal windows. I squinted, trying to readjust and focus my eyes, finding Grandfather standing there waiting, his cases and boxes on a trolley.

"What took you so long?" Grandfather asked.

As we sat on the bench out front of the terminal sharing a smoke ("Rothman, good choice"), I rocked the overloaded trolley full of Grandfather's stuff. It looked to me like a giant caramel sundae with Grandfather's old green army bag acting like a big jalapeno pepper.

Bad English
the III

Both weary after our week's adventure, the seemingly sole survivors of a road trip gone pear-shaped, I took the last drag before stubbing it out with my sneaker or my trainer as that nutcase Loretta called them.

Loretta.

All I knew was how I couldn't wait to get them off for a week.

As my father was pulling up, Grandfather matter-of-factly said to me, "Needless to say, this stays between us two."

"You moving in?" Dad asked as he popped the trunk.

"See if you can get the boxes in first," Grandfather directed us, purposefully avoiding the question.

I did not know what to think. Did that mean my father knew nothing of any of this? That thought had crossed my mind several times throughout everything that had happened. But as my father stood there, his eyes revealed he was as oblivious as Grandfather and I. So together, yet each lost and alone. I saw it. But did they?

The drive home consisted of me cramped between two cardboard boxes. Like, I haven't seen enough of those lately.

"Heart's been all cleared for take-off, obviously," Mr. Jones's attempt at conviviality. He, too, had spent a week virtually by himself.

Grandfather tapped his heart while continuing to look out the window. "Heartless" by Heart popped into my head.

My father looked at me in the rearview mirror. "So, what did you think?" He dropped his gaze back to the road. "What did you get up to?" he asked, eyes shifting from his father to me.

"Yeah, it was good. A lot of time at the hospital holding Grandfather's hand."

"What else? You were there a week."

What is the fishing for? I wondered. *What does he want me to tell him?*

"You know, saw some pubs. Big Ben. All that."

"It's like pulling teeth with you two," Dad said, turning his head to look at each of us. "What did you think of Buckingham Palace? You had to have seen that."

"I couldn't find it," I admitted. Grandfather chuckled.

"Whatchu mean you couldn't find it?"

Grandfather tried to make eye contact with me in the side mirror, but the angle was off. So he peered over his shoulder at me instead, a pained yet insistent look in his eyes.

"Nah, I'm just havin' you on a bit. It was amazing, did a tour and everything."

Grandfather rolled his eyes and turned back to face forward.

"What are you on about?" Dad said, scrutinizing me. "They don't give bloody tours."

(He was right. Buckingham Palace would not open its doors for tours for another month and four years.)

"Oh, that's right. It was St. Paul's Cathedral." That was true. Well, sort of. One afternoon, I had innocently joined a tour group of the historic church and was on the second stop when the priest presiding over the tour caught me cowering in the back of the crowd without the proper credentials. I was politely expelled.

"Well, I've got some news for you, my son. Some good news. And some bad news. Possibly."

Oh no.

"Ready?"

"No, not ready, really," I said, exhausted at the mere thought.

"Well, it seems," Dad said, clearly not caring. "They made a mistake at your new school. You *are* going to graduate."

Grandfather perked up when he heard that, nodding and smiling at me.

"But you have to take all your exams on Friday."

I felt like I was back in Grandfather's circus trailer. I had forgotten all about school. I figured I'd be in my father's garage in the—

The garage—I had forgotten all about the Jaguar. I could not believe my father had not said anything about it yet.

And then it occurred to me: if I graduate, I get *a* car!

That car?

All shredded to shit?

Major backfire.

Well played, Dad. Well played indeed.

"Mom, I'm home!" I said as soon I swung open the door. The dog met me at the door, happy to see me, it seemed. "I can only imagine what you've been going through," I said, scratching its head as I eased past inside.

"What's this dog's name, anyway?"

"I named him after your three-favourite people: Sidney for Sid Vicious, Oliver for Oliver Twist and David for David Jones. SOD for short."

Still trying, and failing, at being funny.

By the time we got all of Grandfather's stuff inside, I had retired to my bedroom, where once my head hit the pillow, I was dead to the world.

Grandfather and Mr. Jones whipped up something in the kitchen and had a bite to eat out by the pool while the bug zapper crackled and popped nearby. The two men remained mostly quiet, only speaking when complimenting the food or commenting on the warm weather.

"Did, um, David meet his uncle and cousin?"

"Briefly," Grandfather replied, wiping his mouth with a paper towel.

Soon after, the older men made their way to their respective rooms, and they, too, retired for the night, each putting the week's events behind them.

It was 9 o'clock.

———

Chapter
XVI

Okay, stop me if you've heard this: Guy walks into a jewelry store. He spots Stan pointing a machine gun at a masked man. The man pulls his mask off, revealing my mother, Polly Jones. I screamed out as I tried to stop the madman.

BLAST!

I jolted up in bed as another BLAST occurred.

It was the crack of noon. I looked outside to see a garbage truck outside backfiring. The driveway was empty, however. I turned and spotted my bag wide open. I could not remember opening it as I didn't need a thing before my head hit the pillow, *but* my pillow.

I bent over to get a closer look and saw the "Highlander" video box; it, too, was open. *That's strange*, I thought before venturing downstairs. But not before passing the spare room, where I snuck a quick peek inside only to find it, too, was empty.

For the first time, I got a sense of what my father had been up to while I was away. The house was completely decorated. Walls were now covered with our old skylines, pictures of my mother, my parents, and the family all together. And, of course, my mother's African motif.

I felt as if our old apartment's walls had stretched like Kevin's room in "Time Bandits," and that last week was all but a memory, a dream even. I traced the new metallic insert in the wall on my walk down the stairs, finding a chair inserted into an elaborate steel mount at the bottom.

Walking into the rec room—I had a rec room!—I found my mother's urn, now illuminated under a single beam from a ceiling track; it made my heart skip a beat.

"Let's take a walk," I said, picking her up from her pedestal.

I carried her outside on the front stoop and gently set her down, sitting beside her.

"It's been a hell of a couple of weeks since you've been gone," I said, conscious of the fact that the last four words were the name of a Rainbow song. "I never knew I could miss someone so much."

I caught a single tear as it rolled down my cheek, taking a long hard look at it on the tip of my finger.

"If you *did* cast a spell, *please break it.*"

———

Inside, the phone rang; I kissed the teardrop, losing it on my lips as I went in to the kitchen. There was a long pause after I said hello, as I saw what else my father had been up to: the sink was littered with dirty dishes and empty booze bottles.

"Why ain't you tell me you were going to England? Huh? No phone call, no postcard. Am I still your girl-friend or what, David?"

"Hey, Shari. Baby," I said, wincing. It was the last person I wanted to speak to right now, though neither of us had any idea how much we needed each other.

"Don't 'Hey Shari baby' me. Answer my question, motherfucker. Am. I. Still. Your. Girlfriend?"

I honestly was at a loss for words. "I don't know anything anymore."

"You can kiss my black ass, David Jones!" she shout-ed before hanging up.

That was easy, she thought as much as I did. At least, that's what I convinced myself. So I didn't waste one second, after getting a dial tone, in calling Veronica.

"She's not home," Veronica's mother informed me.

"D'ya know when she'll be back?"

"No, I sure don't," her mother replied, a bit tersely, I thought.

"Would you be so kind as to tell her DJ called, please?"

"Sure," she said, before hanging up without so much as a good-bye or a 'take a flying fuck.'

Bad English
the III

I watched through the kitchen window as the post-man walked up the sidewalk to find an urn sitting omi-nously on the porch. He stopped in his tracks momen-tarily, looking around, probably in search of cameras. Then, turning up nothing, he eased past the urn, sol-emnly nodding out of respect, and put the mail in its box, repeating the same on his way out.

I returned to sitting down on the front step, catch-ing a glimpse of the postman's bag as he turned past the bushes back out onto the sidewalk.

"Mom, I don't know what to do with my life. Everything is so crazy."

The phone rang inside again.

"Oh man," I thought.

"Hello?" I asked, answering the phone.

"You did a good thing taking your grandfather home. He has nothing but good things to say about you. So, I figured I'd let you sleep in."

He really has no idea, does he? I thought. "Cheers."

"I'd suggest cracking those books, refreshing your memory," his father said.

"Yeah, okay."

"You got a lot at stake here."

The car! I had forgotten all about it.

Dad revealed that Grandfather was at the shop with him before we wrapped up our conversation.

I bee-lined to the garage. All the boxes from before were gone—just another weird, distant memory. But, there, along the far wall, under a gray cover, looked to be a car. I peeked enough to find the green Jaguar still there!

Only now, as I pulled it back farther, the roof that I had single-handedly destroyed (with the help of a Black & Decker saw) had been replaced with a ragtop. All the shredded metal had been buffed out and, more importantly, repaired.

Was I dreaming?

I pulled the cover back the way I found it and backed into the house, nearly tripping over the step leading in.

On my desk in my bedroom, my father had strategically placed my textbooks for me to review. Taking a seat, I opened the history book first and briefly perused the Table of Contents.

After roughly a minute and a half, I said: "Sod this!"

Sod raised his head as I stood up. "Not you."

I remembered something Veronica had said: "Find a way to honor her memory." It gave me pause.

Pulling up to the front of her house, I stepped off the scooter like a cowboy come home to roost. I patted the dust off my jeans before moseying on up her front steps, where I gently knocked on the door.

Much to my surprise, Veronica answered. I felt relieved when she smiled. Just as quickly, though, she recalled being mad at me, scowling instead. She took me by surprise when she looked back into her house before stepping outside.

"'*Ello*," I said, trying to recapture our earlier moments.

"Save it. I know you're not English. Duke showed me your yearbook picture."

Fucking Duke.

"Lookit, I'm sorry, things just got way out of hand. It started out as, like a, I don't know what you would call it, like a—"

"A lie? That's what we call them here in America. In fact, anywhere in the world. Everywhere in the world. Lies."

"I just wanted to be someone else. Anyone else. I didn't think I would be accepted for who I am. But, you know, fair enough. Look, I dig the shit out of you," I said, taking note of the literalness of the comment.

"Lying about yourself, or where you're from is one thing, but to lie and say your mother just died, that's-- and saying I have crabs!"

She punched me hard in the chest.

"It was bed bugs! I had bed bugs from this tent! Oh, never mind. What's the use? I can see you're super-pissed." I turned to walk away, rubbing my stinging chest. "How do you know Duke, anyway?" I asked after descending one step.

Fuck, I thought. Duke.

"He's a friend of the family, worked at my dad's shop for years."

I nodded, stepped down another step. *Fuck.*

"By the way, my mother did die." I choked on the words. "Three weeks ago."

"You won't blame me if I don't believe you. But, I mean, like, you told Lisa and Jill, both of your parents are dead," she said in Valley-speak again.

Why does she do that? Was it a nervous thing?

I nodded. "Yeah, well, my father was dead to me. I blamed him. For everything."

I turned and stepped off the bottom step onto the sidewalk. *Fuck.*

"So that *was* your father that took me home that morning?"

Sullen, I did not turn to face her but nodded. "He tried to kill himself by driving into the back of a city bus."

"Oh my. I'm sorry. And about your mom," Veronica, sounding skeptical, but with sincerity.

I raised my hand with a peace sign (technically, it could have been the British flip-off gesture, but I did not do the double wrist thrust) as I slinked back to my scooter. Once on, I looked back in Veronica's direction, but only at her feet.

"I took your advice."

When she didn't respond, I raised my eyes to hers. She was off in la-la land before stepping to the edge of the porch.

"What advice was that?"

"You said to find a unique way to honor her memory. I have."

Bad English
the III

"What is it?"

Just as I began to answer, a motorcycle screeched to a stop behind me, ramming my scooter and thrusting me forward violently. I looked back, expecting to see a Mack truck.

The motorcyclist pulled his helmet off, revealing himself to be Duke Warfield, of course. I was furious.

"The bust is out on you, motherfucker," Duke said, enraged at my mere presence.

We both swung our legs over our saddle seats faced off against each other.

"It's the *buzz* is out on you, not the *bust*," I informed.

"Whatever, they all know you ain't English."

"Well, you beat me to it. That's what I came to tell them."

"Did you tell her your parents ain't dead either?"

"My mother *is* dead, asshole."

"Yeah, right, your mother can't shut up long enough to die," Duke countered, followed by his high-pitched laugh.

"Don't say a fucking *word* about my mother."

"What are you going to do about it?"

With that, I threw my guitar on the ground. Duke watched the Fender Strat in horror as it bounced off the lawn. I charged at Duke, who was not expecting it. We both hit the ground with me on top of him, flailing away with punches.

Veronica ran down the steps. "HEY! STOP! STOP IT!"

Duke screamed like a girl. Finally, managing to push me off, he limped over to his motorcycle. "We shouldn't be fighting! We're black guitar players!!" Duke started his motorcycle up while forcing his helmet on.

I rolled over to where my guitar was, swooped it up, and ran at an angle across Veronica's front lawn. Just as Duke drove past, I spun 360 degrees, swinging the guitar in a roundhouse, catching Duke right in the face-plate of his helmet. Veronica screamed. The force sent Duke flying backward off his bike. It sailed across the street along the side of Veronica's house and up onto her neighbor's lawn, where it dropped on one side, its wheels still spinning.

Approaching Duke, struggling with his helmet and catching his breath, I stepped on his chest.

"Don't ever talk about my mother again! She's dead!"

Upon saying that, I broke into tears. Veronica covered her mouth with her hands at a complete loss.

I swung my guitar over my shoulder and straddled my scooter but stopped. I got off and bee-lined over to where Duke lay. I turned the guitar around and lifted it by the neck high over my head like a giant ax.

This was for everything, every wrong perpetuated by others unto me.

For my mother!

I slammed the guitar down—narrowly missing Duke—where the ground met the pavement. The neck cracked in two.

Bad English
the III

My father!

Slam!

A further crack!

Gramps!

Ian! Veronica! Stan!

Slam! It shattered into pieces; the guitar held awkwardly together by its six strings.

Sharonda.

For the keen observer, just the sort of theatrics one comes to expect of Jimi, Pete, and Ritchie, minus the talent.

I took one last swing of the mangled instrument, throwing it as far in the air as I could. It landed awkwardly, half on the curb, half in the gutter across the street.

I mouthed the word 'Sorry' to Veronica. She broke into a run in my direction.

Or at least I thought so.

She zipped right over to Duke. As she bent down to attend to him, she waved at me, which I took as an understanding one. In the rearview mirror on my handlebars, I watched Veronica watching me as she helped Duke to his feet until I turned the corner.

"I'm a kill 'im! What the hell was that all about?"

"Maybe you shouldn't have said that about his mother," Veronica said.

"Oh, come on, she ain't dead," Duke said, wincing in pain, grabbing his ribs. "But *he* is."

"Well, there's a way to find out. What are you doing here anyway? You *know* my father doesn't want to see you around here." She stepped up on the walkway leading to her door.

"What about you?"

She walked towards her house. "Me?" She opened the storm door. "Even less," she said as she stepped inside.

"I said I was sorry! But, hey, where's he living now?"

Veronica stared at him as she slowly closed the door without saying a further word.

Knowing Duke, he probably mumbled something distasteful or unkind under his breath. He grabbed the handlebar and struggled to pick it up. Finally giving up, he kicked it instead.

Inside, Veronica leaned with her back to the door, wrestling with her emotions. She could not believe she actually had feelings, mixed as they were, for that fool.

I took a long ride throughout the city, taking side roads, looking for city streets that were new, mysterious, hilly and adventurous. Ones with broad turns. I knew fuck-all of my goals, feelings, and intentions. Future? Give me a break. What's happening? I kept it all in the family.

I searched for memories, happier times, but could only recall brief instances, flashes from what seemed like an eternity ago. The comfort of my mother's beautiful black skin. Her strength. Her optimism, in light of all that she faced. She was a trailblazer in a country that, quite honestly, could take her or leave her. Had brought her and left her, as she was apt to say.

"And I ain't never been appreciated up in this mother-FUCKER."

What I would like, I thought to myself, is *a round-about*. Something that could take me round and round, giving me several exits to turn off. Head in a different direction or stay on the same course. A kiss from her on my forehead. Veronica's kiss. No more of those, it would seem. So I began plotting ways to get her back.

By the time the other Davids returned home, they had found me sitting in the dark listening to John Lennon's gut-wrenching "Mother" on repeat; all three unaware the other was drunk, but neither knew the other was. I began hitting the liquor cabinet after my third attempt at reaching Veronica resulted in her little sister telling me that, as frank as little shits can be, Veronica never wanted to speak to me again. For the life of me, I could not imagine why.

The older Joneses had visited The Block, the notorious downtown East Baltimore Street that was famous for its burlesque houses back in its inception in the 1940s. Now, it carried small strip clubs, sex shops, and the like. Ironically enough, all opposite Baltimore City Police headquarters.

"What are you doing sitting in the dark?" Dad asked

as he switched on the lights of the rec room.

The light flickered, and there I was, sitting on the sofa, my mother's final resting place clutched tightly in my arm. Both men stopped in their tracks.

What exactly *were* they witnessing?

"You alright, son?" Grandfather asked.

My old man, thinking he was referring to him, shot a glance at Grandfather, who moved closer to me in an attempt at peacekeeping.

"No. I mean, do I look alright?" I replied, my eyes watery, nose red.

"What's gotten into you?" my father asked, far more aggressive than I thought necessary, as he clicked off the stereo.

"What are we doing here? I mean, mom's not even cold, and we're up and out of the neighborhood I spent my whole life in? You just couldn't wait to get away from those niggers, could you?!"

Grandfather's eyes widened in surprise. He turned to look at his son, whose eyes were also like two sunny-side-up eggs covered in healthy amounts of Tabasco sauce, bloodshot as the others.

"You know *we* don't like that word, David," my father said, meaning business by calling me by my first name.

Seeing where this conversation was heading, Grandfather backed away from us both. "I can see you two have some things to talk about so, I think I'll retire for the night."

"But it's true! When'd you sign the paperwork for this house? The day you burned her to a crisp?!" I pulled the urn a little tighter to my chest; a butter knife tight in my grip, I stirred the contents inside.

Grandfather slowly made his way up the stairs where they curved left behind the wall. His footsteps got lighter as he had stopped out of sight to eavesdrop.

I continued. "Did you sign the paperwork before or after you burned her?! Hmm?"

My old man sat on the edge of his chair; a look of sadness spread across his drunk, weary face. "That's not fair, Dej," he said, trying to soften the conversation by using one of my nicknames.

"You moved us up here to this, this lily-white fucking neighborhood where I don't know a living soul. So I stick out like a sore thumb. And now I'm forced to graduate with a bunch of fucking strangers. So that you didn't have to look at another black person!?"

"Now you know that's not true."

"I got news for you—I'm BLACK! Mom would be fucking gutted. No, on second thought, I think she would shout: Off with his head!"

He dropped his head into those rough blackened hands of his; he was too tired and drunk to get into it.

"I truly hope you never lose someone you love."

"I did."

I recalled the song on the New Music Phone-In Poll

earlier. "Sowing the Seeds of Love." I didn't like the song, but I loved the title. I tightly grasped the butter knife and began stirring its contents. It made an awful scraping sound inside, like fingernails on a chalkboard, causing the old man to look up to discern the origin of the noise. He seemed surprised, more than taken aback.

"Dej, truth be told, it was your mum's idea to buy this house. She picked it, she loved it, and thought you would, too."

"Bullshit!"

"This had been in the works before she went into hospital. So what do you think, you can buy a house the same day?"

"It's been done!" I barked, spinning the butter knife harder and faster.

"Yes, but not this time. Look, could you stop doing that? You're mixing mommy all up."

"Well, join the club," I said, continuing to stir.

"Look," Dad said, standing. "I'll have to make a few calls, but maybe I can arrange for you to graduate with your old school. But make no mistake, you'll still have to take your exams up here. It's all been arranged. Now, give me that," he said, trying to take the urn from my hands.

We proceeded in a bit of tug-of-war. He grimaced while I sneered back; Polly's ashes sloshed around inside before I finally relented. My father yanked out the knife, scraping ash and muck along the rim as if it were a mayonnaise jar, before returning its lid and setting it gently back upon the mantle. He whispered something to her, but I could not discern what it was.

Figuring the crisis was concluding, Grandfather quietly made his way up the rest of the stairs. Dad kissed me on the top of my head, walked over to the chair on the wall, and sat down on it. Then, with the press of a button on the left end of the chair, he absurdly proceeded to escalate up the wall.

"Your satisfaction is NOT GUARANTEED!"

Ridiculous, I thought, as he rounded the wall out of sight. *What does that even mean?*

I fluffed the throw pillow beside me and stretched out on the couch. A moment later, I rolled off, and bumping into everything along the way, staggered to the phone and dialed.

"Meet me at our old hang out."

Stan pushed his way through some bushes and overbrush to find the footbridge over a channel of water with a fierce current. Overlooking it, I sat, my legs dangling over the side of the thick railing. We often snuck off to this most unusual oasis in the middle of the city quite a lot when we were younger. I took a swig from a nearly empty bottle of Jack Daniels before twisting the cap back on and tossing it to Stan.

"Just in the nigga time," I cracked as Stan awkwardly caught the bottle with ease.

Stan scoffed at me after stealing his original line.

"I blew it, man."

"You blew a man? When was this?"

"Not *a* man. *It,* man. I blew it. I lost the fucking plot, man. I lost the girl. I lost the score. I lost everything."

With that said, I turned my body and slid down the side of the bridge, hanging on for dear life.

"A little cliché, even for you," Stan replied, wincing from the smell of bourbon in the bottle.

"Didn't you tell me once to face my fears?"

"Since when do you have a fear of jumping into knee-high water? What are you talking about? Ain't you graduating in a couple of days?"

"*If* I pass my exams. With a bunch of frickin' white dicks. Whoopty doo. I'd rather be dead. I wish those *dicks* were down there so I could jump on 'em all--that's it!"

"*What's* it?"

"Maybe, that's what I need. I mean, *obviously*, women aren't working for me. They either wanna hurt me or split altogether. Now, you're gay, aren't you?"

This was not the time Stan wanted to get into a conversation about his sexuality.

"You're drunk. What, did you have a fight with Sharonda?"

Sharonda.

"You can tell me. Come on, face *your* fears."

"You might recall, I was hanging from a *street*

sign when I said that."

"Sounds like a challenge." I awkwardly pulled myself back up onto the bridge, flipping my legs over and falling, first to my knees and then flat on my back. "Last one there is a rotten egg!" I yelled as I climbed to my feet and exited stage right.

"Shit!" Stan yelled, dropping the bottle on the ground where I heard it smash into a million pieces before running after me. "Don't even think about it!"

Stan chased me down Baltimore Street, me on my Vespa, him in his Pinto, with me having the edge as I slip-streamed through cars and ran red lights. By the time Stan arrived on the overpass, he drove past my scooter and ran to the nearest phone booth.

"What? I just left David downstairs. He's probably sleeping. He what?!"

Mr. Jones burst into the study. "Dad! David's hanging off the Jones Falls Expressway!"

Grandfather opened his eyes. "What? You sleepwalking?"

"Come on. We've got to hurry!" Mr. Jones limped slowly out of the room as Grandfather, far more slowly, turned his legs over the side of the sofa-bed. Mr. Jones limped back in with as much urgency as he could muster. "COME ON!"

Stan peered over the aluminum-sided fence to find

me standing petrified behind the St. Paul Street exit sign, cars whooshing underneath my feet on their way downtown.

"How's that fear-facing going?"

A car horn honked below, jolting me.

"Did something happen in England?"

I peered slowly over my shoulder. "Bad people, they're bad people."

As more cars spotted me while passing underneath the sign, I awkwardly twisted my neck to find Stan gone. I then heard some rustling and saw Stan emerging from the bushes to my left.

"You know I was at St. Paul's Cathedral this time last week?" I shouted, referring to the street sign I was standing on. Stan shrugged. "Getting kicked off a tour I hadn't paid for. Say that three times fast!"

"I'm gay!" Stan shouted out of the blue. He now had my attention. "And I've always fancied you!" And now he lost my attention.

"We're cousins, Stan!" I said, reminding myself of the line in 'Highlander,' where McCleod is rescued by one cousin from being beat by another: 'He's your cousin, man!' It was the line that preceded the one Ian used at the airport.

I suddenly began swinging an imaginary sword, Stan told me later, killing my perceived enemies; I loudly sang one of the Queen songs from the movie: "Who Wants to Live Forever?"

Slice. Swing. Slice.

"I miss her, man!" I was not even sure who I was speaking about, Veronica or my mother.

"I know you do. We all do."

Off in the distance, a helicopter was coming in our direction, flashing a spotlight as it drew closer.

As the light enveloped my face, I stopped swinging my imaginary broadsword, and Stan later described my face as becoming serene as if a particular understanding washed over me.

The helicopter approached closer as I struggled to navigate the metal rungs that attached the St. Paul exit sign to the concrete overpass.

And that's when my foot slipped off, and I looked up to Stan, terrified by fear of heights. I sure as shit didn't want to end up a stain on some poor sod's windshield.

"Just kidding, a bit of *Thom-fuckery*."

Stan helped me off the sign and onto the paved concrete slope separating itself from the embankment.

"Stop right there!" boomed the B.C.P.D. helicopter's loudspeaker as we disappeared through the over-brush, eluding capture.

"What do you mean you fancy me?"

Stan shrugged. "Just give us a kiss."

I stopped dead in my tracks, remembering who recently said that to me.

"What *were* you doing that night?"

"What night?" Mr. Jones answered as he looked both ways before turning onto Pratt Street.

"You know damn well," Grandfather said, noticing the name of the sign, eliciting childhood memories of his roaming those Depression-era streets.

"I went to see a girl and got into a little race."

"I knew you were drag-racing!"

"It wasn't exactly drag-racing, Dad."

"Oh yeah, what would you call it then?"

Neither could believe this was the topic. "Evading the Old Bill."

Another long pause. "What's the name of this street?"

Mr. Jones could see exactly where this was going. "Pratt."

"Bloody well right."

After racing down I-83, or the JFX, as often referred, Mr. Jones took the St. Paul exit and waited for the traffic light to change before turning onto the overpass, where he slammed on the brakes, jumped out, and hobbled over to look over the fence. By that time, we were long gone. He got back in the car. "He's not there. What the hell was that? I'm going to kill Stan."

When they returned home, Mr. Jones approached his room, no need to check for his son; he could hear the snoring from down the hall.

Chapter
XVII

The following day, I woke up with the worst hangover known to man. I dragged myself into the bathroom, where I hugged the toilet while hurling my guts up several times. I had vague, cloudy snapshot images of hanging off a bridge or overpass, but I did not know whether it happened or if it was just another dream.

I drove my Vespa to Essex High. Except for the occasional teacher or administrator moving robotically about the halls, the school itself was virtually empty due to the last day of activities going on out on the football field. I was led to a small room usually reserved for Detention and took my exams.

Just as in class, I struggled with Algebra, the toughest one of all. Finally, after four grueling hours, I dropped my pencil, pushed my seat back away from the desk, and outstretched my arms, stoked it was all over.

Bad English
the III

Here lieth David Jones's school career.

And then I did something I had not done since I was a kid, not even when my mother was in the hospital, I prayed.

It would be a few days before I got my test results, but I passed. Barely. Except for English. I got a 98, raising my final grade to a C.

Arriving at home around five o'clock, I pulled up the driveway and spotted Grandfather standing in the door frame. I veered off the concrete and across the lawn. A lawn, I might add, that was in desperate need of mowing.

Caught off guard, Grandfather quickly shoved an oblong object into his pants pocket.

"Is that a mezuzah in your pocket, or are you just happy to see me?" I asked with a chuckle.

Grandfather spoke, four nails in his mouth: "Oh, yeah, ha-ha, trying to get this attached before Sabbath, or you'll be hanging it."

"Why is it okay for me to hang up?" Grandfather tilted his head to the side as if to say, take a guess. "Hey, I was bar mitzvahed. I'm as Jewish as Youish," I protested.

Grandfather conceded with a solemn nod. "Here, give me a hand," he said as he carefully removed the case and held it up to the frame, tilting it towards the door, as is tradition. It was beige in color with hand-painted flowers, birds, the Hebrew letter Shin and The Star of David, and, from within, it gave a slight rattle.

———

"Hold it just like this." Then, reciting the Hebrew blessing assigned to the mezuzah hanging, Grandfather lined up the first nail and hammered it in.

"I take it, it's meant to be crooked like this. What's inside of it?"

"The mezuzah, of course. This is just the case. And yes, it should tilt towards the room you are entering."

He lined up the second nail, hammering it.

"I thought the mezuzah was the case."

"No, inside is the mezuzah. It's a tiny scroll called a 'klaf' with prayers from the Torah." The third nail. "Just like you read at your bar mitzvah."

I nodded, grateful for the lesson. Finally, grandfather hammered the fourth and final nail. He lowered the tool, put his hand on my shoulder, and stepped back to admire his handiwork. He then gently touched it with his index and middle fingers before kissing them and led me inside.

"Guess we'll wait to see what your father wants to do for dinner."

He followed me upstairs before retiring to our respective rooms, simultaneously closing our doors behind us.

I plopped down and sprawled out on my bed. On the opposite side of the wall, Grandfather emptied his pockets, where the actual mezuzah, the tiny scroll intended for the case downstairs, rolled across the dresser, stopping at his candy bowl full of change. Grandfather kissed it gently and slipped it into the top dresser drawer behind his neatly stacked set of socks.

Later, when Father arrived home and informed me I would not be able to graduate with my old school-mates, I stomped upstairs, slammed the door, and plopped back onto my bed to pout. Eventually, I put some Pink Floyd on to soothe my soul and tried to gather my thoughts but found it impossible to do without my guitar to strum on.

What had I done that for? I wasn't sure. What I *was* sure about was how satisfying it had been getting my years-long frustration out on my archenemy.

I looked around at all my haphazardly hung posters—posters for Priest, Purple, Floyd, Stones—and thought, What Would Mick Do? Just then, I got an idea, though it seemed wildly familiar, and had a brief flash again of hanging off a bridge or overpass. I grabbed the phone.

"Stan, Stan, my main man, what's up?" I shared my idea with him. He just laughed, dismissing it.

"Come on, I need this," I pleaded with my cousin.

"Let me make a call, but this is going to cost you, cuz."

While I sat there waiting for Stan to call me back, I thought how diametrically opposite they were from each other. I wondered what Ian was up to at this moment—probably hustling some poor sucker at billiards.

Stan called back twenty minutes later. "Hundred bucks."

"A hundred bucks for *that*?"

"No, sixty dollars, I'm charging forty dollars for my finder's fee."

"For a phone call? Where am I going to get that kind of bread, man?"

"Have you tried selling that stuff? He needs to know no later than tomorrow."

I had forgotten all about the coke money, having spent it all and then some in England. "Okay, I'll see what I can do. Or I'll come up with a new plan, Stan. Or you can go fuck a bus, Gus."

I ran scenario after scenario through my head. I had no guitar to pawn now. I picked up my jeans and withdrew the necklace Ian smashed and grabbed. It had to be worth tens of thousands of dollars.

My car!

I dropped the necklace and ran downstairs, where I found my father mucking about.

"Well?"

"Well, what?" Mr. Jones replied.

"Did you hear from the school? You said, they said, if you didn't hear from them that I graduated. So? Did you hear from them?"

"As a matter of fact...no, I did not."

"So the car is mine?" I said, more than asked, almost exploding with glee.

Mr. Jones reached into his pocket and removed a key ring with two keys on it, and tossed it to me.

"Can I?"

"I've no doubt you can. May I, is what I think you are asking?"

"Look, I graduated." We had a staring contest; I blinked. "May I?"

"Go on then."

Father followed his very excited son to the garage just as Grandfather was coming down the stairs.

"What's all the ruckus?" Grandfather asked.

"David's getting his graduation gift," Father informed, a certain mischievous twinkle in his eye.

I pulled the cover from the car, dropping it on the garage floor, and ran my hand across the soft-top before getting into the driver's seat.

"Start her up. It's that little thing that looks like a key," Father said, obviously referring to the screwdriver that I used to hijack it home.

I put the key in the ignition and slowly turned it. Nothing happened. I shot a look at Father, one full of confusion and disappointment.

"Hmm, that's odd," he said. "Pop the bonnet. Let's have a gander."

Searching around underneath, I looked over the dash and down the front where my father was standing. He pointed in the direction of the latch, which I eventually found, and popped her open. I climbed out and assisted him with opening the hood, which opened in the opposite direction. England.

It was empty inside, with no engine whatsoever. I looked up at my father.

"Oh, yeah, I needed that to pay for the roof," he informed. Grandfather laughed. Dad's eyes darted from me, disappointed, to his father, delighted. He, too, began to laugh.

I slammed the hood back down. "Very fuckin' funny."

Grandfather carefully positioned his yarmulke, strategically covering his bald spot, and took a seat to observe Sabbath. The Temple itself was as a synagogue should be. The room is understated, the mood somber, no display of opulence as exists with some churches. A young couple with their two girls sat on the far end of his bench. They smiled politely at him as he returned a solemn nod.

"Shalom, shalom," the Rabbi said as she took her place at the podium. "Deuteronomy tells us a positive commandment to give charity, as the Torah states, 'Open your hand generously, and extend to your needy brother or sister any credit he or she needs to take care of their wants.'"

Grandfather was taken aback at the sight of a female Rabbi, but he could not imagine having heard the Torah read by anyone *but* a female Rabbi by the end of the service. God's words on charity hung especially heavy over his heart.

"I can't come up with the money."

"Come on. You must have something. Pawn that damn guitar you got," Stan said.

"I ain't got it anymore."

"Say what? Why not?"

"I just don't."

"Well, you better figure out something fast, 'cause he needs an answer by three o'clock today. He has a couple interested in a tour."

I hung the phone up and scrambled around my room, trying to come up with something. I kept going back to the necklace, but something told me not to. I scampered out of my room, poked my head into the study, and scanned the room in disbelief. I wondered, even if there was any money here, could I really steal from my family? Tell that to the Jaguar in the garage.

"It's just a loaner. You can always get a loaner in Piccadilly," I remembered Ian saying. And now look, it was mine, I reminded myself as I started rifling through Grandfather's dresser drawers. Underwear. Socks. Ties. Handkerchiefs.

A mezuzah.

A *mezuzah*? Why would the mezuzah be here in his drawer and not in its case downstairs?

And if it is here, what was that rattling in the case?

As I was now prone to do, I grabbed Mother from the mantlepiece. I took her outside, where I removed the lid and strategically placed her under the direct rays of the morning sun. Each day between four and five, it arced over the entirety of the house, as it set in the West.

I turned my attention to the mezuzah case, looking under it, over it, along the sides. I tried to nudge it, but it would not move. Of course. I helped to nail it in place.

I continued to push and pull in different places. I thought about removing the nails but seriously considered whether it might be bad luck or blasphemous.

And then, with just a gentle push on the bottom that resulted in a click and disengagement, the case jutted forward, and something dropped out onto the ground by my feet. I bent down to see what it was. Small and round, it glistened in my hand. I swallowed, almost choking at my discovery. I pressed the bottom in, and again it pushed out towards me; a small, square gold bullion, no larger than a thumbnail, dropped out. I picked it up and looked at both in the palm of my hand. Not sure how to react or what exactly to do, I turned in a near three-hundred-and-sixty-degree angle, stopping when I was back to facing the urn.

"You didn't see that, did you?" I asked Mother.

I put my leg up and spun towards the sidewalk before stopping again. Mouth agape, I turned to go inside but stopped again. "Or did you?"

———

Either way, I thought, *we got to go*. I threw the lid back on the urn, scooped it up, and ran inside, kicking the door closed behind me.

"That was quick! What'd you rob somebody?"

I gave the question considerable thought. "So we got a deal?"

"I'll tell him," Stan assured me.

"And you're going to do the other thing, yeah?"

"*Yeah?*" Stan mimicked. "What are you turning into your father?"

"Yes, I'm turning En-glish, I think I'm turning English, I really think so," I said, parodying The Vapors song, "Turning Japanese."

"Do I have to?"

"Just like I described it."

"Just give me the address," Stan reluctantly said. "But you're going to owe me big time."

After I provided Stan with the pertinent details of how I wanted him to approach my little scheme, I did a quick skim of the Yellow Pages and set out on my scooter.

As I pulled up to the curb, the first thing that caught my eye in the pawnshop window was a black electric Fender Stratocaster connected to a portable amplifier. But I was not there for that.

After filling out the requisite paperwork and showing my license, I placed just the diamond on the glass case before the elderly shop owner.

"Very nice," he said as he picked up and raised his loupe to get a more magnified look at it. "Pawn or sell?"

I had not considered there would be two options. Therefore, I shrewdly asked, "How much would I get?"

The owner weighed the diamond. "Just a little over one carat," he said, running his finger along a chart that lay flat on his desk. "Two thousand to pawn, twenty-five hundred to sell."

"Dollars?!"

"May I ask where you got this?"

I hesitated. "Do I *have* to tell you?"

"No, no, you don't *have* to tell me. But if it is stolen and the police come asking, I have your information here."

"I think I just want to pawn it."

"You said you had some gold, as well?"

"No, that's okay. I'll just take the..." I said, pointing at nothing, although something did catch my eye.

The owner eventually laid out stacks of hundreds, fifties, and twenties totaling two thousand dollars (the owner looked happy, but I could see he would have rather bought it outright). I folded them over into to a massive wad, stuffed it in my front pocket, and turned to walk out of the store.

I stopped, considering something. I then turned and pointed to the wall behind the owner, "Is that a real machine gun?"

The owner looked over his shoulder. "Why, yes, of course, it is."

———

"Veronica, there's a black guy at the door asking for you!" Dana shouted out before walking away, leaving the door ajar.

The door swung open where Veronica's father stood intensely, surprised to find someone he did not know standing there wearing a black bow tie over a tuxedo shirt. "Can I help you?"

Stan held up an envelope with Veronica's name written in calligraphy on it. "I have a special invitation for Veronica."

Veronica's father seemed satisfied with his explanation. "She'll be down in a minute," he said before walking away.

A few moments later, Veronica appeared. She even took Stan's breath away.

"This is for you," Stan said, holding the card out for her. She reluctantly reached out and grabbed it with some apparent confusion.

"Do I know you?" she asked.

Stan merely turned and walked down the stairs, looked at her blankly one last time, got into his Pinto, and drove off.

Veronica opened it to find an invitation to meet a secret admirer atop Federal Hill Tomorrow, Saturday, at 9 p.m. She wrinkled her nose up with an intrigued smirk and looked around the neighborhood before closing the door.

I got home before the others and found a package on the front step. I tore the box open to see the ultimate endgame, my graduation gown. I ran upstairs and called Stan to confirm that everything was good to go. He assured me it was.

"Did you see her? She's lovely, isn't she? So, how did she react? Was she, like, surprised?"

"To answer your questions in order: Yes. Yes. I Don't know. I guess. You going to church tomorrow?"

"I hadn't planned on it."

"Well, if you ain't going to your own surprise party, you best be going to church."

Hanging up, I recalled the promise I had made to myself in England that if we did not get caught, I was going to go straight, not do anything deceptive again. And here I was taking something that wasn't mine. I had rationalized on the way home that I would try and put the gold piece back, stash the rest of the money, and hopefully, Grandfather would give me a graduation gift of some cold hard cash, at which point I could repurchase the diamond and put it back. Somehow.

I ran my new purchase up to my room and stashed it under my bed. Those SOBs are going to remember me for the rest of their lives.

Their short lives.

Returning to the porch, I carefully and methodically as humanly possible, steadied the gold chunk at the bottom of the mezuzah case and, pressing on the bottom as I had done before, tried to jam it back inside. It proved impossible. Instead, a silver block dropped out, rolling down the back of my forearm before falling onto the ground.

Growing frustrated and not wanting more pieces to fall out, I decided to remove the case altogether. I ran inside and grabbed a hammer while parodying a Bad Company song with the lyrics "Give me Silver, Diamond, Gold."

Noting the time, I knew I had to act quickly. So I painstakingly removed the nails one by one, constantly looking panic-stricken over my right shoulder at every car that passed by.

I did not know that Papa de Papa had just gotten off the bus and was walking at a steady pace up our street.

Prying the case open, I squinted to eye the contents inside. The DAGAS, as they had referred to them back in the circus trailer, sparkled in the afternoon sun. I dropped the gold and silver chunks inside before holding it up to the wall for remounting.

Initially, I pointed it in the wrong direction as I started to hammer the first nail. Then, recalling the lesson I received, I quickly turned the mezuzah case to its proper direction and nailed the top left, followed by the right one, into place.

As Grandfather approached, he could hear banging going on nearby. As it was a rather gruelingly hot walk and getting closer to home, he picked up his pace, alternating between swinging his cane and clutching it tightly in his hand.

I nailed the third nail in. Then, as I shifted the fourth and final nail in my hand, I dropped it on the porch and watched in horror as it bounced into the hedges.

"Jesus."

Grandfather rounded the corner onto the sidewalk only to find me down on my hands and knees, hammer in my hand.

"Afternoon," Grandfather said.

My head jerked up, followed by my legs as I leaped to attention, trying to hide the hammer behind me, but who was I kidding?

"Oh, hi."

"What are you up to, then?"

"Oh, doing some housework, thought I heard something in the garden." Grandfather's eyes followed mine to the hedges. "Could be mistaken. Did you find the synagogue? How was it?"

"I did, wonderful service," Grandfather said, gently touching the mezuzah and noticing the missing nail before slowly kissing his finger.

Gramps pushed the door open while I followed him inside before shutting the door behind us. He grasped my shoulder and spun me around, pushing me up against the wall. "What's all this, then? Think I wouldn't see a nail missing?" His hand gripped the handle of his cane. I swear I could see his knuckles turn white as the cane separated ever so slightly at the gold finish. Was there more than meets the eye?

My heart raced, not entirely sure of what he was capable. One thing was for sure, we both heard my father's car pull into the driveway. Grandfather's demeanor changed like a flicked switch when the car door shut.

"What's all this then? A welcoming committee?" Father asked when he walked in. *Another corny dad joke*, I thought. *But at least he's better? And home. We had a home!*

With the tension eased, I took the opportunity to side-step the situation and ran about trying to assemble all the things I needed for my big night. Finally, I packed all I needed in my mother's favorite picnic basket and headed out the door.

"See you guys there!" I shouted.

"Right-O!" Mr. Jones shouted from downstairs.

"Young man," Grandfather whispered as he steadily approached from the kitchen. Finally, he led me out onto the front porch, and my heart pounded as I recalled our brief encounter earlier.

"Have a seat, would you?" Grandfather said, indicating the front stoop.

"I don't have much time, Grandpa," I said, sounding like Professor Potts, or more likely, the grandson, Jeremiah from "Chitty Chitty Bang Bang."

"I won't take long," he assured me. I reluctantly set my picnic basket down, leaning my new purchase, in the case it came in, awkwardly on the ground against the wicker basket and had a seat.

"I know I haven't been in your life very much over these eighteen years. I strong-armed your father into you having a bar mitzvah and then couldn't even make it over for it. I've given you fuck-all in the way of money or presents over the years," Grandfather went on to say. I discreetly checked my watch again. "But I want you to know how very proud I am of you. The first man in the family to graduate high school."

I stood up. "Thanks, Grandad."

"I'm not done yet. Inside this case," Grandy started, then stopped, as if in search of just the right words to convey.

Are silver, gold, and diamonds you stole.

"Are the very souls of our people," Grandfather continued, "I have spent half my life, and often at great expense, searching for the families of those very souls."

I had no idea what he was on about, but I was running short on time. "Yeah, I know, slave traders in South Africa, right? Ian told me," I said, trying to speed things up.

"To the contrary," Grandfather said, disappointed at the interruption. "Inside are the gems of beautiful souls lost to fascism."

What's fascism again? I thought. I knew I should've paid better attention in history class.

"I told you of taking part in the liberation of the concentration camp in Germany,"

Rechecking my watch, I jumped to my feet. The definition of fascism aside, had I not already passed my history exam?

"Grandad, I'm sorry. I have to go. I have so much I have to do before graduation. I'm sorry."

Disappointed, he shrugged his shoulders and held out his arm as if to say Go. "I promise, we'll catch up later." Grandfather nodded solemnly.

Whatever he's on about, I thought as I hopped on my Vespa, *it's probably bullshit anyway.*

Grandfather spotted the nail on the ground and picked it up. He went in, grabbed a hammer, and started to pound the last nail in when his curiosity got the best of him. Grandfather removed the three nails and, taking the case in hand, he opened it, pouring all the gems into his aged hand. After counting them, realizing it was one short, the elderly Jones looked towards the street with absolute fire in his eyes.

I arrived at the Hyatt, where Stan jumped from one of the retaining walls out front and took the picnic basket from me while returning my skateboard.

"Can you keep it a little longer for me?" Then, handing him a stack of twenties, "Here, your half of the return on our investment. I am officially out of the drug selling business," I told Stan. He eyed me curiously while counting the money as I hopped back on my scooter and headed over to Federal Hill. Once there, I parked my Vespa, ran down the flights of stairs, and stood at a bus stop, checking my watch. I was running a few minutes behind but felt good about the time.

What had Grandfather been trying to tell me?

The bus arrived, and I headed out of the city and back to my new neighborhood.

I arrived at Martin Hall, where the graduation ceremony was nearly underway. Kids in caps and gowns and their doting parents stood, taking pictures with their friends and family. It made me want to vomit. I ran inside and found the guidance counselor who had told me that I was not going to pass. *Idiot.*

This is really happening, I thought. I went into the bathroom and, pushing through a few students, who looked at me as if I smelled like shit, I slipped into an empty stall. I set my nylon case from my broken Stratocaster on the toilet seat. I put my cap and gown on, opened the case, and tried to hide my new purchase under my black graduation gown discreetly. It was bulky and awkward at best.

This is going to be a night these motherfuckers will never forget, I thought as I came out of the stall and squeezed back through what I could only assume was the same students from before.

An administrator ran about, gathering all the parents and students, and directed everyone to take their seats. The students were rounded up like cattle to be seated, as well. As the commotion began to settle in the large auditorium, the administrator, which, it turned out, was the Vice Principal, led the students in and pointed to the section of seats cordoned off for us graduates.

After everyone was seated accordingly, with the occasional straggler coming in, the graduation ceremony began. There were speeches galore, and I checked my watch again, wondering how this was all going to time out. I spied around the family section, finally finding Father and Grandfather. They were craning their necks, trying to locate my exact whereabouts.

How can they miss me? I thought, with my bushy blonde hair poking out in all directions from under my cap.

I started getting paranoid when yet another student, this time the President of the Student Body, went to the lectern to give a speech. I rolled my eyes in the back of my head, awkwardly clutching my purchase tightly under my gown.

Finally, it was diploma time. The V.P. started calling one row at a time to come up to the side of the stage, beginning with A's and B's. *By the time they got to J's*, I had started to think, *this could all go pear-shaped. Let's go, let's go, let's go*, I kept repeating through my head. *This is taking forever.* One by one, the Principal called out the names of each student, and they strode across the stage, shit-eating-grins stretched impossibly across their excited faces. I continuously checked my watch. It seemed to be going at a snail's pace. *I got places to go*, I thought. After every student received their diploma in a sturdy leather case of some sort, they shook the Principal's hand and returned to their seat amongst the claps and cheers of their respective family members.

By the grace of all that was holy, my row was finally called on. I stood up, my gown displaying the unusual contours of my oblong purchase underneath, and shimmied down the row along with the rest of my fellow students lining up on the side of the stage. I made impatient rolling gestures with my hand as they continued calling out names of people I never knew and would *never* know after tonight.

I slowly stepped one step at a time up the small set of stairs when I heard it—

Outside, what sounded like a succession of machine-gun shots firing resulted in sounding like the school was under siege.

Panic setting in, I counted the students in front of me—four—and looked at the stack of diplomas, counting down to the fifth.

I shoved past the graduates in front of me and ran across the stage, pulling the fifth diploma from the pile, causing the top four to slide backward, knocking over the pile behind it. The Vice Principal's face grew cross, uncertain at precisely what was happening. I opened the diploma case confirming it was mine: David English Jones.

Bad English
the III

Curiosity had set in for some, but for others, terror was all over their faces, as the machine-gun-sounding helicopter combined with not only my theatrics but the large ominous lump under my gown. I ripped it open to reveal not a gun, as some of the audience may have feared, but my new black Fender Stratocaster as I switched on the amp. My t-shirt, in reality, Ian's T-shirt, read: BOLLOCKS TO THE POLL TAX.

Feedback whistled and screamed through the hall's p.a. system. I then turned to walk off the stage prematurely, as the steps were about another twenty-five feet to my right.

Screw it. I flipped the crowd off English style, shoved the diploma case between my teeth, plucked a particularly high note, and yanked on the whammy bar. The amplifier on my hip squelched the note, which, fortunately, also caught the hall's speakers. Everyone covered their ears as I jumped off the stage, dropping down to one knee, and ran up the aisle leaving everyone there wholly bewildered.

From outside, a light shone through the front windows as I barreled through the double doors of the auditorium to find what Stan and I had arranged, the Hyatt's helicopter! *I could not have timed it better if I tried,* I thought as the helicopter came to rest on the lawn.

Turning to see faces in the windows, I flipped them off again before ducking my head and climbing inside through the already opened passenger door. I shook hands with the pilot, whose name escaped me from all the excitement. On the floor was my picnic basket. The pilot handed me a headset, instructing me to pull the door shut and strap in. I tried to slide it on over my cap, but it wasn't having it. Instead, I stepped out, remembering to switch the tassel to the other side, and flung the cap up into the air, where it got shredded into a million pieces by the copter's blades. I quickly hopped back in, pulled the door shut and the harness over my shoulders.

"You good?" the pilot asked.

I gave him the thumbs up; the pilot manipulated the flight controls, and we lifted over the hall's grounds. I grabbed my stomach nervously as my fear of heights kicked in. In a matter of seconds, the helicopter was breaking back over Baltimore City as we flew over the Inner Harbor, which looked magical from my vantage point.

"Did you ever see the movie '...And Justice For All?'" he said into his microphone. All I could do was nod as my stomach was in my throat. "Remember Jack Warden liked to go out just a little further every day?"

Oh, god.

The hall, meanwhile, was in complete chaos. Attendees and students had rushed to the window to figure out what the hell was going on. The Principal tried, unsuccessfully at first, to quell the chaos and restore some sort of order by pleading with people to return to their seats. The Vice Principal demanded to know who that student was and, in doing so, elicited a cuss word that was heard over the intercom, taking several parents by surprise.

"I get the distinct impression he's not coming back," Grandfather succinctly said.

According to Grandfather, Dad was completely livid.

Chapter
XVIII

Easing out of the helicopter, I grabbed my picnic basket and guitar, keeping my head down. The pilot touched the side of his nose as I shut the door and moved away from the propellers.

Was he? Of course, he was.

The helicopter lifted off, and I watched as it headed back to the hotel, shrinking as it headed towards eleven o'clock. Total time away from the hotel? Twenty minutes tops. Not a bad little taxi ride for all of sixty dollars.

It was exactly nine p.m., and no Veronica was in sight. Nevertheless, I set the basket down as onlookers watched in awe, laughing and whispering to each other at what they had just seen transpire.

"Nice move, man," the guy of a couple walking past said.

I spread out a blanket on the grass overlooking Rash Field, beyond which the lights of the Aquarium reflected off the harbor. I continued setting up my nighttime picnic, which included a glass-encased candle, cheese, crackers, a bottle of sparkling blush, and two plastic cups (after how I felt when I woke up, I was *not* in the mood for alcohol). After lighting the candle, I sat down and was determined to enjoy what I brought, whether she showed up or not.

I scanned the area, but it was becoming clear that I had overshot that. Then, from behind a nearby tree, I spotted Veronica poking her head out before slowly emerging. I stood up as she reluctantly approached, looking ravishing in a yellow sundress but noting that she was not smiling.

"Hell of an entrance," she said matter-of-factly. "I got to tell you, I thought for sure, that was a Harley off in the distance."

"Cheap theatrics. An F-You to school. I just graduated." I said, my arms extended from my graduation gown.

"I knew there had to be a good explanation," she said, drawing closer. Then, pointing to the display on the grass. "Is this all for me?"

"If you like." Another line from "Highlander." "Care for some sparkling non-alcoholic wine? I stopped drinking today."

"No, I can't. But, look, I just came to say I'm flattered that you went to all this trouble, but to be honest, I, uh, I could never have a relationship with someone who, right off the bat, lied to me."

"The English thing."

Veronica scoffed. "Yeah-ha, the English thing. And the father/uncle thing." I nodded, lowering my head in disappointment. "And you're probably not going to like what I have to say next." I braced myself.

"Maybe I should have some," I said, grabbing the bottle. I worked the top off and turned away until it blasted off over Key Highway below and poured myself a glass. "Sure I can't interest you in some?" Veronica shook her head. "Cheese and crackers?" For the first time, she smiled yet shook her head again.

"I'm late for my period."

Pouring the fake wine into the plastic cup, I looked at her only to watch her gaze lower to the ground. I gulped the whole cup, now wishing it *was* the real thing.

Being green about women's cycles, I had no choice but to accept it at face value. "But I didn't...." I started to say but relented. "You know this has no alcohol," I said, holding up the bottle.

She leaned over and picked up the other cup. "Let's get this over with."

I proceeded to pour the fizzy pink juice into her cup. "Am I the...?"

"Well." My mind rambled as I stared across the harbor. I was unaware the sparkling wine was spilling over the rim, dripping onto the grass.

"Your cup runneth over," she pointed out. I stopped pouring and started sucking the rim.

"Tasty."

"Sucks to be lied to, doesn't it?"

I gulped as I searched her face for some indication of where this was headed. "Whaaaa?"

"I like your real accent. Your English one sounds, to be completely honest, sounds kind of feminine."

Ouch.

Veronica smirked and dropped to her knees on the blanket. While that hurt, I let out a sigh of relief that could probably be heard as far as Essex. Essex, England.

"You said the other day that you had taken my advice and honored your mother. How?"

"I planted her favorite flower in her memory," I said proudly.

Veronica smiled. Her first genuine smile of the night. "Nice."

I smiled. And for one brief moment, all seemed right in the world, as if the axis finally aligned for me.

"By the way, I owe you an apology."

"Me?"

"I should have never done that to you that night. I was drunk. Not that that is an excuse."

"No, *I* was wrong. Of course, I was drunk, too, but I knew what I was doing."

"Yes, you certainly did," Veronica countered, without a hint of irony in her voice. "But it wasn't fair to you."

I thought about it for a moment. "It's like reverse *rapism.*"

Veronica erupted into hysterical laughter, covering her face with her hands. "You're funny. The truth is, I was rebounding. Boyfriend. You know."

"Duke?" *Why did I ask that?*

Veronica confirmed by lowering her hands with a nod along with a bite of her lower lip.

I was gutted, my head dropped backward.

Sharonda? My body followed my head as I rolled backwards down the hill. I tried to stop but had too much of a roll going!

The hill.

My feet.

The road below.

The hill. My feet. The road below. The hill. My feet. The road below.

Sharonda approached the blanket, not for a loss of words. "Was that David Jones? Is this his blanket? His mother Polly's picnic basket?"

Sensing something wrong, Veronica stood up and stepped back off the blanket.

"Who the fuck are you?" she asked Veronica menacingly.

"It's not what it looks like."

Sharonda grabbed Veronica by the hair, and they swiftly got to tussling, pulling each other to the ground by the other's locks. Not lox.

Bad English
the III

Well, in my mind, anyway.

"SURPRISE!" came the roar from within the dark house that quickly illuminated by Mr. Jones' flick of the switch, almost giving Grandfather a legitimate heart-attack.

Inside were Stan and his parents, LeRoy and Nola Williams, standing under two banners. One read HAPPY BIRTHDAY, the other CONG*RAD*ULA-TIONS.

"Where's Davey?" Nola asked.

"He had to fly," Grandfather succinctly told the strangers.

As he was the only one with knowledge of my plans, Stan laughed, still irked he was forced to attend as promised.

Everyone made their introductions to Grandfather as Dad apparently went to the liquor cabinet, frantically searching for something. "Where's my bottle of J.D.?"

"Where's your DJ?" Stan countered.

After everyone in attendance had some of my birthday cake, Uncle LeRoy picked up my presents and made his way to the door. "I'll give these to him after church tomorrow. You guys *are* coming, right?"

My father's eyes shifted to *his* father's, who did not respond. Relenting, Mr. Jones nodded his head.

I got home around midnight, coming into a quiet house, confused at finding what looked to be a party that had been celebrated. I ran my finger across the icing of a half-eaten birthday cake, licking it off, before heading up to bed.

The next morning, my old man gathered us three together, all wearing our Sunday best. We both grumbled all the way to the car. If this was a film and, again, the camera lifted up--it would reveal the lawn was cut to read CUNT!

"My wallet," my dad uttered, turning to go back into the house.

Grandfather checked to see that the coast was clear before turning with a wad of cash and handed it to me. "This is for your birthday, boy. Thirteen and eighteen."

I was in awe as I counted the money.

"Get it back," he said, looking over his shoulder to spot my old man walking across the still-butchered front lawn.

I returned a quizzical look at Grandfather.

"You know." He turned back to face forward as I contemplated, but I knew exactly what he meant. Dad took his place behind the wheel next to his father, looking at me in the rearview mirror.

"Well, I never thought I'd be saying this to my father and my son, but let's go to church."

"Maybe we can stop at a mosque on our way home, too," Grandfather muttered under his breath. Twirling my necklace, the Star of David, and the Crucifix side by side, I wondered if Muslims had their own symbol I could get for my chain. *You can never be too safe.*

Dad started the car up; Aretha Franklin was in the middle of her chorus for "Chain of Fools." Not lost on me, I let the pendants drop back onto my necktie before stuffing them back into my shirt.

Back to the old neighborhood we went. After just a couple of weeks, and having been abroad for a week, it now seemed small, even desolate.

Of course, the church was no different as we climbed the stairs, joining the line to shake the Pastor and his wife's hands.

The Pastor gripped my shoulder when it was my turn and looked deep into my eyes, almost as if to hypnotize me. "We have missed you, young brother. How are you holding up?"

At an unusual loss for words, I nodded "Okay" before dropping my chin to take in the Pastor's shoes, focusing on the stylish gold buckles.

"David," I heard the Pastor say as I felt his grip release from my shoulder. He had moved onto my father as I sidestepped to the Pastor's wife. She pulled me into her giant pillows, where I focused on the one flower in my direct view while being rocked back and forth.

"We're all going to miss Polly. She was an amazing spirit," the Pastor said, holding Dad's hand in both of his. "And who is this? Your father?"

Dad nodded before stepping to his right.

"It is an honor to have you here."

"I'm a Jew."

"Ah, one of the Chosen People," the Pastor said, chuckling sincerely. "Then it truly *is* an honor."

As the three Generations of Joneses walked down the aisle of the opulent but somber House of God, opposing thoughts went through each of their minds. On the one hand, Mr. Jones had not been to church since his wife had passed away and was now met with handshakes and hugs. On the other hand, grandfather *had* to be thinking, *What in the world am I doing here?*

It's no St. Paul's Cathedral, I thought before my attention turned to the back of one certain girl's noggin in particular.

As I followed my father and Grandfather into a row of pews where Uncle LeRoy, Aunt Nola, and Stan sat, presents piled up on their right, my eyes locked with that girl's side profile two rows up and over.

Sharonda. She smiled but quickly recalled that she, too, was angry with me. I was getting quite accustomed to that emotion.

I mouthed the word Hi as I took the seat next to Grandfather.

She relented, mouthing Hi back, and quickly turned to face forward at the behest of her mother tugging on the sleeve of her dress.

The service was of its usual Baptist bombast. The choir belted out lively gospel tunes, and the Pastor shouted from bible passages such as Leviticus.

Bad English
the III

I watched Grandfather out of the corner of my eye, solemnly nodding his head and mumbling, "Old Testament."

"'It is forbidden to rob, steal or illegally hold on to any property or money, as we are commanded, 'Do not steal...Do not unjustly withhold that which is due your neighbor. Do not rob. One must therefore be extremely careful not to take illegal possession of any money or property in any manner, no matter how trivial its worth, whether it be from an adult or a child.'"

I think it safe to say, at least I *hoped,* that that was not lost on *any* of us Jones men.

And while Grandfather didn't have the sort of revelation that Jake Blues had upon hearing James Brown in "The Blues Brothers," I could see something, a conversion of sorts, slight but observable, was reaching the old man.

At the end of the service, I left Grandfather and Dad and walked over to Sharonda and her family. Her brother, Anthony fist-bumped me before slapping me on the back; her parents shook my hand and hugged me, expressing their condolences, before leaving us alone to talk. We had a brief conversation before we fell into each other's arms and held each other tight while churchgoers squeezed around us on their way out.

Mr. Jones clutched his wife, who was quietly sobbing. "We're going to get through this together," he assured her. "I

---

will do anything...beg, borrow, steal...kill. To make sure we get you through this. By any means necessary." If she could have held him any tighter.

"'Ere Dad? Can you hear me? It's your son! No, the other one, the good lookin' bloke! Yeah, yeah. No, truthfully, we're <u>not</u> good—anything but good. Look, I need your help. It's Polly. Do you still have that stash? Yeah, yeah, I know but hear me out. I've come up with this idea."

Chapter
XIX

Surprisingly, twenty years later, on March 7, 2009, old Mr. Tannenbaum passed away. According to authorities, he passed away, technically, due to the injuries he sustained on that fateful bank holiday. He had 21 surgeries, everything from his left eye, chest, heart, and lungs in all that time. Nevertheless, Thomas Jones had religiously taken care of him until the day he passed. Though he claimed he had no memory of the lot of it, he exhibited signs of guilt by feeding him, bathing him, and essentially taking care of his every need. After all, it *was he* that literally, as well as figuratively, pulled the trigger when he deviated down his own dark path.

Some might say it was his due Karma.

Either way, his ruse prevented him from ever seeing a dime of the insurance money on which the whole scheme was predicated.

———

Just as it had done ten years earlier, the show "Crime-watch" rebroadcast its episode featuring the robbery in one of its segments. Still, few new leads came through on the tips-line, further frustrating police and authorities.

In 2021, an anonymous source placed a full-page ad in The Evening Standard, offering a ten-thousand-pound reward for any tips that could shed light on the identity of any of the robbers.

With no assistance from Scotland Yard or its agencies, it is difficult to say precisely where the investigation, or lack thereof, went. After Thomas and Irving were released from the hospital, they returned to their modest Tudor cottage in Golders Green. Doctors maintained that Thomas suffered from "Retrograde Amnesia," an affliction that found him unaware of not only who he was but of his entire past as well.

Irving, though, most likely had suffered a stroke during the robbery, rendering him incapacitated before he was gunned down. Confined to a wheelchair, he suffered blindness in one eye, the use of only his left arm and was unable to speak.

While there were still several unanswered questions for Ian, Detective Brompton retired from the police force three years later in 1992. His partner, Detective Erskine, quit the police force or was forced to resign, depending on whom you asked, in 1995, after a brief affair with a female colleague.

What we do not know, however, is where the investigation led them after the Joneses disappeared or headed back to America.

One might be led to believe one of the following occurred:

1) Through their investigation, they, too, discovered more than met the eye regarding the CCTV footage, as Ian had pointed out to DJ later that night. Possibly, Detective Brompton berated Detective Erskine for allowing two men aboard a flight bound for the US with the last name Jones. "One was a baby-faced teen accompanying his decrepit old grandfather!" the younger of the two detectives probably protested in his defence.

2) With 95% of robberies in London unsolved, the two detectives moved on to other crimes occurring in the city. And, boy, were there plenty of them. Bank robberies, with much larger payoffs, were on the rise.

3) Maybe (and this is my favourite) the two grasped each other's hands tightly and skipped down the hallway and out of Scotland Yard singing a Gary Glitter song along the way, determined to make it home in time to watch a rebroadcast of "Only Fools and Horses."

With Ian going off the grid and Thom taking care of a bed-ridden Irving, newspaper reports of the crime became fewer and fewer until it became a side-note in the annals of British crime stories.

Epilogue

Three months later, the toll-free phone number, received hundreds of calls, all false accusations, just people turning in their family and friends in hopes of obtaining the sizable reward money. But nothing of substance. That is until one call was received where the caller possessed some unusual and unrevealed facts.

An interview was arranged with one of its reporters, Britt Starling: The Standard's darling, as she was often referred.

"And how are you privy to all this?" Ms. Starling asked Robbin.

"We were flatmates. That is to say, I was living with Ian at the time. David, DJ, came back to London the next year and spent the summer writing all about it."

"He showed it to you?"

She pushed her hair behind her right ear, followed by her left. "Not exactly. We knew he was writing something. He would write at work, on the tube to and from, and then when we went to bed, he would stand at the ironing table writing into the wee hours."

"An ironing table? Peculiar."

"Said he did his best writing standing up. Only asked one *fing* of us that we respect his privacy and never read what he was writing."

"But, you did."

Robbin chuckled. "Well, there was this one weekend, DJ brought this Scottish bird home from the pub he worked at. The next morning, he did a disappearing act on her. He left without even his trainers. Ian and I pored through the entire thing. That's how I know it so well."

Starling stared at her but pretended to continue writing.

"Did he ever suspect you guys had read it?"

"Not when he lived with us. But after he went home, he *had* to have known. It couldn't have been finished when he went packing back to the states. Ian switched it out. Sent him back to the US with nothing but blank notebook pages. DJ called one day, absolutely livid.

Ian acted like he didn't know what he was talking about.

"And that's it?" Starling asked.

"Yeah, that's all I know," Robbin stated.

———

"What did you think when you read this story?"

"What did I *think*? You couldn't help but feel sorry for David. DJ. I mean, his family really did a number on him."

Yeah, I suppose you're right."

"There was one uva *fink*. He told Ian he was going to get him for that. But, I mean, I would have been cross, as well."

"And you've had no contact with Ian Jones?"

"Oh, not in fifteen years, at least."

"No idea where he is?"

"Not a clue."

"Never looked him up on Facebook? Instagram?"

"Well, yeah. But do you know how many Ian Joneses are on the internet?"

Starling nodded, chewed on the end of her pen. "So, David put this all into motion. The father, that is."

"*A-Parent-Lee*." (A further "Lee" joke?)

"Do you know what happened to the grandfather?"

"He died the summer David was with us. So that was the catalyst that sent him packing up. Didn't even say good-bye, just fucked off out his bedroom window."

"Well, certainly Ian couldn't have switched his writing if he didn't know he was leaving. Or, as you put it, fucked off out the window. So what was he using to write on? Or in?"

"Just white notepads."

"And Ian?"

"I asked him, and he just said he could see it in his *bleady* li'l eyes."

431

"It sounded like you said *bleedin' li'l lies.*" Robbin nervously chuckled. She flinched for her purse. For the flask inside?

"And what about the Traffic Warden?"

"You're the reporter. You tell me."

Starling nodded and leaned forward, turning the tape recorder off. "OK, well, that's that, unless you have anything more to add." Robbin shook her head to the contrary. "Thank you. I think I've got enough for-- something here," she said, chuckling.

"Bloody 'Coronation Street,' innit?"

"Guess you don't want what to give your surname." Robbin tilted her head. "An initial?"

Robbin considered it. "K."

"K," Starling repeated.

Robbin laughed. "No, not K. I was saying, Okay, as in text. G."

"G" as in initial? Or G as in, Gee, mister."

"Just G."

Starling flipped back to the first page, wrote the letter G; she darkened it by going over the same lines a few times.

Robbin and Starling both stood up at the same time. Starling started to offer her hand but offered up her elbow instead due to the pandemic, which was similarly met with Robbin's joint.

"Well, we'll be in touch should anything arise or come to light," Britt said.

Robbin nodded. Starling walked her to the hotel room door, opening it.

"Cheerio," she said, pushing her hair back behind her ears again as she stepped out into the hallway.

"Do you happen to know the type of flower DJ planted?"

"A sunflower, if I'm not mistaken." Acknowledging her mask was a sunflower. "My favourite, too."

"Well. Good-bye," Starling replied before closing the door behind her and returning to the settee where she had been sitting. She picked up the tape recorder and fast-forwarded it to the end.

"What do you think? How did I do?"

A heavy-set older man with menacing eyes rushed in from the adjoining room, the lower half of his face covered by a mask, illustrated by The Blues Brothers' iconic phrase: "We're On A Mission From God."

"You were great," he said, quickly counting out several ten-pound notes, shoving them in her hand. "Can't believe she didn't mention they had to tent and gas his new house for bed bugs. He left *nofink else* out. If you haven't figured it out yet, that was *not* my old girlfriend. Her name was Sarah," he said before running out of the hotel room.

"Britt" wondered what she got herself into. She counted her money, took one last around the room, and shoved the wad inside her bra. Robbin crossed the hotel lobby, taking note of the lilac fragrance combined with the more pungent smell of gin. She made way for a model Japanese family of four scurrying behind their rolling luggage on the way to check-in.

Stepping outside, where a light drizzle was beginning, Robbin reached into her handbag as she approached a 2019 Jaguar XF. Her blue eyeliner was starting to run. She beep-beeped her keys, and the lights blinked on and off where she slid across the driver's seat, which, being in London, was on the right side. Then, leaning over to pull the door shut, she let one last spate of falling rain splash across her face.

Robbin flipped the visor down, illuminating the small vanity mirror, took the handkerchief, and began to wipe the make-up off from her eyelids. Under her eyes. Her cheeks, her forehead. She put the cigarette out in the ashtray and coughed slightly. It was a deep, wheezy cough, a manly cough. Then, as the make-up lessened and the freckled, aging skin underneath became more prominent, she pulled her hair from the roots, revealing it was nothing more than a wig. The hair beneath, a gray bush, told definitively that she was clearly a he.

And not just any man.

David Jones.

In the flesh.

Suddenly the car door flung open, and DJ found himself being yanked violently out by his collar!

Landing on his feet, DJ was spun like a country and western dance partner and found himself facing a man of about fifty-odd years. It took a long second before he realized who this balding, somewhat over-weight man was.

The eyes, the hawkish nose.

Ian.

"Nice tits, love!"

The older cousin proceeded to wrap his arms tight around DJ, pulled him in close. "Last Joneses standing."

"Wait," DJ asked, pulling away. "Does this mean there's no reward money?"

Ian flashed a big toothy grin; the missing one re-placed long ago.

"Thirty years later, and you cunts got me again."

"You're still in America!"

I was aroused from a sun nap as I lounged on the back patio beside the jacuzzi.

Rick, the beefy doorman, stood peering over the fence. "Looking for a little of that...." Rick tapped his nose. "Can I come in?"

I got up and reluctantly let him into the backyard. "We're out of the business," I said with no accent but my *Baltimoron* one.

Rick nodded, scanning the sizable backyard before his eyes landed on the pack of Rothmans on the table. "Hey, you found your brand. Can I pinch one?"

"Yeah, of course. Look, Rick, I should, uh, probably tell you, I'm not really from England."

With that, Rick dropped the pack, picked me up, and flipped me upside down into the jacuzzi. *I guess I had that coming*, I thought, completely submerged.

When you are underwater, are you wet?

I peered up through the surface and saw Rick looking down at me in the hot tub, the light of the afternoon sun surrounding him.

Mr. Jones clutched his son as they watched the cardboard box entering the incinerator on a slow-moving conveyor belt. DJ could not bear to watch and sunk his face into his father's shoulder.

"Deji. Wake up."

DJ awoke to find the audience pouring out of the movie theater to the pounding sounds of Public Enemy's "Fight the Power."

"Is it over?" he asked.

"How do you fall asleep during a riot scene?" Sharonda asked, standing up.

"Tired, I guess," he said as we followed the crowd out.

They joined the back of the line of the all-black audience members making their way out, all buzzing from the excitement of the movie. As they made their way outside, the sun was an orange glow atop the Baltimore World Trade Center.

DJ squinted, adjusting his eyes from the darkness to the light. He placed his arm around Sharonda, turning the necklace—yes, *that* necklace until the clasp was on the back of her neck. A couple standing in line to go inside caught DJ's attention: Veronica and Duke, their arms around each other's waists. DJ pulled Sharonda a little closer, who gazed suspiciously up into his eyes.

They embraced under the The Downtown 6 marquee for "Do The Right Thing" before making their way to a green Jaguar, the top flipped back on that late June summer evening.

A delicate tinkling sound, a slight distinct scraping noise that, of the lid of her final resting place, made way for the spirit within. Raising up with a slight tilt to the left, the cover rose from its cylinder, eventually dropping onto the mantle, where it spun like a coin for a second until it came to a stop. The stem stretched out from the confines within, a leaf directly underneath. And while it would be another two weeks before the yellow petals of the flower started to give way, a sunflower had taken shape.

The Queen rose from her final resting place, swooping and soaring like a Phoenix rising. She ascended towards the warm glow of the sun.

COMING 2022

Bad English the II: More True Tales of a Son of a Brit
Excerpt:

"So, have a seat. You're David, yes? Applying for the barman position?" the Governess said, taking a seat behind a small cluttered oak desk.

"Yes," I said, thinking I needed to say more, so she wouldn't question me or my accent.

"Tha's corre't. David.

What was that? I sound like a robot.

She withdrew a 3x5 card from a small black file box on the corner.

"Surname?"

I pondered it for a moment. *"Sir David."*

For the first time, she looked up directly into my eyes. "You're last name. You're family name."

"Oh. Jones."

COMING 2023

Bad English the I: The Mostly Questionable Tales of a Son of a Brit

Excerpt:

"Truth is, a few of us became aware of a bank behind enemy lines with a sizable account that the Nazis were not going to let go without a fight," Grandfather said with a straight face.

He does know I know the plot of "Kelly's Heroes," surely, I thought.